T0196305

The Common Threads Trilogy

Common Threads II

L.A. Champagne

iUniverse®

THE COMMON THREADS TRILOGY
COMMON THREADS II

Copyright © 2013, 2016 L.A. Champagne.

All rights reserved. No part of this book may be used or reproduced by any means, graphic, electronic, or mechanical, including photocopying, recording, taping or by any information storage retrieval system without the written permission of the author except in the case of brief quotations embodied in critical articles and reviews.

Certain characters in this work are historical figures, and certain events portrayed did take place. However, this is a work of fiction. All of the other characters, names, and events as well as all places, incidents, organizations, and dialogue in this novel are either the products of the author's imagination or are used fictitiously.

iUniverse books may be ordered through booksellers or by contacting:

iUniverse
1663 Liberty Drive
Bloomington, IN 47403
www.iuniverse.com
1-800-Authors (1-800-288-4677)

Because of the dynamic nature of the Internet, any web addresses or links contained in this book may have changed since publication and may no longer be valid. The views expressed in this work are solely those of the author and do not necessarily reflect the views of the publisher, and the publisher hereby disclaims any responsibility for them.

Any people depicted in stock imagery provided by Thinkstock are models, and such images are being used for illustrative purposes only.
Certain stock imagery © Thinkstock.

ISBN: 978-1-4917-8689-5 (sc)
ISBN: 978-1-4917-8690-1 (hc)
ISBN: 978-1-4917-8688-8 (e)

Print information available on the last page.

iUniverse rev. date: 01/21/2016

The
Common
Threads
Trilogy

Is Dedicated to My Daughter
Beverlee and her family

Contents

Dedicated to my dear cousin,
Gone so long before his time.
Scott
1971 – 2015

Acknowledgements

FIRST AND FOREMOST I WANT to thank my wonderful family and friends. Without them all constantly saying to me over the last... almost seven years, "Are you done the second installment yet?" And, "How're the novels coming?"...this trilogy would never have been finished! Their constant love and support, is what kept me going!

To my only child, my beautiful daughter Bev who has always been the light of my life, I wish to give a very special thank you. You have inspired me to do many things, but when you encouraged me to write the novel that was in my head, which lead to this trilogy; I felt I could do it, as long as my health holds up.

The day my second granddaughter "Turtle" was born, I went home from the hospital after seeing and holding her. I later fell asleep and this entire novel-turned-trilogy popped into my head and I got up and started making notes. Thank you sweetie!

My daughter was very patient during the writing process. Although we live 300 miles apart, we were on the phone almost every day... usually from me to her!

Let's face it; being my adult child, it was more recent that she went to school than me. I felt she could be an invaluable source of knowledge. She was and always is! She helped with formation of sentence and paragraph structure, along with punctuation (although, I have to give spell-check a thank you here too, for my many errors). Bev's computer skills and assistance with research was invaluable.

She constantly gave me courage and strength to finish the job. Even when I had to take a year or so break in publishing this book two of the Trilogy, for a traumatic, extensive surgery which was in many ways a serious downfall to my mind, body and soul. But she helped pick me up, dust me off and point me in the right direction, again. For this I admire and love you my dear!

I thank you for being there in the mornings to pass ideas to, in case they were ridiculous. Thank you for the afternoons I called, just to say, "My brain is exhausted…talk English to me; without slang or an accent!" Then there were some late nights to discuss all the baby and childhood developments. She is a great advisor, since she is the mom of two very active, beautiful girls. I always felt she is a much more experienced mother than I. She already had an almost 2 year old daughter, "Kiki", when Turtle was born, so I tapped into all the knowledge she had about new babies and toddlers. She had more bravery than me: to have more than one child…I salute you dear!

She could give me great insight into siblings growing up young, together. I had three older siblings, but don't remember what I felt at such an early age. She could tell me so much about 'kids' and stuff; many things I'd forgotten about. Also, things were not the same now, as when I was a kid! I was so out of touch. My daughter has the greatest experiences at being a mom. As busy as my daughter was and is, she always has time for me. Same goes for my son-in-law, Randy and 'our girls'. Thanks for everything Bev! I love you!

I Thank Bill, my other half…for over 21 years you have cared for me, believed in me and helped me with every aspect of my life from the day we met. During the time I was researching and then writing the Trilogy, you were very patient, distractively quiet at times, (which can drive someone nuts, dear!) and you are always helpful!

It is funny that you can know someone for over a decade or so and you never realize the knowledge your mate holds! He has told me more than once that he "has all sorts of useless bits of information", but in this case, much of his knowledge was quite useful for my project! I am not surprised really…thanks honey, for all your help.

A huge thank you has to go to Dr. Joseph A. Zadra, BSC, MD, CM, FRCS(C) Urologist. Without his help, this novel would not be written with the medical and golf knowledge, it contains. This man was a wealth of knowledge, when it came to all the medical facts; and I credit him for writing the famous 'Honeymoon Golf Game, with The

Bet', at St. Andrews Ancient Golf Course, in Scotland 1850's, which appears in section 1, chapter 4...

Without Joe's help, this would be a mundane, average novel, but with his infinite energy, dedication, enthusiasm, and great encouragement, it is a novel filled with intriguing medical and golf information; as well as an incredible story. Thank you, my dear friend...Dr. J. Zadra!

The other writing assistance I received came from Reverend Donald French (Ret.). I wasn't much on writing funerals, so Rev. Don came to my rescue. He wrote a very dignified funeral for a major, beloved character in section 2, chapter 17. Thank you Rev. Don.

To Rita Quinn, BA., - My great proof-reader, who took on this massive project. It was her wonderful reviews, after she read each section, that also kept me going. She encouraged me to keep writing and helped keep me positive. After the first section, she told me I was her new 'favorite author' and couldn't wait to get the next section. Thank you Rita, for your belief in me!

I also wish to acknowledge the following people, who helped in their areas of expertise. Their knowledge was invaluable. Thank you.

Esther Ofori, BSc N, RN, Toronto Western Hospital - Toronto, ON (Twi Translation) - As I was a patient on the Neuro-Surgery Ward in this hospital, Esther was one of my nurses. I learned that she came from the Ashanti Tribe, and when she walked into my room, she was my character, Afua (Mary). She is a beautiful lady, who brought my character to life. Thank you, and your family, Esther.

Rev. Bruce Musgrave, M. Div., Certified Chaplain, CAPPE, RVH - Barrie, ON

Susan J. Booth, Funeral Director - Steckley-Gooderham Funeral Home - Barrie, ON

Dr. Russell Price, MD FRCP (C) FCAP - Medical Director Dept. Laboratory Medicine, RVH - Barrie, ON

Dr. J.J. Scheeres, MD FRCS (C) Obstetrics & Gynecology, RVH - Barrie, ON Sergeant Sandra Gregory, Toronto Police Services

James Sweeney, Reg. N. - Patient Representative, RVH - Barrie, On (My wonderful Scottish connection)

Carolyn Moran, M.R.C.S.L.T. Speech-Language Pathologist, RVH - Barrie, ON

Caite Harvie-Conway, BSc IBCLC Certified Lactation Consultant, RVH - Barrie, ON

Patricia McAllister, Seed Potato Specialist, Alberta Agriculture and Rural Development, Crop Diversification Centre North

Liz Taylor - St. Andrews History

Terry Reimer, Dir. of Research, National Museum of Civil War Medicine

Frances McLay, PA to Deirdre A. Kinloch Anderson, Director - Kinloch Anderson Ltd. (Marriage Kerchief)

I also want to acknowledge the following web sites, and contacts, belonging to them.

http://www.wikipedia.org - My biggest source of information for so many subjects

http://www.electricscotland.com/burns/burns_boy.htm - Scotland

http://www.eiu.edu/~localite/britain/scotland.htm - Scotland

http://www.ashanti.com.au/pb/wp_8078438f.html?0.98850289123 6146 - Ashanti Tribe

http://www.bbc.co.uk/history/scottishhistory/enlightenment/index. shtml - Scotland

http://www.scottishradiance.com/archive.htm#history - Scotland

http://www.scotshistoryonline.co.uk/burke.html - Scotland

http://www.ww1cemeteries.com (Brent Whittam and Terry Heard)

http://www.languagemarketplace.com, Kimone Morgan - Translation

Forward

I T IS MY PLEASURE TO bring you part two, in *"The Common Threads Trilogy"*. You are embarking on the continuing journey of the MCDONALD, MCGEE and ALLEN families. Many common threads are discretely woven into book one *"Common Threads"* and they continue to wind their ways through this, book two, *"Common Threads II"*; and later the third and final installment, *"More Common Threads"*. They are subtle, but see how many common threads you can find.

The first book: "Common Threads" introduced us to many members of the two large Scottish families and the African couple kidnaped from their country, while both were children; all in the 1850's.

During the first book, you will question your own thoughts on rape, murder and justifiable homicide, regardless of race, religion or color. You will read about their turbulent times as well as their happier times, living and growing generations of families, in Chatham.

You'll learn of the Kente Cloth Robe which was made by a little girl (Afua Kakira), sitting happily in Africa without a care in the world. The one thing she had on her mind was being with her father, daily after school lessons to learn the special art and design of the Kente Robe. She proudly sits with her beloved father learning to make a robe for herself. She picked the dyed colors that her mother taught her to make from roots, seeds and flowers.

Her favorite colors were light blue, with other colors woven in, such as green and red. Black thread would be used to define her robe's pattern. Afua chose a design which pleased her father. She chose to symbolize antiquity and heirloom.

During her young life, Bonny Lass, Diana McGee had never seen the new world, but heard wonderful tales of prosperity. She never thought she would ever leave Scotland. She was so happy there and one of the last things her precious mother did was make a sash for her daughter's wedding, using the McGee family tartan. Diana often watched her mother work with the tartan, which her own family made for generations, from scratch. It was a beautiful piece of material: Depending on the season it could be made with yarn, or cotton; which was dyed light blue. There was also red and green for added color and black thread outlined the family's pattern. – Get it?

Her beloved strong lad, Johnny McDonald, from down the way becomes her betrothed. There is a beautiful, classic Scottish Wedding, alas without mum. Afterward, is a wonderful honeymoon at Scotland's famous; The Royal and Ancient Golf Club of St. Andrews. Diana and Johnny play golf every day and there is a contest and…a bet between them. Read who wins and who pays the piper… After a year or so, the couple's potato crop fails they sail on a two-masted brig to Canada: Its name…the Destino.

The African children; Berko Yaba and Afua Kakira both belonged to the same Ashanti Tribe. They were kidnapped at different times and both suffered an ocean voyage of suffering and torture, on a two-masted Brig called The Destino – Get IT, only to land in Jamaica…BUT the man who bought them both, Jacob Marcus was a kind sugar plantation owner. He renames each slave he buys. Berko becomes Jed Allen and Afua becomes Mary Belle.

Jacob Marcus has a disease of some kind that starts to impair him. Jed is in love with Mary and she's very pretty. While on board the boat from Africa a sailor raped and impregnated her. Still, this doesn't stop Jed, who marries Mary (by "jumping the broom" in traditional African fashion), and says that he will father her baby as if it is his own.

Eventually after murders, rapes, 'accidental' deaths and the Underground Railroad, Jed and Mary arrive in Canada, where they meet John and Diana McDonald. John and Diana grow attached to Jed and Mary, who they look at as their friends and paid workers.

Fast forward 100 years; births, deaths, plagues and diseases unknown. But the medicine, the sciences, home and garden and the industrial revolution advance as per history, hence the genre of "The Common Threads Trilogy" as fictional-historical.

Book one, "Common Threads" ends in 1946. The story continues in book two, "Common Threads II" in 1947, after one of the Scottish white family, marries a member of the African black family members. There is a pregnancy and a change of jobs. The young couple is off to Philadelphia Mississippi.

I hope that I have not given away too much of the first book, "Common Threads". You may still acquire it through my publisher, iUniverse.com or Amazon.com, etc. Please pick it up and read it before you open the pages of my current novel, the continuing story "The Common Threads Trilogy" – *"Common Threads II"*

L.A. Champagne

Chapter 1

A New Home - New Life

AFTER LIZ MCDONALD AND JOSEPH Allen were married in the mid 1940's, when things went terribly wrong on the family farm in Chatham; there was a great deal of sadness for everyone. The deaths of doctors George McDonald and Marteen Allen proved to be a test of strength, in regard to the relationship between God and man. The McDonald and Allen families struggled to come to terms with their losses. They saw each other through the tragedies, like they always had through the generations.

At the same time, business couldn't be better. 'Olde McDonald's Potato Farm' and 'Olde McDonald's Golf Course', were making money, hand over fist, even though both businesses were seasonal.

Eleanor (now the McDonald Matriarch, by widowhood) was not only faced with the tragedy of losing her husband and Joseph Jr.'s loss of his mother, but with losing her best friend and daughter too, as they moved away to Mississippi: She wasn't sure she would be able to handle this. She needed strength. As she often did most of her life, she turned to her Bible and to God.

The first book of Chronicles 16:11 teaches, "Seek the Lord, and his strength, seek his face continually". She'd always relied on God to see her through her life's trials and tribulations and this was a time she needed His love to help her find the strength to let Liz go. Liz had her own life and her own child coming into the world soon. Eleanor had to let her daughter go and find her own way, with her husband. It would be a challenge, since a multi-racial couple, a black husband and white wife, were very unusual for the 1940's, anywhere in the world.

When Joe applied for a job in Mississippi and was offered a position, he and Liz decided to accept and make the move. He would be designing bridges and overpasses around the city of Philadelphia, Neshoba County and outlying areas in this region of Mississippi. There were roads, highways and new interstates that needed both.

In Mississippi there were three major rivers. The Big Black, the Pearl and the Yazoo, which all needed bridges at so many places. The firm he was joining was always busy and he liked that prospect. He knew he would always be busy and never out of work.

Joe and Liz were excited to be starting a new life in a new country, just as grandparents Diana and Johnny had, around ninety years earlier when they'd moved from Scotland; clear across the ocean to Canada. Liz and Joe weren't going quite as far as Liz's great-grandparents or Joe's great-grandparents; from Africa to Jamaica, then to Mississippi and on to Canada. But it still was an exciting and significant move.

While both John and Diana's and Jed and Mary's journeys had taken sixty-seven days to complete, Liz and Joe's journey would only take them about forty-eight hours or less. Technology over the near century had greatly improved. Now, it took only around a week or less to sail across the Atlantic Ocean.

George Sr. bequeathed his wife, Eleanor and each of his children a substantial inheritance, including a large share of the businesses: the farm and golf course. Marteen left Joseph the house that Johnny and Diana had given Jed and Mary nearly as that many years earlier: As well as the 320 acres that Diana had willed to Marteen upon her death. The 320 acres was the original 'west field', which the McDonald's bought, when they moved to Canada. It would always belong to the Allen family. Marteen had not sectioned off her land, as El suggested earlier. She decided to let the family just keep working the crops on her land and they would pay her that land's portion of the profits. *That* money would go to Joe and Liz now.

Liz and Joe appreciated the inheritance and profit checks but they wanted to save that nest egg for their future and family. They invested some of their money right away. They wanted to be able to stand on their own four feet. When they moved away, they wanted to be the first of the family to be successful in their own right.

Their plan was to live off Joe's salary at first. But Liz would also be teaching at some point in time, bringing in another income. Joseph wanted to be the sole provider for their family but he was not stubborn enough to go against Liz's plans. She wanted to work and bring another income to their family too; a family that would include a baby in less than five months. They'd be ready...for him, or her.

They set aside their inheritance money and it would be there when they needed it, or wanted it; for something like a new house, vehicles, holiday, or their children and grandchildren's' future and education. They were determined to make it completely on their own. Eleanor understood and was very proud of them. Each of their lost parents would have been proud too. It was sad; but the grandchild Liz carried, would only have one grandmother. Most of the older generation from the farm had passed, by this time.

The day came when they set off on their journey. There were a lot of tears. Most of them were between Liz and Eleanor, especially with Liz pregnant! El was sure she wouldn't see her grandchild much: But Liz did some research recently and told her mother, "Mom, it's not like the old days of horse and wagon. Here in Canada we have Canadian Pacific Airways. You can fly out of Toronto and come directly to Mississippi, in only a few hours. You also have the option of crossing over to Detroit and flying out of there. It's likely shorter if you go out of Detroit, instead of Toronto." Eleanor was reassured and she said she'd come, as soon as the baby was born; and anyone who wanted to join her for the trip was welcomed to come, too. This was a grand family event and she wished to share it with everyone, so she would gladly pay. She was going to be a grandma!

Joe had to practically pry Liz and her mom apart. He wanted to get on the road as soon as he could because it was going to take them at least eighteen hours driving time, alone. They would keep the speed down to the proper limits, since they were driving with such a large load in the truck. It also depended on how comfortable Liz was. After all, she did have a baby sitting on her bladder. After finally prying Liz from her mom and her brothers, they were off for the adventure of their lifetime...whether it was to be good or bad.

Liz would need several bathroom breaks along the way and they both needed to stretch their legs once in a while. Liz didn't want Joe to know, but she would need a nap, too. She knew she just couldn't get comfortable sitting in the truck that long. He did realize this without her saying so. On the way he said, "Honey, I would like to stop and have a couple of hours to take a nap. I don't know why, I guess I just didn't sleep enough last night. You know the excitement of moving and all. Would you mind?"

Liz looked at him with great relief and said, "No sweetie. I wouldn't mind at all. If you like, I can drive for a bit." She hoped he would refuse her offer, for now.

He said, "No dear I'd like you to have a rest." They stopped at a motel. It was late afternoon and she was so glad that Joe mentioned it first. He was smiling inside but not letting Liz know he was doing this just for her.

After driving over nine-hundred miles from Chatham, Ontario to Philadelphia, Mississippi; Joe and Liz were relieved the trip was finally over. They had left the farm about forty hours earlier. Liz was also relieved about another thing - she never had any morning sickness.

The 1946 GMC CC-101 truck that Joe bought and put all his faith in drove like a champ. Even after this long trip, he felt there were many good years left in her. Joe was the first one to break with family tradition. He did not buy a Ford vehicle. Instead, he bought a General Motors pick-up truck. He was relieved that Liz's father or his grandfather weren't around to witness his decision.

His beautiful 'baby blue', as he called her, moved them and as many belongings as they could fit into the truck's box. Eleanor let Liz take some things from the McDonald house, but much of what they took came from the Allen house. There were things in the Allen house that were still there, from the day Jed and Mary Allen bought them at Lavalle's Mercantile, almost a century ago.

The pick-up's box had thirty square feet of space and they made use of every inch, but still they couldn't bring all of their large furnishings. They would have to buy a sofa and chair for the living room and a dining room suite, but they were able to move their double bed; including the mattress and the frame, spring and headboard. They could live out of their suitcases until they bought dressers. El insisted on Liz taking the large mirror, which Diana and Johnny found in their attic, the first night in their new house almost a hundred years earlier; to their own surprise then. It was the one that Diana had fallen in love with. Liz's mom knew that her daughter had admired that mirror all her life and thought she could take it with her. Their kitchen table and four chairs fit on the truck, since they could be taken apart and reassembled. The coffee table and two end tables, all their lamps, and Joseph's favorite, dirty old beat up recliner (fondly named old reliable)...which he would never part with, made it in the pick-up with no problem.

This was the infamous recliner he even managed to take to Queens University; and squeezed into his dormitory room. They were also able to fit their antique china cabinet and hutch in the truck. There was room for their dishes, silver and all smaller items, all their clothes and delicate and personal belongings, in the cab of the truck between them.

Eleanor had recently let Joe refinish one of the cradles and a rocking horse. She was letting the couple take both pieces with them to Mississippi. But it would be the first time that the set of two horses and two cradles would be split up. After Joe had refinished the set they were taking with them, Liz and Eleanor liked the job he did on them, so they asked him to refinish the other set. He didn't mind and it had been some time since it had been done. Everyone on the farm wondered who would need the other cradle and horse next. The two sets of finely crafted horses and cradles had held McDonald and Allen babies for almost one hundred years.

They could never leave their most cherished piece of furniture behind. They made sure they had room for it. When they married, one of the nicest wedding presents they received from their families was a beautiful console Victor Victrola radio and record player. This model played both AM and FM Radio with wonderful sound to it. The turntable was the most updated model and they loved to play all of their 78 rpm records which they had been collecting over the past few years. Since the 78's were a very breakable collection, they were difficult to move so they were stowed in the cab of the truck, between the two of them, all the way to Mississippi.

To top it all off, Joe purchased a large tarpaulin to keep everything dry. Albeit rare, there had been some freak snow and rain storms in the northern states, as well as in Chatham in past years, at this time of year.

They wanted to be ready for any and all kinds of weather so as to protect all their belongings, while moving south. As always, they consulted their Farmer's Almanac which revealed that they had picked an excellent couple of days for their trip...sunny! While Joe had been busy, wrapping up small details, packing, lifting, and making sure everything was looked after, Liz mapped out the route. She loved doing this.

After leaving Chatham, they headed to Windsor and then crossed the Ambassador Bridge, which took them from Windsor, Ontario to Detroit, Michigan. There was a delay at the border, however. The guards held them up for quite a while so they could check out why a black man and a white woman would be traveling together and claim they were married and relocating to Mississippi, of all places. The guards' laughter, gave way to concern. They thought that there had to be trouble.

After three hours, proof of their births and their marriage and a few phone calls; one being to Eleanor to confirm that this was her daughter and that she was married to Joe and he was not kidnapping her, the border guards eventually let them go on their way. One of the guards waved at them sarcastically saying, "Good luck folks. You're gonna need it where you're goin'!" Joe and Liz couldn't understand what the problem was, or what they really meant.

The Ambassador Bridge was Joe's favorite bridge when he was growing up. He memorized the details of this huge suspension bridge since around the age of eight or so. Its length was 7,500 feet which spanned the Detroit River. Construction on it started in 1927, when he was just eight years old. It was completed in 1929 and opened in 1930. Whenever opportunity allowed, he would take off from the farm if anyone was going into Windsor and he would go just to look at the bridge. They were also building a tunnel at the same time, which opened in 1930. The Detroit and Windsor Tunnel was constructed under the Detroit River. It was 5,160 feet long, just short of a mile long. Growing up, he was always telling Liz that someday he would become a structural engineer and would build bridges and tunnels.

True to his word, after graduation, Joe had a hand in the construction of overpasses and assisted on some bridges in Toronto. He loved the work. He was well respected in the industry in Ontario and for a black man; that was very rare. He was always hearing of major projects coming up worldwide. His boss in Windsor kept him apprised of job openings on other structures, although he did not want to lose him from the firm.

Then one day, came word from Mississippi. There were overpasses and bridges to be built in the Mississippi area. He applied for the job and received a glowing reference from his boss and Liz told him, "Wherever you go Joe, I do! We're in this life together, forever." He loved her so much. Her patience and dedication to him was unparalleled by anything else in his life.

They made their way through Detroit and then forged on to Ohio where they went through Toledo, Findlay, Lima, Sidney, Dayton and Cincinnati. They had to stop a few times for gas and rest stops. They only took time to buy cold drinks or coffee, since Caroline had made them many sandwiches for the journey. After Cincinnati, they went on to Louisville Kentucky, where they found a motel for the night. That first day, Joe had driven for almost ten hours total and Liz eventually drove two, just for a change of pace.

They took about six hours off the road when they arrived at a motel in Louisville. They slept well and got an early start the next morning. In Kentucky, they passed through Elizabethtown; where Joe teased that his wife was so special, they named a town after her. She blushed as she smiled at him. Tennessee was the next state on the trip.

When they hit Nashville, Joe surprised Liz with a stop at Ryman Theater, The Grand Ole Opry. Liz was so thrilled. They both had been brought up on country, gospel and bluegrass music. Both families listened faithfully to the Opry shows. Some of Liz and Joe's favorites were The Carter Family, Bill Munroe, Roy Acuff and of course the comedy of Minnie Pearl.

They stopped for a few hours. It gave her time to rest and stretch while walking around. His stop here was a big surprise to her; so she could take in and feel the history of the place. She had always hoped to visit someday. They walked around the theater and then a bit of the town

After Nashville they drove through Athens and then came to the Alabama border. The next main towns were Cullman, Birmingham and Tuscaloosa. Joe asked if she needed to stop and she told him, "No love, let's just keep going." They finally arrived at the Mississippi border. They drove on through Meridian and DeKalb and finally, Neshoba County, and their new hometown of Philadelphia.

When they arrived they put behind them the rudeness and accusations made at the Canada and U.S. Border. The border guards couldn't believe that Joe was not a kidnapper taking Liz across the border by force. And, what did they mean with their final comments?

After crossing the border, they questioned their decision to move, but then eventually laughed it off. Surely the whole of the United States of America did not hold the same bigoted attitudes as the border guards. After all, they were just a family of two, awaiting their baby's arrival and moving south to begin a new job.

This was the right time for them to leave the farm which they had grown up on. They wanted more independence than their parents and family predecessors. They needed to get over the tragedies. They wanted to reach out and go somewhere new, have their own family and start a new branch of the family tree...away from Scotland, Africa and Chatham. They loved growing up on the farm and working, going to school, university, church, learning the farm business, the golfing, skating, hockey, everything about the lives they had grown up with. But, they had other aspirations than to become farmers.

Farming was a noble living, but they wanted a different life for themselves and their children. Liz imagined that they were following in the steps of their great-grandparents, Diana and Johnny and Mary and Jed, on their journey to another life. Would they be successful? Only time would tell.

Growing up, Liz and Joe both loved learning about their families. Their mothers, Eleanor and Marteen kept their histories alive. From Berko and Afua, and John and Diana, right down to their own lives: Elizabeth and Joseph would listen to all the stories passed down through the generations with great interest. Sometimes when they were growing up, they would talk about what they learned about their families and were fascinated. They never got tired of the history and their parents wanted to tell them as much as they could. They wanted this history to pass down through the ages. Liz, in particular, wanted to know everything, every detail that could ever be remembered...about the great ship Destino, both families landing in a Port Royal in two different countries, Berko and Afua both being from the same tribe, living a few miles apart, but never knowing each other until they were slaves. They wanted to know how both sets of great-grandparents picked October 10 as their wedding date and many other "common threads" as Great-grandma Diana had called them.

The most important pieces of their family history were now being taken away from Chatham, where they had been for almost one-hundred years: On to another country again. The McGee tartan and the Allen Kente Cloth Robe were very well taken care of by each generation of each family. When Joseph and Elizabeth were married both of these pieces of history were passed on to them and they in turn, would hand them down to their children. Since now the two separate families, the Allen's and the McDonald's, had become one; their son or daughter, would be entrusted to be the keeper of these "Common Threads". The McDonald and the Allen family history were indeed rich and well-traveled.

The tartan had traveled from Scotland, through half of Canada and was now on its way to Mississippi, U.S.A. The Kente Cloth Robe which Afua made herself, journeyed from Africa, to Jamaica, onward to Mississippi, up to Canada and now back to Mississippi. The McDonald and the Allen family history were indeed rich and well-traveled!

In their new home town of Philadelphia, they found a motel that not only had rooms, but they also had cabins to rent. You could pay by the week. This was perfect for them. They would stay there until they could find a house they could afford to rent. Liz went into the motel office and both the motel manager took a shine to her and so did his wife. Liz always said that being pregnant usually brings out the best in other people.

They told her, "Ma'am, if we can do anything for ya'll, just let us know." She thanked them as they gave her a complimentary, daily newspaper and she went to the cabin assigned and gave Joe the key. It was a sort of secluded, private one bedroom, living room and kitchenette. They were one of the few motels in the mid 1940's in this region to boast indoor plumbing, too.

This was now Wednesday and Joe had to report to his new office on Monday. He wanted to move in to a place before he started working, if it was at all possible. Joe would get to his new office and meet George

Benson; his new boss, the owner of the business, Benson and Associates. The associates were actually the staff of engineers working for him. His company was small yet diverse. He hired different types of engineers. Joe was a structural engineer, his specialty being bridges.

Liz and Joe were looking forward to settling in for their first night. Liz made dinner for them and Joe read the houses for rent ads in the newspaper. There were three good possibilities he circled. He called two of them for now to make an appointment to look at them on Thursday. After they ate, Joe said, "Darlin' why don't we go take a peek at the other one to see if we want to pursue it as well. I need some air." She agreed. It was only a few blocks away and they found it easily. They liked the exterior and so decided to make the appointment to see the inside. As soon as they got back to the cabin, Joe lay down on the bed and crashed. He was sound asleep, in minutes.

Thursday morning they had breakfast and started out to look at the first two houses. The first one, the landlord told them to, "Go to hell you fuckin' stupid coon, you don't think I'd ever rent to no fuckin' Nigger and a white whore! Leave now before I get my shotgun!" With that, Joe and Liz were horrified and jumped in the truck. They couldn't believe what they heard.

The second appointment went much the same. They drove up to this address which they were to see and got out of the truck. There was a man on the porch who yelled to them, "Are you the ones who want to rent the house?"

Joe said, "Yes sir."

He took a look at Joseph and yelled again to them, "If you know what's good 'fer ya', you lousy Nigger, you'll get back in that truck o' yourn and go back ta' where ya'll come from." They heeded this advice and got in the truck and sped off towards the next appointment. Liz asked Joe to stop at a park they were driving by. He did, not knowing what she had in mind. They now believed they were very sheltered about life and racism, when they lived in Ontario. Even though at university Joe came up against a little bigotry: It always seemed to work out okay for him and he had many friends there. Being an athlete; the star player on the hockey team helped, he was sure.

Liz looked at him lovingly and said, "You know honey, I think we're going to get the same response at the next house, too. I think we have to change our tactic. I know it may seem a little dishonest, but I think you should go back to the motel and let me go to the next appointment alone. Let me look at the house and talk to the landlord, sign a lease, pay the rent...and just tell him my husband will join me soon. I know what we're looking for, what we have to spend and I'm sure I can pick a place we'll both love to live...and our baby, too. What do you think?"

Joe was downhearted, but he thought she may be right. He said, "I love you sweetie. Yeah, I think it's the only way we're going to get a home in this town. Let's do it. Actually, it will give me time to call Mr. Benson to let him know we've arrived and I'll be in the office first thing on Monday morning."

Their plan went into action. Liz dropped Joe off back at the motel. Elizabeth gave him a kiss and said confidently "This next one is ours! I can feel it!"

She drove to the third house and a man and his wife greeted her cordially. "Hello dear, are you the lady that would like to rent the house? We're Mr. and Mrs. Diamont, and you must be Elizabeth." Liz smiled and felt good about this.

"Yes, I'm Elizabeth Allen. Please call me Liz." She told them about her long trip to Mississippi from Ontario, Canada and that her husband was wrapping up business there and she was in charge of finding a place to live and he would join her shortly to start a new job. She hoped God would not strike her dead for her lies. As Mrs. Diamont took Liz through the house, she talked constantly, while Liz listened and looked at everything. She loved everything about the house. The three bedrooms, a good sized fenced yard, big farm-style kitchen and the living room was a little smaller than they were used to, but the dining room was a good size. There was a large basement and indoor plumbing. The people who moved out were moving overseas and they were limited on what they could take with them: So there were some furnishings that came with it, if they wanted them. No extra cost.

The rent was reasonable and Mr. Diamont asked if her husband would sign a one year lease. She told them he would, but with him not here, she'd be happy to sign it. Her husband wouldn't mind. Mr. Diamont was a little more business minded. He said to Liz, "Now I don't mean to offend Mrs. Allen, but down here we take the word, the handshake and signature of the man."

She said, "Well how about I sign now, I have the money to pay you right now, for two months and when my husband gets here, he can sign it too. Would that be alright with you Mr. Diamont? I really love this house." Mr. Diamont rubbed his chin and was pensive.

His wife said, "Dear, I think this will be fine. She obviously has the money and needs a place to live."

Liz continued, "Do you play bridge, or euchre? Maybe we could make it a social evening. You could come for dinner and we could play cards. How does that sound?" She hoped they would agree. She wanted to find friends and maybe she could start with them. Mr. Diamont looked to his wife and she smiled with a nod. He did agree and let her sign the lease and she paid two months in advance. The rent was $125.00 which included heat and power.

As Liz signed the lease she said, "How about this Sunday evening? My husband will be here and probably nervous about starting his new job the next day. This will help keep his mind off it. Please, you'd be doing us a big favor?"

Mr. and Mrs. Diamont smiled and nodded as he replied, "We would love to Liz. Please, it's Alvin and Agnes." They shook hands on the deal and she thanked them both. Liz took $250.00 out of her purse and Mr. Diamont gave her the keys to her new house. He promised her a receipt when they came for supper on Sunday; he had forgotten his receipt book that day.

Mr. and Mrs. Diamont asked if they could help her because they could see most of their belongings on the truck. Although it hadn't occurred to her, she thought yeah, why not let them help unload for her. Mrs. Diamont thought she could see that Liz was pregnant and told her husband not to let her lift anything heavy. It only took a half hour to unload everything off the truck. She thanked them gratefully and they told her to let them know if there was anything they could help her with, until her husband arrived, but she said that she would be fine. She excitedly got into the truck and was so pleased with herself. She couldn't wait to tell Joe. She pulled in to the motel parking lot and drove over to their cottage. In front of their cabin were two police cars, three policemen, an ambulance and the motel owner; and Joseph in handcuffs, with a bleeding lip.

After she had dropped Joe off, the manager saw a black man go into the cabin and he called the police. Joe told the police that management had rented the cabin to a really nice, white lady the day before; and now the truck and she were both gone. The manager couldn't believe there was nothing to her disappearance. He was certain that she must have met with foul play at the hands of this Nigger. He wanted to have Joe charged with break and enter...even though he had the key.

As Liz got out of the truck, she ran to Joseph's side and asked, "What is going on here? Who hurt my husband?" She got her handkerchief out of her purse and started to dab the blood off Joe's lip. The policemen and the manager all dropped their jaws. Joe was telling the truth after all. He really WAS married to her. There was really no crime to charge Joe with, since he had the keys and Liz was fine, so the police took the handcuffs off. The manager told them that they could no longer stay there and they would have to leave immediately. Liz asked for a refund, since she paid for a week, but the manager refused.

She looked at the police and said, "Officers, please tell this... gentleman he owes us some money back since he is making us leave today. We only arrived yesterday and we paid for a whole week."

The officers laughed at her, as one of them said, "Lady, you just be thankful we don't run you outta town. You'd best be gittin' your shit out of that there cabin and get on the road, before we do find somethin' ta' charge ya'll with. And I gotta tell ya', you'se ain't gonna have too easy a time here wit' your...husband! Ya'll might wanna think 'bout movin' ta' 'nother town." The officer spat out the tobacco he was chewing and it landed on Joseph's pants and shoes.

The policemen got in their cars and left laughing, while the manager stood near the doorway of the cabin, watching them gather their belongings and quickly put them in the truck. Liz hadn't had time yet to tell Joe the good news. As they were gathering everything up, she looked to her husband and saw the hurt and disappointment on his face. She leaned in close to him and whispered, "Honey, we got the house let's just get out of here and go to our new home."

As they drove away from the parking lot she asked him, "Joe, who hit you, and why?" He said nothing. She regretted asking him when she saw the shameful look on his face, but asked again.

Joe told her, "I guess I deserved it. I got a little defiant when the policeman asked me what the hell I was doing here. I told them, 'Well, I don't see how it's any business of yours sir' and all of a sudden one of them punched me in the mouth and with that, I told them I'd paid to use this cabin for a week, if you don't believe me, ask the manager. The cabin is paid for. The next thing I know, another one of them punched me again, for sassing back at them. I'm glad that was the extent of it. How would that look? Bruises and cuts on my face, showing up for my first day of work on a brand new job! I should have kept my big mouth shut!" She fell silent for a few moments, not knowing what to say. She embarrassed him and she felt bad.

Joe changed the subject, "So, Mrs. Allen I see not only did you find us a place to live, it looks like you also found people to help you to unload the truck, too...someone did help you, right? You didn't lift anything heavy, did you?"

She smiled her devilish smile that he loved so much and said, "Of course I didn't lift anything heavy, dear. I know better and please don't worry so much, we'll be fine. Oh honey, the landlords are a lovely husband and wife, Mr. & Mrs. Diamont. They were temporarily satisfied to let me sign the contract, but I had to promise them that you would sign as soon as possible. Mr. Diamont insists on that. It's the way of the south apparently!

So, I did the best thing I could possibly do; I invited them to come to dinner on Sunday, to have you sign the lease and to play bridge. They thanked me, agreed to come and out of the blue, they offered to help unload the truck and of course, thinking of my hard working husband, I gratefully accepted their help. I figured if we just took everything inside, you and I can take our time getting unpacked and organized. Oh Joe, you should see our house; you're going to love it...the yard is big and fenced in, the three bedrooms are a good size...Joe, it's beautiful."

As they were stopped at a red light, Joseph said, "Will you please come up for air honey? Take a break, catch your breath and remind me what the address of our perfect new home is?"

They both laughed. Liz said, "It's 2 Gilbert Street? Let's just forget about the bad morning, put it behind us, chalk it up to ignorance and enjoy the rest of the day. Oh yeah, they said we could wallpaper or paint if we want to. Mr. Diamont said to go ahead and buy what we want and give him the receipt. He'll reimburse us.

They just put in a new Frigidaire and stove. Never used yet. Oh Joe, I'm so excited. Our first house, well it's our first rental. Maybe in a year or so, we might buy one of our own. What do you think? It's going to be so wonderful here honey. I think the kitchen could use some paint and maybe wallpaper in the bedrooms. Honey, I know just how I want the nursery to look. It's too bad people couldn't find out what they're having in advance; you know, boy or girl, so you could decorate in pink or blue. Wouldn't that be neat...just imagine that you would be able to know, so you could pick out the perfect name and buy the clothes the right color and people would know what kind of gifts to give. I'll just bet science someday will be able to do that...just imagine ..."

Joe interrupted his wife, "Liz, we're here. How about you stop talking about the house and we'll go inside it?"

They laughed. Suddenly, Liz was swept off her feet and he carried her across the veranda. She had the keys, unlocked the door and her prince charming carried her across the threshold...again. This was the fourth time she was carried across a threshold. After they married, he carried her across the hotel threshold in Windsor, at the farm; he carried her across the threshold of the room they used in the McDonald house and the Allen house. Now she was being carried across the threshold of their house in Mississippi. Although they only rented this house, it was different. They felt it was theirs.

They kissed passionately. Joe set her down in the living room. She had forgotten to tell him that there were some furnishings that also came with the house. She told him that the sofa was actually a hide-a-bed which opens up to reveal a double bed and there was a matching chair. He smiled his sexiest smile and he pulled it open and unfolded the bed.

It was in very good shape and the mattress looked like it hadn't been used. Joseph locked the doors, found a box of blankets and placed some temporarily over the windows, all the while, Elizabeth stood there in the middle of the room watching him, thinking how much she loved him.

She had loved him since they played together as toddlers on the farm. Her earliest memories were of him, her best friend. He finally turned to her and gave her a most loving look. He kissed her hard. It had been a while since they made love. The move had been the only thing on their minds, of late. Liz fell deep into his arms; it was like melting with him to make two bodies become one.

She liked to nibble on his ear. It drove him crazy. As she placed his earlobe gently between her teeth, he moaned. She was wearing a skirt and blouse. Joe started to unbutton her blouse and unzipped the zipper in the back of her skirt. Her skirt dropped to the floor and he slowly pushed her blouse off her shoulders and let it drop, revealing her slip. He kissed her shoulders; one, then the other. She lifted her head back to give better access to her neck. She loved to have her neck kissed and nuzzled. She kept her arms around him as he kissed her more. He pulled her slip above her head as she lifted her arms to help. He sank to his knees, gently kissing her growing stomach. She took his hands as he stood up again. She unbuttoned his shirt and pushed it off. She slowly lifted his undershirt over his head.

She kissed his neck and chest. She was so aroused that she could barely contain her excitement. She quickly opened his belt, unbuttoned and unzipped his trousers. As everything fell to the floor, he helped her get out of her bra and underwear. He picked her up again and placed her on the hide-a-bed. He kissed her lips and slowly made a trail of kisses as he moved down her body. He placed his lips over her hard nipple. He teasingly sucked on it and he slowly moved down over her stomach, with more kisses. As his chin got closer to her soft pubic hair, it tickled. She was breathing heavier now and was starting to moan. She wanted him, now. She couldn't wait much longer. Neither could he. He was so hard and ready. He thrust his penis gently into her; yet at the same time, being careful to not be too rough because of her pregnancy. Her anticipation for this moment was all she could think of. As he started to move in and out of her, feeling her wetness, she couldn't stand any more. She exploded into the greatest climax she had ever experienced in her life, up until now. Joseph followed very quickly with his.

They were both out of breath, but Joe managed ask if he had hurt her. In between heavy breaths, she told him, "No, not at all." She smiled at him as she tenderly touched his cheek. She said, "Oh love, you were incredible and gentle, as always. I love you so much." He smiled back, as he was thinking how lucky he was to have someone who loved him so much. They kissed and fell asleep in each other's arms, for a couple of hours that afternoon.

Their first day and night in their new house, the hours flew by. Liz had Joe help her wash shelves, cupboards and floors. He put up all the curtains on the main floor and the blinds in the bedrooms upstairs. Liz knew she would want them put up right away, for privacy, so she washed and dried all the curtains and wiped down all the blinds before they left Ontario. They were all ready to put up. All of them were the right size, with the exception of the living room curtains. They needed to be shortened by almost one and a half feet. There was a big difference between farm house windows and the windows in a town style house.

Farm houses traditionally had six foot long windows, while town and city house windows were only about four to five feet long, at the most.

One of the first things Liz would need to set up was her sewing machine. She had a Singer manual, treadle model. Johnny had bought it from Lavalle's General Store in Chatham, as a Christmas gift for Diana one year. She loved to sew and passed down her sewing machine to the next generation. Dora inherited the machine; then Eleanor and she passed it on to Liz. Each generation also received the skill and the lessons from their mothers.

Liz's sewing problem was always the double yoke in a nightgown or shirt, for that added layer of warmth around the neck and shoulders. She always needed help with it. Liz always got it turned backwards and inside-out. It took her lots of practice to get it right. She helped her mom make many of the clothes her family wore. When it came to hemming curtains, Liz was a pro. She could do it in her sleep.

Joe unpacked boxes and put things away, where Liz wanted them: All the while, discussing paint and wall paper. He reassembled the table and chairs and set up the house, with Liz's advice and help. When it came to his chair, it had to be in the right location. Joe had to 'position' it just right. He would place it somewhere in the living room and sit in it and try it out. If it didn't 'feel' right, he moved it somewhere else and tried it again. He did this several times. After a half hour and four different spots, he was happy. Each time he tried a location, he had to get Liz to sit on his lap, to make sure the chair was easily accessible and comfortable for her, too. After he was happy with the right spot, he decided to go get the paint, so he could have the downstairs painted before their company, on Sunday.

They decided on what colors of paint they would like for the downstairs and they would like to change the wallpaper upstairs in the bedrooms. She got Joe to park the truck in the Piggly Wiggly parking lot, since the hardware store was only down the street, half a block away. That way, it was closer for her to get the groceries to the truck.

While Joe was being his jovial, friendly self, he had said hello and good day to people on the street and in the hardware store. He was met with cold stares and some ignorance. He just chalked it up to being the 'new kid in town' syndrome. Some people took time to warm up to strangers.

While in the grocery store, Liz picked up the food for Sunday night and what they would need for the next week, which included makings for Joe to take for lunches at work. For Sunday supper, Liz decided to make a nice roast beef, salad, corn and potatoes. She would also prepare a lemon meringue pie, for dessert. The grocery bill was unexpected, for different reasons. It seemed high to Liz, because at the farm there was little to buy, because they had, or could make almost everything on the farm. But, it was low compared to Canadian prices. In the next few days, they would learn many lessons, in their newly adopted country.

Sunday, Agnes Diamont called Liz and asked her what time they should come over. When Liz and Joe moved in, there was already a working telephone. Agnes knew the number, since she and her husband had it put in and they fixed the cost into the rent. Liz said, "How about you come around four-thirty? Supper will be ready around five, or shortly after." Agnes agreed.

As they hung up the phone, Liz told Joe that he should wear a suit, to make an impression. Joe was in a romantic mood again and tried to get Liz to go to bed. She told him, "No, get out of my kitchen and let me make the pie!" As he started to undo her apron and kiss her neck, she started to laugh.

Joe stopped and asked, "What, may I ask are you laughing at?"

Liz said, "I was just wondering how you would look in meringue?" She quickly spun around, took a hand full of meringue she had whipped up, grabbed the bowl and started to chase her husband around the house. She threw it, while he tried to dodge it.

He tripped over his recliner, yelling, "Who the hell put that damn chair there?" Liz laughed even more, for him asking such a stupid question. As he sat on the floor, he remembered, HE placed his chair in that spot, he started to laugh.

Liz said, "Now, please let me finish getting supper ready and whip some more meringue." She snickered at his as he went to change his clothes.

As four-thirty arrived, so did their company. The doorbell rang and to the horror of Mr. and Mrs. Diamont, a black man answered the door. They were speechless. Liz ran out of the kitchen, to the door, so she could make introductions. As she got to the door, she said, "Hi folks. Honey, I'd like to introduce you to our landlords and our new friends,

Alvin and Agnes Diamont. This is my husband, Joseph Allen." Joe put out his hand to shake Alvin's and he refused it. Joe started to feel very awkward. Liz, too.

Alvin said, "Mrs. Allen, you seemed to have deceived us. You never said your husband was a...a...black man." Liz said, "Oh, I didn't know I was supposed to. Is there a problem?"

Alvin said, "My first instinct is to kick you out of our house, right now."

Agnes interrupted, "Alvin, why can't we let them stay for as long as it takes to find another house. They need somewhere to live." Joe stood there and he felt like an alien that just landed here from Mars. He didn't know what to say, or do.

Alvin rubbed his chin and said, "Well, I don't know. You should have told us you were married to a black man. They don't accept that relationship down here you know."

Liz said, "What do you mean? We've been married over a year and it's perfectly fine in Southern Ontario, where we were born and grew up. What is the problem?"

Agnes said, "You are in a new country now dear. The south, in particular, doesn't accept black people, no matter if you're married, or not. You should have moved to the outskirts of town, where the rest of them live. Didn't you know that about Mississippi, before you moved?"

Liz said, "No, we really didn't know. The bible says we are all God's children. Now, won't you please come in?"

Alvin hesitated for a few seconds, taking in the situation. He put his hand out to Joe and said, "I never cross the threshold of any man's home, without an introduction and a handshake. We've already had the introduction from your wife." He put his hand out to Joe, who took it immediately. Joe started to sense that he needed white people in their corner here.

As the Diamont's came in, Agnes and Liz gave a little hug to each other. Both women were relieved. You could tell both women wanted things to work out between them. Liz excused herself to go in the kitchen and Agnes asked if she could help. Liz thought, no time like the present to leave the men alone to see what happens. The ladies went into the kitchen and the men sat in the living room.

Alvin started the conversation, "I here you're starting a new job tomorrow. Where? Benson's was it?"

Joe was relieved that Alvin started to talk, first. He said, "Yes, Benson and Associates. I'm a structural engineer. I design and build bridges and overpasses. I was invited to apply for the job, and I was accepted." Alvin was very impressed. He thought, if that bunch of white bigoted men can accept and work with him, Joe must be ok! Alvin got a good feeling and he started to talk and carry on a conversation, starting with congratulating him on his job and that they didn't have to look for somewhere else to live. He did not know that Benson and Associates and Joe Allen had never met face-to-face. Alvin accepted Joe, being none the wiser.

Liz said, "C'mon guys, supper's ready." As she and Agnes brought the food to the table, the men were still talking.

As they all sat down, Joe asked them to all hold hands while he offered the blessing. "Dear Lord, we thank thee for the food we are about to receive and for our new friends. God bless them and keep them in the hollow of thy hands, Amen."

They all repeated Amen and Alvin said, "Thank you for the kind blessing Joe, but I am afraid we are not worthy of your kind words."

Liz said, "Nonsense, you're our first friends here. We'll always be grateful for your friendship." They ate and everyone commented on how great dinner was. The ladies washed the dishes, while Joe got the table ready to play cards.

Alvin asked, "Do you mind if I smoke my pipe?"

Joe chuckled and said, "Well Alvin, it's your house." They relaxed and chuckled. The tension was over and forgotten!

Alvin lit his pipe and said, "No Joe, it's your house."

They played cards until about ten-thirty, when Agnes suggested that they stop and leave, so Joe could get to sleep and get ready for his first day on the new job. Later, as Liz and Joe got into bed, Liz asked if he was alright. He told her he was a little nervous, but okay. He kissed her and did not let her know, he was starting to get a little worried. He finally fell asleep, wondering what his first day on the job would bring, and he prayed.

Chapter 2

The New Job

A s MONDAY MORNING ROLLED AROUND, Joe had butterflies in his stomach. Liz was a nervous wreck for him. It was the first day of his new job. As Liz always liked to, she helped Joe with his tie. She said, "Honey, don't worry, you'll be fine. Remember, you're a top structural engineer and you're going to wow 'em!"

He smiled and said, "I'm glad you're so confident! I wish I was as calm as you are." She finished with his tie and she put her arms around his waist and kissed him.

She said, "I made your lunch. You have roast beef sandwich, some of your favorite cookies I made yesterday, an apple, and I'm sure they will have coffee, or a Coca-Cola machine, so you can get a drink." As she walked him to the kitchen to get his lunch, she reached up and kissed him again, and she started to tear up.

Joe said, "What are the tears for?"

Liz said, "Honey, I am so proud of you. Please remember, I love you so much."

Joe gave her another kiss and said, "I love you too, sweetie. What are your plans for the day?"

Liz said, "I thought I'd go to the library and look up what kind of community history there is to learn, here. Also, I want to check out the Board of Education, to see what I have to do to qualify for teaching here. If I have to study before exams, I want to start right away. I'd like to get in a school somewhere, before the baby comes, so I can get my foot in the door. That way, I'll be able to work whenever I am comfortable leaving him OR her, with someone. The other thing at the library, maybe I can get some advice, where to find a housekeeper too, oh yeah, one other thing, I want to do a bit more grocery...oops, I mean marketing. You know, stock up."

Joe said, "Now, don't you do too much there, lady. I don't want you getting exhausted, walking around. As a matter of fact, do you want to drive me, and you take the truck, today?"

She said, "No honey, I can walk."

Joe pulled out his wallet and got some money out for her, saying, "Here you go, you can take taxis."

Liz said, "I'll walk a bit for exercise and when I have to take a taxi, I will. I promise. Please don't worry, dear. I'll be fine." She kissed him again and said, "have a good day, darlin'. See you tonight."

He waved back at her, saying, "I'll call you later and let you know how things are going." He left and got in his truck. As it started, he said a little prayer hoping God was listening and would be with him, for whatever today held for him.

"Benson and Associates"...his new job was with the firm of Benson and Associates. He would now be one of them. George Benson's Associates were men who were top in their field. He had two geotechnical engineers and three other structural engineers, which Joe would be working with. He also had two transportation engineers and four hydraulic engineers. That made for a compliment of twelve highly qualified engineers in the office. The boss, George Benson, was also a civil and a geotechnical engineer. He was able to supervise all the projects he had going.

The only other person in the office was the secretary, Maria Mendoza. She got her job at Benson's after George's wife passed away from cancer, the previous year. She had been his secretary, since they started up the business twenty years earlier.

Regular office hours were Monday to Friday, 8:30 a.m. to 5:00 p.m. There could also be occasional overtime on some projects: Mostly the ones out of town. George bid on projects within a hundred mile radius. Before each man was hired, he knew this and accepted it.

Joe was proud of himself. He was so happy. He had a great wife, who loved him as much as he loved her, a new job doing what he loved to do and was trained for at Queen's, a great house to live in and a baby on the way. He thought to himself, I've got it all! Then, his thoughts turned to his mother. He missed her. He wished she were still around. He knew she would be proud of him. He was sure his father would be, too.

As he pulled into the parking lot of Benson and Associates, his happiness gave way to nervousness again. He grabbed his briefcase, with his lunch and some designs and specs of the previous work in Toronto, including many photos. Joe liked to take photos of his projects. He used them in his portfolio. He took them from ground-breaking ceremonies, when applicable, right through to the finished product, so to speak.

Along with these, he also brought another couple of letters of reference, from his boss, the clients and some people he worked over. He had a great working relationship in Toronto. Everyone there respected him and his talent.

When he pushed the door open, he heard lots of banter between the men in the office and the phone ringing. He had a good feeling, at first. He walked to the front counter. As he did, the whole office fell silent. The only sound heard, was the female secretary, talking quietly on the phone, as she stared at Joe. A man came to the counter and said, "Yeah boy, what do you want?" Joe was a little shocked by the slight ignorance he heard. He chalked it up to a Monday morning, 'I really don't want to be here' state of mind.

He stuck out his hand to the gentleman behind the counter and said, "Good morning; am I speaking to Mr. George Benson?"

The man said, "No BOY, you ain't!" He refused to shake Joe's hand. George came to the counter.

He told the man at the counter, "Just get ready for the meeting, Ray. I'll take care of this." The man walked to a desk and sat down. Everyone started to talk and work, again. The man had a bit of a sneer on his face. Joe was a little nervous again.

George said, "I'm George Benson. How can I help you?"

Joe said, as he put his hand out, "Well sir, I'm Joe Allen, your newest structural engineer." Everything went silent again. As he looked around the office, everyone was staring at him. Now; he was starting to feel a little sick with butterflies, again.

George shook his hand. But, it wasn't a sincere hand shake; and all of a sudden Joe felt like he had the plague. George said, "Are you sure?

I mean, you're the talented engineer from Canada that came so highly recommended? You did the jobs in Toronto?"

Joe nervously nodded his head, "Yes sir, that's me. I brought some of my designs, along with photos, so you can see my work. I also have more letters of reference for you, if you like."

George said, "I'm sorry for staring, but I honestly thought I was hiring a white man. Uh, yes, I want to see your designs, photos and references."

As Joe took the papers out of his briefcase, he said, "I'm really sorry, I can't change my color for you, but I assure you, you hired the right man for the job."

All of a sudden, the man named Ray got up from his desk saying, "Now don't you be sassin' boy. Ya'll mind your place, or I'll mind it 'fer ya'."

Joe now wanted to turn around and run right back to Chatham, but he didn't want to be a coward. He apologized to George. George waved his hand, as to let Joe know he wasn't bothered by his comment. But Ray was still coming toward the counter: As he did, George put up his hand, to Ray this time, not to bother him.

George said, "Looks like you did great work and you have great designs. I'll give you that."

Joe said, "Thank you sir, I'm sure you'll be pleased with my work here, too. I'm anxious to get started on some of your projects."

Ray said, "Oh c'mon George, you gotta be kidding! You expect us to work alongside a fuckin' 'coon? No God Damn way!"

George said, "Ray, sit down and shut up. Get your notes ready for the meeting. All the rest of you; do the same." George opened the half swinging door at the end of the counter so Joe could come in.

As Joe came in to the inner 'working' office Ray stood up again. He yelled at George "No George! No way am I sittin' here with a Nigger! No fuckin' way!" He looked around to the other men who were silently making it look like they were working. He continued "C'mon you guys you ain't gonna to put up with this bullshit either, are ya'?" No one answered him. They put their heads down to do their preparations for a meeting.

George scowled at him and said, "Then Ray, are you prepared to submit your resignation today?" Ray sat down, grumbling. George knew he had to let Joe start the job. He couldn't back out of their agreement. He hoped Ray would simmer down.

The office was set up; so that the engineers who were in the same field, sat together. There were four groups of large desks. There were two sets of two desks facing each other; and there were two sets of four desks. These were; two desks side by side, facing the other two desks, which were side by side as well. The secretary sat at a desk just behind the counter and George had a private office.

Ray was sitting again and mad as hell. Before the introductions Joe wasn't sure what to do when being introduced to the other men. He had to make a snap decision. He decided not to put his hand out, again. He would nod an acknowledgment for each man and say, "How do you do, sir?" If they offered their hand, he certainly would take it.

George said, "We have several projects in the works right now. You'll be placed on our newest project. As a matter of fact, its day one for everyone assigned to this one. You'll get right in with the guys, on the ground floor." George started the introductions with the secretary, "This is Maria Mendoza. You'll detect a little accent. She's from Mexico and she looks after us all." He said this with an almost paternal smile.

She just said, "Hi", as did Joe.

George took Joe around and started the rest of the introductions. He started at the first set of four desks, where Ray sat. He said "These guys are my crack team of hydraulic engineers. Uh, you already know Ray Halden, born and raised here in Philadelphia." Joe did not make the mistake of putting his hand out for a greeting, again. Joe and Ray were two totally different specialists and it would be unusual if they had to work side-by-side on the same projects. George made a mental note to himself, not to assign Joe and Ray, to the same projects, if it could be avoided.

George carried on to the other hydraulic engineers. "Here we have Jesse Snow, from Tennessee and we have Bubba Shep and Rick Gills, who come from Louisiana." Each one nodded a hello to Joe, and he reciprocated.

They went on to a set of two desks and George said, "These fellas are my geotechnical engineers, Graydon Carlton from California and Daniel Cooms, from British Columbia, Canada. Many times the projects cross over from geotech, to hydraulic. We've done a lot of river, levee, dyke, the odd dam over the years. You know jobs like that."

George went to the third set of two desks and said, "Over here are my transportation engineers. I'd have to say that these guys are the busiest in the office. They are never out of work. These guys design roads all over the county. They'll never be without a job. Here's Brian Marsh from Santa Monica, California and Walter Bryant from Toronto. If there is a place for traffic, road construction, or highway building on this earth, it's those two cities; and these guys are the best. Oh yeah, you're not the only guy I hired from Canada...as you've heard."

The last set of desks, the last four, had three occupied and an empty one. This was to be Joe's desk. George said, "Here are my structural engineers and this is your team. We have Carroll Byers, another born and bred here in Philadelphia." He nodded, but did not offer his hand. "Here is Lorne Sheffield. He hails from Toronto."

Lorne stood up and said, "Hi, Joe is it?" He reached his hand out and took Joe's, as Joe nodded to him and said hello to him. Lorne said, "Great to meet you Joe. Maybe you can fill me in on what was up in Toronto, when you were working there."

Joe said, "Yeah, sure. I just finished there, a month ago. No problem. I'd be glad to, Lorne."

George then introduced him to the last man. "Last but not least, this is Jerry Jones, from Nova Scotia." Jerry stood and shook hands with Joe. He said, "Glad to have yet, another Canuck down here. We're few and far between, lad. Have you settled in here, yet?"

Joe said, "Yeah, my wife and I drove down last week and found a house to rent right away." As he let go of Jerry's hand, Joe was starting to feel better.

George told Joe, "I'm putting you on the new job. I just won the bidding for it, on Friday. You will be working with your fellow structural engineer, Lorne and hydraulics man, Rick. I picked up this job to build a bridge over the Big Black River, west of town. You'll work together and once I see your work, if I need a man for another project, I just may take you off this one and you can head up another one. Now mind you, it depends on the results I get from you on this job.

Today you, Lorne, Rick and I will be here in the office, going over all the details and getting started, while Carroll and Jerry go to the job site, to check things out. I have my own designs, but I will get all of you to submit your own designs and we'll discuss which the best is. We're not fiercely competitive with each other. We work as a team. All my men here are pros and I've heard you are, too.

We have another bridge in the works, too. That one is on the Pearl River. It is farther out of town, than Big Black River is. You won't be asked to work on that one. You're needed on the new one. So, I hope you're not afraid of hard work. I'm sure we'll all get on together... RIGHT GENTLEMEN!" Everyone sat at their desks and they each nodded, without saying anything, except Ray.

Ray said, "You can't be serious; he's actually going to work here?"

George said, "Yes Ray, he is our newest structural engineer. Get over it and get ready for the meeting." Joe put his briefcase on his desk and George then showed Joe where the lunch room was, at the back of the office and the washroom was there, too.

Ray jumped up and in a loud, blowhard voice said to George, "That's where we draw the line, George. There is no way in hell we're sharing the bathroom with a Nigger. The entire State of Mississippi has separate toilets and water fountains for Niggers. He ain't usin' our toilet!"

The men never minded Marie using it, or George's wife, when she was there. But, this was different. Black is black and white is white. There was no such thing as gray. At least, not in Mississippi!

Ray was right. No business or buildings in town had colored and white, using the same facilities. George rubbed his chin and said, "Sorry Mr. Allen, he's right. That's just the way of it around here."

Joe said, "I see. I saw a filling station on the corner when I drove in. Would I be permitted to leave and use their facilities?"

George thought about it and said, "I guess that would be best. They're equipped for coloreds, there. That would be fine. Just remember, you have to sign out every time you go out of the office; and sign in, every time you come through the door."

George showed Joe the board where they sign in and out. It was a white board with their name and a slider that indicated whether you were in or out of the office. Also, it would let George and Maria know, if they were going to be back at the office at the end of the day. The guys were always in and out to so many different jobs, all over the town and the county. The board was so George could keep track of where his men were, and the secretary used the board as an indicator, to keep track of who was in or out for phone calls, messages and such.

While George was instructing Joe on signing in and out, Ray walked towards them. He looked at George and said, "How much does the Nigger get paid, George?"

George said, "Well now Ray, I don't think that you should concern yourself with that. What Mr. Allen gets paid is a private matter, between us, dont'cha think?"

Ray bellowed, "You best not be getting the same pay as we are, Nigger...I mean MR. ALLEN!"

George said in a very loud voice, almost yelling at him, "Ray, get your shit together and get in to the God Damn meeting, now. I'm not telling you again. Mr. Allen's pay is no one's business."

Every Monday, George would hold a short meeting, about a half an hour or so, with all the engineers. They would each discuss their project's progress and whether there were problems, or needed more assistance. This was the meeting that George must have told Ray to get ready for, Joe thought to himself.

George said, "Okay guys, let's get at it." They all went in to another large room where they all sat around a large banquet table, each ready with their own project notes.

Each man or group gave their status reports on the projects they were working on. Sometimes there was more than one type of engineer working together on a project and their speciality would cross over. There were times that the hydraulic engineers might call on the geotechnical engineers to work with them. The odd time, they would also include a structural engineer to assist, if the project was big and complex. There was nothing simple about any of the jobs that George bid on.

He knew that his men could handle whatever he brought in to the firm. Most people knew George Benson and the reputation of his work and his men. George never had a problem in the twenty years he'd been in business. There was a couple of times that there were weather delays, like the tail end of a hurricane blowing things around and lots of rain during those seasons, but his company always managed to get the jobs done before their deadlines.

The meeting wrapped up a little later than usual, this Monday morning, because of the fuss Ray made over Joe being hired. Everyone that had to leave the office did so and there were a couple of men who stayed behind to do paperwork for their projects. George's men were in and out of the office so often, he kidded about needing a revolving door put in.

Structural engineer, Lorne Sheffield and hydraulic engineer, Rick Gills stayed behind to start on the new bridge over the Big Black River, while the day got started for everyone else. George and Joe stayed, too.

George Benson was the Project Manager, on every one of their jobs. He eventually picked someone to be second in command, after things got rolling well enough and he would back down, so he could spend more time checking on the all the other projects, to see how things were going. If all was well everywhere, he might even bid on another job, if he felt it could be done. He had confidence in all his men and he hoped he could say the same about Joe someday.

He bid on this Big Black River Bridge project knowing that he had this new hot-shot, highly recommended structural engineer, from Toronto. Now, he had to sound out the client about having a black man on the job. Would they accept him, or cancel their contract. He didn't know them well enough to say, one way or the other.

Joe was happy that he would be working with Lorne. Rick too. Joe and Lorne would eventually have their talk about Toronto and get to know each other. George was staying in the office to work on the new project, too. Joe was very relieved to know that Ray was to be out for the day and he might not even see him until the next morning.

When Liz finished washing the breakfast dishes, she bathed and got dressed to go out. She headed off to the town library. She went to a lady sitting at the main desk. She was the head librarian. She dealt with reference and information, too. Liz approached her saying, "Hello, my name is Elizabeth Allen. My husband and I just moved here. We're from Canada. My husband got a job here. I'd like to ask a few questions, if you don't mind."

The lady said, "Certainly Mrs. Allen, what can I help you with?"

Liz said, "Oh please call me Liz. Well first of all, I'd like to do a little bit of research on our new town, county and state. But also, I'm a teacher. I'd like to teach here someday and I'd like to know where the Board of Education is located. I'd like to get information on what requirements I need to fulfil, to be a licensed teacher here. The other thing is I'd like to know if you have any suggestions on where I can find a housekeeper. Can you help me?"

The librarian said, "That's not a problem. Let's start with setting you up with some basic information about Philadelphia, Neshoba County, and Mississippi. I'm sure being a teacher; you already have some information about the history of the United States." Liz smiled and nodded.

The librarian continued, "I'll get a few of the books which have been written on this area, which will be very useful to you. The Board of Education for Neshoba County meets here in the library. I can actually help you out with the requirements; I'm on the board, myself." Liz was happy to hear this. She continued, "My name is Nancy Anderson." Liz shook her hand and Nancy gave her four books to take home, after registering her for a library card.

Nancy's phone was ringing and Liz told her she'd be sitting at a table, looking through the books, until Nancy was freed up again. Liz sat and started to read about the town of Philadelphia.

When Nancy was off the phone, she dug out information from a thick file. She took it to Liz. She sat with her and said, "Here are the qualifications for teaching here in Mississippi. Each State has their regulations and qualifications to become certified. We're not as stringent as most states, mind you. So, even if you're a qualified teacher in some states and move to another state, they could also have you fulfil their requirements, before certification."

Liz took a glance at the material. She was very surprised at how little she had to brush up on. She said, "Oh Nancy, thank you so much. I really appreciate it. You have no idea how happy I am, thank you. When do I get to write the exams?"

Nancy said, "You can write them any time you like. We haven't had anyone write around these parts for many years. The board will be excited. You see Liz there are still so many old ways around here. Most of our teachers are quite old and soon ready for retirement. There is one who is to go on maternity leave shortly. She is the grade three teacher." The phone was ringing again and Nancy got up to answer it.

Liz read over the requirements and she became so excited. She knew all the subjects to write the exams. She was sure she could write them and pass with high marks and ease. She wanted to find out where to write and when was the soonest she could do it.

Nancy came back to Liz after she helped several people find books and she had also looked at her calendar. This was the morning that the children from the school were coming over for a library tour. As a matter of fact, it was the grade three class she mentioned to Liz. Nancy smiled as she thought about Liz. She really liked her enthusiasm and dedication to her career. Nancy thought she and Liz could be very good friends; and she hoped they would. She also expected that they were very close to the same age. Nancy was employed at this library; right out of the University of Mississippi, two years earlier. The librarian she replaced, retired and Nancy got the job.

Nancy said, "Now Liz, we have a few other applicants and we have to offer the jobs on a first come, first serve basis. Mind you, some may have moved away and we just don't know, until we call them in for an interview, which they of course have to pass, too. We have to see if the prior applicants still live here, or are still interested in the job; or, if they'd gotten too old and are retired themselves." Liz smiled confidently.

Nancy continued, "You sure enough came here the right day. The grade three class I mentioned with the teacher; you know, in the family way, is coming fer a tour of the library. You can stay and meet her. You could even go through the tour with them if you like. I'm giving the tour."

Liz was getting more excited. She said, "I'd love to stick around. When are they coming?"

Nancy told her, "About ten thirty. She only had a half hour to wait. The phone was ringing again and Liz said, "I know you're really busy, how about I just pour over this information and you can get back to work. I've taken too much of your time already." Nancy told her she'd have to prepare for the kids coming in. While Nancy went back to her desk, Liz went over the information and the more she read, the more excited she got. She was very confident that she would be teaching in Mississippi, soon. Maybe even before Christmas.

The grade three class came in with their teacher, who Nancy was acquainted with. Her name was Mrs. Geraldine Emms. Nancy introduced Liz to Geraldine and about her being new in town and writing the exams to teach, soon. Mrs. Emms was very happy to meet her. She asked Liz if she could possibly help her keep the kids in line during the tour. It was a Monday and they were all excited about their field trip! Liz was more than happy to help.

After the tour, Geraldine Emms and Liz were going to be friends... Liz was quite sure about it! The children all thanked Liz and Nancy for the tour, as they were leaving. Nancy and Liz commented on how well behaved the children were, after they had settled down.

When the class left, it was about noon and Nancy said to Liz, "I get an hour for lunch. I usually go to the diner on the corner. Would you please be my guest and we can talk more?"

Liz gratefully accepted. She could use something to eat and drink. As they left the library, Liz collected the books Nancy gave her and they went to the diner. Nancy was happy she agreed, because she wanted to help Liz get the job replacing Mrs. Emms for her maternity leave and she wanted to fill her in on more information.

As they talked over lunch, she told Liz she could write the exam any time she liked. The Board of Education would meet a week from today and then the next time would be in another month. All applicants wrote the exams in the library, under Nancy's supervision. After that, they would be given to the school principal, for correction. He was also the head of the school board. At the next board meeting, after Liz wrote and became certified, it would be brought up and voted on, as to accepting the applicant, for consideration to teach in their state.

During lunch, Liz noticed that there were a lot of white people eating, but there were only a few blacks there as well. They had to eat in a separate, small section of the diner. There were only a couple of tables for them. Some of the people were even eating their food, standing up; while whites took up all the tables. Liz was bothered by this, but didn't say anything.

As they were ordering dessert, Nancy was getting around to helping her with finding a housekeeper. Nancy asked, "Are you looking for a black or a white housekeeper?"

Liz hadn't thought twice about it. She said, "Oh, black, if you know of anyone qualified."

Nancy said, "There is a place on the edge of town. It's actually a rooming house for blacks. It's called Minnie's. She gets to know the people she has living with her and she recommends them for jobs around town, whenever she can. I'll point you in the right direction when we leave; and you can talk to her whenever you like. She's never failed to get her borders a job yet. She's quite a nice lady. I think you'd like her. She's down to earth and she can make you laugh sometimes." Nancy looked at her watch and said, "I have to go Liz. Do you think you want to write the exams soon?"

Liz was confidant. She said, "Is Friday okay with you?"

Nancy said, "Yeah, what time do you want to write?"

Liz said, "How about I come at ten, Friday morning. Do I have time for it to get to the principal to grade before the board meeting, Monday?" Nancy told her that would give the principal the weekend to correct it. Nancy was sure when she told him all about Liz, he would be happy to grade it over the weekend and get it to the meeting, Monday. Liz had a great feeling. After lunch, Liz thanked Nancy for taking care of her and her needs. Nancy gave her Minnie's address and they parted company, until Friday.

Liz went to Minnie's. She told her Nancy sent her and why she was there. Minnie was a character. Liz liked her right off. Minnie brought Liz in to have a cup of tea. Minnie did not have anyone at the present, to recommend. She told Liz, "'Tings change all 'da time, 'round here. I never knows when I'se gonna find someone ta' tell ya' 'bout. I'se gonna take yo' telephone number and I'se be sure ta' calls ya' when I'se gots somebody. It don't usually take long befo' I gots someone in mine."

Liz thanked her, gave Minnie her phone number and started to leave. She turned around and asked, "Minnie, would you mind if I used your telephone to call a taxi? I've been out all day. I'm getting a little tired and I still have marketing to do."

Minnie said, "You juss' wait gal, I'se be right back." When Minnie returned to the kitchen, she had her purse in her hand and a set of keys. She told Liz, "I drives ya' home. Where ya'll live?"

Liz was very surprised for her kind offer and told her, "Oh Minnie, no. I can take a taxi."

Minnie replied, "You hush now, gal. What sto' you be wantin' ta' go 'fer, ta' shop?"

Liz said, "Just to the Piggly Wiggly." She and Joe laughed about the name a few times, but it was the best market for miles around.

Minnie said, "'Dat be juss' fine. I has ta' go 'dere, too." They both left and got into a car. Minnie told Liz she was lucky she had a friend that loaned her, her car for the day. Her friend worked nights and let Minnie use her car once or twice a week, for her marketing. Minnie told Liz that she'd been saving her money to buy her own car and she almost had enough, now. She was so proud of herself. Liz was happy for her.

As they drove to the market, Minnie said, "Now gal, when we goes in 'da store, ya'll juss' ax' like I'se yo' maid, hepin' ya'll wit' yo' shoppin'."

Liz was uncomfortable with this, but Minnie said it would be better for both of them. Liz grudgingly went along with Minnie. In the store, they had no problems and whenever Liz spoke, Minnie just kept saying "Yess'um," all the time. People stared a bit at Liz, but then she was someone new in the town. She was very pleasant to everyone and they were slightly guarded, but polite.

Minnie never started any conversation in the store. She waited until she was spoken to first. Liz seemed to be getting quite an education; just by watching, listening and learning about the ways of these people. While shopping, Liz filled Minnie in on her visit to the library; and meeting Nancy. Minnie was happy to listen to Liz's enthusiasm; and happiness about moving there; and writing the exams on Friday. Minnie told her that she would pray and keep her fingers crossed for her.

They talked about Nancy. Minnie said, "She be such a sweet lady. We meets right here in 'dis here store, we did. I be in a hurry and racin' 'trough my shoppin' and I'se comed 'round an aisle, an' we juss' bumped our carts t'gedder. She went flyin' back on ta' her backside. I be scared ta' deat'. 'Da manager 'tought I done it on purpose. He d'int wanna b'lieve me. Nancy told him it be an accident and I done nuttin' wrong. Nancy even started laughin', girl. It be funny, ta' her. I be nervous, still. Nancy tole' 'da manager it be her own fault an' 'dat be 'dat. He finally went away.

I'se still scared as I done my shoppin'. She 'den be finish and gone. 'Da manager, he be fallowin' me 'round an' I get's out 'da door quick as I could. I be followed by 'da manager, an' what'chew 'tink happens next?"

Liz said, "I don't know, what?" Just as Liz and Minnie both went through different checkouts, they stopped talking and the Minnie did not continue until the groceries were in the trunk and they were safely in the car.

After Minnie got Liz's address, she continued with her story, "Well, 'da nex' 'ting I knows, 'dere be two 'udder mens wit' 'da manager. Outside 'da store, 'dere she was. Nancy be sittin' by her car, waitin' 'fer me. I guess she s'pected sometin' might happen, so she comes ta' me an' says, ' it be 'bout time you'se got out here. I been waitin' 'fer ya'.'"

Minnie continued with her story as she drove, "When 'da manager seen us talkin' like we was friends, 'dey juss' stands 'dere an' watch 'fer a spell. She juss' kep' talkin' ta' me. We was tellin' each 'udder our stories an' 'da men all gives up an' 'dey goes back inta' 'da sto', 'dey did. We still talks mo' for a few minits an' 'den Nancy tole' me she din't 'tink 'dey would come after me, if she be 'dere. She lets me get into 'da car an' drive away an' 'dere be no trouble.

I be so grateful, 'dat 'da nex' day, I makes her a pie an' I takes it to 'dat 'dere library, where she done works. Blacks ain't 'lowed ta' go in 'dere. So, I waits 'till I'se sees someone goin' in an' I 'ax 'dat 'dey could give da pie to 'da lady named Nancy. I starts walkin' home an' juss' a few minits later, she comes up behin' me an' says 'tank ya', ta' me. We's be friens' ever since 'dat time an' I ain't had no mo' problem at 'dat store after 'dat, but I am careful wit' 'dem men."

Liz was touched by the story and Nancy's kindness. She was learning so much and started to feel funny about the town. She wasn't sure, but she felt that there must be a tie to gangs, or even worse, Klan. Liz tucked the notion away in the back of her mind. She didn't want to be getting paranoid. She knew Klan existed in the south, but she wasn't sure about this town. She wanted to get started on reading the books Nancy helped her get. Maybe she would find out what she needed to know, without asking someone and maybe getting someone into trouble, or herself.

She asked Minnie to come in for coffee, but she had to go home and start supper for her borders. She did help Liz bring her groceries into the house. Minnie admired the house. As she looked around the living room, she saw a wedding photo of Liz and a black man. She turned to Liz and said, "Who be 'dat black man wit'cha?"

Liz said, "That's my husband, Joe. Isn't he handsome?" Minnie had a scared look on her face, all of a sudden. Liz asked, "What's wrong Minnie?"

Minnie told her, "Lawdy gal, you folk's juss' bought yo'sef a whole peck o' trouble in 'dis town!"

Liz's eyes widened as she spoke, "What do you mean, Minnie. What's wrong? What kind of trouble am I asking for? We've only just moved here, my husband got a new job. I can't think of what trouble we'd have. Now Minnie, don't you worry; there's nothing wrong. I assure you, we'll be fine."

Minnie said, "Don't 'chew knows gal. You'se in Klan country now. How did ya'll get 'dis house. Niggers ain't tol'rated, 'cept 'fer 'da udder edge o' town. Where ya'll say you'se husban' got hisself' a job?"

Liz looked a little worried, "Um, he is employed by Benson and Associates. My husband is a structural engineer. He builds bridges and overpasses."

Minnie was shaking her head, "Yo' husban' he not be workin' 'dere long, I'se can tell ya'll 'dat. 'Dese men 'dat works 'dere, 'dey all be white. Some o' 'dem be bad men! He's gonna have a hard time. I pray ya'll be okay. You juss' be careful now missy. "Tanks 'fer comin' ta' see me, Liz. I 'tinks I can prob'ly has a housekeeper 'fer ya' inside two weeks. I hope 'dat be okay."

Liz said, "Oh, I guess you'd better tell them that there will be a baby in a few months, too."

Minnie said, "I kinda' 'toughts ya' might be in 'da family way. Dat be no problem. I'se find ya' someone 'dat likes babies, too." Liz hugged Minnie and thanked her for the information and for taking her shopping, she was so grateful.

Minnie turned and said, "What'chew say I takes ya'll marketin' ev'ry week. We's can go t'gedder, whatever day be bess' 'fer ya'. I don't mind none pickin' ya' up and takes ya' wit' me. What'chew says gal?" Liz was flabbergasted. She had had such a full day of folks being so kind and helpful to her and they made their plans for the next week. But... Liz still couldn't believe that Minnie said what she did about Liz and Joe having trouble living there.

As they said their good-byes, Minnie left and Liz put her groceries away and lay down on the sofa. She started to leaf through the material Nancy had given her. She went through the subjects she had to refresh her memory in; but, it hadn't been that long since she left teaching: Only a few weeks.

She was fine on most subjects; like Mathematics, which in the states was referred to as Arithmetic. There was basic spelling and reading and she discovered they were still using the McGuffy Readers. Just like her great-grandmother Diana, Eleanor; and Liz had used at the Chatham Public School 101. Because she was now in a new country she needed to give herself a crash course on Geography. She needed to know town, county, state, country, the whole nine yards...and government!

The biggest part to know was history. She had nearly two-hundred years to refresh herself on, but she knew American history quite well. She was interested in history around the world. They did teach a second language in her district, but had qualified teachers who taught it. In the

Deep South there recently was a need to teach children Spanish, because of the close proximity to Mexico. They had many people coming to Mississippi to work so those who did not hail from Mexico were taught Spanish as a second language, just like French is taught in Canada, as a second language.

After looking more thoroughly at the material she brought home, Liz started to think; maybe she bit off more than she could chew, by committing to write the exams Friday. Then she thought to herself, 'a McDonald or an Allen doesn't quit'. She had the determination and she said to herself out loud, "I'm going to do this! I owe it to myself, my husband and our child! I will write the exams on Friday and I will become certified to teach in Mississippi. I am going to be very proud and my family will be proud, too!"

A huge smile came over as she sat there. She was thinking about Christmas on the farm, in 1944. She wasn't thinking of Joe's marriage proposal, but his gift. Not the golf clubs, but the encyclopaedias and the new dictionary, the atlas and the globe. She chuckled, remembering what a bad present she thought it was. Maybe Joe had a premonition, but as soon as he got home from work she would have him drag that box out of the garage for her. She needed it, NOW! She couldn't wait to get her hands on the books and study. She chuckled and smiled. She would be sure to tell Joe what a wonderful, thoughtful present he gave her that Christmas. She lay on the sofa and stretched out. It was only about five minutes, before Liz was sound asleep, until the phone rang at four.

She was a little disoriented at first, because she was so tired, but she picked up the phone and it was Joe. He said, "Hi honey, how is your day going?"

Liz said, "It's been really productive. I'm studying to write the exams to get certified to teach here. I've met the town librarian and a really wonderful lady that is trying to get us a housekeeper, within the next two weeks. How is it going for you, sweetie?"

Joe just held it in, and said, "I'm getting to know the men I'm working with and I'm on a new project; A bridge. Anyway, I'll be home after five. I love you." Liz blew him a tired kiss. She got up and started to make supper.

Chapter 3

Life is Busy

J OE PULLED IN THE DRIVEWAY at about five-fifteen. When he got in, supper was almost ready. Liz went to him and threw her arms around his neck and kissed him, a very seductive hello. She was in a mood and he smiled a wide smile; and told her she'd have to wait, he was starving.

As he washed up, she put supper on the table. After saying the blessing, she asked him about his day. He looked at her with a bit of a tired look and said, "How about you tell me about your day, first. So, have you started studying to write the exams, yet?" He was being facetious, not thinking she'd done anything about it, yet.

She told him, "Yes. I got the information from Nancy at the library. She is on the school board and their monthly meeting is next Monday. I'm writing on Friday and it will be graded on the weekend hopefully and I just know, I'll get my certificate! I just know it." He kind of choked a bit, since he was kidding. He was shocked, pleasantly surprised and very proud of her.

She kept on talking, "Honey, there is something I've been keeping from you since Christmas 1944. You know you how you gave me the encyclopaedias, dictionary, globe and atlas?" He nodded his head as he ate. She said, "Well honey, I thought at the time, it was the most insensitive, stupid gift, you could have ever given me." As Joe kept eating, he grinned and let her carry on. She said, "Now honey, I apologize for thinking that, because I had told you wherever I teach, that those items would be supplied, in whatever classroom I teach in. Well, sweetheart, dear, honey; if you can forgive me for thinking that and I noticed you did pack them and brought them here, and…Sweetie… would you mind getting it all out of the garage for me? Everything in that box is what I REALLY need to get ready for my exams on Friday."

Joe finished eating and pushed his plate back a bit and he was grinning again. He started drinking his tea. He leaned back on the chair and gave her the look. It was a look she didn't see often. It was one that made her eat crow and he loved it!!

He said, "What was that now, I think you said my gifts were insensitive and stupid? Yep, I'm pretty sure that's what you called my gift insensitive and stupid." He had a very satisfied smile.

She slapped his arm and said, "You know, as much as I love you, you can be a jerk at times!"

"Now I'm a jerk, huh?" he grinned again.

There was no way that Liz could win this one. She started to do the dishes, Joe came up behind here and kissed her cheek, still grinning and laughing. He went out to the garage and found Liz's box of books. They were very heavy and he was glad she hadn't tried to lift them. He was still smiling to himself.

As he pulled the box out, he started to think about his first day at work. How much should he tell Liz? She was just so excited and it sounded like she had such a productive day and she was so happy. He didn't want to worry her, or spoil her excited mood. He often felt that his wife was not only a fireball, but her enthusiasm and perkiness, was contagious. People loved to be around her.

He remembered the double hockey games in Kingston against McGill. Everyone loved her and wanted to be around her. She seemed to make people happy. She made it seem like 'fun and enthusiasm' were diseases she wanted to spread; and people wanted to catch. Even through the rest of university, everyone knew and loved Leapin' Liz McDonald! Joe felt he was the luckiest man on earth: To not just know her, but to have her as his wife.

He carried the box into the house as she was finishing the dishes. She thought back to the farm. There were always so many dishes to wash. Now, it barely took any time to do them, since it was just the two of them. She smiled thinking even though she was planning to breast feed she thought that she might be washing some bottles and eventually baby spoons and little dishes. She gave a silent giggle.

Her thoughts turned again to the exams. She was confident about the Arithmetic and Language, but she knew the largest part would be history. Just like the exams she wrote for the Ontario Board! A lot of the history section was Canada and the Mississippi Board exams would mostly include a lot of history of the United States. She laughed to herself, thinking, by the end of Friday, she'd be an expert on most of North America.

Although she was a great student of history she would have to study more. She knew a fair amount of U.S. history, but now she needed to know state, county and town, too. And, she had to learn it all by Friday morning!

Joe had set the box in the living room. He opened it for her and started to take the books out and place them in stacks of six, or seven, on the coffee table, so she did not have to do any bending, digging, or lifting out of the large box and everything was easily accessible to her, while sitting on the couch, or chair. Joe was so proud that she was doing this and so quickly too. He had no doubt she would be certified within a week or two.

He sat in old reliable, in the living room and turned on the radio. As he listened to some news, Liz came in the room. She thanked him for getting the box out for her and setting everything out for her. He smiled at her again. She sat on his lap and put her arms around his neck. He gave her a little squeeze and a kiss. Liz asked, "Honey, what went wrong today? Please tell me about it."

Joe looked at her and he turned the radio down. He had placed it right beside his chair, so he wouldn't have to get up when he wanted to turn it on, or off. He liked to hear the news and sports. Liz was the one who loved to play the 78's. During their trip, they only broke two records. Not a bad average, since the nine-hundred mile trip was bumpy at times and the records were so breakable. The two that didn't survive the trip were: Tex Ritter's "Have I Told You Lately That I Love You?" and Kitty Welles' "Release Me". Liz was disappointed, since they were favorites, but she was sure she could replace them. Surely Philadelphia had a store that sold records.

Joe started to tell her about his day, "Well my love, I got there on time. I went in and came face to face with an asshole...a loudmouth schnook. You know, the kind that has to hold court, always be right and don't dare piss him off!

Including me, there are twelve engineers, plus George Benson and a secretary. George seems okay and the secretary is very quiet. She is Mexican. We have four hydraulic engineers, that's what the asshole, Ray is. There are three other hydraulics' guys, also. One is Rick Gills, I'm working with him. He's from Louisiana. He seems young, but he knows his stuff. We have two geotechnical engineers. One of them is Daniel. He is from British Columbia."

Liz was impressed that there was another Canadian. "That's great I thought you'd be the only Canadian."

Joe started again, "There are two transportation engineers...they are the busiest, because they work on and design highways, roads, interstates and all that. One of them, Walter, he's from Toronto. He seems friendly. As a matter of fact, you won't believe this; but, he helped design the roads in Toronto that I designed some of the overpasses for. He completed his part of the job a couple of years before I came on the scene. Hey hon, remember the photos I took, to form a portfolio, of my work?" Liz was intensely curious and nodded. He said, "Remember I took them in to work this morning?" She nodded again. "Well, I showed he and George and right away, he knew exactly where those pictures were taken and he said it looked like I designed a great overpass, to compliment his highway!" Everyone in the office was excited and interested. They all looked at the photos. All that is, except Ray. They congratulated me on the nice work I did. All that is, except for Ray, again!"

Liz said, "Wow, what a small world!"

Joe continued, "My group of structural engineers seem okay, too. We have Carroll, from right here in Philadelphia and Lorne Sheffield, who's from Toronto too. The other structural guy Jerry Jones is from Nova Scotia."

Liz was quite impressed with the firm. She said, "I'm sure that's quite a rare 'place of business', for these parts! There is one Mexican lady, eight Americans and five Canadians. That really is impressive."

Joe said, "You said it. Around here, they really stick together. Most businesses in these parts, are community and family based and don't like outsiders. Now, here I come, not only an outsider, but a black one!

They don't get more outsider than me!" They both smiled, but knew he was right.

He went on, "I'm sure that George Benson is considered somewhat of a maverick. He doesn't care what the public thinks, he has hired the best men in their field and he has no serious bias, from what I gather about him. 'Benson and Associates' are considered one of the best engineering companies in Mississippi!

Monday mornings, everyone goes into a large board room and we discuss each group's or individual's progress on the project they are assigned to. This is a time that if you need more help on a project, George can re-assign someone if he needs to. Everything usually works out well on all their projects.

Mr. Benson holds two degrees. He is certified as, both a structural and geotechnical engineer. He heads up and helps on all his firm's projects. After their weekly meeting everyone scatters to where they are supposed to be and sometimes you spend part of your day in the office.

Maria seems to be the glue that holds the office together. She is really good at her job apparently; and she gets a lot of respect, from all the men: Even Ray. He has no problem working with a Hispanic woman, but he does with a black Canadian. Anyway, Maria seems busy with answering the phone, constantly. It is a very busy office. She does the bookkeeping and anything else that needs to be done, you name it and Maria takes care of it. She seems nice, but shy. I understand that George's wife did Maria's job from the day she and George formed the business, until she died of cancer over a year ago.

Lorne was so excited to meet me. He wanted all the gossip from Toronto. I think our group will get on okay. We can sometimes work together, or by ourselves, depending on how big the job is. Right now, I am being put with Lorne, Jerry, Carroll and Rick on a new project and after I got settled, we went over the plans on the bridge. I brought my ideas and the new perspective and techniques I learned in Toronto to the job. Lorne and Rick were delighted and told George, despite Ray's ignorance; he really DID hire the right guy.

There are some great projects these men are working on. I am happy to be working with George, Lorne and Rick. We stayed working in the office, while Carroll and Jerry went out to work at the site. We get along pretty good...other than Ray being a jackass!

The other uncomfortable thing in the office is that they won't let me use the washroom. I have to go across the road to the filling station to piss. But, they pointed it out to me that, that's just the way it is in Mississippi. So there is one bathroom for all of them, including Maria, who they have no problem letting her use it. I guess because she's the one who cleans it!"

As Joe was talking, he was not looking at Liz's face. When he paused, he heard a sniff and he looked at her. She had tears rolling down her cheeks. He kissed her cheek and said, "Hey, now...where's the chirpy little sweetheart girl I married. The one who always has a smile?"

Liz looked at him and she turned his head with her hands and she looked in his eyes and asked, "Do you want to go home?"

He tenderly kissed her nose and said, "Over the use of a toilet? You know me better than that babe. Besides, have you ever seen me back down before? Did I back down from hockey, with my disease? Did I back down when I bought a General Motors pick-up, instead of Ford? No! So we are going to stay right here and make a wonderful life for us and our family." He tenderly patted her tummy and she smiled as she wiped her tears.

She said, "I love you Joseph Allen! You are the best! I hope tomorrow goes better for you." She kissed him again.

Joe said, "Now, fill me in more on your day, love."

Liz was back to bubbly again. She said, "I went to the library, as you already know. There I met the librarian. She got some history materials I wanted; you know I wanted to read up on the local history and such. She was really nice.

I also asked her about the Board of Education and what I needed to do to get certified to teach in Mississippi. She gave me the entire package of what was required." Liz got off his lap for a moment and picked up the materials and let him glance at them. She continued, "The only thing I have to really cram for is the history. I checked the Math; oops, I mean Arithmetic...the Language, Grammar; and I know I can do them in my sleep for grades one through eight.

I'm going to be studying history and government most of the week: Mostly U.S. It occurred to me that, by the end of Friday, between studying Canadian history, to write the Ontario boards, and the U.S. history for the Mississippi boards, I'm going to be an expert in North American history! Wouldn't you say?

So, I write the exams on Friday at ten and the board meets Monday night. Hopefully they'll ask me for an interview. Then she told me that the grade three class was coming in for a library tour. Honey, I was in the right place at the right time. The grade three teacher is pregnant and needs to go on maternity leave, shortly. Nancy introduced me to Mrs. Emms. She is so nice."

Joe interrupted, "Who is she?"

Liz replied, "The grade three teacher. She's just getting to know her students, because they just started back to school recently. She's never taught these kids before. Anyway, she asked me to help keep her class in line while they were on the tour. I told her I'd love to, so I did.

By the time the tour was finished, both ladies told me, if I get my certification, they would both recommend that I replace her when she takes her maternity leave. Honey, isn't it great? I Know I just taught grade one so far, but I'd love the experience of teaching grade three.

After the tour, Nancy had some work to do, but she said she'd be going to the diner next door for lunch, and would I like to go, and I said yes..."

Joe held up his hand to her mouth to shut her up for a minute and said, "Darlin' how long is your story?"

She said, "Awe Joe, come on, let me tell you."

He said, "Honey that's fine, you can finish your story, but for the moment, you are sitting on my bladder and I drank lots of coffee today, because I was a little nervous...I need to go...now!" Liz started laughing and jumped off his lap. As he went to the bathroom, she called out that he should try having a baby on his bladder constantly for months and then laughed. When he came out of the bathroom, as he walked by their bedroom he looked and saw Liz lying on their bed with nothing on. She smiled coyly.

He enjoyed what he saw and went in. He lay on the bed beside her and she asked, "Would you like to take a break from my day and do... something else, or should I just continue, telling you about it now." He rolled on his side and put his arms around her. She started kissing him and she was unbuttoning his shirt. When it was opened, she started to kiss his chest and kept kissing lower, and lower.

When she reached his pants, she opened them, too. He was already hard with excitement. She was just as excited as he was. She wanted him. She climbed on top of him and they made love. As they finished, he rolled over on top of her and they kissed again and stayed in each other's arms for a few minutes. He was in pain, now. He started to get a little concerned. He hid the fact, as best he could, that he his erection was not going down. Every time he experienced the priapism symptom of Sickle Cell; lately, he noticed it was lasting longer than the last time. It was sore, but he didn't want her to know.

Liz said, "Can I tell you about the rest of my day now, lover boy?"

Joe turned to her and laughed, "Haven't you tortured me enough today?"

Liz sat up right away, "Torture, torture, I'll give you torture, buddy." She picked up her big feather pillow and brought it down on his head. He was shocked, and so he decided to do the same. The two ended up in a pillow fight, but Liz finally gave in. She said, "I guess pillows are stronger today than in our great-grandparents' day. I remember the stories about Diana and Johnny having to make new pillows each time they had a pillow fight, because they always broke open."

Joe laughed, "Oh yeah, I'd forgotten that story. Can you imagine having to make your own pillows and mattresses too, sometimes?"

Liz said, "Okay, I give up, if you don't want to hear my..."

Joe started, "Okay sweetie go ahead and tell me about the rest of your day...can you do it here, or do we have to go back to the chair?"

She lifted her pillow to hit him again and he said, "Okay, okay, just go ahead and tell me about it."

Liz turned over and pushed him away saying, "No...I know you're really not interested. Maybe I'll find someone who will care how great my day was. You're too busy. I think I'll sleep on the sofa tonight."

As she got up out of their bed, she put her robe on and he said, "Awe, honey, you know I didn't mean it that way." As she went into the bathroom, he followed her. She stopped him by closing the door and locking it.

He said through the door, "C'mon Liz, please come out. We'll sit and you can tell me about the rest of your day, I really want to know how things went for you. Sweetie, please...come out and talk...please?"

After a few minutes of pleading, he heard the door unlock and she slowly opened it. As he pushed the door open, she couldn't help it, she was laughing. She couldn't stop.

When he discovered that she was just putting this on he said, "You brat. I'll get you back. And, don't think I won't." He started laughing, too. He had his robe on now and since it was covering his erection, she never noticed it.

He went down stairs still laughing, while he was thinking of something to get her back with. As he went into the kitchen, he looked in the fridge for something to drink. He noticed that Liz obviously had done more grocery shopping. He pulled out a Coca-Cola and opening it, he said, "Honey how did you get the groceries today?"

She was coming down the stairs and she answered, "Well Mr. Allen, I was going to tell you about it, but you don't seem to want to hear about the rest of my day..." She walked past him and then sat on the sofa. They were both laughing. He was glad she sat on the sofa. He would not have been able to hide himself, if she was on his lap. He didn't want her to know he was suffering.

She said, "Seriously honey, when Nancy and I went to the diner for lunch, she told me that there was a boarding house on the edge of town." She quickly said, "Oh by the way, remind me to tell you about the diner." He just had this smile on his face, but never said a word. "Anyway, this place Nancy told me about, it's called Minnie's. It's a boarding house for black people and, so is the lady that runs it and owns it. Her name is Minnie."

Joe couldn't help it, he said, "Well, isn't that clever! Who would have thought?"

Liz glared at her husband for interrupting her, again. She said, "That's enough smart-ass. Let me finish." He gave her the motion that he was zipping his lips and throwing away the key.

She couldn't help it she laughed again and said, "Nancy told me that if anyone could find us a housekeeper, well Minnie knows a lot of people, in and out of her boarding house. So, I went to see her and told her Nancy sent me. She's a fairly tall, heavy set black lady. I really like her hun; she gives me a back home feeling. You've got to meet her.

Anyway, she made me a cup of tea and we talked. She asked if I had a housekeeper before and I told her we were both brought up with a housekeeper, all the time on the farm. She asked if I wanted a white or black woman. I told her black. She said she should have one for us in the next week, or two. I thanked her for her help and gave her our phone number.

Then I asked to use her telephone, to call a taxi. She wanted to know where I was going. I told her about being pregnant and I was starting to get a little tired and I still had marketing to do, before going home...I remembered not to call it grocery shopping and she insisted on driving me. She said she had her marketing to do, too. So we went together to the Piggly Wiggly. Honey wasn't that so sweet of her?" Joe nodded, paying full attention.

Liz continued, "Minnie asked me to make it look like she was my maid and she was helping me do my shopping. I didn't like the idea, but she said it would be easier on her. The manager has a problem with Minnie, even though she did nothing wrong.

Minnie and Nancy had originally met there, at the Piggly Wiggly. Joseph, you're laughing at me! It's not funny. That's just the name of the store, now behave; you said you were zipped and threw away the key." She scolded him while he was laughing.

She quickly continued with her story, "Now, Minnie and Nancy crashed their carts together at the end of one of the aisles. Nancy was knocked down, right onto her ass. The manager thought Minnie did it on purpose and he was angry. He helped Nancy up and she told him it was her own fault. He didn't want to believe her.

Minnie and Nancy each went on with their shopping and the manager followed Minnie all over the store. She was nervous. Nancy waited outside, just in case there was some trouble. When Minnie went out to the parking lot, Nancy stood and talked with her until the manager went back inside. That's how they got acquainted.

They became friends and found out that maybe they could help each other out with something. Minnie told Nancy that she knew of people who were looking to do domestic work. Nancy told Minnie she came across people all the time who wanted someone for babysitting, or housekeeping. She would keep her ears opened, for people needing help and Nancy would refer these people to her. They've been friends ever since. All the matches that they made with employers and employees have been long, successful relationships. Honey, I know she'll find someone great for us. Minnie also told me there was another person in town that sends people her way. I think she said it was a man at the bus depot. It's funny where you find people to connect with, isn't it?" Joe was smiling and nodding and still keeping his mouth shut, for her to continue.

Liz started up again, "So, after Minnie and I finished our... marketing... she drove me home. She helped me bring the groceries inside. I let her look around the house, so she'd know how big the house was and what to tell perspective housekeepers, who apply for the job. She came across our wedding picture and said the strangest thing. Minnie's smile disappeared. I asked her what was wrong. When she found out you were black, she said we just bought a whole peck of trouble by moving here.

Honey, she told me that we're in Klan Country now. She also said that you won't be working here for very long. When she was leaving, she said she'd pray for us. She also suggested that we market together every week, that she would pick me up and bring me home. We talked about the baby and she said it would not be a problem finding someone for us that loved children. Wouldn't that be great. Honey, what do you think she meant when she said we had a whole peck of trouble for ourselves?"

Joe started to get more concerned, now. He said, "Dear, she's right. I suspected we had Klan around, but wasn't 100% sure. Well, hearing it from a black woman, I guess she would know."

Liz asked, "Do you think there will be any trouble?"

He took her in his arms and hugged her tight and said, "Sweetie, I know we want friends here, but I think we should lay low, so to speak. I can't believe, if we keep to ourselves, anyone would bother us. All we want to do here is live, work and raise a family." He smiled at her and kissed her.

She felt better, but a little disappointed. She said, "I guess you're right. Do you think maybe things were exaggerated? I mean, we're just a very happy couple, making a living, about to start our family. We certainly don't want any trouble, or to cause any."

Joe said, "Yeah. Okay, what about the diner?"

Liz said, "Oh yeah, thanks for reminding me. When we went to the diner, I've never seen this before, but if you're white you get the best seats; but if you're black, well, some people were eating...standing up. Now, explain to me, why it is like that?"

Joe told her, "Honey, it's just the same as me having to go to the bathroom at the filling station. That's just the way things are in Mississippi. It seems that Mississippi has not grown into the 20th century, like the rest of the country is attempting to. We have to get used to and accept it, okay darlin'?"

She said, "I guess you're right. Okay honey, I'm going to bed. I have a lot of studying to do tomorrow?"

Joe asked, "Are you going out at all, tomorrow?"

She replied, "No, I'm just going to study my little heart out. Don't forget to lock up." She stopped in her tracks and continued, "It seems so strange. All our lives growing up, our families never locked our doors, ever. Now, here, we have to make sure we do, for our own safety." She climbed the stairs and was quickly sleeping, dreaming about American history.

Joe still had his erection and it was so painful. By now, he also had chest pain. The sickle cell symptoms were acting with a vengeance, tonight. He was glad Liz went to bed. He was in too much pain to go to bed, just in case she wanted it again. He wouldn't be able to hide the pain from her.

About an hour after Liz went to bed, Joe was able to go to bed, too. He laid there for a little while. He looked at his beautiful wife, wondering what have I done to our lives? He prayed, "Lord, please keep us safe and guide me to make the right decisions for my family." He finally fell asleep after midnight.

After Joe went to work in the morning, Liz hit the books. She started with Mississippi. It was the 20th State in the Union, in 1817. Its name was taken from the Ojibwa Indian word for great river.

After she went through Mississippi history, she went through the county history, then the local history. She was really excited about everything she was reading. All except for the parts about how the Klan had been in this area for over a century. She read about Klan killings and it scared her a lot.

After that, she took a look at each state, learned the main details, their capitols, main historical events, and anything else she thought was noteworthy.

She already knew the Declaration of Independence and the National Anthem. She was almost perfect at their list of presidents, but she could not remember all their dates. She knew historical highlights, for strategic presidents. She took the atlas and she tried to memorize the U.S. map, to the best of her ability, but she always had trouble with the eastern seaboard. There were so many tiny states in there. She hoped there was room for errors on these exams.

She looked at her watch and it was four-thirty. She'd studied all day, even missing lunch. Joe would be home soon. She got up and started dinner.

When Joe came home, they ate and she asked about his day and he told her, "We were out at the site today. It's going to be a great bridge. They chose a design I used around Toronto. They are really enthusiastic about getting this project going. We started to take measurements and we were out there almost all day, studying and planning. It was really great out there, doing what I do. How much studying did you get done, hun?"

She said, "I really got a lot done. I think I'll spend tomorrow on more history and government and the next day, I'll review the Arithmetic, Language and Geography. Honey, do you think I can write on Friday?"

He smiled at her and said, "Yes! I have confidence in you, honey. You know you can do it."

She smiled and said, "You know, I never realized it, but remember me being your cheering squad?"

Joe said, "Of course I remember."

She said, "Well, you're my cheering squad. I wish you could come with me for my exams."

Joe told her, "I'll be there...in spirit. I promise I always will be! Just keep the faith honey. You can do it!" Liz didn't know how much those words would comfort her, someday!

Chapter 4

A New Teacher, Again

FRIDAY CAME AND IT WAS about 9:45 a.m. when Liz walked into the library. Nancy was happy to see her. She asked Liz, "Are you ready Liz?"

Liz said, "Nervous. But, I think I'm ready."

A gentleman came into the library and he went to Nancy. She brought him over to Liz and said, "Elizabeth Allen this is Mr. Vincent Kirkland, the school principal. I told him about you and that you were taking the exams today. He wanted to meet you."

He shook Liz's hand and said, "It's a pleasure to meet you, Mrs. Allen. I've heard from Nancy and from Mrs. Emms that you would be a great teacher for us to have in our school. You come very highly recommended."

Liz blushed and said, "Please, call me Liz. Thank you for the kind words, but we really didn't have a long time to get acquainted."

Vincent said, "Actually, I prefer to go with people's first impressions and gut instincts."

Liz said, "Thank you. That sounds like someone who has a great trust in people."

He said, "Now Liz, are you sure you want to write today? Are you ready? If not, you can write another time if you prefer; maybe next month"

She nervously said, "I really believe I'm ready for it. Are you going to be here today?"

Vincent replied, "Sorry, I have to get back to the school, but I am the one who keeps the exams under lock and key, for the school board. You know dear lady we haven't had anyone write the exams for quite some time. But be assured they are updated. I have a new set of exams every two years.

We are so pleased to have you here writing. Now, when you begin, you will be timed on some tests. The first section of the exams takes two hours, but it is not all one subject. There will be a one hour break and after lunch you will spend two hours on history. Are you ready?"

Liz got out her pens, pencils, sharpener, ruler and eraser. She was given a pitcher of ice water to drink. Vincent said that there would be leeway, if she needed to use the facilities, since he understood she was pregnant.

Liz said, "Yes, but please don't let that dissuade you from accepting my application for employment."

He said, "Oh no, we wouldn't. Anyway, it's almost ten o'clock; so good luck and I'll be back after three to see you."

He left and Nancy gave Liz the first part of her exams. It was Arithmetic. She covered it, like she did with all the subjects, from a grade one level to grade eight. She preferred primary students, but she would have to be prepared for any grade. Math came easy to her, all levels. This section was timed.

Next she had her favorite, Language. It covered spelling, grammar, punctuation, reading, novel study, plays and poetry. She wasn't really challenged by the questions and sections, since she loved it all so much.

Next was Geography. She was knowledgeable about many countries. One of them of course was Canada. She enjoyed that section, although it was small. She had questions for each continent. She had to identify countries and provinces all over the world. She second guessed herself on a few places.

Noon came and she was asked to stop. She had finished a few moments earlier though and she was reviewing her answers. Nancy asked, "How is it going, Liz?"

Liz jumped up and said, "I'll tell you after I get back from the bathroom!" Nancy let out a giggle.

As Liz walked back in from the bathroom, she had a relieved look on her face, she said, "I think I'm doing well."

Nancy said, "Please give me all your papers. Do you want to go to lunch with me?"

Liz said, "Am I allowed to leave, in the middle of the exams?"

Nancy said, "Well, I'm the supervisor and I have the test under lock and key and I'll be with you. I don't see a problem."

Liz laughed. She said, "I never thought of that angle. Let's go!"

They went to a different restaurant this time. It was a really nice place, great atmosphere. Liz really liked it. Nancy knew the waitress and introduced Liz. They ordered and Liz mentioned to Nancy, "I don't see a 'colored' section in here like, the diner."

Nancy replied, "You won't ever see a colored in here." Liz was stunned. Nancy continued, "They are not allowed in this restaurant at all." Liz choked on her drink.

Nancy asked, "Are you alright girl?"

Liz didn't want to start anything and she just said, "Went down the wrong way." She turned the conversation to small talk. It was best so that she wouldn't get upset and spoil her afternoon history exams. She put it out of her mind and they had a really good lunch.

They had ten minutes to get back to the library. They made it back just a couple of minutes before one; Long enough for Liz to empty her bladder, again. Nancy gave Liz her history exams and she started.

After one and a half hours, she asked if she could go to the bathroom. Liz drank a glass of water and two cups of tea at lunch. Nancy told her to go ahead. She was only a couple of minutes and got right back to the exam.

She was finished by 2:55 p.m. and she re-read some of her answers. At three o'clock, Nancy came to her table and collected all the papers. She asked, "How was that section?"

Liz said, "There were times I had to stretch my brain and find the answers, but I think I did well; over all. Should I leave?"

Nancy said, "No, you don't have to. Here comes Vincent. He's planning on marking it right away, so if you want to stick around and see whether you made the grade, so to speak, you're welcome to."

Just then, Vincent said hello to them and took the tests from Nancy. He asked Liz, "Well, how was it? Did you complete some sections?"

Nancy piped up and said, "She completed the entire set of exams. I didn't even see her sweat once."

Vincent took the exams and went to a table. He opened his briefcase and got the answers out and started to grade her exams. He had the answers with him so that he could properly mark her papers and he would make no mistakes.

Nancy suggested that they go in the lunchroom, since the assistant librarian had made a pot of tea for them. Liz said, "That sounds wonderful. I would love a cup of tea. That's something I grew up on. On the farm, there was always tea on the stove, any time of day, or evening. Lead me to it, please." She gave a very relieved smile.

They drank their tea, Liz relaxed and stretched and then they went back out on the floor. Vincent was busy, still grading and he paid no attention to them. Nancy poured him a cup of tea, too and took it to him. He looked up, long enough to say, "Thanks" to Nancy, and got back to the papers in front of him.

Liz wasn't sure how to read his face, but she had a good feeling. She thought about her mom and all the other teachers in the family. She thought they would be proud of her to be certified to teach in Ontario, like all the women teachers in her family AND in United States: Well... at least in the state of Mississippi. It would be just like her mother. She was certified to teach in Ontario and in Scotland.

She thought about Joe and hoped he was having a good day, closing his first work week. She never thought any more about Klan, for now. She thought maybe it was exaggerated. But, now she started to remember the restaurant. No colored allowed. Come to think of it, she never saw any signs to indicate their rule.

"Hello, earth calling Mrs. Allen; are you there?" Vincent was waving her papers in front of her face, indicating he was finished marking her tests.

She said, "Oh, forgive me I was off in a dream world for a minute. You're finished?"

He said, "Yes I am; and I can say, this is the most impressive scores there have been recorded in all of Mississippi, I'll have you know. I checked before I came here to see what some of the highest scores were. I had the feeling you might give us a run for our money. Well Liz, congratulations. You have earned your teaching licence for the State of Mississippi. You are invited to join us at our School Board Meeting, Monday night and you can meet the other board members. You will be presented with your certificate, then. At this same time, the board can get to know you and decide whether to hire you. It will also serve as your interview."

Liz was in a daze. She said, "I made it? I made it? Nancy, I made it! I'm going to be certified? Oh My Lord. Nancy, Vincent, thank you so much. Oh Lord, you're smiling on me today. Thank you!" She lifted her eyes and her heart toward heaven. She knew the Almighty was with her, in her triumph.

They both let out a little laugh. She was so happy and enthusiastic. At the same time, she was tired, too. The studying and the stress of writing, took a lot out of her. She couldn't wait to tell Joe, then her mom.

She said, "Thanks so much, both of you, for the encouragement, and your time to let me write. I think I better go home and lay down, before I fall down. I'm so excited, my legs are like jelly. Nancy, could you call a taxi for me? I don't think I should walk home."

Vincent said, "Liz, don't you want to hear your mark?"

She put her hand over her mouth and said, "Oh yes. I forgot to ask."

Vincent said, "You passed with a 98% overall mark. The highest mark ever, in Mississippi's history. Any school board would be so proud to have you, and I'm sure this School Board will get the chance to tell you that on Monday. Congratulations, again. Where do you live, I can drive you home."

Liz said, "It's okay, I can take a taxi."

Vincent said, "Where do you live?"

Liz said, "Gilbert Street." He told her that was not a problem, he knew that area of town and he'd take her. They both said goodbye to Nancy and went on their way. As they pulled into her driveway, he congratulated her, once again and told her the School Board meeting was on Monday at 7:00 p.m., at the library.

Liz thanked him for the drive and for letting her know the news before the weekend. It might have driven her crazy. She thanked him once again and said she'd see him Monday night.

She looked at the clock and she started supper. She wanted to call her mom, but she just had to tell Joe first. She was so anxious for him to get home. It was about four forty-five, when the phone rang. As she picked it up, she had a sad feeling. She said, "Hello."

"Hi honey," Joe said, "I'm sorry baby, we're going to be working until dark and all day Saturday and Sunday. I'm so sorry darlin'."

She said, "No problem. I knew when we moved here there would be overtime on new projects. You sound happy and it's great to hear you like that. I haven't heard that in your voice since the Toronto jobs. Honey, I'm proud of you and so happy. Your parents are smiling on you, too. I can feel it darling." He fell silent for a few seconds. She always knew what Joe needed: Even when he didn't. A tear filled his eye. He felt their presence, too. He was happy.

Liz continued, "So, you said you have to work till dark?"

Joe said, "Yeah babe, we're not stopping to eat so if you can have something for me when I get home, I'm sure I'll be hungry. Anyway dear, I'm on a pay phone. We're not even in town. We're at the job site. I have to go now hun, bye."

She said, "Bye dear, I'm a certified Mississippi teacher, see you when you get home." She didn't even know if he heard her, or not. As she hung up the phone, she started to cry. She turned the oven down he'd be a few hours before he gets home.

On the site, Lorne said, "So, how did the little woman take it?"

Joe said, "Oh Liz has no problem with me doing overtime. She's very supportive of my job and I am of hers. As a matter of fact, she just told me she is now certified to teach in Mississippi." Joe had a coffee in his hand and dropped it. "Oh my God. Oh Shit!! She did it! She wrote the exams today and she told me as I was hanging up that she was now licensed to teach in Mississippi."

He started to whoop and holler a bit, but then he saw George Benson getting out of his car. He straightened up, but could not contain his smile. He was proud of his wife. Lorne and Rick were, too. Lorne patted Joe on the back and asked him to pass on his congratulations to his wife and so did Rick.

Joe felt like a heel, not staying on the phone to congratulate her, but he was in a hurry and didn't clue in, right away. He wanted to call her back and he couldn't. The boss was there and they had to get back to work.

Liz placed a phone call. Eleanor picked up her phone and said, "Hello."

Liz was trying not to cry as she said, "Hi mom. How are you?"

Eleanor said, "Elizabeth honey, it's great to hear you. We're all fine here, love. How was Joe's first week at work?"

Liz said, "Oh, he's quite busy. As a matter of fact, he's working until dark tonight and all day Saturday and Sunday. He loves it, mom. His bridge design was chosen for the project they're working on. It will span the Big Black River out of town, to the west."

El said, "Well, it's a job he loves, honey. How are you feeling about it?"

She replied, "Oh mom I'm fine with his hours, you know that. I understood marrying a structural engineer consisted of some overtime and I accepted it and I support his job..."

El jumped in and said, "Then tell me girl, why you're crying!"

Liz said, "Mom, I have a surprise and just before Joe hung up the phone I told him, but he didn't even congratulate me. Mom, I'm certified to teach in the state of Mississippi. I wrote the exams for my certification today and they've already been graded. I'll get my official certificate on Monday evening, at the Neshoba County, Board of Education meeting. I received a 98% overall score on the entire set of exams. Mom, that's the highest mark in the history of Mississippi."

Eleanor started screaming in the phone. She was so excited for her daughter and so proud. She said, "Oh my baby, I'm so happy and proud...oh my Lord, you have made our families so proud, honey." Eleanor started to cry.

Just then, Liz's' twin brothers came in to see what their mom was yelling about. After she told them, they each grabbed the phone to congratulate their big sister. They all went on for a while talking and laughing. They each told her how proud they were and that they loved her and missed her and Joe. By the time she got off the phone, she was getting really tired.

She estimated it was about forty-five minutes to sunset, so she turned Joe's dinner back on. She was smiling and singing to herself. She could always count on her family to cheer her up. Just then, the door quietly opened and Joe sneaked in, came up behind her, turned her around, put his arms around her and lifted her, swung her around and said, "Baby, I am so proud of you." He kissed her and gave her a lovely bouquet of wildflowers.

She said, "Oh Joe, I love you so much. Thank you sweetie. These flowers are beautiful. Where did you ever get them?"

Joe said, "Well to be honest, once it sank into me what you told me, about passing the exams, it was too late to say anything. I was already off the phone and George was on site. I told Lorne and Rick what was going on and they both said to congratulate you.

George Benson came along and found out, too. He sent his best wishes as well. George said to me that I could knock off around seven and get home to you. He said the three of them could handle the last hour and get me caught up Saturday morning.

I wasn't sure what to do, but Lorne and Rick gave me the nod. If George said go early, it was okay. Luckily, I drove the truck with Lorne and followed Rick out to the site. They said it was always best to take two vehicles to the sites. You never know what can happen through the day. George drove his own vehicle everywhere. It all worked out great.

While I was on site, I came across these beautiful blue flowers and I picked them for you. I know any kind of blue flowers are your favorite. As I was driving home, it seemed like I came across such a variety of flowers, I kept getting out of the truck to pick some for you. I knew you'd like them. I think I probably would have been home at least fifteen, or twenty minutes earlier, but you would never have had a bouquet of wildflowers. Making a long story short, I love you and I am proud of you, honey!" He kissed her passionately and asked, "Can you take dinner out of the oven, or turn it down? I have something else in mind I'd prefer to do." He kept kissing her as she turned the oven down, again. He picked her up and carried her to the bedroom.

They made love as passionately as they had a few nights earlier; his symptoms did not bother him this time. Afterward, Joe said, "Alright teach, can a guy get some supper around here?"

She smiled and said, "Right away, love. I'll be eating with you."

Joe said, as she dished up their supper, "Didn't you eat yet?"

She told him, "I really haven't had time. I was on the phone with mom, Abe and Simon..."

Joe said, "Say no more...that explains it."

As they ate their supper, Liz told him, "I'm going to the school board meeting, Monday and I will get my certificate then. I already have some recommendations and the principal said I could very well be hired on, but I still had to meet the rest of the board. My interview will be then too. Anyway, how did your day go?"

Joe had a good day and after getting over a few bumps on his first day at work, he was happy with his first week on the job. Joe told her about the site that the bridge was going to be built. He was so enthusiastic. He was in his element talking about the bridge. Liz couldn't be happier, too. They talked about their concerns about the black and white issues. They felt they were going to be okay living there, after all. Maybe they were wrong about their concerns.

Joe was out most of the weekend while Liz rested. When he came home Saturday, he told her that he had to work late for the next two to three weeks, including Saturdays, at least 8 to 5 and Sundays 8 to 4. They had to get ready to bring in the big machines to start getting the land ready.

Liz spent a lot of her time that weekend, thinking about the board meeting on Monday night. Joe would be working late again, while Liz attended the meeting at the library.

When she arrived Monday she was introduced to the rest of the board members. There was tea and coffee, along with some sandwiches and cookies, for after the meeting. Liz was surprised.

When she was formally introduced to the group, they all applauded. They were all so impressed. They asked her questions about her life, background, family, but none of the questions were, "Is your husband black, or white."

There was a gentleman who showed up just after the interview. Liz didn't know who he was. When the actual meeting came to order, they started with New Business. This was the presentation of Liz's certificate. Vince introduced the man who had just come in. He said, "Ladies and gentlemen, I'd like to introduce Mr. Thomas L. Bailey, Governor of Mississippi." Liz was stunned. As the man stood, the board rose and applauded, as did Liz. She was hoping that she wouldn't pass out!

As he stood, he said, "Mrs. Elizabeth Allen, it is my privilege and honor to present you with your certificate to be an Elementary School Teacher, anywhere in the State of Mississippi. Along with the honor of presenting this certificate, I understand that you passed the examinations with an overall mark of 98%. That is the highest score for certification of any teacher in the entire history of Mississippi. It is truly a pleasure to give you this certificate, along with my congratulations." They applauded again, as he handed her the certificate.

"Now, that was from me." As the Governor continued to speak, no one else on the Board knew what else he was going to say as he went on. "Over the weekend I had an opportunity to make a few phone calls. These calls were regarding you and your incredible mark on the teacher examinations."

He pulled a letter out of the inside pocket of his suit jacket. In front of everyone, he unfolded this letter and everyone remained silent. He asked Liz if she would step up towards him so he could read it to her.

The Governor started again, "Mrs. Allen this letter was couriered to me this morning and it comes from the Oval Office, of the White House. It comes from the President of the United States. It reads:

> Mrs. Elizabeth Allen
>
> I wish to take this opportunity to congratulate you on your recent success in becoming the latest Elementary School Teacher, entitled to teach anywhere in the State of Mississippi.
>
> Your overall grade of 98% on your exams is indeed impressive. I commend your determination in becoming a teacher in that great State. Being a teacher in Ontario, Canada, surely prepared you for your success, south of the border.
>
> It is my hope that you become very satisfied teaching in Mississippi. Teaching, being such a noble profession, is honored to have such an intelligent, remarkable lady amongst them.
>
> Again, I offer my sincere congratulations, on your remarkable achievement.
>
> Sincerely,
> Harry S. Truman

Mrs. Allen, this letter is signed by the President of the United States."

Liz had her hand over her mouth in disbelief, as to what she was hearing. When the Governor stopped speaking, the board members stood up and applauded and cheered for Liz, calling, "Speech, speech."

After the applause stopped, Liz said, "I don't quite know what to say. I'm actually speechless, wow! My husband thought that was impossible." Everyone laughed with her. She smiled and said, "First, I must say thank you for presenting my certificate in person, Mr. Bailey. It is truly an honor to meet you sir and the letter from the President, um, I'm so honored, but I am really just your average school teacher, trying to be a shining light for young minds, wherever I teach. I thank you all for the confidence you have in me. I promise, wherever I teach in Mississippi, I will do the job to the best of my ability." She was nervous but they applauded, once again.

When they finished, Governor Bailey got up again. "I also would like to say what a pleasure it is that you come from Canada. We are proud that you have decided to join us, here in the south."

Vince rose again and said, "Well we're not to keep you in suspense, Mrs. Allen. We'd like to welcome you as a new teacher for the Neshoba County School Board. We have a placement for you, although temporary. It is the grade three class at Philadelphia Public School. Mrs. Emms is going to have a baby and you will take her place until she returns, in February.

You are to start school next Monday. You can attend her class with her for two weeks, so you can get up to speed and get to know the school, the faculty and your students." Liz was so highly thought of and proved herself, that they wanted her!

When the meeting was adjourned Nancy hugged Liz. Everyone turned to the refreshments and they all congratulated Liz. She was so happy she started to tear up, yet again. She couldn't wait to tell Joe everything: Specially the part about the Governor of Mississippi, presenting her with her Certificate and the letter from the President. She would be sure to frame both.

After the meeting Vince asked Liz if she'd like a drive home. She said, "That would be great, thanks." She said her goodbyes to everyone and thanked them all for having such confidence in her.

They left and Vincent dropped her off at home. She was still tearing a bit, but she was so happy. As she went into the house, there was a giant banner across the kitchen saying 'Congratulations Liz'. There were balloons and vases of flowers everywhere. They were her favorites...Red Roses and White Orchids. She was so shocked. In the middle of the kitchen table there was a gift. Joe came in, from where he was hiding in the dining room and kissed his wife and pulled out a chair so she could sit down to open it.

She opened it and inside the carefully packaged gift, she found the hand bell that her great-grandfather Johnny McDonald, gave his wife, her great-grandmother Diana, when she started teaching. She turned it over and found the inscription:

"It is through error that man tries and rises. It is through tragedy, he learns. All the roads of learning begin in the darkness and go out into the light". She would always believe in this, just like her great-grandmother. She too, wanted to be this light...she cried, remembering what she told the board members and the governor and asked, "Honey, how did you get this?"

Joe said, "It wasn't me darlin'. Your mom shipped it down over the weekend. She wanted to give it to you in person someday, but you surprised her by getting certified so quickly. Anyway, it arrived here on the same day you became a certified Mississippi teacher."

She hugged him and held him for a moment crying. She told him all about Governor Bailey and showed him the letter from the President. Liz looked in his eyes and said, "I know the Lord is watching us, Joe. We were meant to be here. I love you." As he kissed her, he gave her his gift. She opened it up. It was a beautiful set of two gold plated fountain pens and a matching gold pencil, with refillable leads. Inscribed on each one was, "Mrs. Elizabeth Allen (1947)". She loved them. It was the most beautiful set she'd ever seen. One pen had red ink and the other, blue. She was so thrilled. She would use them and treasure them, forever.

She hugged her husband again, still having tears running down her face. She was so happy this night, but she was exhausted. He helped her up the stairs. As she got ready for bed, Joe went back down to lock the door. She turned the light on and looked around the bedroom. He had even put flowers on her night stand. She was touched.

She lay down and smiled. She had so much to be thankful for. She said a silent prayer and quickly fell asleep, before Joe got back to the bedroom. When he went into the bedroom, he saw her sleeping already and tucked her in. He too, smiled and said a prayer. He believed they were going to have a great life in Mississippi. He was just as happy as her.

But it wasn't last. As Joe worked hard, over the months, strange little things kept happening and stupid pranks. He knew it was all Ray's doing. He was turning out to be a real asshole. Especially since George

Benson had another bathroom built, just for Joe. Maria asked to use it too; Joe and George had no problem. It was a little cleaner, although she cleaned both. No man in the office ever said anything about her using it. Joe felt like something was coming to a head, in the office. He just didn't know what...or when it would be!

Chapter 5

Joseph's OWN Project

MONDAY FEBRUARY 24, 1947 WAS a beautiful sunny winter Mississippi morning to remember. There was no snow through the winter and they missed it and the Chatham winters which they were used to. Joseph thought he would let Liz sleep in, since Etta was there permanently now to watch over her. Liz was up a lot during the night with heartburn and painful rumblings in her very large abdomen. She slept very little the last few nights. She could not get comfortable and was restless. On her last visit to the doctor the baby had dropped dramatically and he told her she could give birth any time...that was two weeks earlier.

Liz missed not getting up early and ready for school. She had been substituting for the grade three teacher at Philadelphia Elementary School for the last few months. Liz missed teaching, already! Mrs. Emms returned at the beginning of February and it was now time for Liz to take her maternity leave.

She was just a substitute teacher for now, but hoped to return to that school; some day when her child was old enough and she felt she was ready to leave him, or her, at home all day with Etta. Liz made friends at this school and she loved her experience teaching there and wished to actively pursue it full time when she was ready; hoping they would have a spot for her, at this school. If she had to travel to another school to teach, she would; as long as it wasn't too far away. Queen's University and Chatham Public School 101 prepared her for all of this and she was so excited about it. She had a lot to live up to, though. She had the School Board, The Governor and the President behind her, too.

But now, she was finding it hard to fill her days, until the arrival of the baby. Liz and Joe had hired a housekeeper and Joe liked her being around to look after Liz, when he was at work.

Etta had been with the Allen's a few months. Etta arrived in Philadelphia Mississippi, not too long after the Allen's did. She was born in Arkansas about twenty-three years earlier. Her father left her mother before she was born and her mother died in childbirth. She lived and worked on one of the last rice plantations left in the United States.

Most rice farms had evolved into big business and had been mechanized, but the farm Etta was born on, named the "Olde Tyme Plantation", still existed in the Mississippi Delta Region of Arkansas. Etta had been cared for by several of the black women who worked in the house. She had no formal education, just what the women of the house taught her and when old enough, she was put to work in the house.

Since there was no slavery by law, blacks had to be paid for their services now. They were paid pittance, in comparison to whites. After she had been raped several times growing up, by both black and white men, she decided that she wanted to leave. She knew there was a place somewhere out in the world where she could be safe. Maybe she could find it in another state. She thought she might like to try Mississippi. She knew she never wanted to see Arkansas, ever again.

Etta took her pay, cried with the women she knew as her mothers, trying to say goodbye and bravely got on a bus. She had saved her money, for all the years of working, but she didn't have a plan, or a place in mind; she just got on a bus to 'somewhere' Mississippi, as she referred to it. As the bus pulled into the town of Philadelphia in Mississippi, she got off the bus; and headed towards the ticket counter, at the depot. She said, "Scuse me sir, can you tell me where I mights find me a room ta' rent?"

Without looking at her, he kept his head down looking at the newspaper, he said, "Leave the depot, turn right, go down a block, then look to the left, an' ya'll will see a place that rents rooms." He brought his head up and looked at her. He said, "Oh, ya'll mean a room 'fer Niggers. That's different. Ya'll leave the depot, ya' still turn right and walk about a mile and a half and you will find a house on the edge of town that'll take ya', if they have room. The place is called Minnie's. Can ya' read?" Etta said she knew her letters and some words. He wrote the name Minnie's, on a piece of paper and said, "You match up the name on this paper with the sign on her front porch."

He looked around and when no one was paying attention to him he started to write something on the back of the paper. He asked, "You here lookin' for work, too?" Etta nodded her head. He continued, "Where'd ya come from?"

Etta said, "I'se from a plantation in Arkansas. My name is Etta, no lass' name, sir. I lives 'dere all my life, til' now, 'dis day."

He gave her the paper and told her to give it to the lady at the house. He reminded her to match the paper, to the sign on the house. It was a large two story, yellow house. People were staring at him, taking a while talking to her so he gruffly told her the directions again and told her to go away.

She set off, with a good feeling. It only took her under an hour. She always walked fast and she was very fit. She didn't even think it was as far away as the man said. She saw the sign on a large yellow house. It matched what he wrote on the paper, "Minnie's". She climbed the few steps and rang the doorbell. The door was opened by a heavyset black woman about six feet tall, an intimidating figure.

The woman said, "I'se Minnie, I 'spect you'se need a room? An' a job, right?" Etta was a little nervous all of a sudden. She could only nod her answers. Minnie continued and said, "What's yo' name, girl?"

Etta said, "It's Etta, no lass' name ma'am. 'Da man at 'da depot gives me 'dis paper. Minnie read it and smiled as she took her up to the second floor. Etta noticed that there were many rooms. She stopped at the room at the end of the hall, and opened the door. They talked and chattered, while Minnie told Etta the house rules and they found out a little about each other. Minnie had a good feeling about her.

The next day, Minnie took Etta in her very own car which not many blacks owned, in this town. Minnie had just finally bought hers, a few days earlier. She drove to 2 Gilbert Street. Etta was wondering what this day would bring and what had the man at the depot written on the paper, to Minnie, the day before. Was there some connection? She could not read it, but some day, she hoped her questions would be answered. Where was Minnie taking her? Minnie just told her she was going for a visit and interview, to see about a job and asked if she had experience with babies.

As Liz opened the door she said, "Good morning Minnie, how are you today?"

Minnie said, "I'se fine today ma'am, how's you and 'da mister?" Minnie had met Joe and she liked him and she liked them as a couple.

Liz said, "We're both just fine, thank you. This must be Etta. How do you do Etta; please, won't you both come in?" As Liz let them in, she brought them into the living room and served coffee and cookies.

Liz asked Etta about her experience and wanted to know if she would like a trial basis of working there for a couple of weeks. She would come at 6:30 a.m. and leave after supper dishes were done. They usually ate around five-thirty, at the latest. Everything sounded fine to her and Etta asked if she could start working right then.

Liz said, "I love your enthusiasm Etta. That's okay with me. I'll show you around and; oh by the way, we're going to have a baby in February. Did Minnie tell you?" Etta nodded her head and smiled. Liz continued, "Have you helped with the care of babies, before?"

Etta said, "Yes ma'am. I sho' does. I hep'd wit' many babies 'round 'da farm and in 'da main house on 'da 'farm, too. I loves 'em ma'am." Liz felt good hearing that.

Minnie excused herself and asked if Etta remembered her way back to the boarding house. Etta wasn't sure, so Minnie said she'd pick her up in the evening. She asked Liz to call her when she Etta finished and she would come and get her. Liz said she would call and they both said goodbye to Minnie, as she left.

Joe and Liz and Etta all got on so well. When Liz worked, Etta's help was needed in the house. They appreciated her, so much. When Liz wasn't working and stayed home, she felt that she wanted to do the cleaning and laundry and make Joe's lunches, herself. Etta felt like she wasn't doing enough work to get paid for, but that was fine with them. They let her stay anyway on those days, to help Liz out and keep her company.

Liz finally decided in the last few weeks of her pregnancy; while she was home and waiting for the baby, to relinquish most jobs around the house to Etta. She was letting her make breakfast for Joe and prepare his lunches for work. To be honest, Liz was finding it difficult to get close enough to the kitchen counter to do almost anything the last few weeks.

It seemed to her that her tummy was there at least five minutes before the rest of her was. She teased herself about that often, which made Joe and Etta chuckle along with her. She was certain that boy or girl, this baby was not going to be a football linebacker; he or she already was one! Including, being ready for college and everything, to boot!

They decided to have Etta live with them full time, if she would accept the idea. Liz would need her lots more, soon; and since Etta had no family of her own, she was more than happy to be moving in with them.

A couple of weeks before Christmas, Liz and Joe asked Etta, to stay after supper one night, to sit with them and have coffee before she went back to Minnie's. As she sat down, Liz started, "Etta, we want to tell you that since you came into our lives, we have come to know you, rely heavily on you and trust you and we're very satisfied with your work. We'd like to make a proposition. Joe suggested that we build a bedroom and bathroom for you in the basement and have you move in with us, permanently. We would really like you to consider it. You would still have Sundays off, as well as Tuesday and Thursday evenings after 5:00 p.m., for your personal time and to attend your meetings and church gatherings and such; and you will not be expected to do the dishes those nights, we will.

You'll still have two weeks off in the summer, like we discussed when we hired you; as well as all the legal, government holidays. When the baby comes, I'll need you a little more and with you here, Joe won't worry so much about me."

Joe continued, "We thought about just giving you one of the bedrooms upstairs, but we would like to have another baby someday and it would be easier to build your own room now; and not have to bother building it and moving you in around a year or so from now. Would you be willing to consider our offer?"

Etta was caught off guard by all of this. She had an eerie feeling when they asked her to sit with them and have coffee that evening, that maybe she was being dismissed, but was not sure why. She always did the best work she could for the Allen's and she was very fond of both Joe and Liz.

Etta loved children and wasn't sure what the future held for her in this way; so she thought, why not devote herself to this friendly couple, who seemed to have adopted her and cared for her? She was proud of her position with the Allen's and was honored and thrilled when they asked her to live with them. She said, "Oh my Lawdy, ma'am, sir, I don't know what to say. I'se so 'fraid you and my missus din't want me 'round no mo'." Liz took her hand compassionately and Etta pulled it back quickly. The last time a white person touched her, she was raped. She felt a little foolish being startled, but Liz understood.

Liz took her hand again and said, "We care for you very much Etta and would like to consider you part of our family. If you need a few days to think about it, we understand."

Etta was overflowing with emotions and she started tearing up, "They'se really nuttin' ta' 'tink over, you folks is just so much like family ta' me, I sho' 'nuff would love ta' live here."

Joe told her, "Don't worry about your pay, Etta. Just because we'll give you your own room and meals, your pay won't go down. You'll still make the same wage, $25.00 a week. There may be times when we might need you to help with the baby in the middle of the night, or to babysit and you'll be right here for us."

Etta told them, "I wouldn't care if ya'll never paid me 'agin, I'se so happy ya'll wants me 'round...I won't be trouble 'fer ya', I'se always gonna be here 'fer ya' and 'da missus...always. I look after all yo' babies whenever ya'll needs me, I'se gonna be right here, yessir, I'se always be here 'fer ya' bote' and you'se little ones, no matter how many chil'run ya'll has!" With that, Liz gave Etta a warm, yet gentle hug as Joseph shook her hand and the plans were set.

After Christmas, their first away from Chatham and the family; in the evenings, Joe was busy building a bedroom and bathroom, in their basement, for Etta. She was now to become a member of the Allen family, of Gilbert Street.

NOW, this February 24th, a bright Monday morning, started out just like any other. Joseph awoke, had his breakfast, showered, shaved and dressed in his blue suit. He went into the bedroom and as quietly as he could he kissed Liz on the cheek, saying goodbye, and he softly called out as he left the room, "Don't you do anything sweetie, you just let Etta do for you and have her call me at the office if anything happens, or if you need me for anything. I love you, Mrs. Allen. Now you take care and behave yourself darlin'."

With one eye open and a smile on her face, Liz said, "I love you too Mr. Allen and don't forget you said you'd take me to see the movies tonight!"

Going through school, Liz excelled at English studies. She read voraciously. Right from the time she learned her alphabet, on the farm. Her mother taught Liz and Joe to read earlier than most children. Eleanor loved teaching her daughter and Joe. They made great students. Joe's mind was elsewhere sometimes and she would laugh. She knew he would get serious about school sometime. She never worried about him. With his mom being a doctor, she knew he was going to be a very intelligent boy. The same with Liz and her brothers.

Liz would read anything she could get her hands on. She loved the classics. Her favorite author was Charles Dickens. She was excited in 1946 when David Lean's "Great Expectations" premiered in theaters. She was so anxious to see it. It would be nominated for eight Academy Awards in 1947. She was also thrilled because her favorite British actor, John Mills, played the leading roll.

This was to be their first outing to the movies in their new community. They expected they would have to sit in "colored section", to sit together; Liz was fine with that. They had been so busy working on the house and preparing for the baby, that they set aside very little time for socializing, except when the Diamont's came over to play cards, once in a while. They were having very few problems so far, mostly because they had not appeared out together as a couple, they seemed to do things individually and not had time, even to meet their neighbors yet, other than to say 'hi'. They never responded with a 'hi' in return, to either of them.

In Ontario, it was okay for colored people to go places with white people. Go out to dinner together, the theater, use the same bathrooms and drinking fountains...it was accepted. They really had no idea what Mississippi held for a mixed-race couple, before they moved. They heard stories, but they didn't want to believe them. The Diamont's and Minnie told them what their life could be like. They were still fairly new here and would very soon find out how different things REALLY were!

With their goodbyes said, Joe grabbed his lunch and was out the door. As he got into the pickup, he wondered what sort of bullshit he would be dealing with, today at work. His co-worker, Ray, still was not very friendly towards him, but what else was new?

The pranks had been since that first week he arrived there, fresh from Chatham Ontario; bright, eager and willing to do his best in Mississippi. He wanted to succeed. Legally, there was no recourse to fire Joe his work was exemplary, so Ray used other methods to try to get Joe out of their office.

Ray tried to get the other guys in the office to join with him, since day one. The guys were too busy to be pulled into his games...except, Bubba Shep. Ray was recently nominated for the recruitment committee, within his order of the Klan and he was elected. He managed to get Bubba to join. Ray was really feeling proud and now had an ally at work. Bubba really didn't want to, but he helped Ray with some pranks. Bubba did like Joe, but could never let Ray know.

Not long after Joe was there, Ray started with juvenile pranks; like gum and thumb tacks on his chair: Then hiding important files, making him look incompetent.

Just on the previous Friday, he had put salt in the sugar bowl beside the coffee machine. Since Ray knew Joe took two spoons of sugar in his coffee, this was plenty to ruin his cup. He laughed and Joe just ignored him. He dumped his coffee and got a Coca-Cola from the lunch room machine and said to the guys, "Don't use the sugar bowl, it's salt." The guys just looked around at each other and then at Ray, who was snickering. They just went back to their work, shaking their heads at Ray-ashamed for him.

When Ray didn't get the reaction he wanted, he would conspire with Bubba, about the next prank they may pull. These childish pranks were done to Joe almost daily. Ray was always pulling them just to annoy Joe, but he would never give in. He wouldn't satisfy them, with anger. That would give Ray and Bubba the 'right' to retaliate! He worked daily in this dangerous environment of men belonging to the KKK. They were trying to break him and get rid of him...maybe run him out of town, or worse. Ray didn't like Mr. Joseph Allen and made no secret of it.

The other men only talked with Joe in a jovial way, out of the office. No one was buddy-buddy with Joe, in front of Ray and Bubba; who was now under Ray's thumb, too. Truth be told, the men did not want to be on the bad side of Ray either. Joe felt that the exception might be his boss, George Benson. He thought that George liked him, or at least 'accepted' him a bit, but could never show it in front of the rest of the staff.

The five that worked on the bridge, for months, Rick, Carroll, Lorne, Joe and Jerry, were fine on the job site. There were no problems there, but in the office, things were a little cooler. Joe knew the real score. Joe remembered back to the day he realized that George Benson really was alright with him.

Thursday February 6th George left a note on Joe's desk, before he got in. It said, 'I have a real big problem! Come to my office as soon as you get in?' When Joe found the note, he was worried. He tried to think of what he had done wrong. Was there a problem with his designs; was there something wrong with his work, on site? Or, what had Ray done to him, this time? His mind flooded with all kinds of scenarios of what was going to happen in George's office.

Joe took a deep breath and knocked on the office door. George grumbled out a loud, "Come!" He stood and motioned for Joe to close the door. As Joe turned around and closed the door, George continued, "Sit!" Joe sat down. George got right into it. "Joseph, I have a serious problem in this office. Everyone is assigned and working hard, you included. This week, I received a phone call because someone wanted to hire our services. My problem is; everyone is assigned to all our jobs. Not wanting to ever let a good job go by, I told them I'd take it on.

Therein, lays my problem. I thought about it for three and a half seconds and decided how I would handle it. Joseph, I know you love your bridge, but I'm taking you off it and assigning you to your own new project! I know you're up to it and I have every faith in you, that you can handle it." George reached out to shake Joe's hand. Joe was stunned, but stood and took George's hand. George said, "Can't you muster a smile, son?"

Joe grinned from ear to ear, saying, "Yes sir, I sure can! Thank you so much Mr. Benson. Thank you for your confidence in me. You're right, I do get attached to my bridges and I know it's silly."

George said, "No son, I understand. Each project I accept is like a new baby, to me. I've been one hell of a great father for twenty years." They both laughed. Joe still couldn't believe it: His own project, after being there a few months. Liz was going to be so happy and proud.

George drove Joe out of town to the site, as he filled him in on the job. He told Joe, "There's a company that needs to build a few bridges. Not motor bridges; foot bridges." Some engineers might have been insulted, but not Joe. He hadn't done them before, but he was up to the new challenge. He was excited by it.

George took Joe to meet the head man at Pakos Industries. It was a small group of four factories, built around a large parking lot. They wanted the buildings now being connected by a series of heavy duty, secure foot bridges. The head of Pakos, Roy Pakos was very unimpressed with Joe being black. He asked George if he had a normal engineer, he didn't want a black one.

George told Pakos, "Roy, I assure you that I have taken this man off my largest project, where his expertise is needed. He is the best man I have: And you are damn lucky to get him. I guarantee you will be impressed with his work. He's the best in Mississippi. This man comes highly educated and a seasoned engineer, designing bridges and overpasses in Canada. So, if you're going to have a problem with him, let's get it out in the open. If you want out, say so now and I'll drop your contract!"

Joe couldn't believe what he was hearing. He was thinking to himself, 'Shit, now I know how Liz felt about the letter from the president!'

Roy Pakos said, "Well, can you bring your design ideas and estimates in on Monday?"

Joe said, "Yes sir, I could do that. I'm sure I can design something you'll like and is efficient for your purpose. But, what I'll need from you first, is to go over your needs and your ideas of what you want to see built. Show me where the bridges are to go, do you want actual foot bridges, or catwalks, or what do you think about tunnels to connect all the buildings together. I'll need to know your budget and all of that is needed from you before I can even start the designs and estimates, Mr. Pakos."

Roy Pakos took George and Joe around the grounds of the complex of factories. Joe took extensive notes. He wrote everything down that Roy wanted, or suggested. Joe had his own ideas, but this was not the time to voice them. He wanted Pakos' ideas and George's too. George brought their basic tools with them and Joe got right to work, taking his measurements, while George and Pakos talked. When Roy went inside, George helped Joe and they just did a lot of smiling at each other.

By the end of the day, Joe had everything he needed to draw his designs and estimates, for Monday. He'd have to tell Liz there would be overtime, again. He thought about the baby. Hoping it would come, when he was home. He was excited and on his way home, he stopped and bought Liz red roses and white orchids. He also bought Etta a few carnations. He was happy.

When Joe walked in the house that day, Etta was in the kitchen making supper and Liz was lying on the sofa. She was just resting before eating. She certainly was getting quite large. When he came in with flowers, she was thrilled. She tried to get off the sofa and failed. She called, "Etta?" Etta popped her head out of the kitchen and saw that Liz needed help off the sofa. She smiled.

Joe said, "It's okay Etta, I'll get her." As he went to help her get up, he said, "Hey sweetie, how are you doing today?"

Liz said, "I'm fine. The baby on the other hand, is running a race."

When she sat up on the sofa, Joe went into the kitchen, where he had laid the flowers and gave the smaller package to Etta and kissed her on her cheek. He brought the large package to Liz and gave her a loving kiss and the best hug he could, without disturbing the baby's activity.

Etta was standing in the kitchen speechless, holding her package.

Joe said, "Okay ladies, you can both open your packages." They opened them up and Etta started to cry. Joe and Liz weren't quite sure what kind of a cry, but they thought a happy cry.

She said, "Mr. Joe, ain't no one ever's give me flowers, in all my life. I'se 'spect all my life, I had ta' dies ta' git' some. I 'tanks ya' sir, 'dey's beautiful. Mrs. Liz can I use one of your lovely vases ta' puts 'dem in?"

Liz nodded her head. She opened up her package and she said, "Joe, they are so beautiful. I think this means you're REALLY happy about something! Etta, could you please get another vase for mine?" Etta brought her carnations in to show Liz and set it on the coffee table and put Liz's flowers in the other vase.

Liz said, "Etta, they are lovely carnations. You can put them anywhere you like in the house."

Etta, still in a bit of a daze and tears flowing, said, "I 'tinks 'dey goes in my room, if it's okay?"

Joe said, "That's a wonderful idea." He took her hand and said, "I hope you like them and I just wanted you to know we love you and you're part of our family." Etta couldn't help it, she cried and she hugged both of them.

Liz said, "Honey are you going to keep me in suspense, or are you going to tell us why you're floating on cloud nine?" As he helped Liz off the sofa, to go eat supper, he carried her flowers into the dining room to use as a centerpiece.

He said, "You won't believe me Liz, but this morning, George got me in his office and I was nervous, I didn't know what he wanted; I was expecting Ray had done something to get me fired.

Well he started with 'I have a serious problem'; I was sure it was something Ray did to me." They both were eating and Etta was listening, too. "He said he got this call to do a job. He took me off my bridge and assigned me my own project." Liz leapt out of her chair, as quickly as an almost nine month very pregnant woman could-and hugged him. Etta was excited too. She put out her hand to congratulate him. While still keeping Liz in one arm, he put out his hand to Etta and pulled her into a family hug. The three couldn't be happier.

After a moment, they told Etta to bring her supper to the table and Liz told her, "From now on Etta, you will eat your supper with us, IF you want to."

Etta said, "I 'tanks ya' Mrs. Liz, I'd love ta'. But I'll not do it in front of comp'ny, it wouldn't be proper." That was settled. Etta brought her supper to the table for herself and sat down to eat with Joe and Liz.

Joe continued. "Honey, I am going to build three foot bridges, catwalks or tunnels, depending on what the man decides, from my designs and estimates. George took me out of town to a complex, called Pakos Industries. It is four buildings, factories. I don't know all they manufacture, but anyway, he wants all the buildings connected together by outdoor bridges and I am to design them."

Liz said, "Sweetie that's wonderful. At least it's a new challenge with something you haven't done before."

Joe said, "Oh but I have, sweetie. At Queens, remember I built that class project where I built the tunnel and the bridge, on top. It was over and under a river. I know it was a motor bridge, but I know I can adapt it into foot bridges and tunnels between buildings. What do you think?"

Liz was wide eyed as she spoke, "You're right. You got a great mark on your design and the model. I never thought about adapting one you already designed: Honey that's brilliant."

Joe said, "I know how you felt with the presidential letter you received. Pakos doesn't want me because I'm black. But, George sat there and raved on how great I was and that he was fortunate to get me. He just kept going on and on and Pakos backed down and we started the tour of the exterior of the place. George helped me all day with measurements and ideas and I never let it out, that I already had the design in mind.

Out in the garage are all my designs from Toronto and Queen's. I know I can adapt the motor bridges, to foot bridges. He has a good size budget. It's a lot harder to do the tunnel and more expensive. George took samples and he's going to let me know as soon as he can, geologically, if the land is sound enough for tunnels. Honey, it will mean overtime, for a while."

Remembering that February 6th day, when Joe got his 'own' project, she was smiling when she told him, "Dear, I know you'll do it and don't worry, Etta is going to be here with me constantly. I'll tell the baby to wait until you're home, if you like." He smiled and kissed her. This was the happiest day they'd had, since moving to Mississippi. It was all coming together...then as he got back to the present...came the rest of the day...February 24th. And what a day it was going to be!

Chapter 6

February 24th - A Day Never to be Forgotten

WHEN JOE ARRIVED AT THE office this Monday February 24, 1947; he wondered what he was in for today. They all had their Monday morning meeting and a few of the men were not needed on their job sites that morning. They stayed in the office, to do paper work.

Joe was due out at a meeting at his project site out of town at two that afternoon...or so he thought. It had been written on his calendar before he arrived at work and when he asked Maria about it, she said she never got the call or wrote anything on his calendar.

Ray butted in with, "I was in here first this morning and the phone was ringing and I answered it. I took your message and I wrote it on your calendar...MISTER ALLEN!"

Joe said "Thank you did he say what the meeting was about?"

Ray said "I dunno just bring all materials and files on the project. Mr. Pakos is not happy with your work, somethin' like that. Seems like you're not going to stay in the budget and he's decided the tunnels are going to be crap and he's not sure about your flimsy bridges!" Joe was really upset and nervous, now.

Ray told Joe, "You shoulda' come to me, boy. I coulda' told you your design wouldn't work. I expect George ain't gonna to be happy at all 'bout any of this, is he, boy?" Joe went to his desk, worried.

After lunch, Joe gathered everything up and put it in his briefcase. As he signed out of the office, Ray had put a slightly closed bottle of blue ink in Joe's briefcase and closed it. Joseph grabbed the briefcase and unlocked the door of his truck and opened it. Inside his truck on the floor, was fresh manure! Now what was he to do? He couldn't go to a meeting like this. Ray was watching out the window of the office laughing at him. Joe was angry as hell, but could not show it. He would have to take taxis everywhere until he could get the truck cleaned out. He would leave it there until after work. He slammed the pick-up door and went back into the office. He didn't say a word.

Ray said, "What's the matter Joe, problem with your truck?" He didn't respond. He was set up good this time, but now he needed to call Pakos to let them know he would be a bit late for the meeting. He opened his briefcase to check for the phone number and there was ink all over his files. Not one page was untouched. There was more laughter in the office from Ray...he had outdone himself this time with more to come.

Joseph was furious and almost broke with this one. He could put up with the harmless stuff, but now it meant his job could be on the line. His hard work on this project so far, was ruined. He had no idea what was in store for him the rest of that horrible Monday. He just wanted to go home...maybe all the way back to Chatham! He was giving it serious thought right about then.

He stopped and took a deep breath and asked the Lord for some guidance and strength to endure the rest of this horrible day. He remembered God's advice to Joshua in the bible, in The Book of Amos 1:9 "Have not I commanded thee? Be strong and have a good courage; be not afraid, neither be thou dismayed: for the Lord thy God is with thee withersoever thou goest". George came out to see what Ray was laughing at. No one else was laughing, except Bubba was snickering a little. George saw the mess of ink and papers, but no one told George about the manure.

At that moment, the office phone rang. Maria answered, "Good afternoon, Benson and Associates, how may I help you?" She put the caller on hold and told Joe, "Mr. Allen, it's for you."

It was Etta. "Hello sir, I'se juss' lettin' ya' know the missus is on her way to 'da' hospital, by taxi. 'Da doctor tole' her ta' goes and he'd be meetin' her 'dere. She be in labor sir and she be juss' a hollerin' no less 'den five minutes apart. She wanted I should call an' tell ya'll ta' go ta' her."

He replied, "Thank you Etta. I'm on my way."

As Joe hung up the phone, his boss overheard him and said "And where do you think you're going, Allen? It's not five o'clock yet. This office closes at five o'clock."

Joe implored, "I'm sorry sir and I know it's not five o'clock, but my wife is in labor and on her way to the hospital. This is our first baby and the pains are five minutes apart. I need to be with her." Joseph's boss, George Benson was the one man who had, what he thought was a small speck of real compassion for him. He hoped that George would understand.

He did understand, but George knew there would be trouble for Joe, if he let him go early. He said, "I'm sorry, but you'll have to wait until the end of the day. You can't just leave any time you want." Joseph was shocked: Absolutely speechless! George said, "You get back to your desk now, you seem to have a mess to deal with and if I'm not mistaken, I heard someone say this morning that you have a meeting out of town, to get to. If there's a mess at Pakos, you let me know."

Joe slowly returned to his desk and his briefcase and started to clean it up, along with what he could salvage of the files that were in it. He would have to go through it page-by-page and recopy everything. As he started through the papers, he found the phone number for Pakos. He called and said he had to re-schedule their meeting.

Roy Pakos asked him, "What the hell are you talkin' about? We had no meeting today. You know its tomorrow at eight forty-five, as usual. If you can't get this job done right, I'll have to get you removed from the project and insist on your replacement by a white man, who was supposed to be assigned to the job; not just some fuckin' Canadian Nigger!" He slammed the phone down. Joseph couldn't believe how bad his day was going.

Ray had set him up again. There was nothing wrong at his site. As hard as it was, he did not go and knock Ray's head off. He would have given anything for a hockey stick at that moment. But, he had other concerns. He was so worried about Liz: so much that he felt like walking out right then and telling George Benson where he can shove his job. But, he couldn't! He needed this job: Now, more than ever. Sometime today, his family was going to welcome a new member. He smiled at that thought.

By 2:00 p.m. Elizabeth was at the hospital and in the labor room of the General Hospital. As she suffered one contraction after another, she longed to see Joseph by her side. The doctor arrived and told her to expect to be maybe another hour or so, since she was not quite ready. As he checked on her dilation, he realized her water had not broken yet.

"There may be a few hours to go yet, Liz," he told her. By three o'clock she was contracting at four minutes apart. All of a sudden at three-twenty, her water broke and she dilated a few centimeters within a half hour.

Joe was busy still cleaning up his briefcase, files and his desk, while trying to dry his paperwork. He was trying to remember all his work that had been covered over with ink and he was worried about Liz. She knew some of the troubles he had at work with Ray Halden, but he tried not to worry her, so kept most of the worst pranks to himself. She didn't know how bad he really had it there.

He hoped she would understand that he couldn't be there by circumstance, not by choice. More than anything else in the world, he wanted to be in that father's waiting room, waiting for news from the doctor.

He imagined the doctor coming through the door, with his hand outstretched, saying, "Congratulations Mr. Allen, you're the proud father of a healthy baby boy!" But he kept his wits about him and thought, he might also say "baby girl!" He had to be ready for either. Deep down (and he would never let Liz know), he hoped for a boy. What father didn't?

Four o'clock came and went. Liz was in very hard labor now. She asked the doctor and nurses if Joseph was there and they said there was no word of him yet. The doctor had never met Elizabeth's husband before and the nurses didn't know him, either. It was customary for the fathers to sign in at the admitting department and they would then be taken to the waiting room. Mothers-to-be were told at this time that their husband had arrived and was awaiting news.

The doctor observed the baby's cap showing now. Pale white, with light hair....it was almost there. Dr. Atkins said, "Okay Liz, one more big push and I think we're there." With that, Elizabeth took a big breath and grabbed a hand of a nurse, on each side of the delivery table and pushed with all her might. Out came the head and with another push the shoulders slipped out, within seconds. Their baby had arrived, at last. The nurses gave her a cheer and as soon as the doctor aspirated him and with a smack on his tiny bottom, he said, "Well Liz, this little boy looks like he wants to see his mama." With that, Dr. Atkins held him up to show Liz and she started to cry tears of joy; at this beautiful, perfect little boy. She was exhilarated, ecstatic, exhausted and relieved... then the afterbirth arrived.

When that was done, she was sad that Joseph was not here yet, to be told and share in her joy. She knew it must have been that he could not get away from work yet, or he was on the job site. Maybe there was a problem with the Pakos job he was in charge of. She was understanding, but disappointed. She knew in her heart, if he COULD be there, he would. A nurse took the baby to the examining table to wash him, weigh and measure him. He was so small to be coming out of such a large womb. He was only four pounds, eight ounces and sixteen inches long. He was born at 4:25 p.m.

As the nurse placed him in her arms, Liz gave another yell. To the doctor's horror and surprise when he looked; there was something black showing. Liz screamed again and what looked like a black head appeared. Liz was scared and she did not know what was going on, but she needed to push again. She yelled louder than the last time, probably due to the added fear she was feeling now. The nurse took the baby from her arms and the doctor said, "Elizabeth, I don't know quite how to tell you this, but you appear to be the mother of twins!" He was shocked. So was Liz. They never even had an inkling that she was pregnant with twins.

This would explain her large size. But; Dr. Atkins never heard two heartbeats. He explained, "In obstetrics, there are cases where one twin could hide behind the other and it's difficult to detect a second baby until they are actually born." At that moment, she remembered the story of Jacob and Mina's twins, about fifty years earlier. It was the same circumstances. She couldn't wait to tell Joseph! Dr. Atkins could only hear one baby's heartbeat, not two. It was assumed that she was having one very large baby, never even indulging in the thought that she was going to give birth to twins.

Liz watched the doctor's face. "What's wrong...why do you have a strange look of concern?" He quietly told one of the nurses to get the hospital administrator and have him come to the delivery waiting room and wait for him there. He needed to talk to him and it was urgent. As soon as he was finished with this delivery he would need to see him. Again, he stressed to his nurse, it was urgent and extremely important that they talk right away; and she was to tell no one about this on the way to his office.

Again, Liz saw a look on his face she couldn't understand and she didn't hear what he and the nurse were whispering about. Along came another big contraction and she only had one nurse's hand to hold this time. She was nervous.

Liz needed to push, it was time again. She was confused, she was happy, she was worried and suddenly very lonely for Joe and scared. Dr. Atkins had become silent, she wasn't sure why.

She asked him, "What is it Doctor? There's something wrong...I can see it on your face. What is it?" Another contraction came and she couldn't help yelling as she pushed. Out came the head and with another small push, the shoulders. Liz's other baby boy was born.

Dr. Atkins said sternly, "Mrs. Allen, you have another boy." Although she did not want to, the nurse took the boy without Liz seeing him and she washed, weighed and measured him. He was four pounds, twelve ounces and fifteen inches long. His birth was clocked at 4:45 p.m.

Liz asked, "What is wrong, why are you so quiet? What's wrong with my other boy?" The nurse brought him over to her and held him up for her. She and Joseph were the parents of twins: One black boy and one white boy. She smiled and wanted to hold her babies. She was so happy, she could not wait for Joe to arrive; she was so excited!

She was confused by the look on the doctor and the nurses' face. Sure, it was a little unusual, but after all, Joseph was their black father and she was their white mother. She thought for a moment, then she realized that in Mississippi, maybe this would not be easily accepted, but they would deal with it as a family and hopefully after a while, their friends and neighbors would accept the boys, too.

She had a lot of faith in her fellow man. All her past bible study came back to her and she thought of the scriptures. Leviticus 19:17 "Thou shalt not hate thy brother in thine heart: thou shalt in any way wise rebuke thy neighbor, and not suffer sin upon him" and also 19:34,

"But the stranger that dwelleth with you shall be unto you as one born among you and thou shalt love him as thyself; for ye were strangers in the land of Egypt: I am the Lord your God". She firmly believed in 'Love Thy Neighbor', just the same way, these little boys' great-great-grandfather, Jed Allen, did. She never anticipated any troubles with her unusual family as long as they trusted in God.

The nurse put both twins in Liz's arms. She cried more tears of joy. She was a very proud mother and knew their father would be as happy as she was. After only about five minutes, the nurse told her, "You better give them to me now and I'll put them in their bassinets." As the nurse took them, Liz gave a small groan as the last contraction came, delivering the second afterbirth.

At that moment the other nurse came back into the delivery room then; and quietly told Dr. Atkins, "Sir, the administrator will be in the waiting room to see you as soon as he can, he is dealing with a problem at the front door of the hospital. Can you believe a Nigger is trying to get in. He is claiming his wife is having a baby here." Right then, the other nurse and Dr. Atkins looked at each other: They both understood this was true. They just helped deliver this man's baby. A Nigger baby!

Dr. Atkins said "Thank you nurse," as he washed his hands. He instructed the nurses to help clean up Elizabeth, and whispered to one of them, "Just work slowly and keep her and the twins in the delivery room until I am back, I'm sure you know what I mean!"

The Nigger at the door of the hospital was the father of the white twin and the black twin: The husband of Elizabeth Allen. No one at the front door knew about the mixed race couple yet, or the twins. The boys had been born in a "WHITE ONLY" hospital. Liz did not hear anything that was going on, she was just longing to hold her boys again and wanted to see Joseph.

The administrator of the hospital had been called by security to assist them with a problem at the front door. They asked a black man, who was attempting to enter, what his name was and why he was attempting to enter the hospital.

He answered, "My name is Joseph Allen and my wife is Elizabeth Allen. She came in here this afternoon to give birth to our child. All I want is to get in to see her and the baby if it has been born yet. Why can't I see them?" The administrator assured the black man that no wife of 'his' would have been allowed into this hospital. She surely would have been taken to the 'other' hospital, just on the outskirts of town. Joseph could not understand this. He was sure that Dr. Atkins worked out of this hospital. He was beginning to lose patience as a security officer began to push him around. The administrator had called the police to come and assist, in case of real trouble. They arrived just as Joe was pushed to the ground by one of the guards.

At the same time the police arrived, Dr. Atkins arrived at the front door and told the administrator he needed to talk to him, NOW! He looked at Joseph, lying on the ground and the security guard standing over him with his foot on Joe's chest, which was now in severe pain, from his Sickle Cell Disease. Dr. Atkins told the administrator, "I believe this man is the father of a baby I just delivered." The administrator, the guards and police were dumbstruck. He continued, "That is why I sent my nurse to get you. Mrs. Allen did deliver a baby. As a matter of fact, she delivered two babies." Joseph heard this and started to smile. He continued, "She gave birth to twins, two boys: One white, one black. Mrs. Allen is white and I believe this black man on the ground is their father." As the doctor looked at Joe, he asked, "Mr. Allen, I presume?" Looking at the administrator, the police and the security guards, Dr. Atkins next said, "I'm sure you all can see the dilemma at hand."

They let Joseph get up and he brushed off his clothes. As he stood up, he expected them to let him go into see his wife and boys. He couldn't be more wrong. As he walked toward the door, the security officers stood in the doorway and blocked him from entering the hospital. The policeman asked, "Are we going to have trouble with you boy, or are you going to leave peacefully?"

Joe was shocked. He wanted to go in to be with his family. But the administrator said, "There are no Niggers allowed in here, Mr. Allen."

"What about my sons?" he asked. The administrator instructed the doctor to bring the black baby to the door and Mr. Allen would either have to take it to the other hospital; if it needed care, or take him home!

He told all involved, "Mrs. Allen and the white baby are of course, allowed to stay in our hospital as long as the doctor deems necessary."

Dr. Atkins went back to the delivery room with the administrator in tow, while security kept Joe outside. The police stayed, too. As both men suited up and went in, the nurses were just finishing cleaning Liz and the babies were now sleeping.

Liz and the nurses listened to the doctor speak, "Liz, your husband is at the hospital now." Elizabeth smiled and was relieved.

She breathed a sigh of relief and said, "Oh thank God he's here. Does he know that we have two healthy boys? Does he know they're fine and I'm fine? When can I see him? When can he come and see the boys? Doctor, please tell me what he said when he heard the news."

The doctor said to her, "Elizabeth, he can't come in and see you or the boys. Didn't you know this was a white's only, hospital?"

Liz stopped smiling, "No, Dr. Atkins, we did not know! Please tell me you're kidding! Please tell me this is a horrible joke!"

The administrator introduced himself, "Mrs. Allen, I am Charles Weston, the hospital administrator. I assure you that Dr. Atkins is not joking. We have never treated or allowed a Nigg... uh, black person here, ever and we are not about to change this policy now. You will have to send the black baby to the front door of the hospital, where it will be given to his father and from there, Mr. Allen will have to either take him to the Nigg...uh, black hospital, or if he is healthy, he can take him home.

Frankly Mrs. Allen, we don't care where he takes him, but this baby cannot stay here and has to leave immediately. You will not be receiving a birth certificate for the black one. He was never born at this hospital." He turned to the doctor and asked, "Doctor Atkins, is the other baby healthy enough to go home, or should he go to the other hospital for some reason?"

The doctor told them, "Mr. Allen can take him home, if he wants to. He's small, but seems healthy."

The administrator looked at Liz, again and said, "You and your normal son are allowed to stay here as long as Dr. Atkins says you should. Of course we'll make you and your son very comfortable while you're here."

Elizabeth Allen was horrified! She yelled, "NORMAL SON, how dare you!!" She couldn't believe what she was hearing. She could not utter a word. She was in shock. While she was silent, one of the nurses was getting the black baby wrapped up warmly in a blanket, trying not to disturb him and gathered him up to hand to the administrator. He and the doctor were going to take him to the front door, to hand over to Joseph.

Liz said, "STOP RIGHT THERE doctor, Mr. Weston. You will please put my son down and hand me the small suitcase that I brought with me." All four of them looked at her.

The nurse put the baby back in the bassinet and said to the administrator, "I'll just get her bag; it's in the labor room, just outside."

Mr. Weston said, "What is your plan Mrs. Allen?" She sat up on the delivery table, swung her legs over and waited for her head to stop spinning. She hopped down off the table, as the nurse came back with Liz's suitcase. Elizabeth had already stripped off her hospital gown. She didn't care who was there; she was standing there, in the delivery room, with only a large Kotex pad belted to her, to stop the bleeding. She took the suitcase from the nurse and placed it on the bloody delivery table.

The administrator was embarrassed and said, "Excuse me ma'am, I'll just leave..."

She said in anger, "No Mr. Weston, don't leave on my account." She looked through the case to find her bra and tried to put it on, but it was painful. Her milk was getting ready to come in quickly and her breasts were getting hard, already. The bra hurt, so she angrily threw it back in the suitcase. She put on her slip and maternity dress. She walked over to the administrator and slapped his face as hard as she could. She took one son in each arm and had the nurse put the suitcase handle in her hand and she left the delivery room and walked toward the front entrance of the hospital.

The security officers and police were still monitoring Joe's actions, until the administrator came back. To everyone's surprise, this small feisty woman holding two babies and a suitcase pushed right past them and she saw Joe outside. He ran to her, took one of the babies and the suitcase. There were a few taxis around, so Joe kissed his wife, in front of everyone and they got in a cab, then on their way home.

On the way home, Liz asked, "Honey are you okay? Did those men hurt you?" She had tears in her eyes. When she looked at her husband sitting beside her so hurt and frustrated, he looked like he could almost cry, himself. He almost did! His chest was so sore, but he couldn't let her know. He hid his pain.

Joe pushed her hair back for her and said, "I love you with all my heart, Liz." He paused, then looked at her square in the face and asked, "So, tell me dear, what kind of day did you have?" They both laughed, as the taxi pulled into their driveway. Etta was confused that they both were home; in a taxi no less. But she ran out to the car. She was so excited. Joseph handed her the baby he was holding so he could pay the driver. It was only .55 cents, but he gave the man one dollar and said, "Keep the change. My boys, who were born only a couple of hours ago want you to have it."

The driver tipped his hat and said, "Thanks mister and congratulations to you and the missus." He nodded towards Etta, but wasn't sure what the white woman was doing there. He only got a peek at the black baby. He scratched his head and left, while all three went in the house, with the newborn twins.

Etta was crying. She couldn't believe there were two babies and that they were home, only a couple of hours after their births. She did have supper made, but they couldn't eat. It was still warm, but she would keep it warm as long as she needed for Joe and now Liz. She asked what happened and Liz told her she could stay in the room and listen to her conversation, on the phone, to her mother. That way she could hear what her day was like.

Etta had one baby and Liz had the other, while Joe went upstairs to their bedroom. He came back downstairs right away and he was carrying the family cradle. The boys were so tiny; they both fit in the same one. Etta smiled and she served Joe some supper. He was a bit hungry. Both babies were still asleep as Liz made her phone call.

Liz got her mother's number and said, "Hey mom, can you do us a favor?" Eleanor was thrilled to hear her daughter. She said, "Sure honey, is it time to come down there yet? Are you in labor?"

Liz said, "Well mom, you're going to need to ship the other cradle and rocking horse, down here." El screamed into the phone. She was so excited. Liz had to hold the phone away from her ear for a moment, until her mom calmed down. Etta and Joe were laughing.

When El finally stopped screaming, Liz told her, "Grandma, you have two very small twin grandsons." After Eleanor stopped screeching deliriously, her own twin boys came running in the house to find out what was going on and Liz said, "Mom, please calm down, we're all fine."

Abe and Simon both called into the phone over their mother's shoulder, "Congrats, sis! Good job!" Eleanor smacked both of her boys on their bottoms, while Liz told her mom everything about her day and whatever part of Joe's day she knew. Etta was in tears through parts of it, Eleanor too. Joe was hurt to hear everything Liz went through. How could he ever tell her about his day, now?

When Liz hung up the phone, she told Joe, "Mom's going to be here in the next few days. Instead of going to Toronto to fly down, she's going to Detroit. Honey, where is the truck? Did you have an accident?"

Joe couldn't avoid it any longer, "Ray" he paused for a second before continuing, "And I suspect Bubba, decided to pull the ultimate prank today. They put manure in the cab of the truck and destroyed the paper work on the Pakos project, by dumping ink on it." Liz started crying. She couldn't help it. It was a number of factors. She cried for Joe, for herself, for her babies and for Etta not knowing anything that was going on for hours. She couldn't stop crying. It seemed that post-partum depression may be starting right away.

The whole family had such a bad day, with the exception of the twins being born. While the boys slept in the one cradle, Joe took Liz into the living room and sat her on the sofa. He just held her. Not saying a word; just holding her and letting her cry.

Liz was sore and bleeding, but she couldn't stop crying for at least fifteen minutes, while Joe held her. Etta slipped out of the dining room and cleaned up in the kitchen, keeping some food hot for Liz, but doubted she'd eat it.

Joe said, "I guess I better go get the truck and try and do something with it. I'm not sure what. I don't know if I can get the smell out love." Liz rested her head on his chest as he held her.

She said, "I seriously doubt you can. You know from the farm, it's just as bad and as permanent as skunk."

Joe said, "Well love, I guess we may have to scrap it and buy a new vehicle. I know we have money for one, but I don't think I should drive it to work anymore. I should check out the bus schedule. I'll check which one goes by the office and start taking it, or it is a nice walk; just to work out my frustrations." He thought for a few seconds and said, "Cancel that. I forgot, I need to have a vehicle for the job site, I don't know what I was thinking."

Liz still held him tight, and started to cry again. Joe took her into the kitchen to see the boys. He said, "Do you want me to move them to the bedroom, so you can lay down with them?"

Liz said, "Yes, I think I need to go to bed." Even though his chest was still a little sore, he picked up the cradle and went up to their bedroom, while Etta helped Liz up the stairs and helped get her out of her clothes and into a nursing nightie she'd bought recently. Etta went back downstairs, to fix a fresh snack for Liz. Maybe she would be hungry, soon.

Joe looked at Liz and said, "Well mama, what do you think they would like for names?" She looked at him and stopped crying. They threw a bunch of names around for a bit and then they called out to Etta to come up to their bedroom. As she came into their room, she brought up Liz's snack. Each of them was holding a baby. Etta smiled at the beautiful family.

Joseph said, "Etta, you have the distinct honor of being the first person to be introduced to our sons." Joe held up the white boy and said, "Miss Etta, I'd like to introduce you to James Joseph Allen."

Liz held up their black twin and said, "Miss Etta, I'd like to introduce you to John Jacob Allen. Someday you will be in complete charge of them, when we're both working. We know you will love them both. Miss Etta is what we will teach them to call you. You deserve their respect right from the start."

Chapter 7

The Day After

J OE DECIDED, SINCE THEY BOTH had a really long trying day, he would leave the truck in the parking lot at work overnight. He thought it would be safe enough there. He smiled, thinking about it: Anyone who would try to steal his truck would have second thoughts once they broke into it and smelled the cow shit. He planned to go to work early in the morning to deal with it. He would have a taxi take him to work and he would take gloves, something to put the manure in and a small garden trowel. He wasn't too sure how he was going to get the odor out, but he'd think about that overnight.

His alarm went off and he didn't want to get up. He was up earlier than usual, because he had to go clean up the truck. He was hoping George Benson was in a better mood, today. The day before, he was surprised that George took a really nasty tone towards him. Everything that happened was not Joe's fault and if he had a little time to talk to him, he could maybe explain.

As he lay there thinking; he could smell French Toast. His nose was trained to guess what Etta was cooking for breakfast each day and he was very seldom wrong. Liz always chuckled about it, but he knew. He kissed Liz and the boys, who were lying on the bed because she was trying to feed them. She estimated that she had a grand total of two hours of sleep. She was trying to feed the boys, with limited success.

As he showered, the boys went back to sleep and so did Liz. After his shower, he dressed in casual clothes which he used around the house and took a suit with him to change into when he was done with the truck.

As his taxi pulled into his work lot, his truck was nowhere to be seen. He couldn't believe it. Someone stole his truck! Although it was quite early, there were lights on in the office. Someone was there already. This was good.

He had been never given a key to the office. He couldn't go in early to do some work, unless someone was already there. Most of the time there would be no one going in early. A couple of times, another structural engineer on his project went in early with him.

With the lights being on in the office, he tried the door and it was locked. His boss was in and Joe saw him through the window, so he knocked on the door. George Benson opened it and said, "What are you doing here so early?"

Joe said, "I came here to clean up my truck. I can't believe someone actually stole it! What the hell kind of moron steals a truck with cow shit in it?"

George said, "Well that isn't exactly what happened. When I was getting here, about an hour ago, there was a tow truck getting ready to take it away. I figured that you had arranged for it. So I just went about my business. So, you didn't arrange it?"

Joe said, "No, I didn't. What the hell is going on?" Joe's boss told him the name of the towing company that picked it up. George also asked him if their baby came.

Joe said, "Thanks, I'll call them and see about the truck. Uh...we had twin boys, late yesterday afternoon: John and James."

George smiled, slapped Joe's back and put out his hand and said, "Well congratulations, Joe, my boy. That's wonderful. Is your wife alright?"

Joe took George's hand and replied, "She had a hard day of labor and she was mistreated. We had to take the boys home last night. I'll fill you in on that later. They were doing okay this morning when I left the house."

George said, "I feel bad about the cruel pranks yesterday. I had no idea what Ray was up to with the cow shit. If I did, it certainly wouldn't have happened. I'll talk with Ray, today. I'm getting pretty fed up with his crap. He's such an ass and I should fire that sorry ass, but I need him.

He's talented and a great engineer and he knows it. To be honest, he's getting too big for his britches. But, he's Klan; and now he's recruited Bubba. I have to consider that, too. Not that I'm Klan, mind you. Them assholes scare the bejeezers out of me." He handed Joe the phone book to look up the phone number of the towing company. Joe took the phone book and thanked George.

As Joe was looking up the phone number of the towing company, he asked George not to talk to Ray; it might just make him retaliate. He would rather it just be left alone. George told him, "Okay, but whenever you want me to, just let me know. I really am in your corner Joe: Even when I have to be a prick to you. I'm sorry you couldn't get to your wife sooner, yesterday. I couldn't let you go early; you realized that, didn't you? I would never have gotten a moment's peace, if I did. I'm so sorry son." Joe nodded. He thought it was something like that and he smiled. George did like him.

Joe called the towing company and gave the information about his truck. They asked him to wait a moment. When they came back on the line, they told Joe that they towed it on behalf of the Sheriff's Office and it was towed to the impound lot.

Joe thought that was strange; why would the Sheriff's Office tow his truck out of a private parking lot? He called the Sheriff's Office, next. When he finally got someone who knew what was going on, he was told that George Benson called early this morning and asked that it be removed from his parking lot.

They told Joe that there was a fine and he had to pay for the towing and an impound fee, before he could get it back. Joe asked them to hold on for a moment and told George what they said.

George took the telephone and told them that he was George Benson and that he never made any such call. He knew the truck was in his lot last night and he gave permission for it to be there, overnight. There was no reason it should ever have been removed. The Sheriff's Office told him; if he found out who made the call, they could be arrested; but regardless, Mr. Allen still had to pay the fine and fees. George hung up the phone and he told Joe, he still had to pay to get his truck back.

They looked at each other and they knew. Ray! George was fuming enough about the condition of Joe's truck, but now that he had the nerve to impersonate him…he crossed the line, but there was no proof. It would be George's word against Ray's.

It was getting on to opening time in the office, so George told Joe, "Stay a little late, after everyone clears out this afternoon and I'll drive you over to take care of things. Do you have the money to cover the fees?"

Joe said, "George you really don't have to do that, but thanks for the offer and yes, I can cover it, no problem."

George said, "I WILL take you my FRIEND! I'm so sorry this happened, Joe. I can't tell ya' how sorry I am. And, it all started on the day your twins were born. How about you get into your suit and as far as we're concerned, nothing is out of the ordinary today. We'll just act as nothing happened and really piss off Ray. It will drive him crazy-you just watch. He will pace and chain-smoke. He'll pretend that he is doing work, but he really won't be getting anything done. He will concern himself with what is going on with you. Just wait and watch!

Oh by the way, I talked to Pakos. He was pissed, but I smoothed it over; told them there was a mix-up in phone messages and it was NOT your fault in any way and reminded him you were the best man for the job and they are damn lucky to have you. They're okay now. I told Ray, in no uncertain terms that if his pranks affect one of my projects, he not only does it to you, he fucks me up too. I took your files on the Pakos project and all last night and this morning, I've been able to help get as much recopied for you as I could. I'm helping you the best I can, Joe. Are you sure you have enough money for those fines and the towing? It could be costly. I mean; I can float you a loan. Just between us. I feel kinda responsible. I don't mind."

Joe said, "Mr. Benson, we have the money. That is the least of my concerns right now. Really, I'm fine."

His boss apologized again, "I'm so sorry. Please, when we're alone, call me George. I guess I have somewhat stereotyped you, haven't I? I mean, thinking you don't have enough money."

Joe smiled, "It's okay George. No problem. Thanks anyway." He was very surprised about George's offer.

George said, "As far as the re-copying and stuff on the paper work, you did it all by yourself." Joe understood. He went into his washroom and changed. As he did, he thanked the Lord for listening and helping him through this troubled morning. He had a better feeling, after talking to George. He now knew someone was in his corner.

When everyone got into work, Joe was already there, so Ray piped up, "Who let you in, Uncle Tom?" The others chuckled a bit. Joe was looking through a different perspective, this morning. He saw the look of fear in the other men he worked with. He saw it all, now. They were just as afraid of Ray as George was, even Bubba. They all felt that they had to go along with Ray, or there may be consequences.

George stood behind Ray and said, "I let him in. And the man's name is Joe; address him either that way, or Mr. Allen!" He told everyone in the office to get busy. George never said anything to Ray about the pranks, or about him probably being the one that made the call to the Sheriff's Office, earlier that morning.

He and Joe went on like nothing happened. It finally got the better of Ray and he asked, "Hey Joe, I didn't see your truck this morning. How did ya'll get to work today?" He was not getting the reaction from Joe he'd hoped for. That always pissed him off; when he couldn't rile Joe up.

Joe said, "I took a taxi this morning. I got here just fine, thanks for asking Ray." Ray just grumbled and went back to his desk, to stew.

Joe continued trying to get his files cleaned up and reprinted, for the Pakos project. He concentrated on his drawings that day, more than the notes. When he looked in the file, he knew how much work George had done for him. He was surprised and very grateful for his help. Joe figured it must have taken George hours to copy so many notes for him. He was very grateful.

Joe would make sure to thank him again for his help and kindness, behind the others' backs, of course. He would not mess things up for George and Joe felt he had an ally now, albeit a secret one.

By noon, Ray hadn't thought of something else to do to Joe. George noticed that Ray was not doing any work and asked if he had a problem, or if he needed help with anything. Ray said, "Hell no George, I'm busy enough: Just taking a break." In the office, anyone was allowed to smoke. Ray had just thought of something to pull on Joe. He lit a cigarette and wandered to the coffee machine. He made a coffee for himself and asked, "Hey Mr. Allen, would you like a coffee?"

Joe said, "No thanks Ray, not at the moment. But thanks for asking." Ray took his coffee and wandered around the office for a few moments. Joe got up and went to the cabinet where the pads of papers were kept. He ran out. As he went to the cabinet, Ray went to Joe's desk to look over something, but it was just a ruse. He set his lit cigarette on Joe's seat and walked away.

Joe didn't see it. There was always so much smoke in the air, that he didn't pay attention to the smell around his desk. He sat right down on the cigarette. He jumped up and hollered, "Holy Shit!" Not only did it burn his behind, it burned a hole in one of his best suits. Ray laughed.

George asked Joe what happened. Joe told him, "Ray must have accidentally dropped his cigarette and it landed on my chair. I didn't notice and sat on it."

George was mad. "Accidental my ass! Ray, you did that on purpose. What the hell is your problem? Are you fucked in the head, or just an asshole?" Everyone stopped working. There wasn't a sound in the office, at all. You could have heard the proverbial pin drop. Everyone stared at George. They knew he was mad and no one dared say anything.

Ray started to laugh. He couldn't believe that George yelled at him, defending Joe Allen. He said, "You stickin' up 'fer the Nigger now... eh...boss-man, Massa?" George spun and scowled at Ray. No one in the office ever heard George get this mad, or had seen that look before.

George Benson had his Engineering business for twenty years. A couple of the guys had been with him that long and Ray had been with him eight years. The other men were with him anywhere from a year, to fifteen years. He had prided himself on picking talented men. When it came to Ray, he was highly recommended and he was good at his job. George looked the other way because of the KKK, until after Joe arrived.

Ray laughed some more, lit another cigarette and sat back down at his desk. He started working, still snickering. Everyone went about their business, waiting for something else to happen. They didn't know when; but they were sure, Ray Halden was going to get even. No one talked like that to him and got away with it.

Joe had sudden fear hit him. Not for himself, this time. He feared for George. Ray already had impersonated him to the sheriff's office that morning. They were sure it was him, now. What would be next? George was angry.

At home, Liz was having a little trouble with James. He didn't seem to want to latch on properly to breast-feed. John was no trouble at all. He was a little piggy; Liz secretly giggled. Etta was so happy having the twins around. She was so excited and did everything Liz wanted with the boys. She was really a big help to her. Liz thought by noon, she would never have handled them alone. Etta was needed and much appreciated.

Etta was worried because the babies were so small. Liz and Joe were concerned as well. Liz knew she would never go back to Dr. Atkins. There was nothing visibly wrong with them, but she still would feel better if she had a doctor to look them over. She had an idea. She called Minnie. Liz told her about the boys and the trauma she had endured the day before, with their birth. She asked Minnie if she could recommend a good doctor that would look at both boys. Liz didn't care if he was black, white, or green. Minnie said, "You leaves it ta' me, gal. I'll 'git back to ya' as quick as I can 'fer ya'. How's Etta doin'? She still be okay 'fer ya'?"

Liz said, "Oh Minnie, she's just perfect. We love having her here. She is a true blessing to us. You come and see our boys anytime, you hear? I'll wait for your call and thanks, Minnie." Liz felt better. If Minnie couldn't help, she would try Agnes Diamont; maybe she would know a doctor who was not prejudiced.

At lunchtime, James latched on just a little bit better than he had previously. The littlest one was hungry. He fed for about fifteen minutes. Liz was relieved that he ate more this time. She was becoming more concerned about his feeding, than Johns. John had no problem and a big appetite.

About two in the afternoon, the doorbell rang. Etta answered it and Minnie was standing there with a man who was carrying a black bag. Etta welcomed them in, giving Minnie a big hug.

Minnie said, "I sho' misses ya', gal. Why you not come see 'yer ole Minnie?" Etta told her that she was busy helping to get ready for the baby and her Mrs. was getting so big, she needed lots of help, recently.

Liz was lying down in her room, when she heard the doorbell and she came to see who it was. She was so surprised to see Minnie standing in her kitchen, with a tall good looking black man.

Minnie said, "Good day to ya', Liz. You'se look like you'se havin' yo'sef a bad time, love. I'se glad we's here! Hon, 'dis here be Doc Robert Hathaway. He do work out of 'dat 'udder hospital, 'dose doc's tole' ya 'bout. He has a private practice too, an' he says he come ta' look at 'yer young'uns."

Liz held out her hand and shook the doctor's. She was so happy. She never thought she would have someone at the house. She thought they might even have to go to another county to get the boys looked at. She said, "Dr. Hathaway, how can I thank you for this? We really appreciate your help. I could have taken them to your office."

Minnie said, "You hush now gal, an' don't you worry none 'bout his time: 'Dis here be a real fine man, 'da finess' in all Mississippi an' a good Christian, too. He loves his work, he does."

Dr. Hathaway said, "Now Mrs. Allen, please feel free to call me Robert. Minnie told me a little about your terrible treatment, yesterday. When she explained your situation, I felt you needed my help, quickly. I just rearranged my schedule and I'll tend to everyone a little later, today. There aren't any seriously ill patients that couldn't wait a couple of hours. Now, please tell me a little background, on their birth yesterday. Oh' before you tell me that, did you receive a birth certificate for your Negro son?"

Liz said, "Please, it's Liz; and when you meet my husband, it's Joe." He thanked her for the informality. She told him, "No, they wouldn't issue one, because they didn't acknowledge him, or his birth, but I got one for James."

The doctor told her, "I thought as much. Under those circumstances, this is going to seem awkward, but legally, I can issue a birth certificate, but only with today's date. I can't put their hospital's name or ours on it. I have to say it was a home birth. That will mean your twins, legally were born a day apart. You realize later in life your boys can't do much without a birth certificate. What would you like me to do about this?"

Liz hadn't thought of that. She said, "Oh, I don't know. I guess if that's the only way we can get one. Please, can I just talk to Joe first. I'm sure we will want you to, but I'd like his input too, if that's okay?"

Robert told her, "That's fine, dear. Even in a few days I can do it and it will still have today's date on it, February 25, 1947 as the date of his birth. There would be no problem with me doing it in a few days."

Robert continued, "Now, let's talk about and check you and your little ones. Are you always this pale, Liz? Did you hemorrhage yesterday? How is your flow, today?" Liz told him she was paler than usual and she did not hemorrhage much after the births, but she was bleeding heavier, today.

Etta cut in, "'Scuse me sir, but my Mrs. is real pale today, now. I'm sorry Mrs. Liz, but I juss' has ta' tell him, you looks like a ghost, t'day."

Liz didn't mind her speaking up. She smiled at Etta to let her know it was okay. She continued with everything from the day before, during their birth; and that she and Joe felt that they had to bring the boys home. She told him she wasn't sure if the 'other' hospital took whites.

He told her, "We won't turn any human away, regardless of their color, race, creed, religion, or political preference." He grinned after the last part. Liz was relieved to hear this. He asked her about her and Joseph's health.

Liz's eyes dropped. She had forgotten about Joe over the last couple of days. She told him, "Joe has Sickle Cell Disease. He's not just a carrier, he has the actual disease. He has mostly had the chest pain, priapism of the penis and bad chest colds in the winter, the odd time. He didn't have one this year, but we're not in the middle of a Chatham, Ontario winter." They both smiled.

She asked if he knew Canada and he told her he came from Canada, and that he knew where Chatham was and he understood the winters. He mentioned that he had friends that moved there many years ago and he visited, when he could.

Etta and Minnie made tea, coffee and got out some cookies and cake, to serve. Liz was appreciative, since she didn't have any lunch, yet. She had been too exhausted to eat.

Robert asked, "How bad are your husband's symptoms? How frequent?" Liz told him everything she knew. Everything she could, about her husband being the hockey star at Queen's University and how he skated and golfed and worked on the farm. She tried to include every symptom she knew of, or at least, every serious one.

She also told him of their family history. She told him that Joe's father had it, but died of Spanish Flu, not the disease; and he only had minor chest pains and the priapism as well and that he'd died in his twenties. She went on about his African great grandfather Jed, dying at twenty-three years old. Liz's Joe was now twenty-six years old. She also told the doctor about Joe's grandfather, on his mother's side, dying of it at the age of thirty-six.

Robert continued, "I can't tell you how impressive that is, that Joe participated in sports, to that degree. Not many with the disease can handle that kind of activity and cardio-vascular workout. You do realize there is no cure for Sickle Cell, yet?"

She let a tear fall down her cheek and quietly whispered, "Yes, we know."

Robert patted her hand and continued, "We'll test the boys as soon as we can. We need to know." The thought of, maybe having one child with it was terrible enough, but two. It overwhelmed her a bit.

The doctor brushed her tear away and said, "Don't worry mama: They'll be carefully followed by me as long as I'm around and able to look after them. I'm not going anywhere."

She told him they read everything they could about sickle cell disease and since her dad and Joe's mom were doctors, they had access to the latest reports and progress on the disease, up until they both died in the last couple of years.

After they finished talking in the kitchen, Liz took everyone upstairs, where the boys were just starting to stir. Etta and Minnie were in awe of the twins. They were so beautiful and neither Minnie, nor Robert had ever seen black and white twins before. Robert said, "These twins are called Fraternal Twins. Even though they have very similar facial features, the difference in the color of their skin, is what makes them Non-Identical Twins."

James started to cry first. Liz told Robert about James' feeding problem and he said he would examine John first, while she tried to get James to eat. He wanted to observe them together and see if he could suggest anything to help.

John seemed strong enough and he wasn't dehydrated. James latched on to Liz slightly and was eating as quickly as he could, he was hungry. The doctor told Liz, "Some women with twins learn to feed both at one time. I give them credit. But I've been told, sometimes you learn to feed both at the same time; or listen to the other one scream waiting." They all laughed.

Liz smiled; she was not quite ready to try it. She was feeling weak. She was exhausted, but needed to feed the boys. Robert told her, "Now Liz, I am going to take you and the boys to the hospital. Don't panic, but I want to keep you there, in case I need to give you blood and the boys need to have tests and we'll make sure they're not losing too much weight. Now, don't you argue, you're coming with me!"

Just then, the phone rang. Liz answered, "Hello." Robert went to Minnie and Etta and asked them to get the boys ready to go to the hospital; and that Etta should plan to stay at the hospital with Liz until her husband arrives.

She listened on the phone as Joe said, "Hi honey how's my big family this afternoon?"

Liz said, "Sweetie, there is a doctor here and he says the boys and I should go to the hospital. You know; the one at the edge of town; where they'll take and treat everyone. I may need some blood and the boys need blood tests. But honey, the doctor says there is nothing to worry about; he would just feel better if we were there."

Joe said, "Baby I'm sorry, I'll be there when I can. I have to take care of the truck tonight…it's a long story and I don't have time to get into it right now, love. My boss is helping me after work. Sweetie, I'll get to you and the boys as soon as I can, okay?" Liz understood.

The doctor took the phone from Liz and said, "Hi Joe, your wife said I should call you that. I'm Dr. Robert Hathaway. Please call me Robert. I just want to reassure you, that your family is doing okay, but I'd like them in the hospital for a week or two. If you can't get there to see your wife until after eight tonight, please give them your name at the reception desk and I'll leave instructions to let you in, even if visiting hours are over. Please don't worry son; they're in good hands and I'll let Miss Etta stay with Liz while she waits for you."

Joe said, "Well Dr…Uh…Robert, thank you so much. Please understand, I can pay you, that isn't a problem. You're sure they're all okay? Did we do something wrong trying to care for them at home?"

Robert told him, "No son, under the circumstances of what you both went through yesterday, I probably would have taken them home, too. So, I'm just getting Etta and Minnie to get the boys ready and I'll drive the family to the hospital. Do you know where the Lincoln Hospital is?"

Joe said he'd find it and Robert gave Liz the phone again. She said, "So you'll be there later this evening to see us?"

He said, "Yeah, I'll try not to come in smelling like shit, I'll likely take a taxi to see you after I get the truck home. I'll have to shower and change before coming to see you. There's getting to be too many ears around here. I'll see you tonight, babe. I love you and you do what the doctor tells you. He sounds like a great guy to have on our side, bye."

Minnie had her own car and she went back home to make supper for her borders. Etta and the twins and Liz got into Dr. Hathaway's car and he started to drive towards the hospital. Liz thanked him again, for all the help he's been and getting them to the hospital. She asked where he was from. She already knew he was from Canada.

He said, "I was born in the little town of Barrie, Ontario and suffice it to say, in the latter part of the last century. Liz and Etta let out a giggle. The hospital opened in 1891. It is about sixty miles north of Toronto: Royal Victoria Hospital, in Barrie. It was named after her Majesty, Queen Victoria.

My parents told me, I was one of the only black babies to be born there, around that time. Most women, black and white, had their babies at home, with a midwife present. My mother started labor on our farm and was bleeding profusely. My father took her to the nearest hospital.

Royal Victoria in Barrie was the closest and you know; they only had four beds, when they opened. Isn't that something? Anyway, my father didn't know if they would accept black folks. The hospital was so new, he just didn't know. There were so few of us blacks in the area at that time, he just wasn't sure. But, he had to take a chance. My mother needed a doctor right away. My father had to try. It meant my mother's life and mine.

Their doctor assessed my mother's condition and they had to admit her, immediately. I was breech and they had to perform a caesarean section. They saved my mother and me. My father was sure the hospital might insist that we go to Toronto, where they treated blacks on a regular basis, but the Barrie doctor wouldn't hear of it.

So, my mother was admitted and had the emergency surgery to deliver me and we both were fine. They let my mother and I stay together in a ward: and they treated her like a person. Not a black person. Not a white person. But, a PERSON! You know Liz, Royal Victoria Hospital in Barrie; the doctors and the nurses, their care of my mother and me; is the reason I became a doctor."

A few seconds later, after turning a corner, he continued, "I heard you say you studied at Queen's University, I studied at McGill University in Montreal." He smiled at her and she smiled back and she said in the familiar, cheering voice she had in school, "Kill McGill!" Robert laughed. Liz started to estimate his age and she asked, "Robert, I don't want you to reveal your age if you don't want to, but you look about my dad's age. He went to McGill and became a surgeon. Would you maybe have known a George McDonald Jr.?"

He was surprised and didn't even have to go back in his memory to retrieve this name. He said, "I certainly do! He was one of the few good chums I had at McGill. When he had to go to war in 1914, I assumed he died over there."

Liz excitedly said, "NO, no he didn't. After the war he married a very lovely Scottish lass named Eleanor, in Scotland. He's my daddy...I mean they're my parents!"

Liz and her doctor had a great, sudden feeling of kinship. As horrible as Liz was feeling at that moment, she felt she had another 'common thread' in her life, only this one didn't come from between the two families. It was such a good feeling to think about her dad, in a happy way. He asked what happened to him and Liz said, "He died a year or so ago and I prefer not to discuss it, if you don't mind, Robert; nothing personal. I may tell you about it sometime when I'm able." He understood.

Robert said, "Here we are ladies and gentlemen. On behalf of Lincoln Memorial Hospital, I welcome you." Dr. Hathaway told both women to stay seated in the car until he came back. He ran into the front of the hospital and emerged within a minute, with a wheelchair and two nurses. He opened Liz's' door and took James and handed him to the one of the nurses. The other nurse helped Liz into the wheelchair and then he went around the other side of the car and opened Etta's door. He took John and handed him to the other nurse, who was now around that side of the car, and he helped Etta out of the car. The group walked into the hospital and the doctor wheeled Liz in. He told the group to follow him.

They went to the elevator and all got in and went to the fourth floor. They went to the maternity floor. He started calling out orders to the evening head nurse. He said, "Tell me which room is empty please and tell lab people to get here. I need blood work on two babies and their mother, right away. I need two warming bassinets, we have twins here, both around four pounds, maybe less."

The nurse told him, "Room 425 is available, doctor." She went about arranging everything he requested. He wheeled Liz in to the room and took James from the nurse as she helped Liz get into bed. As she was getting on the bed, Liz collapsed. She was unconscious.

Robert handed James to Etta and called for someone to get A-Negative blood, as well as an IV of glucose and potassium going. He had asked Liz at home, if she knew her blood type and she told him that the other hospital told her she had A-Negative blood.

She had been bleeding more than she let on, which he suspected at the house. A nurse ran in the room with the blood and IV bottles and he found a vein immediately.

He asked the nurse holding John to take Etta to the nursery and set the boys up in warming bassinets and he'd instruct them shortly on what he wanted done. He said, "If they are hungry, please feed them high protein, high fat formula if we have any; if not, feed them whatever we have. I'm sure they need it, especially the white boy. Also, call down to the front desk and tell them to admit a man named Joe Allen, no matter what time he comes in. He is to be let in to see his wife, ANYTIME he gets here. Do you understand?" The nurse nodded and said she'd take care of it.

Robert stayed with Liz and he had a nurse help him to see how much she was bleeding. She was hemorrhaging, but not dangerously. The nurse applied pressure while the doctor went to get medications that should help slow down her blood flow. He had the nurse get a catheter. Since she was unconscious, she needed a catheter put in to her bladder. She needed to void, but she was unable to relieve herself.

Robert went to the nursery while the nurse stayed to monitor Liz. He saw all the nurses gathered around the two bassinets. He smiled. The boys were a hit! He walked in and they were all doting over them; Etta, too. She told them all about the births and they were so enthralled with the story, but angered at Liz's' treatment, by the other hospital.

Dr. Hathaway cleared his throat. They all turned to look at him and he said, "Ladies please, can we get back to work? These beautiful little boys need our help."

Etta cut in with, "Doctor, how's my Mrs. doin'?" He told her she was still unconscious, but she'd be fine. He told Etta she could go back to Liz and sit with her, until she wakes up and that the boys were going to be looked after by the best nurses in Mississippi. She didn't need to worry.

A nurse escorted Etta back to Liz's' room. She was given a chair and a magazine and the night's newspaper to occupy her time, while she waited. The nurse stopped half way across the room and asked Etta, "Can ya'll read, Miss Etta?"

She replied, "Some ma'am. My Mrs. be teachin' me to read an' talk better. 'Dat be 'da harder part." They both giggled a bit. "She be a school teacher. She been a teacher in Canada an' here, in Mississippi. 'Dat's true." She said this with pride. After the nurse left, Etta sat there and wept. She didn't want to read. She had to watch her Mrs.: Liz looked so pale, having blood being pumped into her. Etta was scared and wished her Mr. Joe was there. She didn't understand everything. Liz never had time to tell Etta why Joe was going to be late and how late, he might be. She wished he would hurry and come.

In the nursery, they were taking blood samples from both babies. They had both eaten about three ounces of a special, high protein formula and the doctor examined each baby thoroughly, including their weights. James lost 11 oz. since his registered birth weight and John had lost 5 oz. The doctor was not pleased about this.

Dr. Hathaway called his office. His nurse was still there. He said if there were a true emergency, he would need them to come to Lincoln and he'd see them there. He did not want to leave Liz or the twins. They weren't in danger, but he wanted to help Liz's' family and honor his good friend, George McDonald. He imagined Liz was daddy's little girl and the apple of his eye!

He smiled, thinking that, when he woke up that morning, he never thought it would lead him back in time to a dear, kind, sincere, friend. He stopped smiling and wondered if Liz knew about the prostitutes.

At five that afternoon, George and Joe lagged behind as everyone left the office. They got in George's car and went to the Sheriff's Office. Joe never told George yet why they took the babies home the previous night. He wanted to wait a bit, until he would not be overheard by anyone else in the office. As far as George knew, Joe's wife had the babies and were fine and the doctor released them early, although a little unusual. He thought it was a bit early, but maybe they were healthy enough to go home.

When they parked at the Sheriff's Office, the deputy was at the desk. He lifted his head out of the newspaper and said, "Well, George Benson, what can I do for ya'll?"

George said, "Oh, it's not me, deputy. Mr. Allen, here needs your help."

The deputy said, "Well, boy, what'chew wants?" Joe told him the story and the deputy said, "Sorry, you were supposed to get this cleared up by four this afternoon. Now ya'll can't git' 'yer 've-hi-cal'. Ya' see, boy, I don't have control over the situation. The sheriff does and he just went home for the day."

Joe was getting hot under the collar and said, "Why didn't anyone tell me about the time I needed to be here by, when I was on the damn phone this morning?"

The deputy replied, "Now boy, don't chew 'git smart with me, or you'll be sleepin' here tonight. We didn't tell you, because ya' didn't ask me...boy!"

George interceded, "If he pays the fine and the towing and the impound fee now, can he come and get the truck in the morning?"

The deputy said, "Nope. He has ta' come back tamorra' and pay when the town clerk and the sheriff are here. Then he has ta' go ta' the towin' company personally and pays 'dem. But they won't release his 've-hi-cal', because you haven't paid your fees and fine, yet. Now, ya'll have a good night, George. Boy, I guess I'll tell them ya'll be back in the mornin'...oh, by the way boy, since it will be there another night, your fees and fines double and I do believe, since you didn't pay the towing company today, ya'll is gonna have ta' pay double ta' them, too!"

George saw red. He started to raise his voice to the deputy and said, "Look here, deputy..."

Joe put his hand up and said, "George, let's go. I'll come back tomorrow." They left the Sheriff's Office and got back in George's car. They were both angry. George asked Joe if he wanted to be taken over to the hospital, now.

Joe said, "No, I still need to change: Now that my pants have a hole in them. Not to mention a very sore burned spot on my ass. Man that sure hurts but I won't give Ray the satisfaction of seeing me in pain. If you just drop me off at my place, I can take a taxi to the hospital."

George said, "No, I won't hear of it and maybe I can meet your wife and take a peek at those sweet baby boys of yours, papa. What's your address?"

As they started to drive, Joe told him, "It's 2 Gilbert Street. George, I best tell you something. George, my wife's name is Elizabeth

McDonald, Liz. She and I grew up together in Chatham Ontario. It was on a potato farm, of all places. It was started by her great-grandparents. My great-grandparents worked for and with her family. Both families were close through the generations. Her family gave my family our own house and land on that property.

It was and always remained to this day, such a strong relationship between the two families. You would never believe the things that have connected the two families for almost a century. Your head would spin. We have such incredible heritage.

Liz and I were best friends all our lives. Our families lived and worked on the farm, together. We went to Queen's University together, got married and then we came here. We hardly ever had any problems all our lives. We were accepted where we lived in Canada. We had very few problems, until we came here."

George said, "Joe, is this your house?"

Joe said, "Yeah, this is it."

George couldn't help it. He said, "Wow, what a nice house Joe. I'm a little surprised you live in this area: Oh, no offense though, Joe."

Joe opened the door and they both went in. He showed George into the living room as he said, "None taken. Are you sure you want to come to the hospital with me?"

George said, "Is there some reason you don't want me to meet your wife, Joe?"

Joe said, "It's not that, George. My wife...uh...Liz ...is white. Our twins are...well...John is black and James is white. I just wanted to prepare you, if you still want to go. If you don't, I understand."

The news knocked George off his feet and he fell back onto the sofa. He was slightly shocked. Joe had gone upstairs to the bedroom to get changed and George called out, "Joe, are you a drinkin' man?"

Joe poked his head out from around the bedroom door and called down to him, "I thought this was a dry county!" George called back, "I know, but I was hopin'...uh... you were a drinkin' man and had a small stash." He just sat on the sofa, staring into space, until Joe got downstairs in a complete change of clothes.

He didn't go into the living room where George was, he went into the kitchen. He then came into the living room, holding two bottles of beer. He said, "Do me a favor. Don't ask me where I got it."

George looked at Joe and he laughed. He was not trying to be rude, but he couldn't help laughing. He accepted the beer and said, "I'm sorry Joe. I'm not laughing at you, honestly."

Joe said, "Somehow, I believe you."

They both drank their beer, while George talked, "Can you just imagine what Ray...I mean...the look on his face if you show up to a social event, or something?"

There was silence, as they drank. They looked at each other. They both had a cold chill go up their spines, at the same time. They both felt fear: More George, than Joe. George was more acquainted with Ray and Joe, just barely. George said one thing. "Klan; you folks could be in for serious trouble, my boy."

Joe looked at him. "What do I do, George? I'm not going to run and hide. I admit there are times I've thought of going home and Liz reminds me, we are home. I won't hide my wife and my children. But I do thank you for the heads up."

George finished his beer and said thanks to Joe. He said, "Okay Mr. Allen, it's already after seven-thirty, let's get to that hospital so I can meet your wife and your sons."

Joe was careful to place the beer bottles so no one would ever find them; to be disposed of another time.

They got into the car and it was only about ten minutes before they reached the hospital. In the car, Joe told George about the white hospital and the treatment they got; or didn't get. And, about how they were turned away and the black baby was kicked out.

They climbed the couple of steps and went into the main doors to reception. He asked where his wife was and they told him visiting hours were almost over. They asked his name and when he told them, he was given the directions to her room.

Joe and George went to the fourth floor and the nurse's station. He told the nurse his name and they took him and his friend into Liz's' room.

Chapter 8

Hospital Time for Liz and the Boys

JOE POKED HIS HEAD AROUND the door and he saw Etta sitting in a chair beside Liz's bed. She was still weeping with concern; he wanted so bad that her Mrs. and the boys be okay: Liz was still asleep and had not come-to, since she became unconscious. Joe saw the IV and empty blood bottles hanging and tubes going into her arms. He was very concerned for his wife!

He stepped into her room and said quietly, "Etta." She was a little startled and turned. When she saw him, she jumped out of the chair and ran to hug him. He hugged her back. She looked behind him and she saw a white man with him. She stepped backwards and straightened her appearance and she apologized for the hug.

Joe said, "It's alright Etta. This is George Benson, my boss."

George stepped forward and offered his hand to Etta. This surprised her. Joe nodded and said, "He's okay Etta." She accepted it and nervously gave a slight nod.

Liz started to stir. All three stood and looked at her. Joe took the chair and he set it at Liz's head. The other two came and stood beside her bed. As she opened her eyes; the first thing she saw was Joe. She smiled at him. He was so happy to see her beautiful baby blues, again. She said, "Hi. Where are the babies?"

Just then, Dr. Hathaway came into the room. He looked at Liz and said, "Hello there pretty lady. I hope you've had a good sleep. Now, before you panic, your babies are fine. They are having naps, too. And yes, John is eating formula like it's going out of style and James is trying, but he's a bit slower than his brother, but don't worry, he's fine." He was smiling as he put his hand out to Joe. He said, "I'm Dr. Robert Hathaway. I presume we talked this afternoon on the telephone; Joe is it?"

Joe smiled back and said, "Yes Doctor Hathaway how is my wife?"

Robert said, "Please, call me Robert. She looks much better than she did when I brought her in. Isn't that right, Miss Etta?"

Etta said, "Oh yessir. You got 'dat right: Mr. Joe, she had no color to her, she collapse right here in 'dis bed, she did. She looks much better since she had all 'dat blood, you been givin' her."

Joe looked to Robert and said, "How much blood has she had and why?"

Robert said, "She's had two full units today. I think she might not need much more, if any. We won't know for a while. Although she told me she didn't hemorrhage right away yesterday after your twins were born, today is a different story.

From what Etta told me, she was up through the night trying to feed the boys and James wasn't eating. I know what that can do to a mother. She didn't want to worry you I expect and she was under much stress.

You see; stress and worry can do unimaginable things to the human body, as well as the human mind. She was not looking after herself properly. She was changing her pads frequently, but she paid no attention to how much she was really bleeding. That's why I brought her in. So by not looking after herself properly and the boys needed to be fed more; I decided to admit them."

Liz looked at the group and there were now tears falling down her face. She cried and screamed, "STOP TALKING ABOUT ME LIKE I'M NOT HERE! I'M SORRY! I DID THE BEST I COULD. I'M SO SORRY I CAN'T FEED THEM PROPERLY. I GUESS THAT MAKES ME A BAD MOTHER!"

She was at a full cry by this time and she felt so guilty. Joe went to her and tried to put his arms around her and sit on the side of her bed. She started hitting him in the chest screaming, "GET AWAY FROM ME! EVERYBODY JUST GET THE HELL OUT OF HERE! HOW

CAN YOU LOOK AT ME? I CAN'T EVEN FEED MY BABIES. WHAT KIND OF FUCKING MOTHER AM I GOING TO BE? GO TO HELL, THE WHOLE LOT OF YOU! GET OUT OF HERE NOW!!"

She was now shaking. Her sobbing got worse. Joe went to sit on the side of the bed again, but she hit him again and pushed him away.

She was extremely emotional: The last time Joe saw her this emotional, was when they were thirteen years old and she was almost raped. Back then, it was a feeling of terror. She didn't think she would live. She was sure that the worker was going to kill her. That was also the day Joe killed that farm worker; with a pitchfork in the back. He was worried, now. The woman, who screamed out, was not the wife he knew and loved. He grew quite worried about her state of mind.

Robert took everyone out of her room and went into the hall; Joe let his own tear drop. He looked to the doctor as he put his hands on Joe's shoulders, to almost give him a hug. He said, "Joe, what you just witnessed, was perfectly normal. I expected her to react that way. That's why I told you everything I did, while she was conscious. I did it to get her upset and to lash out at us. She needed to get it out so that we can get her to relax and start over again, trying to feed the boys."

Joe looked at Robert with slight relief. He even managed a little smile. He said to the doctor, "So you staged all of that to help her?"

Robert nodded, "Yes, some doctors don't agree with some of my methods, but I have studied psychology and I've found the sooner we can get the patient's anger out, the faster they heal emotionally and get on with a perfectly normal, happy life. I'm sure it's working with your wife.

She is probably feeling guilt at yelling at us, just now. She may cry for a few hours, so you have to be patient with her. Joe, this is a hormonally draining time for any woman, but doubled with the guilt that Liz wasn't able to feed James properly and the traumatic treatment she and the babies were put through yesterday, she's on an emotional overload and lashed out. Please Joe and the rest of you; don't take what she says personally. It happened fast, with your wife Joe. That is good! Let me go in first and talk to her, but stay here outside the door and listen; I'll call you in shortly to see her."

In a few minutes she was wiping her tears away. She looked at the doctor and said, "Oh, Robert. What have I done? Joe must hate me for hitting him. What did I say? Oh my Lord, I must have hurt him. Did he leave? Why I did I do that? How can he ever look at me again? Oh my Lord, I hit him in the chest and it was very painful yesterday. Is he okay doctor?"

Robert walked to the door and poked his head in the hall. He told Joe to come in, but the others should wait.

Liz was crying full tilt now. Joe went to the side of her bed, again. He looked at her with love. He held his arms out to hold her. She leaned into them. They embraced lightly, so Joe wouldn't hurt her. Joe sat for a minute while the doctor stood on the other side of the bed; replacing her intravenous and blood lines which fell out in her outburst.

She said, "Honey, can you forgive me? I'm so sorry. I love you. Please, tell me you forgive me?"

Joe nodded, "Of course dear, you must be exhausted. The boys are going to be fine honey. They are eating better and the doctor has them on formula with extra fat and protein, too."

Liz said, "Have you seen them yet tonight? Are they okay?"

Joe said, "I haven't been to see them yet, but I am going shortly. Sweetie, I know this isn't the most opportune time, but I have someone with me who wants to meet you. And Etta wants to see you, too. Can they come in?"

Liz said, "That's right. There was a man with you." She whispered, "Oh Joe: What they must think of me. Please bring them in. I have to apologize to them too."

Joe brought George and Etta in the room. Etta went immediately to Liz's side and said, "Mrs. Liz is you okay? I been sittin' here since 'da doctor brought us here. You been sleepin' and I been waitin' an' prayin'. He says 'da boys is fine. The nurses, 'dey loves em', bote'." Liz smiled at her as they hugged.

Joe brought George forward and said, "Honey, I'd like you to meet George Benson, my boss. He drove me around to get the truck, but I can't get it until tomorrow, so he drove me here and insisted on meeting you and our boys."

George stepped forward as he put his hand out to Liz. She was still weak from her lack of blood and her outburst. She raised her hand to acknowledge him. He took it and said, "Hello Mrs. Allen. It is a pleasure to meet you. Joe was right. You are a very beautiful lady and I'm looking forward to seeing your boys. Papa says they are the most beautiful twins ever made on earth!"

Liz grinned, "Please. It's Liz. Of course he would say that. I think he's quite proud, wouldn't you say? It's nice to meet you Mr. Benson. Joe tells me that you're a great boss to work for. I'm glad you've been with him today." She looked to George and Etta and said, "Thank you both and please accept my apology for my outburst earlier." They both told her not to worry about it.

Robert said, "Now before the twins come in and you feed them, I need to tell you both something. As you know, James is smaller than John. We are feeding them both formula; seeing as you haven't been awake for a while. John is fine. James, on the other hand is now less than four pounds.

I've put in a tube. feeding tube. The proper name for it is a naso-gastric, or NG tube. It is inserted into a nostril and it goes directly down into his tummy. We use a syringe and we take the formula and inject it into the tube and it goes directly into his stomach. He also has an IV solution of glucose; basically sugar and water. You are going to see these tubes sticking out of him, but please believe me he is NOT in any pain."

Liz, he still needs you. Even though he's getting a bottle in the nursery sometimes and the feeding tube, I still want you to try and breast feed, whenever the time is right for both of you. Now, I'm going to get a nurse or two and we're going to get your sons and bring them in here, so you can feed them. I'll be right back folks."

As they waited, George said, "You do look just like Joe said Mrs... uh...Liz. Pretty as a picture! You'll be a wonderful mother, dear. I know papa here is going to be a great father, too. If either of you ever needs anything and I mean anything! Please ask. I'll be around for you both.

My wife would have loved to have met you, two. We were never blessed with little ones ourselves. So, needless to say there are no grandchildren, either. She passed on some time ago, from cancer." His mind went back about a year and thought about the last painful days, for his wife. Since that day, he poured all his energy into his business. He missed her so much.

Just at that moment the doctor came in the room, again. Behind him came two nurses, each pushing a bassinet on wheels. They had brought the boys into Liz's room. Liz and Joe were so thrilled. Liz started crying, so did Etta. Then they gasped when they saw James: With the tubes sticking out of him, even though Robert prepared them, it was still something of a shock to see this poor little cherub.

Robert took James out of his bassinet and handed him to Liz; he needed to eat, so he let Liz try again at her breast. Robert told Joe he could pick up John. During this, Etta kept crying; she was so happy. The boys looked a little better to mommy, since they had a formula feeding, in the nursery. John's look improved, over the last few hours, but James still has a little way to go, yet.

Robert said to Liz, "James has been eating just 'okay', so we are monitoring his weight very closely. I'm not that happy with his weight loss, that's why I inserted an N.G. John, on the other hand has been eating well. They look pretty good otherwise, but I want them to stay here in the hospital a week, or two; you too, Liz. I don't even want you getting up to relieve yourself right now. No walking around, just yet. Just a day or two, then you can take walks to the nursery at feeding times: Only with a nurse, or with Etta. Etta can stay here in the room with you through the days, if you'd like her to. You may find twins overwhelming. You are lucky to have Etta."

Liz said, "I'm expecting my mom sometime in the next few days, too. She's the only grandparent the boys have and she can't wait to get here. She is going to stay, however long I need her. I'm sure between her and Etta, I'll be fine."

He smiled at her and continued, "That is good. I'm looking forward to meeting her. Wow, being the only grandparent, she has a lot on her shoulders. But remembering Liz's dad, I'm sure he picked a bride who can handle it. Joe, you can come any time too. But don't you get run down. We have to look after papa, just as well as mama."

All of a sudden Liz cut in, "Oh, Oh, Oh, Joe, I haven't had a chance to tell you. Dr. Hathaway went to school with daddy. They were chums in McGill and he and dad studied and hung around together, in Montreal. He was born in Barrie, Ontario, you remember where that is Joe? It is just north of Toronto."

Joe turned to him and said, "That is incredible. I am so happy to know you. Please, we welcome you into our lives and our home any time. We owe you so much for everything you have done for us today. You're family now!"

Robert said, "Well thank you Joe, Liz. That's the best pay a doctor can ever receive. I'm so happy to learn my old friend actually survived WWI and came home to have a family. I know we have much to talk about. Joe, I understand from Liz that your mother was a doctor. Was she a specialist?"

As he spoke, Joe lowered his eyes ever so slightly, "She was a general practitioner, not qualified for surgery; but she eventually studied so that she could do anaesthetic for George, during many of his surgeries. They had an office together, in Chatham. They worked together for many years.

I'm not sure Liz has covered this, but both our families lived together in Chatham, so we literally grew up together. We had a family doctor and a surgeon living on the same farm."

Robert said, "Wow, that's incredible. Well, now, I am glad everyone is feeling a little better. But I have to ask you all to leave, so we can get mama to sleep and the boys need to eat again and we're going to see if mama's milk is ready for them. Joe gave John back to a nurse and she laid him down in his bassinet. Liz kept James in her arms and he sort of latched on and was drinking. Etta came and hugged Liz and George Benson gave Liz a little fatherly kiss on the cheek. She was touched.

Then all of a sudden, he said, "I'm so sorry, that was very forward of me! I think I got caught up in the family talk."

Liz said, "George, you can always be part of our family, as long as you like. Please feel free to join us any time."

George blushed, a little, and said, "Thank you, kind lady. If I ever had a daughter, I could only hope that she would have been just like you. Behave yourself and do what the doctor says." He gave another smile as he backed up; and let Joe get close to her.

Joe came and sat on the side of her bed. Liz was trying to get James to drink, more. He kept letting go and couldn't seem to keep feeding. The tube in his nose was getting in his way, at times. As Joe bent over to kiss his wife, his body weight pressing on her breast; he got shot right in the face with her milk.

Although the others in the room could not see her exposed breast, they clearly saw the milk fly through the air and hit Joe in the face.

The nurses, doctor, George and Etta could not contain their laughter. It was so funny to see and as Joe took the corner of a spit cloth from over Liz's shoulder and wiped his face, he was laughing, too.

Liz was laughing so much that she had moved James around a little. Without her realizing it, he had completely latched on again and was eating perfectly. They all had smiles as they left...still laughing, all the way down the hall.

A nurse stayed in the room with her in case she needed help to switch babies, when she was ready. The nurse was still giggling and so was Liz. After James stopped suckling and after only ten minutes, he dozed off and John was starting to fuss. It was his turn.

The nurse took James from his mother and set him in his bassinet and took John out and gave him to Liz and she put him to the other breast. He ate until he was full, and the nurse put him in his bassinet, too. She told Liz, "I have to take them back to the nursery now Mrs. Allen. You need to rest." Just then the doctor came back in to her room.

He nodded at the nurse and said to Liz, "How did it go? Did you shoot anyone else?"

She laughed with the doctor and then said, "Robert, it was so good. They both drank until they fell asleep. It was wonderful." The doctor wanted to wait to become excited. James needed to eat more. He needed to gain more weight.

Liz was beaming from ear to ear. She said, "Do I really have to stay here? I can come back and spend the days here to feed them."

Robert said, "Liz, I need you here for at least a week. Your mom and Etta can come in as much as they like. Remember, I have to meet the beautiful Scottish Lassie, my dear friend married. Do you want us to wake you up for feedings through the night, or do you want to sleep. Both of your boys can use a bottle fine, if you want to sleep. Remember, there is no shame in wanting some sleep tonight."

She smiled at him and said, "I realize that Robert. But, I would really like to try feeding through the night. If I can't, I'll use the bottle and I promise I won't go crazy on you; Fair deal?" She let out a giggle.

Robert smiled at her and said, "That's fine. The nurse will bring them when they wake up. Now, you try and get some sleep. If you need me, I'm easy to get hold of. Good night Liz."

As Etta and Joe got in George's vehicle, they were still laughing about the shot of milk, Joe got in the face. George was having a pleasant time with Joe and his family. It had been so long since he had laughed this much. But he intended to talk to Joe at the house. George needed to talk about the way things had to be between them at work, or around any of the other employees.

As they drove in the driveway, Etta realized that they probably hadn't eaten any supper. She was right. The men went into the living room and Etta started into the kitchen, to get them something to eat. Joe asked if she would go get a couple of beers, for them. She did. George sat there with a smile. He could see how happy Joe was: A loving wife, newborn twins, house and a good job. He was happy for him. He would have been happier for them, if Joe had been white. George knew that an inter-racial couple, living in Mississippi, was not a safe relationship.

George's mind came back to him as Joe gave him a beer. George said, "Thanks Joe. Look, I said there was something that we needed to talk about. I'll help you out all I can, you know helping you get your truck business sorted out. But I can't show favoritism at work. The rest can't know I've helped you by driving you around and I may grumble a bit in your direction, but you know I don't mean it, right?"

Joe nodded. He said, "Yeah George, I know and I thank you for driving me around today. I do appreciate what you've done for me. Everything! You know, calming Ray down and things like that. Having the other 'can', put in for me. I know you blamed having to do it because I'm taking too much time out of the office, going to the filling station. I always thought you really did it out of a bit of respect and to help me feel human. Thanks George." Joe raised his beer to George and George did the same to Joe.

Etta called the men, "Ya'll come, now 'dere's supper here waitin' 'fer ya'. Come eat while it be hot."

As both men sat in the kitchen, Etta had made a large breakfast for them. She thought it would be the fastest meal to get for them...and she made Joe's favorite, Canadian bacon!

Ever since Liz and Joe got a taste of American bacon, they started to look for a butcher that might be able to order Canadian bacon for them. They found one who would. She also made eggs, hash brown potatoes and toast. They both hungrily ate and thanked Etta for looking after them. She ate after they went back into the living room. Just as they sat down again, the telephone rang. Etta picked it up and said, "Allen residence." She came into the living room and said, "It be 'fer you Mr. Joe. It be Mrs. Liz's mom. She sound worried."

George thought he better get going, so he waved at Joe. Joe said, "Hi mom, can you hold on a sec?" He excused himself from Eleanor for a moment to walk George to the door.

George said, "I'll come by at seven-thirty tomorrow morning and we'll try to get your truck back. Is that okay?"

Joe said, "Well thanks George, you really don't have to, I can take a taxi." Once again, George wouldn't hear of it. He was going to pick Joe up. Joe said, "It sure is appreciated. Okay, I'll see you at seven-thirty. Do you think we can also drop Etta off at the hospital, if she's ready to go, too?"

As he got into his car, he waved at Joe and said, "Certainly. I don't mind at all, good night Joe."

Joe said, "Good night George and thanks again, for everything."

Joe came back and picked up the telephone. "Hi grandma, how are things up your way?"

Eleanor was excited, with worry, "Now Joseph you tell me why I haven't been able to get anyone on the phone since this afternoon? What's wrong, where is Liz, where are the babies? What's going on, Joe?"

Joe said, "Okay ma, I'm okay, really. There was a doctor here today that looked at Liz and the boys and took them to the hospital. Not the one where they were born, but the other one. All three are fine, I promise you, ma." He heard worry in her voice, so he tried to be calm and play down the day. He continued, "James wasn't feeding properly and Liz had lost blood and needed some. I've just come home and had supper and all three of them are doing fine. When I left them, James was eating perfectly."

Eleanor was very worried, but she was calmer now. She said, "Joe I am coming down by airplane. I am coming tomorrow. I know there is no airport very close, so I will have to fly into the Jackson, Mississippi Airport and rent a car there, then drive to Philadelphia. I'm catching a flight out of Detroit, instead of Toronto. It's closer. Are you sure my baby girl is alright? Did she have a problem bleeding?"

Joe said, "Yeah, she seemed fine after the birth and then today, she hemorrhaged. She's been given two units of blood today and the doctor thinks that's plenty, but he said they can't rule out more, if needed. He's monitoring her very closely, mom. Don't worry he seems to be really good. Oh mom, you'll never believe this, but have you ever heard the name Robert Hathaway?"

Eleanor thought for a moment, "Yes, it seems to me that George went to medical school with someone by that name. Wait, he was one of the first black doctor's to come out of McGill. Why do you ask?"

Joe said, "Mom, are you sitting down?"

She replied, "I am now. What's this about, Joe?"

Joe said, "Mom, Robert Hathaway is our family doctor, here. He remembers George really well. He lost track of dad after the war and assumed that he had died over in Europe. He has been so nice, mom. He is giving us very special treatment and he's looking forward to meeting you. Mom, neither Liz nor the doctor have mentioned dad's past, or how he died. Liz told him she wasn't ready to talk about his death.

Mom, he's so nice, you'll really like him. He's black, single, good looking, kind, generous, and just wait till you meet him. Anyway, ma, what time are you expected to get to Mississippi, tomorrow?"

Eleanor was shocked and said, "I don't know if I'm ready to talk to someone about Liz's dad. I don't know. I guess I should prepare myself. I'd like to know what Liz is planning to say, too. I guess we'll know tomorrow."

Joe said, "Don't worry mom. She is not talking much about her dad, until you get here. You two can decide what you want to say, or not say to him.

Mom, dad's been gone a while. Let's try and put it in the past and deal with the present. You have a beautiful daughter here, excited and wanting to see you again and show off our babies to their only grandma. You just hurry yourself down here and we'll take care of you, mom. Anyway, what time are you expecting to be here?"

El told him, "Taking all methods of travel into consideration, I was told by the people of the car rental place how long it takes to drive to Philadelphia from that airport. So, including getting a drive to Detroit, then the airplane, my estimate is, I should be there by four-thirty in the afternoon. Do I go to your house, or directly to the hospital?"

Joe said, "I think if you go directly to the hospital; that would be best, because our housekeeper Etta, will be staying with Liz at the hospital all day. There will be no one at the house to let you in. I work until five and I will be going to the hospital after work. Sometimes I have to do a bit of overtime, but I'll call the hospital if I can't get there until later. How does that sound to you? El, are you okay? Mom, are you alright?"

Eleanor thought about her husband. She hadn't thought about him for a while. He would have loved to see his grandchildren: Marteen, too. It was a tragedy they weren't around long enough to share this wonderful time. She let a tear fall.

When her mind floated back, she heard, "Mom, mom, mom, are you there? Mom?"

She said, "Sorry dear. My mind just took a short vacation. What were you saying...you think I should go to the hospital when I get to town?"

He replied, "Yeah. You're thinking about my mom and George, huh?"

Eleanor started to cry, "Oh son, I hurt so bad; all over again and honey, it's not your fault for bringing it up. It is so sad that they couldn't have been here to meet their grandsons."

Joe said "I'm sorry, mom. You go right ahead and cry. I'm sorry I mentioned the doctor. Mom I'm really sorry for bringing this all up, again. Can you forgive me?"

Eleanor said, "Honey, don't mind me. I'll be alright. You said nothing wrong and there is nothing to forgive. Anyway, it's late and I have to get some sleep. Grandma's going to need her energy. Okay Joe, is there anything else you can think of before I come?"

Joe said, "No, nothing I can think of. You just get your beautiful self here. We need you, mom. Love ya and we'll see you tomorrow."

Eleanor said, "Don't you worry honey, I'll be there with bells on. No one is going to keep this grandma from her babies. I love you too. If you talk to my girl, tell her I can't wait to be with her. See you tomorrow, son."

As she hung up the phone she thought to herself, she shouldn't be worried about meeting someone who knew George. She started to think she was being silly. But, she did think it was her husband's shame; he and Marteen won't share in the joy of grandchildren. El had enough love for all the grandparents.

Joe hung up and told Etta, "Liz's mom will be at the hospital probably sometime around four-thirty tomorrow afternoon, but don't tell Liz. If she goes crazy on you and you have to, just tell her, but you don't know what time. I'd like it to be a bit of a surprise. Do you think you can handle it Etta?"

She smiled at him and said, "I sho' 'nuff gonna try not to tell the Mrs... You need somethin' else tonight, Mr. Joe?"

He said, "No thanks Etta. Thanks for dinner, it was great. What do you think of my boss, Mr. Benson?"

Etta said, "He sho' kind 'nough: Seems likes he be a nice man. Mr. Joe, where's yer' truck?"

Joe told her about the horrible day he had with trying to get the truck back and he felt that he was going to have to just take the truck to a wrecker's and buy a new car. He'd like to maybe have it before Liz comes home. He said, "Etta, George is going to pick me up at seven-thirty in the morning to go take care of it. If you're ready by that time, George said he would take you to the hospital to drop you off for the day. If you're not ready to go then, I'll leave you taxi money."

Etta said, "You sho' 'nough has real problems at work. Can't Mr. Benson do somethin' 'fer ya'?"

Joe said, "He does what he can, but we can't let the other men in the office know he likes me and helps me. I'm going to turn in, now. Oh, will you be up early enough?"

Etta said, "Yessir, I'se be up early ta' give ya'll a good breakfass', an' ready ta' go ta' 'da Mrs. 'fer 'da day...an' I can't tell her 'dat her mama comin' in 'da afternoon, I gots it all, Mr. Joe. Now, even big strong papa's needs 'dere rest, too. You know, you ain't gonna have a good sleep 'fer 'da nex' eighteen years, or mo'. Good night now, Mr. Joe." She gave a big grin as she excused herself to bed. Joe laughed and he headed off to bed as well. He closed his eyes and thanked the Lord for everything he'd been blessed with. Sleep came quickly.

Chapter 9

Frustrations and Happiness

L IZ WAS AWAKENED BY THE nurse at midnight. James was hungry. It had only been just around three hours or so, since he finished the last feeding. Since he was the tinier of the two; the doctor said to feed him as much as he wants. He needed it. She held him and he took to her breast right away. She was so happy and relieved he was eating well.

When James finished, she got a very large burp out of him and she started to giggle. She said to her son, "Just like daddy!" And, James burped again. She laid him on her bed in front of her. She took his tiny hand out of his blanket and held it, with one finger. A tear fell down her cheek. She loved him so much. He was a miracle, just like his brother.

Just then, a nurse came in with John. He was starting to get hungry, too. His timing was great. She took him from the nurse and laid him beside James. She then took his hand out of his blanket, too. She looked at her sons, side-by-side and they truly were a miracle. They did look identical, except for their color. James was asleep, again and John was starting to let his mother know he was hungry. John still had no problem eating. The nurse said they'd probably be bringing them back in another three hours. When babies are that small, three hours, or sometimes even two, is the normal time between feedings. But, Dr. Hathaway said that if James wanted to eat more often, to let him.

When the nurse came back to Liz's room, Liz asked her, "Do you think you could bring them here before I feed them, so I can change their diapers, too? I'd like to get some practice at changing such tiny bums."

The nurse said, "We don't want you to get worn out, Mrs. Allen."

Liz said, "Dear, it's only diapers. Please?"

The nurse looked at her and smiled. She said, "Alright, mama." As she picked up John and headed back to the nursery, she said to Liz, "I'll just 'git some supplies 'fer ya'. Diapers, plastic pants, powder. 'Dat way, I'll just bring da' babies here as soon as 'dey are ready to eat an' you'll be able to change them before you feed 'dem. Is 'dat okay?"

Liz said "That sounds good. I wish they could stay here in the room with me."

The nurse told her, "Sorry Mrs. Allen, but we are still running tests on them at specific times and you need your rest too."

Although Liz was disappointed, she understood. But she asked, "Would I be able to bathe them in the morning; at least, John?"

The nurse said, "I don't see a problem. We'll check it out with the doctor first, though."

Liz gave an uncomfortable sigh. Her nurse asked if she had pain and Liz said, "Yes, as a matter of fact I do."

The nurse told Liz that she could have a bit of morphine. It would help. Liz told her no, but thanked her. Her nurse suggested she take it, because if she didn't, she would likely be in much more pain in a while. She reassured Liz that there was no problem taking it and breast-feeding. The nurse explained that since it goes through the body and into breast milk, it would only be a small amount to help her with the pain, but a few hours before feeding time, again. The heavy absorption should be past by then and it should only affect the babies a bit, if even at all.

Liz did not really want it, but the nurse told her not to wait until it was too painful. She decided to accept the drug. The nurse came back and injected the morphine into her IV. Within ten minutes, she was comfortable and asleep.

The nurse came back to her room shortly before 4:00 a.m. She had another nurse following her. Each nurse was carrying a baby. The boys woke up at the same time. Liz had to be awakened by the nurse, again. She was sleeping really well, but she still was excited that they both were back. The nurses asked with a smile, if she wanted to try both babies at once.

Liz grinned and said, "Well, let me change their diapers first, then we'll see if I can manage it. She had both babies on her bed and one nurse stayed with her, to help. She was having trouble getting the diaper folded as tiny as the boys needed. The nurse showed her a couple of times, how they fold them in the nursery. The nurse changed James, while Liz followed along and changed John.

When the boys were naked on the bed, they both shivered with the cool air and peed at the same time. Liz and the nurse laughed. James took a little more care than John did. When being changed, it was important to be careful of James' I.V. and feeding tubes. Liz did very well changing John, for her first time. She would need practice on James.

Both boys were crying quite loudly by now. Liz said, "Well gentlemen, there is no time like the present! The nurse helped lift James. Liz took him and put her to her breast. James took to her nipple, immediately. Liz and the nurse were elated. Then the nurse lifted John off the bed and helped place him in her other arm. Liz put John on her other side and he took right away, too. She was doing it! She was so proud of herself, both at once. The nurse was proud of her, too. She had found a comfortable position to hold them both and feed them at the same time.

After both boys ate and were burped, which she had to do one at a time, the nurse took them back to the nursery. Another nurse came in to change her IV bottle. The blood bottle was empty and Dr. Hathaway left orders to check her blood flow after the bottle was empty, and when they did, they discovered that she was still hemorrhaging some, but not near as bad as when she came in to the hospital, the previous day. The nurse hung another unit of blood; her third.

Liz asked if she could have a wet cloth and wipe her face and hands. The nurse asked, "Would you like a bed bath, Mrs. Allen? I have time and if you'd like it, I can help you, now. I can also change your bed and you'll feel so much better."

Liz said, "Oh yes, I would love a hand with a bed bath and change. The nurse got a basin of warm water and soap. She helped Liz to take off her gown and she helped wash Liz head to toe. Another nurse came in and helped change her bed. When they had finished, Liz felt so good. It was great to feel clean and have a clean bed.

When the nurse was finished, she brought back another unit of blood. Liz was a little worried. The nurse told her not to worry that she might not need the whole unit. She had taken two units, in fifteen hours. The doctor would be in a few hours and he might discontinue it. Right now, it was a safety precaution. She asked Liz if she needed more morphine. Liz told her no, that she was fine and being clean felt so much better. She fell back asleep quickly.

As the alarm went off at the house, Joe opened one eye. He felt like he had just fallen to sleep a few minutes earlier. As he rolled over, he smelled something. He sniffed the air and he was sure he could smell fresh coffee and pancakes. He got out of bed and went to the kitchen. Sure enough, Etta was in the kitchen bright and early and she had breakfast almost ready. Joe was glad. He needed that first cup of coffee to get him awake. As soon as he sat down, Etta said, "Good mornin' Mr. Joe. How'd ya'll sleep?"

Joe said, "Good morning Etta. I slept well, but not long enough. I could go back for another couple of hours. So, I take it that you'll be ready to go when I do, so you can get a ride to the hospital with us?"

Etta said, "Yessir. I'se ready when you is. I'se gonna pack a bag for 'da Mrs. Ya'll knows…toilet stuffs an' nighties, dressin' gown…You knows Mr. Joe, you'se just teasin' me. 'Da kinda' stuff a lady hates ta' be wit'out. We din't take 'dem yes'erday, 'cause 'da doctor wanted to get 'da Mrs. an' 'da boys to 'da hospital, right away. He tole' me I could 'gits it today an' take it."

Joe said, "Etta, that's wonderful. That's why I like you looking after us. You know just what we need. I never would have thought of taking her things to her. I hope she slept well and the boys weren't too much trouble for her. Now you remember, don't tell her that her mother is coming this afternoon. If she asks if you know when she's coming, you can tell her yes, she is supposed to be here sometime in the next day, or two; but you have no idea when she will arrive, yet. Downplay her arrival time, if you can."

Etta smiled and said, "Yessir, I remember. I hope she don't ask, so it will be a big surprise. What's her mother like? I expect she be a real nice lady."

As Joe was eating his last mouthful of pancakes, he said, "Etta, you'll like her and I know she'll like you. She is a very nice, sweet lady with a lot of love in her. She's known me since the day I was born. I love her to pieces! Okay, I'll shower and then you can get Liz's' things together. I'll give you a small suitcase to put everything in."

After Etta got Liz's things together and Joe showered and changed the telephone rang, just after seven o'clock. Joe answered it. It was George Benson. He called to ask if they were ready to go, a few minutes early. They were and George said he would be there shortly. It was just about ten minutes after seven; and he thought if he picked up Joe and Etta a little earlier, Joe could see Liz and the boys for a few minutes, before work. When he hung up the phone, he told Etta they were being picked up shortly, so he could visit with Liz for a couple of minutes, before going to the Sheriff's Office to pay the fine and impound fee.

George parked at the hospital and the three got out of his truck and went in together. George wanted to make sure that Liz and the boys were fine, too. Through the night he had such a feeling of contentment. He had a new family. He just couldn't tell anyone about them, for their safety and his.

They went in to Liz's room. Liz was really surprised to see Joe come in, and his boss. She was expecting just Etta. Joe came to Liz and kissed her, being careful not to put pressure on her breast, again. Liz laughed as she said, "Watch out, they're fully loaded." Everyone laughed.

George came to her bedside, took her hand and kissed it. Liz brought him closer and gave him a hug. He was surprised, but happy. Liz was starting to see him as a fatherly figure, just like Joe.

Robert came into the room and said, "Good morning all! Well papa, how was your night? Mama did very well through the night. I'll let you talk and I'll be back to see you in a bit Liz. Joe is there anything that you want to ask me, while I'm here?"

Joe shook his hand and said, "No, I don't think so Robert." I'm sure we will, but not right now. Robert left the room and Joe very cautious not to lean up against Liz's breast again, gave her another good morning kiss. She was so happy to see him.

Liz told him that she had fed the boys three times through the night and there were no problems. She told him about getting to change their diapers, too. She was so happy this morning. Etta placed her suitcase on the dresser. Liz was glad Etta remembered to bring her things to her. As they were all talking, a nurse came in with James. He was crying loud and sounded very hungry.

She handed him to Liz and she got ready to change him. She showed Etta, Joe and George, how to fold the diaper; small enough to fit their boys' tiny bottoms. Joe would need lots of practice. Everyone was awestruck at how tiny James was. After changing him, Joe held him for a moment and it brought a tear to his eye.

This tiny baby now relied on his parents to help him grow, learn and become a son that every parent could be so proud of. The same with his other son, too!

George said, "I hate to say it Joe, but we have to get going."

Joe knew they would have to leave shortly, but he didn't want to put his son down. James had other ideas. He let out a really big scream and Liz said, "Okay papa, he is definitely hungry. You scoot and get to work."

He kissed his wife and son, but just as they were leaving, the nurse brought John in too. Joe took a moment to hold him. He kissed his other son and said goodbye to Liz and Etta, saying, "Etta, don't let her do too much. She needs her rest. You both have a good day. I love you Mrs. Allen." He blew her a kiss and he was gone.

Liz was asking Etta how Joe was really doing. She told her that he was doing just fine. He was eating properly and he slept all night. Etta took a diaper and folded it just like Liz taught her and she changed John. For a first timer on a baby that tiny, Etta did very well. Liz already had James on one breast and after Etta had John changed Liz asked her, "Etta please give John to me in my other arm. I want to show you something."

Etta handed John to his mother and she put him to her other breast and he latched on, perfectly. Etta was so surprised that she could feed both boys at once, now. She was amazed.

As Liz fed the boys together, the women both giggled that she could do it. Etta watched for a moment, as her thoughts went to her own life. She never had a mother to feed her. She had a wet nurse: There were always black women on the plantation having babies.

The white women who had babies used wet nurses all the time. It was considered too genteel for white women to lower themselves to breast feed their own child. So, a black woman was usually the one who fed the babies. It was this way for centuries past and completely accepted in all societies.

Liz knew about wet nurses, but they never had any at the family farm, over the generations. The women all breast fed their own babies there, except for the littlest ones, who were fed by droppers and bottles, only by medical necessity! Liz remembered all the stories and she often told Etta, about life on their family's farm. She was always listening with so much interest to the stories that Joe and Liz told her about their farm life, through all their generations.

Liz and Etta spent most of the day talking. Etta stayed all day: Beside her Missus. That morning, when Etta made Joe's lunch, she made one for herself, so she wouldn't have to leave Liz's side. Whenever the boys fell asleep, the nurses took them back to the nursery and Etta stayed watching over her Missus…even as she napped.

Liz was in some pain by after the noon feeding. After she fed the boys again, she was given another five milligrams of morphine and slept until just before the boys came back for their late afternoon feeding. She had slept for almost four hours, this time.

While Liz slept, Etta crocheted little outfits for the boys and watched Liz sleep. Etta had been feeling very comfortable and happy through the day. As long as Liz didn't mention her mother, Etta would not have to lie, or 'evade' the truth, as Mr. Joe put it to her.

In Chatham there had been a snow storm through the night and the current temperature was twenty-seven degrees Fahrenheit. It was a cold, bright sunny winter day on the farm. The day before, when Eleanor called the ticket agent to book her flight, Abe suggested that his mom ask if the agent knew what the temperature was like in Mississippi, so she would know what to pack for her trip. The agent told her that Mississippi, the previous day, had a temperature of sixty-seven degrees and that El could expect the same in the coming days.

On Olde McDonald's Potato Farm that morning, Liz's twin brothers, Abe and Simon told their mom that they would drive her to the Detroit Airport. From Chatham, it was about an hour to the U.S. Border. After they arrived at the Ambassador Bridge in Windsor, they crossed the border into Detroit, Michigan. It was only about a half hour or so from the border to the airport. They wanted to give their mother a hand, because she had a couple of large gifts to take for Joe and Liz. There were two items that had a combined weight of seventy-five pounds, so the boys came along so their mother would not have to lift the items out of the car and bring them to the airline counter to be weighed and processed. El was getting more excited about her trip as the minutes wore on.

Liz went to the ticket agent and bought her ticket. She only paid for one way, because she didn't know how long she would be visiting. After her ticket, she checked the gifts through. Her suitcase and gifts were then loaded on the cart to be sent out on the tarmac, to the airplane.

While still at the ticket counter the agent helped Eleanor arrange for a rental car in Mississippi. Jackson Airport dealt with Hertz Rental Cars. By the time El left the counter in Detroit, she had her ticket, the gifts checked in and her rental car arranged for her use, while she was in Mississippi.

The boys had to get back to the farm, so as soon as they watched the luggage cart drive out to the airplane and saw everything was loaded into the cargo hold, they kissed their mom goodbye and left. There were farm animals about to be born, which needed their attention.

El only had a half hour to wait before boarding. Eleanor would have been happier if the boys and, or their wives were coming with her. Liz and Joe would love to see her brothers and their families but knew they were all so busy.

Eleanor saw this trip as a great adventure. She was the first of the family to fly commercially. After the plane took off, some passengers fell asleep. Some, like El, read and some just talked to the person next to them. The flight from Detroit to Jackson, Mississippi was about three and a half hours and almost eight-hundred miles. Her total traveling time from when she left Chatham to the hospital in Philadelphia would be around six and a half hours.

The airline provided information for the passengers to read about the airplane they were flying in. El found this very interesting. The airplane she was taking was the Douglas DC-4E or the DC-4. It was made by the Douglas Aircraft Company and it was designed in 1935. The first flight was 1938. The plane had three crew members and seated forty-two passengers. Their top flying speed was two hundred forty-five miles per hour at seven thousand feet elevation. This was the common elevation and speed, for this aircraft and flight.

El was so thrilled to be going on a plane, to see her daughter, Joe and her new twin grandsons. She brought some knitting and magazines to keep her mind busy on the plane; so that she wouldn't go crazy waiting to get there.

After the two men left the hospital George took Joe to the Sheriff's Office, again. As they went to the counter they were at the evening before, they were glad the ignorant deputy wasn't on duty, again. There was a woman behind the counter. On the counter was a name plate with her name and "Town Clerk" on it. She was who they were supposed to make payments to.

Joe went through his story once again with the clerk and she said she had to 'look up his file' Joe asked, "Excuse me Miss, why is there a file on me? This was all a big mistake. Please listen to Mr. Benson, here. My car was removed from his lot, but it was not reported by him; but someone pretending to be him. Please, Miss. I have to pay the fines and get my truck out of the impound lot."

George spoke up. While he was trying to help explain the situation, she walked away to a filing drawer and opened it. She wasn't even paying attention to them, when she pulled a file out and said, "I have it right here, MISTER ALLEN!! You were here after hours last night and you were quite belligerent and caused quite a fuss. Please remember your place, boy. I'm not here to take your crap."

George stepped in, "Miss, all the man wants is to pay his fine and impound fees and then we will pay the tow truck operator. The man has to get to work, or he'll be docked pay. Just tell me what the hell he owes and I'll pay it right now!"

The clerk looked around back of her and the sheriff was sitting back with his feet up on the desk. He now stood up and went to the counter. He knew George Benson and figured they pushed him and Joe as far as they could. The sheriff said, "George, there has been some sort of misunderstanding. Elsie, what is the fine Mr. Allen here, owes." She showed him the file and Sheriff Appleton said, "Okay gentlemen, for the fine, you owe $250.00. The impound fee is $300.00. So, if you have $550.00, IN CASH, this will be cleared up immediately."

Joe couldn't believe it. He was outraged. So was George. George expected them to do something dirty, like this and he came prepared. As the sheriff watched George pull out his billfold, he watched George pull out $550.00. When George pushed the money towards the sheriff, he asked, "May I have a receipt marked, 'Paid in Full' for my records?"

The sheriff smiled and asked the clerk where the receipt book was. She told him in the drawer in front of him. As the sheriff searched the drawer, George grabbed the file on Joe. He opened it up; and there wasn't even one piece of paper in it. As a matter of fact, it was a blank file folder. It didn't even have a name on it. George showed it to Joe and they both were very angry.

Sheriff Appleton got really pissed off at George for doing this and as he wrote out the receipt, he had to write it for whoever paid. He was writing George's name, when George piped up, spelling it out…he said, "The name on the receipt will say, J..O..S..E..P..H….A..L..L..E..N. I hope you followed all of that and I didn't spell it too fast. The sheriff was getting madder, but more at himself, for being found out.

With receipt in hand, Joe and George left the Sheriff's Office. They were still okay for time. It was only 8:05 a.m. and they had to try to be in the office by eight-thirty.

They went to "Wild Willy's Towing & Junk Yard. They had just opened and when they walked into the office, as Willy was just getting off the telephone. As they neared the office, they both overheard him saying, "Don't worry Sheriff, I will. Thanks for the heads up!" He laughed loudly, as the men walked into the office. Willy quickly hung up the phone without even saying goodbye.

While they were there, George did most of the talking. He knew Willy by trade, only. They were not friends, but George knew him to be in the Klan. George asked what the fee for towing was. Willy said he'd have to check the file. He forgot when he towed it, and who for. George grabbed Willy by the scruff of the neck as he jumped over the desk and yelled, "I AM SICK AND TIRED OF THIS FUCKIN' BULLSHIT: HOW MUCH YOU ASSHOLE!!"

Willy was a sissy. He backed down and said, "Give me a hundred and we'll call it paid."

George said, "You'll sign a receipt saying 'Paid in Full'; right, Willy?"

Willy was nervous, but did what he was told. Next, Joe spoke up and said, "How much more do I have to pay you to keep the truck and just scrap it? Compress it and get rid of it: How much?"

Willy was totally blind sided. He said, "Normally I buy a ve-hi-cal an' strip the parts an' then I scrap it." Willy all of a sudden, remembered the sheriff's phone call, he was supposed to 'stick it' to the Nigger!

He said, "I don't know what it's worth, give me the keys and I'll check it out."

George gave him the hundred dollars for the towing fee and waited for the receipt. Joe handed Willy the keys to the ignition. The three walked out to the yard.

Willy let his wrecking yard be the town impound yard, too. He was paid so much a month, by the Sheriff's Office. George and Joe followed Willy out to the yard where he left Joe's pick-up. Joe and George gave each other a playful, evil grin.

As they got close to the pick-up truck, Willy stopped. He sniffed the air. He grumbled under his breath, "God Damn farmer's field, he must be spreadin' shit today." Joe and George were trying to hide their grins, as each walked down a side of the truck. Willy took the key and put it in the driver's side; and he opened the door. George shoved him in the cab and said, "Get a better look, Willy." He closed his door and leaned against it, as Joe was leaning up against the passenger door.

It was warm and the truck smelled ripe. The cab was disgusting. Willy could barely stand it. George and Joe opened both doors and let Willy out. He ran behind the pick-up and puked up his breakfast. Willy said, "For $50.00 I'll tow it to an abandoned gravel pit and I'll bury it there. No one ever uses it. An' don't 'chews be breathin' one word 'bout any o' this to nobody. Do ya'll understand me? Nothin' to no one! I'll just deny it." The three walked back to the office and everything was settled. George got the receipt to show Joseph Allen had paid his final bill, in full.

It was eight-forty and they were ten minutes late for work. It was arranged between the two of them, that George would drop Joe back at home and he would then call a taxi for himself, to get to work. When he got in to the office, George was going to give him proper shit for being late and Joe was to blame it on seeing his wife and new twins.

When Joe got to work, after some ranting and raving on George's part, he yelled to the others to get back to work and told Joe to get into his office immediately, so he could continue with discussing office policy and what time he was to be at work.

After they closed the door, George continued to yell at Joe, who was sitting there, trying not to laugh. After five minutes of George ranting, he told Joe to, "Get the hell back to your desk and get some work done, before I replace you, Nigger!"

Joe was prepared, and knew he had to take it that far. When Joe left George's office, he had put a distressed look on his face and Ray was beaming from ear-to-ear. He felt that Joe had been properly reprimanded for the crime, almost twenty-five minutes late for work.

Joe sat at his desk and brought out his paper work. Inside, he was feeling so satisfied, but he now had to go out and buy a new vehicle. It wasn't that they couldn't afford it, it was the principle. He thought about Liz and how she could use one of her own. He would purchase two vehicles. He wanted to get another pick-up. He liked having one and it would be helpful for work, in case he needed to transport equipment to his work site.

Over the last couple of days, he discovered how wrong he and Liz were, in believing the racism wasn't as bad as they heard it was. They trusted in God and they believed that they would find life in Mississippi, pretty much the same as it was in Chatham. He wasn't sure that Liz could handle how wrong they were. He felt it was too late to turn back. He had to give it about a year, or so. But, he didn't want Liz to know everything he went through, ever since they moved there six months earlier. Joe was losing faith, but tried to keep it together for her.

Chapter 10

A Friendly Face

I T WAS ABOUT 4:15 P.M. when Liz woke up again. This time, she woke up before the boys were ready to eat, again. When she awoke at this time, she looked at Etta's chair, expecting to see her still sitting there, Etta was actually hiding around the curtain and Eleanor sat in her chair beside the bed, waiting for her daughter to wake up. She had gotten to the hospital only ten minutes earlier. As Liz adjusted her eyes to the room, she looked at the chair. Something wasn't right. She expected to see Etta, but instead Liz saw her mother sitting in the chair. Liz sat upright quickly and said, "Mom? Is that really you? Mom? Are you really here? Mom!"

El couldn't stand it anymore. She leapt out of the chair and sat on her daughter's bed hugging her. She knew Liz's breasts would be full, so she avoided squeezing her in that area. They both cried and just held each other. Etta came out from behind the curtain and Liz saw her. She held out her hand to hold Etta's and she took it, like a best friend would.

A few minutes later there were some crying noises in the hall. Two nurses were bringing two very hungry, wet little boys to see their mama. Liz started to tear up a bit. The nurses set the boys on the bed like Liz preferred to have them, for changing their diapers. El really didn't need much of a lesson on folding the 'nappies', as she always had called them, small enough to fit their tiny bottoms. She reminded her daughter that she has twin brothers at home, who were just a little larger than these two.

After both boys were dry Liz said, "James, John, I'd like to introduce you both to the most wonderful woman that God ever made and put on this planet. And, you boys are so very lucky. She just happens to be your only grandma and I can tell you from experience, that there is nothing she wouldn't do for you and she will love you unconditionally, for as long as she lives and even in eternity."

Liz held up James and said, "Grandma, this is your grandson, James." She handed James over to Eleanor, who was crying, by now. Liz then picked up John and said, "John, I'd like you to meet your grandma, too. She will love you as much as your brother and there will be nothing she wouldn't do for either one of you."

Liz handed John to her, while she still had James in her arms. But, she was experienced at holding two at once, from having her own twins. All three ladies and the two nurses were crying and it truly was a moment to remember in their lives; and Liz would remind them of this day, as long as she lived.

When the boys kept crying because they were hungry, Liz showed her mom how she could feed both of them at the same time. Her mom said, "I could never master feeding Abe and Simon, that way. I tried. Honey, you're doing so well, but I see your blood bottle. How many have you had?"

Liz said, "As far as they have told me, almost three full ones, so far."

El told her, "Honey, many women in our family have hemorrhaged. You're just as strong, if not stronger than they were, dear."

Just then Robert walked in the room. He looked at Eleanor and saw the resemblance to Liz and he said, "Well, Lord bless my soul, this beautiful woman has to be the lovely Scottish Lassie that stole Dr. George McDonald's heart, many years ago."

Eleanor stood up and extended her hand; blushing a little. She said, "Hi, I am Elizabeth's mom, Eleanor McDonald." Robert didn't want to let go of her hand. He was captivated. She was so beautiful.

Eleanor continued, while he still held her hand, "Well, I never realized all of you McGill graduates were so sweet, sophisticated and charming, as well as handsome." It was Robert's turn to blush.

As Robert still shook her hand, he said, "Since your daughter told me about you, I was looking forward to meeting you. Welcome to Mississippi, my dear lady." He kissed her hand.

Eleanor was smiling, so was Liz. Liz said, "Did you come in for something in particular doctor, or just to meet my mom? Oh, I guess you couldn't have known that she was here."

Robert smiled, "Oh I knew she would be here." Liz had a puzzled look on her face. Robert continued, "Etta told me."

Etta smiled at Liz. Just then, James decided he was full. Liz handed him to Eleanor to burp. John kept feeding for another few minutes. While Eleanor still held James, she eventually burped John, at the same time. It all came back to her, how she used to burp both of her boys at once. It was so wonderful to remember those times. El was in tears, looking at her twin grandsons. She was so happy and proud of her grandsons and her daughter.

Robert said, "You're too young to be a grandma."

El sniffed a bit then smiled at him for the compliment. Liz liked the way the conversation was going between them. Robert said, "I just want to examine the boys again, if you don't mind mama. I like to look them over, at least once or twice a day, to listen to their breathing. Their lungs are tinier than most babies'. So far they don't seem to be having any trouble, but you have to remember, they're only three days old."

He took James from Eleanor and laid him on Liz's bed and took him out of his blanket, diaper and sleeper, being careful not to interfere with his IV and his feeding tube. Little James was not happy, he was cold and shivering. He was so adorable, grandma started to cry again. Robert asked Liz, "Is daddy coming in soon, to see his boys and lovely wife?"

Liz said, "Yes, but I'm not sure when. What time is it mom?"

El looked at her watch and she said, "It's after five honey, doesn't Joe get off at five?"

Liz said, "Yeah, but sometimes he has to do a bit of overtime, but his boss told us this morning, he would try to make sure Joe was out in good time, so he could get here to see me and the boys for the evening."

El said, "Did you say Joe's boss?"

As she finished dressing James again, El was taking everything off John for his examination. Liz said, "You know, it's been a strange few days. Joe's boss is driving him around and came here to see me and the boys and he seems like a really nice guy. Joe's had a problem with his truck, so George is helping him with rides."

Eleanor smiled as she said, "You know girl, you should have bought a Ford. They both giggled, remembering hearing the story about Johnny

McDonald going into Windsor and buying a Model-T and George Sr. beat him home to the farm in Chatham with the horse and wagon. It felt good to laugh together, again. They missed each other.

After the examinations were done on both babies, Robert was ready to tell Liz how they were doing. Just then, Joe and George walked through the door. They saw everyone there and Joe went directly to Liz and kissed her. He was so happy to see the babies lying on her bed, with her. Then, he saw Eleanor who was standing back, waiting for him to notice her. He looked to her and gave her a big smile. He put his arms around her and they held each other for a moment, not speaking. Finally, Joe broke the silence between them and said, "Mom, you're here. Thanks for coming. I can't believe you're here in Mississippi. Chatham seems like light years away, but you're here. We missed you, mom." He meant everything he said to Eleanor. But, he wished it was his own mom he was saying it to as well. It broke his heart just a little, again.

When Joe and Eleanor let go of each other Robert said, "Mom and dad, it's time we had a talk. Liz, Joe, if your guests don't mind, I'd like to speak with you alone."

Liz said, "Dr. Hathaway, this is the twins' only grandma and our closest friends. We don't mind them hearing the news about our twins. Please go ahead we don't want anyone to leave."

That was fine with him, but he needed to ask. He started, "Well, let's recap the events since the boys' births, three days ago. Mama and papa, as you know, when James was born, he weighed four pounds and eight ounces. He dropped to three pounds and nine ounces within twenty-four hours. As of twenty minutes ago, James' weight was three pounds and fourteen ounces.

John weighed four pounds and twelve ounces at birth. In twenty-four hours he dropped to four pounds and seven ounces. Twenty minutes ago, he was back up to four pounds and fourteen ounces. I'm not worried about his weight. I am however, still concerned about James' weight.

Liz, when you became unconscious I had the nurses start them both on a formula because I had no idea how long you would be in that state and I got them to start an eating chart on each one of them, in the nursery. What they were fed, how much they were fed, etc. John took a four ounce bottle in fifteen minutes, or so. That is really good. I knew when you were ready all he would need was your feeding. That was fine for him. I knew he would be filled up with your feeding alone, after you were awake.

Dear, that's why I had the nurses continue recording their feedings in here, too. You know how much time each took to eat and how long between feedings. John is now eating for about twenty minutes before he seems full. I'm very happy with that amount. He's obviously hungry and getting fully fed by you, now. He doesn't need to be supplemented any more by formula.

James, on the other hand; when I brought you all from the house, you indicated to me that he hardly suckled the first night. He was not getting enough nourishment. I expect it was due to his size and capability, but you also have a slightly unusual nipple shape. You have what we call a soft nipple. John adapted to it right away. James is going to do fine, as you can tell he's latching on better now, isn't he?" Liz, slightly embarrassed, nodded her head. She suddenly felt inadequate. The doctor continued, "So don't worry. Now, Liz, before you start crying at me, IT IS NOT YOUR FAULT, DEAR! Do you understand me? It is a common problem, actually. There are many, many women that have soft nipples and it can cause trouble in some babies, but the problem is never long-lived: As you can see for yourself."

She was ready to cry, thinking exactly that. Everyone kind of chuckled and she said, "Yes, doctor, I understand!"

Robert continued, "Good. We're sure he'll soon be eating as much as his brother; but Liz, Joe, we needed him to eat more and he needs higher protein and fat. Liz, it's not that your milk isn't good enough. You were in a weakened state and it wasn't quite enough for the little guy. He wasn't eating from his bottle too well, so that's why I put him on the IV and an NG feeding tube.

You will still go on feeding him as usual, but we have to keep him on his supplement, in the nursery. I think we should rotate feedings. You feed him now as long as you can and when he wakes up next time, we need him to drink the substitute formula we have for him. We'll bring the bottle to you and you can still feed him, but we have to try and get more weight on him. The IV and feeding tube will stay in, until I'm happy with his weight and his sucking ability, is greatly improved.

We don't want to worry you, but as I told you before, I get a little concerned with babies that are less than four pounds. John's very strong, for his size. I'm very confident that he will need just your breast milk. He'll very likely be over five pounds, tomorrow or the next day.

So, in a nut-shell, James needs to eat as much as we can get into him and between you the formula, feeding tube and glucose IV, he should start gaining more weight very soon. So, please don't worry.

All that being said; I also have blood test results to give you. John's blood is positive for Sickle Cell. He has the disease." Joe, Liz and her mom gasped. They were praying for a different diagnosis. He continued, "James' blood is fine...so far. There are no sickle cells in his blood. We are going to test him again later today and a couple of times tomorrow, just so we can rule it out. Please remember if we don't find any of these cells in repeated blood tests, he could still be a carrier. He may never know, or not until he has children of his own. The chances for his children having it would be about one out of four, or they could also become carriers. You know there is nothing we can do about it?" The three of them nodded.

Dr. Hathaway continued, "Joe, I understand your symptoms did not keep you from playing hockey, for my nemesis...The Queen's Tricolors!" Everyone laughed and he continued, "That is a remarkable feat to perform with Sickle Cell Disease. Maybe John will be just like his daddy and not have severe symptoms. Are there any questions?"

Etta and George didn't understand everything he said, but Joe, Liz and El understood, all too well. Liz said, "Please keep monitoring James' blood. We need to know, but doctor all we ever heard from my dad and Joe's mom, who kept us informed on the disease, was that only black people got it. What's happening?"

Robert said, "My dear girl, it is the heredity factor. You are white and Joe is black. You crossed over genetically and had babies. Believe it or not, you're not the first to do so." He tenderly smiled at Liz, trying to make her feel better and they all gave a little chuckle. He continued, "It happened a long time ago, but it is just recently becoming more common. Not so, in the United States though. There are not a lot of multi-racial families like yours in the world, so there is always the possibility that white children, like little James, here, can carry the disease, or have it himself."

He continued, "Joseph's maternal grandfather and his paternal great-grandfather died of the disease. Right now James' blood cells look great, perfectly round, just the way they are supposed to look. I really don't expect it to change, but by re-running the tests for another couple of days we can be sure, but just whether he has the disease, not the carrier aspect. He can carry it, without ever knowing."

Liz, Joe and Eleanor looked at each other and Liz said, "Thank you doctor. We appreciate knowing. The Lord will see us through. He has blessed us with two beautiful twin boys. They will be loved and cherished, no matter what life has in store for them. We can't thank you enough for everything you've done for us." As she spoke she took Robert's hand and rested it against her cheek. A tear fell on it.

Dr. Hathaway said, "No thanks are necessary, love. God brought us together for a reason. I was meant to meet you wonderful people and help raise your babies and to honor my dear friend, their grandpa George. I've thought of him often over the years. You've brought such happiness to my life, too." A nurse came into the room because it was time to take the boys back to the nursery.

The doctor said, "Now I'm sorry, but I have to get caught up on some office patients, still waiting for me. I will see you ladies in the morning; along with your two cherubs!" As he was taking his leave, he gave Etta a little hug, he gave Liz a friendly warm hug to reassure her and he shook hands with Joe and George. He turned to Eleanor, took her hand and kissed it again, saying, "I hope you will be around for a while to help Liz. I know she has Etta who is very competent, but girls need their mother sometimes. I do hope to see more of you, while you're here." Eleanor blushed. Neither Joe, nor Liz had ever seen her mother turn red like this, before.

She said, "I hope to see you more, too. Thank you for your attention and kindness towards my family. It means a great deal to me, Robert."

Robert smiled at El, only and said to everyone, "Please, everyone get some sleep tonight. Liz needs hers. I'm going to ask everyone to leave here by eight, tonight. Good night ladies and gentlemen." He almost floated out of the room and Liz giggled. Etta joined her and Joe was smiling from ear to ear.

George Benson said, "Joe do you need me to take you home tonight?"

Joe said, "Uh, no thanks George. Mom has a rental car and I'm sure she'll drive us home. Mom, can I get you to drop me around at work tomorrow, before you two ladies come here? I'll explain later."

El said, "Of course dear. I'll take you anywhere you like, any time of day. I am here to help you both and Etta, too."

Etta smiled at Eleanor and said, "I 'tanks ya' ma'am." She couldn't help adding, "Mrs. El, you'se sho' as pretty as 'yer girl, here, an' we's sho' gonna all look after 'dem fine baby boys, ain't we?" El blushed a little again and smiled at Etta. They really liked each other.

Joe told George he could go home and that he was fine with his mother-in-law, there. She would drive him around for a day or two, until he could make other arrangements. George said, "Ladies, I know I will see you again. Liz don't you wear yourself out, I don't need my employee losing sleep and napping at work." Everyone laughed. George said, "Now you get rest, young lady and Joe, I will see you at eight-thirty in the morning. Mrs. McDonald, it was a pleasure to meet you and Miss Etta is right...you are just as pretty as your daughter! Good night, all." Eleanor blushed...again. Liz, Joe and Etta giggled.

Everyone said goodnight to him and Joe thanked him once again as he left. Liz had eaten some supper, but the other three hadn't. Liz said, "Honey, mom, Etta, I think you should all go home and eat something and get some sleep. Joe, please make up the spare room for mom, the sheets are already on the bed. Mom you do look tired. Please everyone, I'll be fine and so will the boys. I would like to rest before they come to eat, again. Besides, you can go down to the nursery to look at them before you leave. I love you all and I'll see you in the morning."

Joe asked Etta to take Eleanor to the nursery and he'd meet them there. El kissed her daughter and Etta held Liz's hand and kissed it. They went to the nursery and Joe sat on the bed. Liz started to giggle and so did Joe. They both were thinking about the breast milk in the face.

Joe said, "Hun I don't want to leave you." She looked at him and he had so much love in his eyes and his heart for her. She knew she was the luckiest woman in the world to have his love. She sat up on the side of the bed and he put his arms around her, careful not to squish her breasts and they kissed. It was the first private, intimate moment they'd had in a few days. It felt nice.

After the kiss, she turned him around and smacked him in the behind and told him to go say goodnight to their sons and get the ladies home. He flashed his smile and waved, as he left to go to the nursery to see the boys, get the ladies and head home for the night.

When the three of them got home, Eleanor was shown around the house and she loved it. While Etta started to make supper, Joe showed his mother-in-law to her room, which Etta had already prepared for her. El asked Joe, "Well dear, now that you have the two boys, are you going to give each one their own room from the start, or both in one for now?"

Joe said, "I never thought about that. What do you think Liz would like?"

She thought for a moment and said, "Honey, that's a hard one. I gave up guessing what my daughter was thinking, when she became a teenager." They both laughed.

El said, "It would be nice if we knew, then as a surprise, we could decorate the second room, before she comes home from the hospital." Joe loved the idea.

He had a smile as he said, "Mom, let's do it! Let's set up the second bedroom, now. Oh darn, I wish we had that second family cradle here. Wouldn't she love that?" Eleanor had a smile on her face.

Just then the phone rang. Joe called down to Etta that he would answer it the bedroom.

Joe picked it up and said, "Hello."

It was Abe. He said, "Hey Joe, did mom get there okay?"

Joe said, "Hey kiddo. Yeah she did. We just got in from the hospital, from seeing your sister and nephews. Everyone seems good today. James is slower at eating, but he'll be fine. Would you like to talk to mom?"

Abe said, "Yeah. By the way...congratulations Joe. We are so happy for you and Lizzy. Everyone is really excited here, about the twins. Are you keeping well, daddy?"

Joe said, "Yeah, I'm fine, thanks. I know Liz misses you guys a lot: Me, too. We wish you could come to see us sometime, but she's so happy that mom is here. Anyway, here's mom. Say hi to everyone for us and we send our love...here mom, it's Abe." He handed her the telephone.

Eleanor was a little surprised, but she was happy her son phoned to check on her. As she talked, Joe gave her some privacy and went about looking in the other bedroom. He started to think about whether he should decorate it the same, or should they make them different? He would ask Mom her opinion when she got off the phone. Just then, she walked into the bedroom that Joe was in and looked around.

Joe asked her, "So, everything is good at home?"

She said, "Yeah, the boys just wanted to make sure I got here safely. You know commercial air travel. It's so new. They were worried and jealous I was flying and they weren't. And, they wanted to know how their sister was doing. Do you think we should decorate this room the same as the other one, or different?"

Joe smiled and said, "You know mom, I think you've been able to read my mind since the day I was born. I was just going to ask you the same thing." He put his arm around her shoulders and gave her a squeeze as she smiled at him. Just then, Etta called up to them and told them that supper was ready.

As they both sat down at the dining room table, Joe noticed there were only two place settings. He said, "Etta, I know you said you would eat in the kitchen when company is here, but please, bring your supper in here and join us. Mom is family. We want you here." She thanked him and moved her meal to the dining room to be with them. After she got seated, Joe gave the blessing and thanked the Lord for bringing mom safely to Mississippi and into their home.

Joe asked both of the ladies, "Well what do you ladies both think? Do the other bedroom the same, or different?" They both thought it should be the same, for now. El was experienced in this field, with her own twins.

She said, "When we had the boys, we decorated their rooms the same. Then as they grew into their own identities, we let them decide what they wanted. I think Liz would agree to treat your boys' rooms, the same for now." The three of them decided that's what they would do.

Joe said, "I just wish there was some way to get the other cradle and horse here, before Liz gets home."

When they were finished eating, El said, "Oh my goodness, Joe would you come out to the car with me. I forgot to give you the present I brought for you and Liz...where is my brain?"

Joe said, "Sure no problem, but mom you really didn't have to buy us a present. Just having you here is the best present you could ever give us." He gave her a hug as they walked out of the house and she guided him to the trunk of the car. As she opened the trunk; there inside, was the matching cradle and the rocking horse. As Joe just stared in disbelief, he said, "Oh my God mom, how did you ever do this? Thank you so much, you're the best." He gave her a very big hug and let a couple of tears fall. He said, "Oh mom, Liz is going to be so happy. I can't believe this, she won't either." He hugged her again and Eleanor shed a few tears too. Joe got them out of the trunk and brought them in the house.

Etta was really surprised when she saw them, too. She said, "Lawdy, Mrs. Liz is gonna be mighty surprised at 'dis. She gonna be tickled pink, she is. They'se a perfect match to each 'udder, ain't 'dey?" Grinning from ear to ear, over his re-finishing job, Joe agreed.

Eleanor said, "The boys helped me in Detroit to get them passed through customs and everything and they left as soon as we saw the luggage cart go to the plane and they were put on board. In Jackson, the porters were really helpful, getting them from the baggage area and into the trunk of the rental car, too. The combined weight of both of them is about seventy-five pounds. You have to pay by weight and how much space they will take up, in the cargo hold. Anyway son, here they are. I think Liz will love this surprise."

Joe said, "Okay here's the plan. We'll decorate the other bedroom the same as the first one, and the horses and cradles will be here waiting for her. So, when she comes home, it will be one of her surprises. The other surprise is, I'm buying her a car of her own. I know she'd want a Ford. So mom, I'd like you to come car shopping with me. I want your opinion." Both El and Etta were shocked at his other news. They both told him that Liz will go crazy about all her surprises.

Just then, Etta said, "What's we gonna do wit' Mrs. Eleanor. She was s'pose ta' sleep in 'da 'udder room." Joe said that she can still sleep in that room, it wouldn't be a problem.

El got excited and said, "Does this mean I get to sleep in with one of the boys?"

Joe said, "Mom, to be totally honest I think Liz is going to want James sleeping in our room beside the bed, for a while. John can have the first room. She may even want them both in our room. After each one is ready, they can be moved to their own rooms." El agreed that he was probably right. At that moment he chuckled. He said, "Mom you should have seen when they were here that first night. Both boys fit in the one cradle. One at each end and not one part of them touched the other."

At Lincoln Memorial Hospital, Liz had changed and fed James four times through the night; and John twice. She was not having any more pain, so she didn't have to take any more morphine. It did concern her to be taking it, while feeding the boys. Although she was told it wasn't harmful, she still was leery. For James's first feeding, he was alone.

John's tummy was still full. During this feeding, Liz was to feed James the bottled formula. She was quite pleased, how well he sucked on the bottle. He certainly was hungry. He finished four ounces in twenty-five minutes. He was not out to win any speed records. His brother took care of this. Although it is very hard to calculate what the babies eat from Liz's' breast, John seemed to fill himself usually within about ten to fifteen minutes. After every feeding, John was always very content. He was a champion burper, and had no problem getting back to sleep. To Liz, it felt like she had been up all night, with all her sons' feedings.

The second feeding for James was on her breast. This time, John was with him. She kept yawning while changing their diapers. The nurse offered her help, but Liz declined. She told the nurse, "Thank you, but I have to get used to this, so there's no time like the present, right?" The nurse smiled and just watched while Liz changed the boys. Liz had been able to fold the diapers small enough by then. She was doing a great job and the nurses were impressed with her. She was getting to be a pro.

She was able to breast-feed James and John both at the same time now, with great ease. She and the boys got into a comfortable position, each time and she would not vary from it, unless there was a problem with one of them. She might have to reposition, on occasion. Most of the time, they seemed like all three were perfectly comfortable and Liz was happy.

When both boys were finished, after one of their feedings and went back to the nursery, Liz asked the nurse, "Would you mind if I gave myself a wash and maybe wash my hair?"

Her nurse said, "No, ma'am, I don't mind ya' washin' one bit. I'll get your basin." When she returned, she said, "How about, you wash now and we'll see to your hair in the mornin'. You know, 'da doctor still don't want ya' out of bed, yet. But, he may let ya' later 'dis mornin', when he comes in. 'Den, we might be able to let ya'll have a shower bath. We'll wash your hair, 'den."

Liz said, "Oh that would be wonderful, thank you. I sure hope he'll let me bathe properly. Okay, I'll have my wash now and a snooze before James comes back, in a couple of hours and I'll do my hair later. Maybe I'll get my mom, or Etta to help me." The nurse had also brought fresh linens and another nurse to help make Liz's bed.

Liz was still not allowed to put one foot on the floor, so she had to have her bed changed, with her in it, again. It worked better when two nurses did it together. After she and her bed were freshened up, she quickly fell asleep and was awakened by a crying baby in her room, two hours later. She woke up with a smile saying, "Oh James, what a fuss you're making."

She changed his diaper and smiled. She sat watching and wondering at her perfect baby. She silently thanked the Lord for James, asking Him to help her littlest one to grow and also to watch over the rest of her family.

She also prayed to Him to keep James from becoming found positive for Sickle Cell Disease. She prayed for Him to watch over John and that he would have an easier time with it, like his daddy experienced, all his life. She prayed that he would not suffer like his great-grandfather and his great-great-grandfather, Jed. She smiled at James, feeling silly at the thought of James having it, too.

She was quite confident that James would not get it...after all, he was white. She picked him up, put the bottle in his mouth and it took him almost thirty minutes to finish the four ounces this time, but he did finish it.

By the time her breakfast came to her, she had only gotten about three and a half hours of sleep. While she ate, Dr. Hathaway came in. He already examined the boys and she heard them both coming down the hall for their breakfast. She smiled at Robert and he smiled back saying, "Well, here comes the troops! Are you ready mama?"

Liz grinned from ear-to-ear saying, "You bet I am buster! Bring em' on!" Robert laughed. He was beginning to really love Liz...her humor and strength.

He told her, "Now mommy, you eat your breakfast! Your boys will have to learn that patience is a virtue. Mama has to look after herself, too. Liz, don't let them wear you out. There's no shame in making them wait a bit. You'll still be a great mother. It's really okay if you leave the wet diaper on, a few minutes longer, love! Um...by the way...um...is your mother coming in today?"

Liz giggled while she sipped on her coffee, almost spilling it, saying, "OH...just try stopping her, doc!" She laughed harder and he joined her.

He said, "That's great, I'm looking forward to hearing about what George was up to, after the war." Liz suddenly looked out the window and frowned a little. The anguish was there on her face. Robert saw it.

As the nurses wheeled the twins into Liz's room, they left them there and then they left the room so Liz and Robert had privacy. The twins were just beginning to cry. Liz had finished her breakfast, but still had a bit more coffee to drink. Robert said, "Liz, I examined them several minutes ago in the nursery and they're looking fine. Last night's blood from James, still showed no sickle cells. They just took more this morning. I'll test it this evening and I think, that will be the last one. We're quite certain both samples today will show normal cells. But remember, he still may be a carrier."

Liz told him, "Dad and Joe's mom were always in touch with scientists, they wanted to be informed about a possible cure. Dad and Marteen...that's Joe's mom, worked very closely, for many years."

Robert saw the look on Elizabeth's face. He pretty much guessed what the look was about. "They were more than working together, if I'm not mistaken and not too bold to say...weren't they?"

Liz felt a tear welling in her eye. She said, "Are we that transparent?"

Robert touched her cheek, where the tear had fallen. "No dear. I just knew your daddy, too well. If you ever want to talk, I'm around."

Liz took his hand and kissed the back of it. She said, "Thanks."

Robert took Liz's hand and patted it. He said, "From what you told me about your family, the way this dysfunctional world is now, the McDonald's and the Allen's are the perfect model for peace and harmony. You are so lucky to have had such a life...until you came to Mississippi. It came crashing down around you both here, hasn't it?"

The tears started to flow faster, now. He hit the nail on the head. He sat on the side of her bed and held her. She filled him in on as much as she knew was happening to Joe at work and he already knew about her abuse at the 'white' hospital. While she finished her coffee, stopped crying and got ready to change diapers, she and Robert hadn't even noticed that the boys stopped crying, and had fallen back to sleep.

Robert said, "You listen to me, girl. You hold your head up and show these people what a happy, wonderful, loving marriage is all about. Including a beautiful family." She hugged him again.

She cleared her throat and Liz asked him if she could finally get out of bed and he told her she could. The hemorrhaging stopped and her blood was discontinued, as well as her IV. She had her freedom, but only to go to the bathroom and to the bathtub room, down the hall. She was not allowed to go to the nursery, for a few more days; the boys would continue to be brought to her room. She was delighted with moving around. Robert also told her if she did not eat or drink properly, she would have to go back on to the IV. She promised that she would happily follow orders and do both, saluting him! He laughed.

Just then, James started to fuss again. Robert helped her out of bed to walk to his bassinet. She was glad to be moving. She picked up James and laid him on her bed to change him. She then started feeding him and John started to fuss, too. Robert said, "Okay mama, what are you going to do now?"

She grinned and said, "Maybe a very kind doctor might help a lady out in this situation?" He chuckled and got John out of his bassinet, changed him and helped put him on Liz's other breast. Just then Etta and Eleanor came in the room.

Everyone was happy to see Liz looking so well and the boys, too. Robert was happy to see El. He was so captivated by her beauty. He wanted to spend time with her and talk. Now that he knew about George's infidelity, he would avoid that subject unless she wanted to speak about it.

Both boys were full and ready for a burp. Grandma took James and Etta took John and then Liz said, "Oh my goodness, I haven't even asked about Joe. How was he this morning, mom?"

A nurse came to the room and said, "Forgive me Dr. Hathaway, I have 'dat report ya'll been waitin' 'fer. Would ya'll please come to 'da desk? It's important, sir." He told her he'd come right away. He said his farewells to all, saying he'd see them a little later and went to the desk. With the nurse's insistence, he was very concerned.

Eleanor told her daughter, "Honey, I thought we'd let Joe sleep a bit longer this morning. We told him you wouldn't be upset that he didn't come this morning. He was supposed to be at the job site for the day. George was driving him."--

Liz said, "Of course I'm not upset. I'm sure he needs to catch up on work; as much as he does sleep. I hope he has a good day."

El said, "He said he'd either call here today to let me know when I need to pick him up, or George will drop him off, here."

Liz said, "That's great. I really like George Benson. He's a sweet man. Ladies, you can put the boys back in their bassinets, now. I'm sure they are due back in the nursery. Mom, Robert said I can shower and wash my hair, can you help me with that shortly?"

El said, "I'd love to dear. Whenever you're ready. By the way, your brothers called last night to see how you, Joe and the boys are and to make sure I arrived safely. They both said to tell you they love you."

Liz was happy and said, "Really, how sweet. Tell them I love them, too. There's hope for them yet, mom!" They laughed together.

On cue, two nurses came back to take the boys to the nursery and they brought Liz some towels, facecloth, shampoo and soap and told her where the bathtub room was. Liz was just like a kid in a candy shop, who had been left to run amok. Eleanor and Etta laughed and Liz joined in. She was so happy.

Just a few moments later, Robert ran into the room. He had a look about him, Liz hadn't seen, since the day he took them to the hospital, very worried about the trio. Something was wrong. He took Liz's hand and he took Eleanor's hand, turned to Liz and he said, "Sweetie, I'm so sorry. James has Sickle Cell Disease. As well as our own lab here - which is good; I decided to send his blood out to a better one. The 'white' one. We don't have the best equipment here. We get no government assistance. They have better, state of the art equipment. I needed to be absolutely sure for you. Honey I'm so sorry." Liz looked at him in horror. She was so sure, still convinced; because he was white, he'd be fine.

Liz looked at El and she said, "Mom...why both. WHERE IS GOD? Why both my boys. Mom, how can I tell Joe? It will crush him. We thought there was no way. What do I tell their father? He already feels guilty for passing it on to John. Why hasn't God answered my prayers? Aww damn, mom..." She wept.

Her mother hugged her and said, "Because my darling, He's decided this is the way your family is going to be. We have to adjust to His schedule, not ours." Robert had never heard anyone explain things this way. So simply and true! Neither had Etta.

As Liz wiped tears from her cheek, she smiled at her mom and said, "You always did know what to say to make me feel better. I don't know what any of us would do without you. But, how do I tell Joe?"

Robert stepped in and said, "If you like my dear, I can be present."

Liz said, "Thanks doc, but I think I prefer to tell him alone, when he gets here tonight." The three of them smiled at her and she mustered one back. She sat on her bed. As her mother came to her and put her arms around Liz's shoulders again, she couldn't help it, Liz started to weep again, holding on to her mother. Eleanor got her to lie down on her bed and she cried herself to sleep, going over in her mind, what she would tell her husband.

A couple of hours later, Dr. Hathaway came into the room and saw Etta and El talking quietly in a corner of the room. They didn't want to disturb Liz, so he walked over to the ladies and sat with them. He quietly said, "How would you two lovely ladies like to do a very big favor for me and for Liz?"

They both nodded and El said, "Anything we can do to help, just ask."

"Robert said, "I want Liz to get some more sleep, so if you ladies will follow me I'll show you what needs to be done." The three of them walked to the nursery. As he took them through the door, there was a loud crying going on. They both smiled. They knew it was James and John.

Robert addressed the nurse who was in the nursery, "Miss Martin, please get these ladies the supplies we discussed."

She smiled and said, "Yes'sir, right away." She went through a door at the back of the nursery and came back with diapers and bottles. Eleanor and Etta were both surprised and smiled at each other.

Robert said, "Okay grandma here's your and Etta's chance to have some private time with our boys. Go ahead and change them and then you can decide who gets to feed who; and get them both to drink as much of these bottles as you can. They are four ounce bottles.

I thought I would give you both some time with the boys before they get out of here and like I said before, Liz needs to sleep. This burden she's carrying around on her shoulders, keeps getting bigger. I wish I could relieve some of it and get her not to take things to heart so much. She's taken on so much in the last few days. I'm so glad you didn't mind my bringing you both to do this for us."

El smiled at him and said, "Doctor, my daughter takes everything on; she hates other people to have to share her burdens. She honestly thinks she's 'Wonder Woman', some days."

The three chuckled as Eleanor was teaching Etta how to fold the 'nappies' to fit the boys' tiny bums. As Robert was leaving the nursery, he told El that he would go check on Liz to see if she was still sleeping. He hoped she was.

After the diaper changes, Eleanor said, "Etta, if you don't mind, I'd like to feed James."

Etta replied, "No ma'am, I doesn't mind at all. I'se a little scared 'round 'dat tube o' his."

El smiled, and took the bottle and Etta took the other one and they picked up the boys. They took them over to a couple of old rocking chairs in the nursery. They were both made very comfortable, for feeding the boys.

Robert walked in to the nursery again and said, "Well mom, your daughter is still sleeping quite soundly. I don't expect her to awaken for a while. We will need to wake her next time, though. She will be getting filled by then; and will need to feed them herself. While she and the boys are here, I'd like this to happen at least once a day. I hope you both don't mind?"

Etta jumped in and said, "You sho' 'nuff' crazy to be askin' us 'dat question. We loves 'dese boys and we don't mind any at all!"

He smiled at Etta and said, "Etta my dear, I think that's the most I've heard you say in the few days that I've known you." She laughed. When the ladies were done feeding, they didn't want to put the boys down. They wanted to keep holding them for a bit. They were comfortable holding them. The doctor came back after a while and said they should check on Liz and that the nurses would bring the boys there, the next time they woke up.

Eleanor and Etta went to Liz's' room again and she was still asleep. They went back to their corner and continued to chat. They were having the greatest time, getting to know each other. The nurse periodically poked her head in the room, to see if Liz was awake. She wasn't. The boys were still sleeping in the nursery, also.

After Eleanor had dropped Joe off at Benson and Associates that morning, he had some paper work to do, before he went to his job site, at Pakos Industries. A little later, George came to Joe to talk to him. After several minutes, George and Joe got up to leave. George issued some instructions to the others in the office and said that he and Joe were going to Pakos. He and Joe signed out.

George was impressed at how well things were going on the project. He was very proud of Joe. They both went into the office and sat down with Roy Pakos, who was immensely calmed down since the incident on Monday.

When they walked in the office, Joe decided: And he was sure George wouldn't mind; that HE take control of the visit. Joe extended his hand right away and very business-like, said, "Good morning Mr. Pakos, you're looking well this morning. I really have to apologize for the mix-up on Monday. Somehow it got on my calendar that you wanted to see me; and well, once again, I'm really sorry. How do you like the way things are progressing with the project? I sincerely hope you're happy with the work starting on your tunnels and foot bridges." When Joe had brought in his designs of both bridges and tunnels; he won over Mr. Pakos on the idea and the safety factor of building both.

As he let go of Joe's handshake Roy said, "I'm well, thank you Mr. Allen. It's me that owes the apology. I said things in anger; and, well...I'm sorry. I was having the worst day and I took it out on you. I had no right to.

I'm very happy with the speed at which things are getting done around here. George, I apologize to you as well. You really have a talented boy here. Let's sit."

He shook George Benson's hand and then the three of them sat in Roy's office. He called out to his secretary, "Miss Sharpe, please bring coffee for these two gentlemen and myself."

Joe was very proud of himself and smiled. Roy sat down at his desk. He continued, "I'm quite pleased. Everything seems to be dead-on with your schedule, Mr. Allen. The equipment rolled in here right on schedule and the men started to work immediately, I just can't say enough to tell you how pleased I am."

Joe very proudly said, "Please sir, call me Joe. I'm glad you're pleased with the progress. I am here for the day to supervise and make sure all elements of the project are going exactly as planned. Once I start sir I like to closely supervise all my projects. To be totally honest sir, I do have to make you aware of something."

As Roy opened his door for the secretary with the coffee he said, "What's that Joe?" She served her boss and his company the coffee. She poured it for George and Roy and turned to leave the office.

Roy Pakos said, "Miss Sharpe you seem to have forgotten to pour a cup of coffee for the head of our construction project, Mr. Allen."

Miss Sharpe turned to Roy and said to him, "Mr. Pakos, sir, I will pour your coffee and for Mr. Benson; but I will not serve any Nig... Coloreds. I just won't do it...sir!"

Roy said, "That's fine Miss Sharpe, you will pack up all your belongings and leave the premises. You're fired. You may pick up your last pay, this Friday." After saying this, Roy poured Joe's coffee.

Joe was feeling very awkward, now. He never expected to cause waves like this before, he was in shock. Needless to say, so were George, and Miss Sharpe. Joe was sure she would apologize to her boss, to save her job. She didn't. She slowly turned and left the office. She did as she was told. She would rather lose her job, than serve coffee to a Nigger!

Without missing a beat Roy said, "Sorry for my secretary's rudeness. Now, what were you saying Joe?"

Joe tried not to let the firing upset him. He explained, "Sir that is sort of what I wanted to mention. I will be spending a great deal of time here on the job and I'm afraid some of this same behavior may occur again with the men on the job out there. I'd like to get your thoughts on how you'd like me to handle this type of situation."

Roy said, "Joe we'll handle it the way I just did now. This is my property, my business, my project and I'll support you. Please I need your expertise on this job. Please, say you'll stay and see it through to the end."

Joe said, "I'm not going anywhere sir. I'm here to do a job and it will get done; to your satisfaction, or my name isn't Joseph Allen."

The three men stood up and all shook hands again as George Benson said, "Well Joe how about you take me on a tour and let's take a look at this top notch project you have going on here." The three men left the office and Joe, very proudly walked them both around the project under way.

This was a monumental day for Joe. It was the most satisfying, happiest day, with the exception of the birth of their sons, since moving to Mississippi.

Chapter 11

Growing Boys

WHEN LIZ WOKE UP, BOTH boys were in her room. Etta and El had already changed their diapers. Liz was quite surprised and said, "Mom, what time is it?"

Eleanor said, "Well sleepy-head, it happens to be just after noon. Your lunch is here and your sons need to eat, too."

Liz was very confused about the time and started to panic a little. She slept too long. Her first thoughts were, the boys must be starving by now. "Oh my God mom; why did I sleep so long, they must be starving." She was starting to cry and feel guilty.

Eleanor said, "Honey, honey, don't worry, it's okay, calm down dear! You were sleeping so soundly and Robert said that he didn't want to wake you up. So, when the boys woke up he took Etta and me to the nursery and we got to change their nappies and feed them both their formula."

Liz was very relieved and calmed right away. When she heard what was going on, she thought it was a wonderful idea; and she certainly didn't mind the rest. It gave the two ladies some practice before the babies get home. She appreciated that Robert was kind enough to arrange it all. As she sat up in the bed, she let out a yelp. Her breasts were very full and extremely rock hard. She needed to be relieved, as soon as possible.

James and John already had dry diapers and Eleanor took James to her daughter and Liz placed him on her left breast. He latched on to her, faster than he had before and he started to eat. They were all pleased. Then, Etta handed John to her and she placed him to her other breast. She got into their comfortable position and she was so happy to have both of them eating together. The pain in her breasts would decrease shortly, as they ate.

Liz said, "Mom, would you please uncover my lunch and let me see what's there?"

Eleanor said, "Sure dear." She took the lid off the plate and it revealed a tuna sandwich and there was also some tomato soup. It was very hot. The steam was rising from it. Her mom continued, "Would you like me to leave the lid off the soup, to cool?"

Liz yawned, nodded and said, "Yeah thanks mom, that'd be great. I had a great sleep. Holy Christmas, I'm famished. Ok watch this ladies. Now mom, I want you to place a half of the sandwich in my right hand please." El smiled and did what Liz asked. This new mama fed both of her boys at the same time: She was able to prop John up with her knee and forearm and she took a big bite of her sandwich. They cheered her on. Eleanor was impressed.

Liz said, "You see mom. I was paying more attention to you and things you did with Abe and Simon, than you ever thought I did."

Eleanor smiled, as she said, "Honey, you're doing great. That's right; I used to take shortcuts, but I don't remember being that talented. I'm quite proud, darlin'! Do you remember some other shortcuts and actions I took with your brothers?"

Liz told her, "Yeah, I do. You know, even though I was only a few years older than they are, I do remember many things you did with them. I was always so amazed and watched everything you did with them. It was fun to watch. Little did I know that education was going to come in handy with my own twin sons!" Liz giggled as she ate and fed the boys, at the same time.

Eleanor was quite happy about this. She said, "You're doing great, love. They are looking pretty good, don't you think? They seem to be eating pretty well, now. I'm sure they are gaining weight. Dr. Hathaway said he'd come along this afternoon and let us know how they're doing."

Just then, Liz remembered...James has Sickle Cell Disease. A sudden frown came to her face. She thought that she was so exhausted maybe it was all a bad dream. She looked at her mom and asked, "Mom, I'm hoping it was a dream but, did Robert tell us James has it?"

Eleanor lowered her eyes a bit, came to Liz and took her daughter's chin in her hand and said, "I'm sorry baby-girl. Yes, he did tell us James' blood is positive." Liz had a couple of tears welling up in her eyes and Eleanor kissed her daughter on the forehead, continuing, "Just remember dear, our families have dealt with this disease; on and off through the generations and our families handled it all head on. You know God will see us through. Your boys may be as lucky as Joe and they'll be hockey stars, too. We'll help them through it and remember... scientists are still working to find a cure. Maybe it's just around the corner. We have to trust in the Lord. He knows what He's doing." She smiled at Liz when she said this.

Etta was quiet, but just then she said, "You know Mrs. Liz...our beloved Lord, Jesus... He made Mr. Joe lass' 'dis long 'wit it, an' he be juss' fine! Now yo' babies is gonna 'git tru' it, too." Etta went to the other side of Liz's bed and rested her hand on her shoulder. Liz felt better. God had a plan for their family and right then Liz decided they were both right! What will be, will be.

Just then, a nurse came in her room. She told Liz, "'Dey's a phone message 'fer ya'll, Mrs. Allen. Yo' husban' don't need a ride 'dis aft'noon. He be comin' here after he done work. May be a little late, he's not sho', yet."

Liz said, "Thanks love. Can I still get up and have a bath and wash my hair this afternoon?"

The nurse said, "Yess'um. Do ya' wants me ta' hep' ya', or maybe yo' mama would like ta'?"

Eleanor said, "Sure, I can help her, nurse. I don't mind."

The nurse continued, "'Dat be okay wit' us. Ya'll juss' wait an' I'se go 'git 'da instruments ta' 'git 'dat catheter out o' ya'll. Now 'dat ya'll can 'git up, ya'll can go ta' da' lav'tory an' pee on 'yer own. But, you be sho' ta' let me know if ya'll can't go, now. We needs ta' know 'dat. 'Den ya'll can have 'yer bath."

Liz said, "Okay thanks, I will."

The nurse watched Liz as she was feeding the both boys and eating her own meal, at the same time. She laughed and said, "Ya'll seems 'sperienced now, ain't 'cha?"

Liz smiled at her as she was just about to leave and said, "Well you see, I have twin brothers. I learned many things from my mom." The nurse nodded and said she'd be back to take the boys away when they were done feeding.

It was about a half hour later when she called the nurse to take the boys back to the nursery. As soon as the nurses took them Liz ate the rest of her own lunch. The nurse came back after she was done, to take her catheter out.

Etta packed a good, bagged lunch for herself and Liz's mom. They had eaten theirs while Liz was feeding and eating her own.

Eleanor helped Liz bathe while Etta just waited for them. She started to straighten the bed. Liz's nurse came back to the room and she brought fresh linens. Etta helped the nurse make the bed, as they talked and joked for a bit.

Liz and El came back in the room and Liz was walking very slowly. She was tired out: But, she was clean and her hair was washed. She felt so good! She was also very happy to be getting back to the bed, too. She was exhausted. Just then, Robert came in and said, "Wow, you're a new woman, my dear. You look beautiful."

Liz started to blush. She smiled and said, "Thank you, Robert. You sure know how to make a woman feel great."

He said, "Well I only speak the truth, my dear lady. How do you feel?"

Liz blushed some more, but told him she's quite tired again. Robert replied, "I think you should sleep some more dear and we should get Grandma and Etta to go back to the nursery and feed them the next time they wake up this afternoon. That way you can nap. What do you think?"

Liz said, "Who am I to disobey my doctor's orders." She snuggled down into her bed and tried to not show pain, on her face.

Robert said, "I know what that look is about. I think you should take a bit of morphine, Liz. You look like you can use it." Liz nodded her head, saying that she became sore from showering and washing her hair and the walk to get to the tub room. She told him she would gladly take the medicine.

As Liz was settling in for another nap, Etta and Eleanor decided that they would go outside and take a walk around the neighborhood, since it was another beautiful warm, February day.

The hospital was located just on the edge of town, where the white neighborhood ends and the black one begins. Etta wasn't sure where Eleanor felt the most comfortable.

She told Eleanor about the area and Eleanor decided, she would be fine in the colored section; and Etta would be accepted in the white area, while walking with each other. So, they decided, as long as they stick together they would be fine in either neighborhood. As they walked and talked, they had no trouble. There were a few stares, but no incidences.

After about twenty minutes of walking and talking, they found themselves at Minnie's door. Etta said, "Mrs. El, how would ya'll like ta' meet Minnie?"

El said, I'd love to, but we can't stay long. We have to get back to feed the boys." It felt so good to El, to hear herself say that.

Etta knocked on the door and Minnie opened it. She had the biggest smile, pulled Etta toward her and gave her a big hug. She said, "I was wonderin' how 'tings was goin'. How be Liz, an' our little ones doin', gal?"

Etta was always happy with Minnie's hugs. She said, "Well, she be doin' better 'den 'da lass' time you seen her, 'dat 'fer sho'. Minnie, we ain't got lots o' time, but I wanted ta' bring someone ta' meets ya'."

Minnie took one look at El and said, "Oh my Lawdy, looky here, now. 'Dis here gots ta' be our Lizzy's mama, Miss Eleanor! Ya'll looks juss' as pretty as 'yer daughter does." With that, she took El to her bosom and hugged her, too.

Eleanor was surprised by her warmth and said, "Yes I am. Minnie, I'm so happy to meet you. My daughter and Etta talk about you fondly. I feel like we're family already."

She welcomed them in and offered them some tea. At first, they said they couldn't stay that long; but Minnie told them the tea was ready to pour and she had fresh banana loaf, right out of the oven. They decided to stay! They both filled Minnie in on the events of the last few days. El couldn't thank Minnie enough: For bringing Dr. Hathaway to her daughter and grandsons. Minnie decided she'd like to go see Liz and the boys. She said, "How 'bout we all 'gits ta' da' hospital. I'll drive. I just gotta see 'dem babies' a'gin."

As Joe, George and Roy started off on their walk around the grounds to observe the work in progress, George was quiet, but quite proud of the way Joe handled himself. He was also glad that Roy Pakos apologized to Joe and himself. He felt that he had made the best decision in awarding this job to Joe. It was small enough that it didn't need any of the other engineers to be removed from their projects, to assist. He could handle it. Joe's experience on bridges and the tunnel design he suggested, showed that the job was thought out thoroughly and Mr. Pakos hadn't even really thought of using tunnels to connect the buildings. George was the only other engineer involved and he was concentrating on the geotechnical, mostly the tunnel aspect of the job.

By Pakos wanting both foot bridges above ground; AND tunnels underground, connecting the buildings, it meant a much more expensive project, but Pakos had the money and it was what he wanted.

George thought, right from the moment that Roy Pakos decided that he wanted both the tunnels and foot bridges Joe was going to get a very large bonus, which no one in the office would ever know about.

As the three were out touring the grounds, Joe went to every person who was involved in the job. He liked to meet and talk with each person on his work crew; and get their opinions and he was always there to field any and all questions and, or problems which had been encountered, or that had not been foreseen. Joe was approachable to all the men who worked under him, and he wanted to keep all his men happy.

As he went around talking to each man, through the day, he only found a few people who would not shake his hand and were very cool toward him. These few Joe wondered, what would they do if the higher bosses hadn't been there? How would they treat him on his own? The other thing that crossed his mind was who might be Klan? Who can he trust? Who might sabotage his project? If there were problems, he would learn answers to his questions, in time.

After touring the site, around two-thirty, George said to Joe, "I think things are going well here, Joe. I'm pleased, what do you say? I have things that need my attention in the office and I'd like to go over some things with you there as well."

This was news to Joe. He had no idea what George was referring to. He grew a little nervous. He turned to look at George, who shot him a quick look, a smile and a wink of his eye. Joe wasn't sure what was up, but he felt better after he saw the wink. Still, Joe wondered, if there was anything up, or whether he just wanted to get out of there.

Roy Pakos brought them both back to the office and they sat around his desk, again. Roy locked his office door. Pakos Industries employed a fairly large office staff. There are several secretaries and they each had several duties. Miss Sharpe was personal secretary to Roy. The position was now open for someone else. There were three women; through the day who talked to Roy Pakos about the position opening and he would interview each of them the next day.

It meant a little higher wages for whoever was the successful candidate. Roy asked one of the other ladies in the office to take over for the day. He asked Mrs. Rice, Pakos Industries Vice President's secretary to take over for the rest of the day. She was delighted to help out. She happened to be the vice president's wife, as well. He was out of town for a couple of days, on business, so Mrs. Rice was able to do Miss Sharpe's job for the day. She also told Roy, she could fill in until he chose his new secretary. That was fine with him. Roy Pakos and his vice president, Allan Rice were close friends outside of the business, too. Mr. and Mrs. Rice often socialized with the boss and his wife.

As the three men sat around Roy's desk, like they had that morning; Roy went to a beautiful antique barrister's bookcase, in the corner of his office, unlocked it and brought out a large bottle of scotch and three glasses. Roy said, "Gentlemen, how would you like to join me in a little libation." George and Joe smiled at each other and nodded that they'd be delighted to join him for a quick one.

It was about three-thirty, when George said, "Well Roy, we really must get going. We still have some work to do, before quitting time."

Joe said, "It's been a pleasure, sir. I'll be back, in a couple of days but, if there are any problems, please call me right away." Joe reached for his pen and then remembered that he had a supply of his business cards, in his briefcase. He reached in and...saw the ink stains, from Ray's practical joke and remembered that horrible day, again. He tried to quickly take a card out and realized that they were all stuck together with blue ink. He got pissed, all over again.

George quickly realized what Joe was trying to do and said, "Never mind Joe, here's mine." He handed his business card to Roy and Joe asked for it back for a moment. He turned it over and Joe wrote down his home phone number. Joe handed the card back to Roy and said, "If you have an emergency, or anything goes wrong, PLEASE, feel free to call me day or night."

Roy looked quite shocked and was about to say thanks to Joe, when George stepped in and said, "Oh, don't feel bad if you need to call him in the middle of the night, he won't be sleeping...at all. Joseph and his wife just had twin boys, born a couple of days ago." Roy had a very surprised look on his face and he grabbed his bottle of scotch and poured another shot in each glass. Roy made a nice toast, congratulating Joe, before they left the office.

As they got into George's car, Joe asked George, "Well George, what is this pressing work we need to get back to at the office?"

George grinned. "We're not going back to the office, today. I'm going to take you home and then we can go see Liz and the boys after that."

George had a surprise lined up for Joe. He was anxious to watch it unfold. When they left the job site, George headed towards Joe's house.

They went over the day's events, with Joe still feeling awkward about Roy's secretary being fired, on account of him. George said, "Don't you worry about it. That's Pakos' business and you have no more control over it, than I do. Joe, it really goes to show you are respected by Pakos, now. That says a lot, my friend!"

George turned his car down Gilbert Street and in Joe's driveway, stood a brand new "Baby Blue", GM CC-101 Pick-Up Truck: Identical to his beloved truck that moved Liz and him, from Chatham to Mississippi, several months earlier. The only difference was, this truck was a brand new one. It was a 1947 model. His original "Baby Blue", was a 1946. As George pulled his car in the driveway, behind the truck, Joe was speechless, as George was beaming from ear-to-ear!

George said, "Now son, you just pay me back whenever you can, but I knew how much you loved her. And, I know how busy you are. So, I thought I'd help you out the best I could. Now, if you want to take her back and exchange her for something a little different, I can arrange that for you, too. Well, what do ya' say, laddy?"

Joe actually had tears welling up in his eyes. He said, "WOW... George, I am absolutely flabbergasted. George, you really didn't need to..."

George put his hand up to interrupt Joe and said, "Now Joe, I thought we could make a payment plan. You can work it off. It doesn't matter how long you take, paying for it."

Joe said, "There's no trouble with paying you, George. You see, Liz and I are...what do the snobbery call it...'independently wealthy'! I can write you a check for the entire amount today, or I can go get the cash, in full, tomorrow, but I won't change a thing. I love it already." George was shocked. Joe continued, "Please don't worry. Liz's dad and my mom left us both generous inheritances and we have an excellent, constant income from the farm property we own. We also have a very large nest egg and I can pay for the whole thing tonight and what I owe you for paying my fines the other day. I'll never be able to thank you enough, for everything you've done for us. We really appreciate it and you; Thank-you, my friend!"

George was still in shock about Joe's true financial status, but delighted at the same time. In all his wildest dreams, he never expected to hear this disclosure. As a matter of fact, George never even heard of a wealthy black man in Mississippi! He was really happy for them, both. He thought at that moment, he'd LOVE to see the look on Ray Halden's face, if he were ever to hear this...not that he would ever reveal Joe and Liz's secret to anyone, ever!

As they went over the bill of sale, Joe wrote out a check for $2685.00 for the truck plus what George paid out, a few days earlier. George took the check and handed Joe the keys. Joe was ecstatic. They shook hands and George said, "Well my boy, I guess I've stereotyped you again. You know, assuming you didn't have the money to pay for it. I'm so sorry. Now, let's go see our girl, and our sweet baby boys."

Joe smiled the biggest smile and said, "George, you're truly one in a million. Who's driving?"

George said, "Well, how about we leave my car here and we go to the hospital in 'baby'?"

Joe said, "Sounds good to me. Let's go, buddy." They got in the truck and drove to the hospital. On the way, Joe said, "Oh, George you can't imagine how this feels. It is wonderful to have my truck, again. How can I ever thank you?"

George said, "Well, with all the crap you and Liz had to endure since you arrived in Mississippi, I feel that no matter what I've done for you, it isn't enough. I just want to help you and your family as much as I can."

Joe said, "Now comes a surprise for Liz. Her mom and I are going out before Liz gets home from the hospital and I am going to buy a brand new car for her. She'll go wild. I have to make sure it's a Ford."

George was surprised and said, "She'll love whatever you pick out for her. Do you have a model in mind?"

Joe told him, "I saw a magazine ad for a 1947 Ford Coupe, 2 Door. I think she'd like it. It seems like it should be a good size for her to handle. I want to find one and take a spin in it and let mom take it out, too. I want to see how it maneuvers. You know, being brought up on the farm, Liz and her mom are excellent drivers. Everyone is. You start out at around the age of twelve. The first thing you drive on the farm is a tractor...after a horse, that is!"

They both laughed and George said, "Sounds great. She's going to be so surprised." They pulled into the hospital parking lot and they both had smiles on their faces.

Joe said, "We better stop smiling, Liz will wonder what trouble we've been up to." They both laughed and got it out of their system.

Liz woke up around 6:00 p.m., after having another great sleep from her bath and morphine. Her supper was there. Liz's mom and Etta were in the room, still. She was shocked she slept so long and said, "The boys seem later tonight, mom. Is everything alright?"

El pulled the table and her supper towards Liz and said, "Don't worry honey, we fed them almost three hours ago. I imagine they'll be here very soon. You missed Minnie. Etta and I went for a walk, and we stopped at Minnie's. She came back here with us to visit you and the boys. She was at the nursery with us when we fed them. As a matter of fact, Etta let Minnie feed John. I tell you darlin' she was so tickled! You should have seen how happy she was to be here and to feed John."

Liz smiled and she said, "Oh Etta that was so sweet and thoughtful of you. Thank you. I wish you would have woken me up to visit with her." Liz looked at her supper tray. She was hungry. El told Liz that Etta and she would eat with Joe, at home later. Liz started to eat.

As Liz ate and the three of them chatted, Joe and George walked in to the room. Liz pushed her tray away from her, jumped out of bed and threw herself around Joe in a great big hug and kissed him. The look on his face was total shock. He never expected it and everyone started to laugh. She nearly knocked him off his feet, like she almost did at Christmas 1944, for the golf clubs.

George said, "Wow young lady, you sure have gotten a lot of energy all of a sudden. What are they feeding patients around here? I think I'd like some!" Everyone laughed, while she kissed Joe, again...a little more passionately than the first time. Her breasts were filling again and as she squashed herself against her husband, she left two wet spots, from her breasts. She noticed it as she backed away from him and she burst out in uncontrollable laughter. As she moved away from him, she turned Joe around, to face everyone and they all saw the wet spots on his chest and they all burst out laughing, too.

Joe said, "What is it about you, and those things? They're loaded weapons." Everyone laughed, more.

Robert walked in the room at that moment and saw what everyone was laughing at. He couldn't help it. He had to join them. He couldn't resist saying, "Liz, you're going to have to get those things licensed as weapons." Everyone laughed even louder and Liz told Robert what Joe had just said about them, too. He joined the laughter, again. Joe finally felt the wet spots, through his clothes and he couldn't help it, he laughed, harder.

Everyone said their hellos to George and Joe, while there was some crying in the hallway. Liz smiled and said, "Great timing, daddy, here come our boys." The nurses brought them, in their bassinets. Joe was elated. He was thrilled to see them right away. He was impressed he didn't have to wait long for them to wake up.

George said to Joe, "Well papa, don't you think it's about time you changed a diaper?"

Eleanor said, "That's right, George. I agree, it is time daddy learned." While Joe grinned, he was nervous.

Liz said, "Okay dad, I'll talk you through it. You take John and I'll change James. He takes a little more care, since you have to work around his paraphernalia," referring to his tubes.

Everyone watched and for a first time, Joe did well. Liz also let Joe feed John his bottle. Liz breast-fed James at the same time and the whole family, Liz feeding James and Joe feeding John, all sat on the bed together. Eleanor said, "What a beautiful family portrait this would make." They all agreed.

Everyone else decided they would leave the room and let them have their first few moments together, as a family, since they were at home the night of their birth. Eleanor remembered, as they walked out of the room, that she had brought her camera. It was in the glove box of the rental car. She went to get it. Etta and George tagged along. It was the end of Robert's day and as they walked outside to El's car, he asked them if they would join him for dinner, as Eleanor got her keys out and unlocked the door and retrieved her camera.

She looked at Robert and said, "That sounds lovely, but I..." She stopped speaking and was dumbstruck. She looked one row over and there was a truck, identical to Joe's, baby blue GM pick-up. She remembered it from the day he brought it home to the farm. He was so proud of it. She started walking over to the truck to get a better look.

The three followed and Robert asked, "Eleanor is there a problem? What's wrong?" George knew she spotted it and he felt he'd be explaining it, shortly. He was sure Joe wouldn't mind, under the circumstances. She did deserve an explanation.

Eleanor said, "I can't believe it. This is the identical truck to Joe's. He bought it to move them to Mississippi. He recently had to get rid of it because of the cow shit! I can't believe it. It's such a shock to see it."

She looked inside the truck window and she spotted Joe's coat. He had gone into the hospital without it and left it in the truck. She looked at George and said, "George didn't you and Joe drive here together tonight?"

George said, "Yes ma'am, we did."

She said, "I'm sure I'm not mistaken. That coat on the seat belongs to Joe. What do you know about this?"

George grinned and said, "You're not going crazy Eleanor. This is identical to his truck. He bought it today. He wants to surprise Liz. He was so busy I took it upon myself to find it, buy it and park it in his driveway. When I drove him home tonight, it was waiting for him. He paid me for it. You should have seen the look on his face when he saw it sitting in his driveway. He really didn't have time to get it himself, so I bought it for him." Everyone smiled and loved the fact that Joe's boss thought that much of Joe, to do this.

As the four went back into the hospital, Eleanor said, "I'm sorry Robert, I guess we should get back to your question about dinner. I'm not sure what Etta and George would like to do, but my thought is, maybe when we go home, you come home and join us. George this includes you, too. How does my idea sound?"

Everyone agreed and decided that is what they would do. They were sure Joe wouldn't mind. When they walked back to Liz's room, the family was still on her bed and still in a beautiful scene, oblivious to the world around them. There was such innocence and honesty to it, Eleanor just had to capture it on film.

Before she took the picture, a tear welled in her eye. She was remembering how much she loved her own George and when he had sat on her own hospital bed, after the births of Abe and Simon, each holding a newborn twin and Liz on her bed too, just being their doting big sister! She wished it would have been captured on film. She wanted Liz and Joe to see what the four witnesses, now saw: Beauty, love, and truth. As a tear fell, she clicked the camera and the flash went off, breaking the beauty of the moment.

Liz and Joe were happy that her mom took a picture. It would be the most treasured photo in their lives. Everyone came in the room. The boys had just filled up and were asleep in their parent's arms. Joe kissed his wife, as he got up off the bed and he placed John back in his bassinet. Liz got out of her bed and took James to his and laid him down, too.

El asked, "Would it be okay if Etta and I take the boys back to the nursery?"

Joe said, "Mom, I'd like them to stay for a bit. I just want to look at them."

She said, "Of course, dear. By the way Joe, we've kind of took it upon ourselves to make supper arrangements. The four of us are going back to your place and Etta and I will make supper for all five of us. Robert and George both said they'd join us. Does that sound okay with you, dear?"

Joe said, "Mom, that's a wonderful idea. I'm so glad you guys will join us."

Eleanor said to Joe, "So, dear, I was just outside getting the camera. It was in the car...in the parking lot. You'll never guess what I saw, parked one row over from my car!"

Joe looked at George and they both grinned. Joe said, "So I guess George explained?" El smiled and nodded.

Liz was in the dark at this point. She said, "What's going on. What's this about a vehicle?" As the four smiled, Joe explained about the pick-up. Liz was so touched she got off of the bed, went to George, reached up on tiptoes and kissed him on the cheek. She said, "George Benson, you are truly a kind, gentle, caring man. Joe and I are blessed to know you. I hope you don't mind, but we'd like our boys to call you Uncle George, if that is okay with you?"

He didn't know what to say, he was surprised. He was happy to have meaning in his life, again. This family adopted him and he was proud. He went to the bassinets and bent over and kissed each baby on his forehead, saying, "I would be very honored, my dear."

Liz said, "Now you ladies, how about you get these men fed. They all put in long days, I'm sure and I know you all must be starving." Joe put his arms around his wife, from behind and kissed her on her cheek. All of a sudden, she was aroused. She wanted more. He hadn't intended it to happen, but he was getting aroused, himself. He had to stop.

He said, "Honey, do you really want us to go?"

Liz turned to face him, put her arms around his waist and said, "Yes darling. Please take everyone home and have a great supper. Everything seems right with the world, tonight. I love you." She kissed him and everyone said goodnight to her and they took the boys to the nursery, while Joe stayed behind to kiss her more. It felt so good to be in each other's arms. He let her get back into bed and tucked her in. She felt a beautiful glow. It seemed like nothing could spoil it. But she was wrong.

Liz said, "Joe, we have news....I'm sorry to spoil the evening honey, but James has Sickle Cell Disease." Joe's demeanor changed. He was very upset, now. She told him everything.

They just stayed looking at each other and a moment later he smiled. As they looked deep and lovingly into each other's eyes Liz smiled, too. Joe said, "We can handle it, right mommy?"

She said, "God will help us through it: Right, daddy?" He held her close and nodded his head in agreement.

He asked his wife, "Is it okay if I talk to Robert about it tonight, honey: Even without you there?" She told him that it would be fine. The four came back to her room and got Joe and they all left together to go home. Liz snuggled under the covers. She knew she'd have to get some sleep while she could.

She laid there thinking about Joe. How much she loved him. How much she loved their boys. She hoped that the three of them would get out of the hospital, soon. She wanted to get home and start being a normal family. Liz smiled, as she fell asleep. She would be awakened by little cries, in only a few hours.

Joe and George drove home in the new pick-up, Robert drove his own car and Eleanor and Etta went in her rental car. When they all arrived, Joe asked Robert and George if they would join him in having a beer. They gratefully accepted.

Eleanor and Etta started to make supper. Etta had taken ground beef out of the freezer, to thaw through the day. She was planning on meatloaf. But now, Etta stopped dead in her tracks and was a little nervous.

She said to El, "Lawdy, Mrs. El...We gots us a doctor in 'da house 'fer supper! What's we gonna feed a doctor? What's we gonna feed him, Mrs. El? We cain't feed him no reg'lar meatloaf!"

Eleanor laughed, "Etta, meatloaf is fine. Doctor's eat regular food, just like you and me. They are just regular folks, I assure you!"

Etta said, "Is ya'll sure?"

El laughed and told her "Meatloaf will be perfect, my dear. Remember, I was married to a surgeon. Honey, he ate everything! You put anything in front of him and he ate it!" Eleanor giggled and it put Etta at ease.

Joe came in the kitchen and asked El, "Mom, I'm going downstairs to get some beer. Would you like one?"

Eleanor said, "Sure that sounds good dear." Etta looked wide eyed at her, without saying anything.

El said, "Yeah Etta, even old gals like me drink beer." She smiled and winked at her. Etta giggled and smiled back.

As the preparation for dinner was done and the table set, El took her beer and went in to the living room to join the men. She asked, "Anyone mind if I crash your party, boys?"

Robert moved over on the sofa, so that she would sit beside him. She did. No one minded if she joined in. They were discussing the boys' sickle cell and then the conversation turned to vehicles. Joe mentioned to El about the Ford Coupe he wanted to look at for Liz. She said that maybe they could go test drive one on Saturday. He agreed.

By nine-thirty, George and Robert were both excusing themselves and thanked Etta for a wonderful supper. They all had an enjoyable evening, especially Robert, who was glad to have the opportunity to get to know Eleanor better, in a more private setting. The men thanked Joe and El for their hospitality. Eleanor and Joe had a great evening with them, as well. Etta came in to the living room and asked if the two of them would like anything else, before she turned in.

Joe said, "Etta I didn't make a big deal about it, but I really wished you had eaten supper with us. You know we don't mind."

Etta said, "I'se sorry Mr. Joe. It juss' ain't proper. You'se pays me ta' work. I'se sorry if I'se made ya' mad."

Joe got up and went over to her. He gave her a friendly hug and said, "No Etta, I'm not upset or mad. I just want you to know, you are family."

She thanked him and said, "I knows I am, but I knows my place when comp'ny's here."

She smiled at him and he took her hands and kissed each one and said, "Good night Etta. You are one in a million. We all love you, very much and our boys will love you, too. Oh, by the way, I guess mom doesn't have to drive me to work, so you two can leave any time you like to go to the hospital. I'll leave it up to you, both. I'll be getting up at my regular time. Good night."

El said good night to Etta and told her that she really enjoyed spending the whole day with her. She left Joe and Eleanor by themselves, in the living room.

Joe said, "So mom, we have two little boys with sickle cell. We can only pray and hope they have a fairly easy enough time with it, like I do."

El said, "I know, dear. I hope so, too. All we can do is hope and pray they won't be stricken with the worst symptoms and get a chance to grow up to be fine gentlemen. We just love them, all the more, right?"

Joe nodded, as a tear rolled down his cheek. Eleanor came to him and knelt down before him. She held his hands and said, "Now son, I know what you're thinking. You did NOT do this to your sons. You're a sweet, gentle, intelligent man, who loves my daughter to pieces, and will raise two, very fine, healthy boys, for a very long time. You lean on us. Lean on your family and God. We stick together through everything, right?" He nodded his head.

They stood up and hugged. He said, "Mom, why my boys? Why both of them?" He sobbed on her shoulder. She just held him and let him cry.

After a moment he said, "I don't mean any disrespect; but I miss my mom so much." He wept some more and she held him tighter.

She said, "I know you do sweetheart, I know. I miss George AND your mom, too! You didn't deserve the hand you were dealt, son. My heart has broken for you, many times over. I tried to be a mom to you over the years, when your mom was so busy working, but I guess I didn't do the job as well as I was hoping I had."

Joe lifted Eleanor's chin, looked her in the eye and said, "You were always there for me, mom...at home and school. I could always count on you. I don't ever remember a time in my life that I didn't love you like a mom!" He wrapped his arms around her and gave her a very big hug. Now she was tearing up, too. They both laughed.

Joe said, "Okay! I guess we leave things up to God, right?"

El said, "I think that's what He wants, son. Who are we to argue with God?" She smiled at him and said, "Good night, dear." She kissed him on the forehead and turned and went upstairs.

He called out to her, "Mom?" She turned back to him, half way up the stairs and looked at him. Joe smiled and he said, "Thanks for loving me, like your own. G'night."

She flashed a smile and said, "I love you, son: Goodnight, dear."

Joe turned off the lights and made his way up to his bed. He stopped and looked in the undecorated room and smiled. He wanted to get it done before Liz came home, with the boys. He went to his room, laid on the bed and fell asleep in his suit, still with two visible breast milk spots. He was exhausted.

By Friday, both boys had gained weight. James had the NG tube and IV taken out. The three women were getting experienced at diapering and bathing. Liz let them both help her when they were visiting. The doctor told Liz and Joe, he may let all of them go home on Monday. They would be a week old. John was over five pounds and James was around four and a half pounds. Robert was happy with that. They both seemed strong.

Liz was excited, until he repeated, "I MAY let you go home Monday, but is it at MY discretion, Liz. But, I don't foresee any problems." She smiled with relief. El and Etta did too. Liz couldn't wait to tell Joe, that night.

Truth be told, Robert could have released them over the weekend but he was giving Joe time to get the second bedroom done and buy the car for Liz. El and Etta had gone out and bought the wallpaper and paint to match other room. All three of them worked on it in the evenings, after supper and visiting Liz. It would be done by Sunday they hoped, but Joe and El had to go out Saturday, to get Liz's car.

Saturday, Etta stayed with Liz most of the day at the hospital, while Joe and Eleanor drove to another town, to where there was a Ford Dealer. He didn't think he should talk first. He thought that maybe El could start, so they could get a feel for how receptive the dealer was, selling a car to a black man.

As they got out of the pick-up, the salesman walked toward them. Joe made a quick change of plans and put out his hand and introduced himself. The man was a little hesitant and taken aback, but shook it none-the-less. He figured, 'as long as I sell a car, I guess I can shake a Nigger's hand'. The salesman asked, "What can I do for you fine, wonderful folks, today? Glorious day for buyin' a brand new car, ain't it? What can I show ya' folks, you just name it and I'll fix ya' up. You won't leave here without bein' totally satisfied, or my name ain't Duncan McBride!" He was the semi-pushy, bull-shitter, with a half of a pound of bryl-cream in his hair, who thought he was God's gift to the women of the world and 'trying' too hard! He directed his greeting toward El only...she was female...and white. This pissed off Joe, a little. El just smiled and stayed in the background and waited to see what would transpire.

Joe very politely took control of the conversation, while El stayed in the background. Mr. McBride made it clear he wanted her to talk to her, but she just nodded and agreed with everything Joe said, ignoring the salesman. He and the salesman talked about the new 2 Door Coupe and that he was buying it for his wife. There were two on the lot, as well as a 4 door. Joe told him that since he was buying it for his wife, as a surprise, he brought her 'friend', Eleanor along, to get a female's opinion and to see how it handles for her. He asked to take it for a drive and the salesman got the keys. Joe drove it first while the salesman was rambling on about all the features and then El drove it. She loved it. She said, "Joe, I think your wife will love it. It drives beautifully and I think she'll handle it just fine. There's lots of room in the back seat, for a car-bed, for the twins, too!

The salesman asked about the children and Joe told him about their new arrivals. They made small talk about babies and families for a few minutes.

Joe was glad to hear Eleanor's comments. He had estimated the price and he brought enough cash to pay for it right away. Joe wanted the very car they test drove. The salesman was quite shocked, but he took them into the showroom, then his office, so he could write up the sale. Joe brought out the roll of cash and salesman's eyes nearly popped out. Joe counted off $2,165.00.

The salesman was a little nervous about accepting this large amount of cash from a black man. Could he trust that they were real bills and not counterfeit. Joe saw the question rolling around in his mind and said, "Don't worry, it's real. It's an inheritance." The salesman looked to Eleanor and she nodded to him. The salesman took the cash and Joe drove home in the truck and Eleanor drove home in Liz's new car.

On Saturday, Eleanor and Joe were only able to see Liz, and the twins, for a few hours in the late afternoon and evening. She had no idea what they'd been up to, all day. Joe told her Friday night that he had to work some overtime at his site on Saturday, and El told her that she had some 'grandma' shopping to do! Liz fully accepted and believed both excuses, without a worry, or a clue, that something was up and it was a surprise for her! She and the boys had a great day with Etta, who had been a big help, to her.

Monday rolled around and Robert came in to her room. He had been over to the house to see Joe, on Sunday morning and asked if they were ready to let Liz and the boys come home, the next day. He also used the opportunity to see Eleanor. He was quite taken with her and wanted to see her more, outside of the hospital. He hoped that when he released Liz and the boys, he would still be able to see El.

Eleanor said to Joe, while Robert was there, "Honey, I think we could use one more day, to get everything cleaned up and the paint smell out...and I want to vacuum the car out and wash it as well." Robert agreed that he would make an excuse and release the three on Tuesday, but would not tell Liz until Monday morning.

When Robert entered Liz's room Monday morning, Liz couldn't wait...she burst out with, "Robert, can we go, please...please...please?"

Robert laughed a little and then put on his 'professional' face and said, "Sweetie, I'm sorry, but I would like you stay for one more day. I'll release you on Tuesday. I'd like to run some more blood work and another urinalysis on you, to make sure you're healthy enough to go home. I feel the boys are okay, now."

She was really disappointed, but said, "Awe...okay...I guess we can wait, one more day. Is there a problem?" He told her it was just a precaution to make sure all her blood levels were normal and healthy, since she had hemorrhaged after the birth. He also wanted to check that she had no bladder infection.

He explained, "You see Liz, when you've had a catheter in, it can sometimes leave you with a bladder, or urinary tract infection, so I want to make sure you don't have one. If you do, you'll need an antibiotic...okay? I just want to be sure, before you leave." Liz accepted his explanation.

By 10:00 a.m. Monday morning, Etta and El were in her room. She was just finished bathing, diapering and feeding both boys, who were now just on breast milk. She was so happy. When the two came in, Liz was quite proud of all she accomplished on her own. They were both very impressed.

Liz said, "Robert won't let us go home until tomorrow. He wants to run some more blood and urine tests, on me. Just to make sure I have no infections, or problems."

They both pretended to be disappointed, but her mom told her, "The doctor knows best, dear."

Joe had been out at the work site all day Friday and things were going well. He was on his own. He stopped by Roy Pakos' office and told him they would be putting a small shack on the property. It would be for himself and the heads of each section of the project. Above ground, and below ground; and Roy could find Joe there most of the time when he was on site. Roy was pleased to see him Friday and asked how his wife and boys were. Joe told him he should be bringing them home on the next Tuesday, if all goes well.

Since the Pakos job was not a rush, Joe and the men did not work overtime. The crews worked from 7:30 a.m. until 5:30 p.m. Work was progressing well on top and a little slower underground. Joe decided that, if Roy agreed, he'd bring in a second digger for the tunnels. He said that would be fine, that way top and bottom should be finished around the same time. Joe also checked with George Benson, since he was the underground expert. He agreed that it was safe and expedient.

Joe had no problems on the job site with the foremen of each division. There were a couple of men on the job who just grunted when Joe was walking around inspecting the work, but for the most part the job was be incident free, racially speaking.

He kept his personal life guarded around the men on the job, with the exception of the news that he just becoming a dad of twins. He thought it was best this way. He didn't want to invite hostility. Joe was really happy on his job site. After the major pranks pulled by Ray on the Monday, Joe was very cautious around the office, when Ray was in.

He drove to the office on Monday, in his new baby blue. Ray was already in the office, so Joe was glad that he wouldn't see the truck right away. He was wrong. Ray was watching out the window. Just then George Benson drove in. Joe thought he saw George's car down the street. As it turned out, he did. George wanted Joe to drive in first then drive in right behind him. George wanted to see what Ray would do.

As soon as Ray saw Joe get out of the truck, he left the window. Joe went in the office and Ray started. Ray said, "Hey, Joe has a vehicle again. Looks like you did a great job, cleaning your shit!" Just then, George came in the office and Ray shut up.

George said "Good morning, gentlemen. Are we ready to start our meeting? I have a lot to do, today."

Everyone gathered their paper work and headed into the board room, with their coffee. George asked, "Ray, what am I going to find in the sugar bowl, or the milk, this morning?"

Ray turned around and went to the sugar bowl and emptied it. It was salt. Ray turned red. It hadn't occurred to him, that George might get a cup of coffee, before Joe. George planned it that way. He wanted to try and help Joe, as much as he could, without playing favorites.

They all sat down and the meeting began. The only project in trouble was the bridge Ray was working on. Over the weekend, the site was vandalized. Joe hated to see that happen, but he was really glad it happened to Ray. He hoped God would forgive him, later. Joe had been taking photos of his job, and they were developed over the weekend. Everyone was impressed with the progress at which his job was progressing: Everyone except Ray. Bubba was still his side-kick.

Whatever Ray thought, or did, Bubba acted the same. He was becoming more, Ray's lackey and this made Ray feel like he had lots of power. George was keeping an eye on Bubba, too.

After the meeting, George had to head out to Ray's site, so that he could assess the project damage, for himself. Joe was going out to his own site, after lunch. He had a few jobs to do in the office. All morning, he thought about Liz and the boys. His family was coming home from the hospital tomorrow. He was so excited. At the same time, he was terrified. He would now be a full-time dad.

Chapter 12

Finally Home Together

T HE SUN SHONE BRIGHTLY ON Tuesday March 4, 1947, as Liz rose, fed, changed and bathed the boys. As she bathed them, her mind wandered. She thought of the second family cradle and rocking-horse. She wondered how they were going to get it there. She thought, maybe when her mom goes home to Chatham, she could send it down the same way she sent her hand-bell down, when she became certified to teach in Mississippi. She wondered if the items were too large to ship. Then she remembered the train. Trains carried tons of cargo from place to place. That's what she'd do when she gets home today. She'd talk to her mom about arranging it.

She bathed the boys, one at a time, because not even 'Wonder Woman' could bathe both at the same time. She smiled as she thought about it. Fortunately, while she was bathing James, John was just lying in his bassinet and he seemed to be watching her. But he was content to wait his turn. She smiled at him and made funny faces.

She thought about going home and she was excited. She knew Etta and her mom would have the house positively spotless. She wasn't looking forward to coming home without Joe there. He had to work all day and she wished that he could have been at the house, when she and the boys arrive. It's not that she didn't have help, she just wanted daddy to be there, too. Oh well, she thought, grandma and Miss Etta will do nicely. Daddy would be home at supper time and to tuck them in...and be awakened for every feeding through the night! She giggled a bit.

Liz couldn't wait to sleep in the same bed as her husband, again. She missed not lying next to him, the past week. No one said much, but she assumed her mom was comfortable in their guest room. There was so much going through her mind, she couldn't keep up with it.

She was glad Joe had replaced his truck, but it was forced, due to the cruelty of a class-A jerk, as Joe called him, sometimes. She worried about what else he'd had to endure, since they moved to Mississippi. Joe never told his wife much, so; she figured he was only dealing with minor pranks and name calling.

She finished drying James and dressing him in his 'going home outfit', which grandma made for him. She took John's blanket off and started to bathe him. The water had cooled down, so she just added some warm water. The nurse came in to see if she needed help and Liz told her, she was doing fine. She asked, "Do the boys have to go back to the nursery after I'm done, or can they stay here until we go home?"

The nurse said, "I 'spect it be okay ta' leave 'dem, here. I'll ask 'da doctor, when he comes in." Liz thanked her as she left the room, to continue her work. James started nodding off right away when she laid him down. She hoped John would, too. She needed a rest. At home, she knew she would have help, but she would still be a hands-on mom. She would be sure to give grandma extra time with them, because she lived so far away and would go back home to Chatham someday, soon.

She finished bathing and dressing John in his outfit and laid him down. He just looked around for a bit and then he started to yawn. Liz saw him. It was the cutest thing she'd ever seen, in her life. She pulled his bassinet over to the bed. She lay down and just kept watching him. It was about every forty-five seconds to a minute, he would yawn again. She kept giggling quietly, as she watched. It was only about five minutes and he was asleep. She nodded off, too.

She wasn't sure how long she was out, but Robert came in and gently called her name, since the boys were there sleeping, too. She opened her eyes and saw him. She smiled. He nodded and she knew it. She was going home with both boys, today.

She sat up and he sat on the bed beside her. He said "The boys are still small, but big enough to go home. James' eating is greatly improved. He has no trouble latching on now, from what I've observed. It just took him several days of practice. Are they both eating at the same time now?"

Liz said, "Just over the last forty-eight hours, James sleeps as long as John does. John eats faster and finishes sooner. That's where Etta and mom's help will come in handy."

Robert looked at her and said, "Liz, would it be okay if I dropped around at the house occasionally? I'd like to keep an eye on the boys and you, too. Your blood and urine tests came back fine and you should have no problems. There are no infections."

Liz said, "Checking up on the kids and me; yeah right." He smiled and was flushed. "It wouldn't have anything to do with a beautiful Scottish Lassie, would it?"

He grinned and said, "I can't help it. She is such a wonderful lady. I'd like to get to know her better. Are you okay with that?"

She replied, "Robert, you are welcome to drop by our house at any time you like. You're one of the family now." He gave her a kiss on the cheek and told her that he had already filled out the discharge papers and she could leave any time her ride arrived, but she'd have to sign papers when she was leaving, too. She was excited. She said, "Do you think I could have a bath before I go home: Could I take them back to the nursery long enough to bathe?" He said that it was not a problem she could take them back any time. He even volunteered to take one, while she took the other.

Liz didn't want to be in the bath too long. She didn't know what time her mom and Etta were coming to pick her up. She was only about fifteen, or twenty minutes and she was back at the nursery to bring the boys back to her room. A nurse helped her and when they were in her room she noticed that Liz was all packed and ready to go. Liz lay down, again. She looked at her watch and it was only nine-fifteen. She hoped they would be there soon to get her. She dozed off.

Around ten o'clock, there was a little sound in the room. She thought to herself, I'm not going to get up, unless they start to cry. Suddenly, she felt someone sit on the bed and kiss her on the cheek. When she opened her eyes Joe was sitting on her bed with both boys in his arms.

She sprung up in bed and was so thrilled to see this beautiful sight. She said, "Okay daddy, how did you do that without them making a sound?" He kissed her on the lips and she was so happy. Etta and Eleanor came out from around the curtain and Liz said, "I see, the troops are here to help." All of a sudden, it occurred to her, "Joe, aren't you supposed to be at work?"

He said, "George told me to come to the hospital, take you home and I could just go to the job site after you get settled. He'll sign me out of the office for the whole day. As far as anyone else knows in the office I'm at my job site all day."

The boys started to wake up and cry at the same time. Liz said, "How about we get them home as soon as possible and I'll feed them there?"

Just then Robert walked in and saw that she was ready to go. He had seen Joe and the ladies come in. He brought the papers for her to sign. He said, "Hello everyone. We're going to miss you all around here. Anyway Liz, if you can sign your release papers, you and the boys can go home." She took the papers and his pen and signed.

Robert handed her a birth certificate for John. It read February 24, 1947. It was officially recorded that John had a home birth, at 7:45 p.m. The time Liz and Joe actually arrived home that evening, after the boys' birth and the fiasco at the other hospital! That meant that he was legally born the same day as his brother. The white hospital would never admit to a "Nigger" baby being born in their building. Robert smiled at her, when he gave it to her. Liz gave him a hug, with a tear in her eye and she gave him a big kiss on the cheek.

Liz said, "Robert, I think we're having supper around six, if you'd like to join us this evening."

He grinned and said, "Well, I am on call, but I'd love to. I'll be there. I'll have to leave your phone number with the hospital, so they can reach me in an emergency and my answering service, too."

Joe said, "Of course, that's not a problem. We'll see you tonight."

Liz wanted to ride with Joe and James, in the new truck. She let Etta take John with her and her mom. They all arrived at the same time and Liz was so happy to be home.

By now, both boys were wailing and hungry. Liz just went in to the house and did not go upstairs. She sat in the living room and started to feed James. John stopped crying for a few moments, so El asked if she wanted John's nappy changed. Liz told her yes and she'd feed him as soon as he fussed, again.

Joe went out of the room for a moment and Liz heard something rolling down the hall. He came around the corner and he had a kind of dresser on wheels and on top, it had a large changing table. In the drawers were change pads, burp cloths, powder, diapers, rubber pants, and everything they used in the hospital. There were also a few sleepers and undershirts. Liz was flabbergasted. She was so surprised.

Joe said, "I thought you could use some help down here to make life simpler."

Liz said, "Honey, where did you ever get this?"

Joe smiled, and said, "George Benson made it for you. He thought it might help make life a little easier on you and Etta, instead of you both going up and down the stairs all day." The look on Liz's face was unmistakable. She'd just found another reason to care for and adopt this man into their family. Liz loved his gift and his carpentry work.

She said, "Honey, please tell him thank you for me and tell him to drop around any time."

Joe said, "Well since Robert is coming for supper tonight, how about George coming, too. They have become good friends over the last week, or so. What do you think?"

Liz asked Etta, "Would it be too much to ask you to make supper for one more person tonight?" Etta smiled and told her that it would be a pleasure. Eleanor was smiling, too.

Joe noticed that James was done eating and sound asleep. He said, "Do you want me to change him?" Liz said, rather than disturb him; they'd just get it, next time he wakes up. She fed John, while Joe held James. When John was full and asleep, Joe said, "Okay honey, let's take our sons upstairs and put them to bed."

Eleanor guided Liz up, while Joe carried James. He held Liz's arm, while she carried John. They came to the top of the stairs. John pointed Liz toward the original nursery they readied. He turned on the light and it was just as she left it before they were born. Liz looked around the room and there were smiles on Joe, Eleanor and Etta.

She said, quietly, "Alright you three, what's up?" Joe led her by the hand and they went into the spare bedroom and he turned on the light. She just stood in awe and amazement. She was looking at a carbon copy of the other nursery. She said, "Oh my God, this is so wonderful." No one spoke; they just waited for her to notice. As she stared, it occurred to her, she was looking at the second cradle and rocking horse from Chatham.

Etta stepped over to Liz and took John from her and she said, "Now you git yo'sef over 'dere an' give yo' mama a great big hug: She done carted 'dese all 'da way from Chatham wit' her."

Liz started to cry, "Oh mom, you did that for us? How can we ever thank you?" She hugged her mom and just held on to her for a moment whispering thank you, in her ear. Joe walked over to them and hugged El, thanking her again.

Joe said, "Okay mama, which of our boys gets which room? I know you might want James in our room for a while, or maybe both, but you get to decide who gets what room."

Liz picked the first nursery for James, since it was the closest to their room. She took John and laid him in the cradle in the room they were standing, in. It would be John's room. Then she took James and laid him down in his room and she took Joe's hand, and his mom's and they headed downstairs. Eleanor grabbed Etta's hand and led her down, too.

When they went downstairs, they were still smiling at Liz. She couldn't imagine there would be any other surprises for her. She couldn't be more wrong. Eleanor quietly slipped out of the house. Liz hadn't paid attention to her. Joe said, "Honey, come outside for a minute." He took her by the hand, placed his hands over her eyes, and stood her on the driveway. She could hear a car coming towards her, and stop. He uncovered her eyes and Eleanor got out of a car. He continued, "Honey, this is your new car. I thought this would make life a little easier for you, too."

El handed her the keys, hugged her and said, "Dear, it drives beautifully. You're going to love it!" Liz threw her arms around Joe and kissed him. She was speechless.

Joe told her, "Honey, I'm really sorry I can't stay, but, I really have to get to the site."

She hugged him again, kissed him and whispered a playful, sexy, "Thank-you," in his ear, and gave it a nibble. He grinned and said goodbye to them. He jumped in his truck and headed out to work. Liz couldn't have had a better homecoming.

George was in the shack on the site. He was talking with the digger operator and Roy Pakos. Joe said, "Hi guys, we got a problem?"

George said, "Well Joe, it looks like I fucked up, on this one! When I did the geological study! I pulled the original geological study, from when they built the buildings, here. It was either faked, or not done properly. This is much rockier ground, than what I saw on the study. We were just deciding what to do about it."

Joe felt so bad for George and for being late. He said, "I am so sorry gentlemen, I didn't mean to be this late."

Roy said, "Don't worry about it. I think taking your wife and son's home from the hospital is a little more important than playing in the dirt with some rocks. I'm happy for you Joe." With a big smile, Roy extended his hand and gave Joe a friendly pat on the back and said, "Congratulations, papa."

Joe said, "Thank you Mr. Pakos, I appreciate you understanding."

George said, "Okay, let's sit down now and discuss our options." Then there was a knock on the shack door. It was the second digger operator. He ran into rocks in the section he was digging in, too.

George said, "Roy, I can't believe I fucked up, this bad. This is totally my fault. I have never made such a stupid mistake before and relied on a previous study. They said the ground wasn't this rocky and I took the report as truth. I should have done my own, more thoroughly. I know better!" He rested his head in his hands, in shame.

Joe said, "Well let's not sit here, let's get out there, assess and regroup: Alright Roy?"

Roy nodded, "Yeah, let's take a look." They both patted George on the back and they all went out to the tunnels. George had all the original reports on the ground from years earlier with him and George cut a few corners, by following the previous study. He'd never done that on a job, in his life.

Quietly, Joe said to George, "Look, it happened and we can't change it. Let's just fix it. By the way, you're wanted for supper tonight. How does that sound?"

George said, "Thanks Joe. Let's fix up my mistake and try and hold our reputations intact, first!" He paused and then looked at Joe, "Shit... we can't let Ray get word of this fuckin' mess!" Joe agreed.

George and Joe looked at the geological reports from years ago and from what he could see, it was incomplete, or untrue. George asked if there were problems building the buildings. Roy told him yes, but he was told all the rocks were hauled away, which is what he paid for.

Joe said, "There's another possibility, George! Roy, do you know if they dug up rock and instead of actually hauling them away, like they were contracted to do, they dumped them in the outer perimeter, right where we are digging now and hauled away good soil and gravel for themselves?"

George looked at Joe and said, "Those sons of bitches. Let's get out there and check it out."

Roy said, "Come to think of it, there was a lot of hauling done, at night. I didn't pay extra they just talked about doubling up on jobs and needed to do some of it, at night. I should have suspected something was wrong!"

After careful assessment of the rocks, it was evident that they were still a bit loose, even after several years of settling. Those rocks hadn't been in their current locations for millions of years, as they should have been. They were dug up and dumped there, within the last couple of decades. George was somewhat relieved.

George said, "Okay we know what we're looking at, let's go sit and discuss what Roy wants us to do next. You guys on the diggers, I want you in on this, too."

They went back to the shack and all sat down. Roy's new secretary had brought out a tray of coffee and donuts. They were ready for a coffee by now; although George could have used something much stronger... he was so upset with himself!

George said, "Roy, whatever other costs incurred on the tunnels, I will cover. Now, first option; do you want to cancel the tunnels and just rely on your foot bridges? Or, to keep on schedule, we get two more diggers here, I'll pay and we haul it away properly, like it was supposed to when the buildings were built. If you can give Joe and me a minute, we can figure an estimate on time to make sure it will be ready on the date promised. Another option is to start tunnels, in a slightly different spot, hoping we won't run into the same mess."

Roy said, "Well, run your figures with Joe and I want you to run expense, too. I'm not letting you pay for it all. If I decide to go ahead, we'll split the cost. This isn't your mistake, George. I had no idea they falsified the reports. I had my secretary pull the original contract. I paid plenty for haulage. They fucked me over, too." He showed George the contract and he was right. He angrily continued, "The Company pocketed that money and they're no longer in business, either. It doesn't surprise me, the bastards. I paid for their fuckin' retirement!"

Joe started to get his papers out of his briefcase to start figuring. George said, "Gentlemen, if you'll excuse us, Roy, can we use your office?"

Roy said, "Yes, I was just about to suggest that. I have an adding machine in there you can use." He looked to the equipment operators and said, "You fellas just hang around and we'll let you know what we're doing in a little bit. Don't worry, you're both still on the clock." They thanked Roy and they left the shack and lit up their smokes and waited. The three men went in to Roy's office. He continued, "Now, if you gentlemen don't mind, I'll just excuse myself; I have other things to attend to. I'll be back."

George and Joe worked out the figures and when Roy came back to his office, he was pleasantly surprised. Even with adding the two extra diggers and haulage trucks, it wasn't as much as he thought it would be. Roy was quite prepared to pay for it and certainly could afford it.

George said, "Roy, you're not going to pay for haulage again. I am, so your cost is low. You pay for the two diggers and I'll pay for four trucks, haulage and no arguing about the haulage, I'll get it. Do you want to go ahead?"

Roy said, "Yes, men we have a deal. Let's get on with it. Now that Joe sold me on the idea of bridges AND tunnels, that's what I want! Let's do it." They shook hands.

Joe took the sheets he used for figuring and offered it to Roy saying, "Of course, we will both sign and date these figures. The cost will NOT change for you, Mr. Pakos. If you'd like to have your secretary witness our signatures, we can call it a deal." Roy told them it wasn't necessary, but George agreed and told him to please do it.

Joe and Roy walked out to talk to the diggers, Bobby and Raife and told them to go ahead, right where they stopped and that they were going to try and have the dump trucks in later that day, or the next to start hauling. They were also getting two more diggers to join them.

While work started on the tunnels again, George called the contracting company to hire the rest of the crew and machinery they would need on the project. They required two more diggers, and four dump truck: One for each digger. He told them to draw up new contracts for them and he'd be in to pick them up within forty-eight hours.

When George went out to join the others, he let them know there were going to be two dump trucks starting after lunch and two more diggers were coming. And, starting the next day, there would be a total of four diggers and four dump trucks. Everyone was pleased. Raife and

Bobby were busy digging rocks and just kept going, all afternoon. The one thing everyone noticed, as before, these rocks came out with ease. They were definitely not in their 'natural' places. They were uprooted and moved to their present location: Probably during the dig, to build the factories.

Joe excused himself and went up to check on the bridges above, to make sure there was nothing wrong. He didn't want anything going wrong up top, if he could help it. As he went in the building, he signed in and went to the inside of the building, where they were readying to cut through the wall to the outside and make the hole for the doorway, leading to one of the bridges.

Things were looking good up top, so he went downstairs to climb the scaffold to talk to the men working on the outside of the building. The foreman was up there and told Joe everything was fine. They had encountered no problems and he asked Joe, if things had gotten settled in the tunnels.

Joe said, "Yeah, we're getting more diggers and trucks and we're getting it all dug out and carted away. We will try to stay within the time frame, with the extra machines on. Hearing nothing was wrong on the bridge building, Joe went back down to the tunnels. He reported to George that everything was good, up top.

At five-thirty, Joe drove in the driveway and George behind him. They went in the house and George was carrying a bag. Liz greeted him at the door, hugged him and kissed his cheek and thanked him for building the change table for her. George appreciated the kindness and affection, after the day he had. He said, "Well, lovely lady, I'm so glad you're home. Here are two more gifts for my boys." He handed her the bag he was carrying and inside were two pieces of carved and brightly painted pieces of wood. One said "James" and the other said "John". They were to place on each door of their nurseries. Joe didn't know about the name carvings and was equally surprised and touched with the gifts. Liz hugged him again as she thanked him.

Just then the doorbell rang. Eleanor quickly went to answered it, before anyone else got there and Robert was standing there holding three bouquets of flowers. One was for Liz, one for Eleanor and one for Etta. He shook George and Joe's hand saying hello and a kiss on the cheek for each lady.

The ladies were surprised and thankful for the flowers. Etta and El, took the three bouquets and put them in vases. Supper was almost ready and the boys were fed, just an hour earlier, so they were tucked in to their cradles, sound asleep. Robert went upstairs and took a peek at them both. He asked Liz how her feedings were, since she got home. She told him, "I fed them on average, every three hours, with no problems from either of them." He was happy to hear it.

Later downstairs, Liz heard one of the boys cry. She said to Joe, "There goes James. I wonder why he's awake."

Joe looked at her and said, "Now, how do you know it's James? They're upstairs and we're downstairs. How the heck can you tell?"

Liz looked at him, snapped a tea towel at his bottom, which she had in her hand and said, "A mother knows, daddy!" Everyone laughed.

Robert said, "She's right, Joe. Mothers have that inane sense which they can tell, usually right from the start, which cry comes from which child." She took Joe upstairs and she was right. James was crying. Joe shook his head, he couldn't believe it...she was actually right! As soon as James heard them in the room, he seemed to go right back to sleep.

Everyone went into the dining room and had the wonderful dinner Etta prepared, with Eleanor's help. Etta was invited to eat dinner with them and after persuasion, she did. It was a great evening. Liz went upstairs to feed the boys, but brought them downstairs' after they were fed, for everyone to see.

The phone rang at eight forty-five. It was for Robert, since he was on call; the hospital called him to an emergency. There had been a lynching and the white hospital would not take the body. The man was being brought in to Lincoln and Robert had to examine the body and declare him dead.

The family overheard the main details as Robert asked the person on the phone questions, and were shocked. Liz started to cry. She couldn't believe she was hearing this. Her first thought was to take the twins and Joe and go home to Chatham. El held her for a moment. Joe came to her and took her from El and walked in the dining room with her. She looked up into his face now and she saw fear. Or, was it a reflection of what she knew was on her own face?

She said, "Oh my Lord, Joe. What are we doing here? This place is barbaric. I don't know if I can stay. What the hell have we done, moving here? Aren't these people Christians?" He held her tighter, trying not to think about the horror, they had just overheard.

Robert said, "I'm really sorry, everyone. I had no intention of you overhearing that. If you'll excuse me, I have to get to the hospital. It was a lovely dinner and thanks for having me: Good night everyone."

Eleanor said, "I'll walk you out." Robert was pleased

As Robert was getting in his car, he said, "El, please don't let Liz get too upset. She is already going to go through post-partum depression; she doesn't need this on her mind, too."

El said, "I agree, I think, between the boys and everyone here, we can keep her busy enough."

Robert smiled at her, took her hand and tenderly kissed it, saying, "Good night, my sweet lady." Eleanor blushed, as he got in his car and drove away. She smiled and suddenly felt warm...all over her body, just from his kiss on her hand!

When she went into the house, Liz had stopped crying. The boys both wanted to be fed. George said, "Well ladies, Joe. Thanks so much for the invitation, but I should get going, too. I'll see you in the office, Joe. Good night, ladies." Joe walked him out and they talked about the tunnels a bit more. Joe reassured George that everything was going to work out fine. When he went in the house, Liz had said good night to her mom and Etta and gone upstairs to feed the boys. He went upstairs to help her, if she needed it.

Joe went into James' nursery where Liz was changing his diaper. Joe asked, "Honey, would you like me to change John?"

She said, "Sweetie that would be great, thanks." After both boys were changed, she sat on her bed and fed them, both at the same time again. She was becoming really good at it and the boys seemed to be comfortable and got enough to eat, each time.

Joe smiled as he watched her. He said, "Do you know how beautiful you are?" She gave him a smile and he kissed her. He was getting tired and said, "I think I'll go down, lock up and say good night. I'm going to get some sleep. Do you want anything from downstairs?" Liz told him she didn't.

When he came back up and got into bed, Liz said, "I'm going to the library in the next few days. I want to do research on lynching. It is such a horrible thought that we live in a country which allows it. I hope they catch the people who did it."

Joe said, "Hun, they usually don't and do you really want to fill your head with that horrible information?"

She looked at him and replied, "I want to know, so I can protect my family. I need to know, what to expect, while living here. Darlin' don't worry; I'm not going off the deep end with this. I just want to be more knowledgeable about it. You're probably right about the people not being caught. We really don't have a lot of police protection in this town, do we?"

Joe never told her much about his experience with the sheriff and his deputy. He didn't want her to worry. He had his suspicions that they knew about the lynching and they weren't about to charge anyone. After all, it was only a Nigger that was murdered.

By the end of the week, things were going well on Joe's job and the diggers and trucks were keeping up with the schedule. Those rocks were getting hauled out quickly and professionally. George had hired an excellent construction and haulage crew. So far neither Ray nor any of the other guys had found out about the trouble on the Pakos site and George and Joe decided, at their Monday meeting, it wasn't necessary to mention it. George didn't want his men to know how he blew it.

Liz was still thinking about the lynching, she couldn't forget it. She was serious about doing research on lynchings. She wanted to understand, or try and make sense of it. She called Nancy at the library and asked what books she had on the subject. She told Liz she had several and she had some legal books as well, which weren't supposed to be let out of the library, but she said she'd let Liz borrow them, if she could come and see the boys.

Nancy hadn't met Joe, or been in their house yet, in the time they'd known each other. To Liz's knowledge, she did not know they were a mixed race family. Liz decided, she'd let her come over. Nancy would have to know about her family sometime and felt Nancy wasn't the prejudice type! She told Liz she would bring the books by her house after work. Liz was thankful, she said, "Nancy would Friday be okay? We'd like you to stay for supper."

Nancy said, "Well, thank you, are you sure it would be okay. I mean, if it's no trouble for Etta."

Liz said, "It's no trouble at all and you can meet my mom, too." As Liz hung up the phone, she wondered if Minnie might have told her about their family. She thought to herself, well I think she'll be okay with it. Anyway, she was so thrilled that Nancy was taking time from her evening to bring the books to her. Nancy was not surprised at Liz's request. It was on everyone's mind that week. The recent lynching was big news and the gossip spread like wildfire!

Robert had called Liz the day after they had supper together and the next, checking up on her. He dropped by the house a couple of nights after their dinner. He looked at the boys and he said, "Well mama, I think you are doing remarkably well. How are you feeling about the boys, feeding and being home? Are you doing alright? Do you need anything, or want to talk about anything?"

Liz thought he was sweet to be so concerned. She said, "Well Robert, the boys are eating great. At least we think they're looking better every day."

Robert agreed, "You know, even after only two days home, I can see improvement and it looks like they gained a few ounces. I forgot to ask, do you have a baby scale, here?" Liz shook her head, no. Robert excused himself and went to the car. He came back into the house with a brand new top-of-the-line baby scale, with a big red bow and ribbon on it.

Eleanor watched him bring it in and give it to Liz. She was touched by the way he cared about her daughter and her family. It was a really sweet thing to do. Liz was speechless, as he said, "I bought this for both of us. I really need to keep track of their weight gains, or loss. This way, you don't have to worry about getting them dressed to come to my office. I want you to keep a chart for me, just like in the hospital." She thanked him and hugged him.

Eleanor came to him and thanked him and hugged him, too. She was really beginning to like Robert a lot. She thought of him in a different way, than she thought of anyone else. Before, or since, her George died. He asked her if he could take her for a drive. She told him, she'd love to. When she hugged him, she felt warm all over her body, again. She was slightly surprised by her reaction. It felt sexually good to her.

He asked if she'd been around the town yet and she told him she'd seen quite a bit of it. He asked her, "El, there aren't very many places where we could go to have a coffee together. I know this is forward of me, but would you like to come to my house for coffee and a talk?"

El said, "I understand. I'd love to go to your place. I love my family so much, but getting out for a bit is nice, too." He gave her a big smile and drove to his house. She was very impressed with it. It was a gorgeous, large, three bedroom house fit for a doctor and a family. The house was located in a white neighborhood. His neighbors didn't mind him living in their neighborhood...after all he was a respected doctor, even if he was a Nigger!

He made coffee and they sat in his living room, which was very nicely decorated and kept. She said, "You must have a housekeeper, right? I've never seen a bachelor have such a clean house." She grinned as he told her he hired someone from Minnie's house, as a housekeeper. They both chuckled.

As the evening went on, she listened to how he traveled around for a bit in Canada, after graduating from McGill and eventually coming to live in the States. He found that Mississippi could use medical skills, treating people in black communities, the most.

He listened while she finally told him what his good friend had been doing since graduating. She told him everything from the farm and farm life, the golf course right down to the kids, the prostitutes and the dozen year affair with Joe's mom, the gonorrhea, the suicide of this good friend and subsequent death of Marteen. She talked till she cried and he held her, not saying a word. He just held her while she wept.

She slowly stopped crying and she felt a little better, getting it all out. She apologized to him for being a blubbering idiot; and she had never told anyone that much before and it still hurt. He pushed the hair out of her face and he kissed her on the lips. She responded. It was a beautiful kiss, which turned very passionate.

As they stopped kissing, Robert rose and he took her hand and she rose, too. He picked her up and he carried her into his bedroom. He laid her on the bed and lay down beside her. She wasn't sure what to do, she felt like she did on the night she and George tried to make love, on their wedding night. She was just as nervous now; and he could tell.

Robert asked, "If you don't want this, please let me know. I want you to be comfortable and we can go back in the living room; and if you prefer, I'll even take you home if you like."

She smiled and said, "To Chatham?" He grinned and kissed her again. She was very responsive. She let him unbutton her blouse and put his hands under her bra. She was excited and her nipples were hard. He kissed her neck and she wanted more. She started to unbutton his shirt and she caressed his hard, hair covered chest. He was becoming so aroused. He needed to adjust his trousers, because he had become so hard. She giggled at him as he opened his belt and his pants.

They quickly helped each other out of their clothes. El was still a little shy and she preferred to get under the covers fast as she could. Robert asked her one more time, "Eleanor is this what you really want? I'll stop if you say so."

She said, "Robert, I want you to make love to me, now." He smiled and he got on top of her. She was slightly tight, to get into. She hadn't been with anyone since George died. But, she was wet. He knew she really wanted him. It wasn't long before they reached their climax, together.

As he slowed down and caught his breath, she took his face in her hands and kissed him passionately. She said, "Robert that was so incredible. I never thought I could feel anything, again. You have given me something so special. You gave me back my sense of being a woman; A sexy, beautiful, happy woman. Thank you so much." She kissed him passionately, again and said, "You know Robert, you and George are the only two lovers I've ever had in my life and I never expected anyone, after George. Thank you...that was very special." She meant every word she said. Robert knew she was a sincere, loving, faithful type of woman. That's what he loved about her!

She did not want him to get off of her. She wanted to keep him inside her, so she locked her legs around his waist. She smiled and kissed him seductively, for a few moments. All of a sudden, she rolled him over and she was on top of him. He was so surprised she did this. She was tiny, but she was stronger than he realized. He grinned at her as she started moving slowly, with him still inside her.

She kept kissing him and nibbling on his ear and neck. It only took another few moments, before he was hard, again.

She noticed he was still very interested. He started growing inside her, again. She remained on top, while he let her take complete control. They both reached another climax, after a short time. As they finished and she got off of him, she lay in his arms for a little while. They didn't speak at first, they just held each other.

After several minutes she said, "I guess I have to go back soon."

He said, "I wish you didn't have to." He smiled at her as she rested her head on his chest. They both felt very satisfied and happy. He said, "Eleanor, would you ever consider moving here?" She was surprised, but she told him she had to get back to Chatham, but would be coming back to visit, often!

She asked him, "Would you ever consider visiting me in Chatham?"

He grinned and said, "How about every other weekend, or every weekend?" She was so thrilled to hear him say it. She couldn't believe that he wanted to see her, that much. He did!

As they walked into Liz and Joe's house, Etta had already retired and they found Joe and Liz sitting in old faithful, in the dark, listening to their Perry Como record, of their wedding song. They wanted to make sure El got in okay, because she didn't have a key to the house. El said, "You didn't have to wait up, dear. How is everyone?"

Liz turned on the living room light and said that they were just enjoying together time, before she had to feed the boys, again.

Robert said, "Well, I have to get some sleep, I am due for rounds early in the morning. Goodnight Joe, Liz, you call me if I am needed." They thanked him. He turned to El and said, "It was a lovely evening, I hope we can do it again sometime...soon." He kissed her on the cheek and she tried really hard not to giggle at his words. She felt naughty and it was a great feeling. She'd never felt like that before. She walked him to the door out of sight of the kids and they kissed passionately, again and said good night. He left and Eleanor excused herself to bed, without stopping, so Liz couldn't ask questions. She didn't want to talk about anything that night. She just wanted to go to sleep; wondering when would be the next time that she would be in his arms again.

Liz and Joe just looked at each other and Liz said, "Well, I think I'll have a talk with mom in the morning, about dating." They both giggled and they saw happiness to her mood. They were happy that she found someone who put such a smile on her face. They hadn't seen one since learning about her husband's infidelity a couple of years earlier.

Friday evening Nancy came for dinner. She closed the library at six and arrived about ten minutes later. She rang the doorbell and Joe answered the door. Nancy thought she had the wrong house. He held his hand out to her and said, "You must be Nancy. Hi, I'm Joe, Liz's husband." She put her hand out to shake his. She was slightly taken aback. She had no idea that he was black.

After Nancy composed herself she said, "Uh...hi yes, I'm Nancy. It's nice to meet you, Joe. I wonder if you might help me bring the books in that Liz wanted." He went to the car with her and brought them in. There were quite a few. Liz finished feeding the boys and she came downstairs to see Nancy and Joe had met and the books were there. She hugged Nancy and then introduced her to Eleanor, who had been upstairs with her and the twins. Etta, she had met before through Minnie.

Etta said that dinner was served and everyone went into the dining room to eat. As Joe said the blessing, he welcomed Nancy to their home, for which she thanked him afterward. They had a great dinner and conversation. Nancy became comfortable with the mixed-race couple and eventually, she never even noticed Joe was black. As the boys cried, right on cue, Liz asked Nancy to come upstairs with her to get them for their feeding. She was excited. She'd wanted to see the boys, but dinner and conversation would go on for some time. But, she knew they would be waking soon, so she could see them.

It hadn't occurred to Nancy, until she saw John, that they could have a black baby. But to actually see them together, a white and a black twin amazed her. Now she understood why Liz was so interested in studying and learning about lynching.

The day after Nancy brought the books over, Liz started reading. The first thing she wanted to learn more about was "Civil Rights", then more on lynching. Civil Rights are simply, "Rights that are bestowed by nations on those within their territorial boundaries." In the U.S., laws protecting civil rights are included in the Constitution, amendments, 13 and 14, which she already knew.

She remembered touching on civil rights, while growing up going to school in Chatham and teaching it. She also covered it on her Mississippi board exams. She wanted more than that. She read everything she could.

Lynching was a fairly new subject to her. The dictionary defined it as "an extrajudicial punishment, meted by a mob, defined by some codes of law as: Any act of violence inflicted by a mob upon the body of another person, which results in the death of that person".

It seemed so simplified and just matter-of-fact. She poured over the literature and learned it's origin was by Charles Lynch, a Virginia justice of the peace. He sentenced members of an abolitionist movement, before the Civil War. They were hung, because they opposed slavery.

After the war ended, southern white people regularly lynched freed blacks, who wanted to vote. Between 1868 and 1871, alone, there were over four-hundred lynching's done by the Ku Klux Klan. They wanted white supremacy.

The Ku Klux Klan and a few others used lynching as a method to control the blacks and forcing them to work on farms and plantations. By the end of the 19th century, lynching's peaked and continued into the 20th century.

After World War I, lynching's' became more frequent, again. Negroes, who served in the war, felt a sense of, maybe having new respect, because of their service for their country. It was not to be. There were riots and lynching's still. Many of the Negroes were lynched while still wearing their military uniforms, with pride. The uniforms meant nothing to the vigilantes

This sickened Liz. The whole sordid, disgusting facts she was finding out, were almost too much for her. As she researched, she found so many photographs that were published. She saw pictures of lynching's with the captors proudly taking pictures of their kill. Often, in these photographs, you could clearly see police sheriffs and officers, in the crowd. She couldn't believe it. Not only did they pose, but they actually participated in these killings. It occurred to her now that no one was ever going to be caught, or convicted of hanging the black man, that Robert attended to, at Lincoln a few days ago.

The next time Robert called, she asked him, "When a person is lynched, is it a quick death, or slow?"

He told her, "Liz, don't dwell on this. Please concentrate on your happy life and family."

Liz said, "Robert, I just want to know this, and I'll drop it, please. I need to know."

He gave a sigh and said, "Okay. If a person is lynched by dropping from a height, the chances of them breaking their neck right away, is high. This 'could' kill them instantly. It may not, but in the act of lynching, the body is left alone to die, anyway: Sometimes for days.

If the mob puts a noose around the neck of a victim, they have several men who pull the other end of the rope, usually over a tree branch. The body is lifted slowly. Death is painful and slow. The neck doesn't usually break with this method, the victim's breathing cuts off and they die of suffocation and that is all I'm going to tell you, Liz. Please, think about other things." He could hear her very softly, quietly as she could, sob at the other end of the phone.

She said, "Thank you for your honesty in helping me understand. I needed to know." As she hung up the phone, she went upstairs and cried in her room. She wondered how many times, lynching's would take place around her town, and touch her life in some way. The thought frightened her and she hoped, she prayed, she would never know any victims.

Chapter 13

Life Goes On at 2 Gilbert Street

LIZ HAD A GREAT OPPORTUNITY to go back and teach at Philadelphia Public School, almost eighteen months after the twins were born. A position came open teaching the grade one class. The teacher retired and the board called Liz first. She took the job right away without even thinking about it. They were thrilled to have her join the school permanently. She was so excited. After speaking to Vincent who was still the principal, she jumped around the house and grabbed Etta and danced with her. She couldn't be happier.

Liz was keeping up with her teaching skills while the boys were growing and she was preparing to go back to teaching school, someday. She had taught Etta to speak better English and to write, although it was still frowned upon to teach these skills to blacks. The idea was to not let them read, write, or vote. She also helped Minnie sometimes, too.

When Liz grabbed Etta, she said, "Mrs. Liz, what are you jumpin' 'bout, for? What's got hold of ya', Mrs. Liz?"

Liz said, "Oh, Miss Etta," Joe and Liz had referred to her this way, since the boys were born. They taught the boys, by example. If they wanted them to respect Etta, they had to show them their respect for her as well. She continued, "I'm going back to school. I have my grade one class. Oh my God, I'm so excited!" She swung Etta around the kitchen and the boys were awakened by her squealing. She laughed and couldn't be happier.

As she went upstairs to the nurseries, she got each boy up, changed their diapers and brought them downstairs. They laughed at their 'funny mommy'. It was an hour or so, before Joe was to get home. But could she wait? As the boys sat up at the kitchen table to have a drink of milk, she said, "Oh Etta, I didn't even consider Joe's opinion. I hope he doesn't mind." She shrugged her shoulders, saying to Etta, "Well, I guess I'll find out at supper. Oh, I really hope he doesn't mind."

After the boys had a bit to drink, they each had an Arrowroot Biscuit. It was their favorite. When they were done with their snack, Liz let them on their rocking horses. Joe had moved them down to the living room, so they could keep an eye on them, better. They liked to get going and ride the horses, rough. They had already had a few spills since they first learned to ride them. James pulled John off his horse one day and it required Dr. Robert to put three stitches on his forehead, just below the hairline.

They were little trouble makers at times. Stealing each other's toys was their favorite pastime. Each one had a favorite hiding place and Liz and Etta loved to watch them play this way.

The boys were best friends right from the cradle in the early years. They were usually dressed the same, but that only lasted about eleven months. From the time they could start walking around; one would get wet or dirty, when the other stayed clean. Liz was not going to change both outfits, when one was still clean. She leaned on practicality after that.

When Joe got home that evening, she met him at the door and put her arms around him and kissed him. He smiled his sexiest smile, pretended he was going to kiss her again but instead he said, "Okay love, what have you done now?"

Liz slapped him on the shoulder, saying, "You brat, just for that I won't tell you until after supper."

He said, "Alright, I'll wash up. Is supper ready?" He ran up the stairs to the bathroom and when he came down, he went into the dining room where their sons were already in their high chairs. When they both saw him, they raised their arms to him and they said in unison, "DADA!"

Joe picked each one out of their chairs and held them together, giving them each a kiss and said, "Now, this is what it's all for: Right, love?" As he said this, he walked to Liz and while still holding the boys, he gave her a kiss too. She kissed him back and the boys, too. They were very cuddly, affectionate boys.

He asked, "Did they eat, yet?"

Liz said, "Nope, we thought we'd let you help feed tonight."

He smiled and said, "Alright guys, who gets daddy tonight?" Both boys started laughing and wiggling around in his arms. He had to put them in their chairs again. While Etta brought the meal to the table, Liz brought the boy's food, she and Etta were canning, that day. Liz loved canning regular foods and baby food. She learned this from her mom, grandmother, Dora and great-grandmother, Diana.

She loved to share her canning, too. She decorated her jars and gave them out as gifts to her neighbors and friends. She still believed in and lived by, 'Love Thy Neighbor', just as she had been taught by her family and her church. This was her little way of telling those around her that she cared about them. It also made her feel good to share the fruits of her labor.

This night, daddy helped feed James and mommy helped feed John. They were quite happy feeding the boys, as they 'tried' to eat themselves. It sometimes made for a long dinner time but, they wouldn't have it any other way. They loved their family.

As they ate dinner, Liz told Joe about the phone call from Vincent Kirkland. He was returned to the Neshoba School Board at election time, Nancy too and he was still the principal of Philadelphia Public School. It was the call she was waiting for and she told Joe she really wanted to do it. It was her favorite grade: The grade one class. She adored teaching the six year olds. Joe knew this. He could see she really wanted to do this. He said, in between bites of his steak and feeding sweet potato to James, "So, let me guess. You told him you wanted to take the job: Right?"

Liz looked apprehensive for a second, but smiled and said "You're darn tootin' I did." He laughed, as James was tugging on his shirt to feed him more. "Do you mind that I want to go back to work, dear?"

Joe got up and went over to his wife, kissed her and said, "Congratulations honey." But he looked towards Etta and continued, "What about Miss Etta, does she want the full time responsibility of looking after the boys until they are ready for school?"

Liz looked at Etta and said, "Oh my Lord I'm so sorry, Etta. I didn't even consider your feelings."

Etta said, "Mr. Joe, Mrs. Liz, there's nothin' I would rather do. I'm proud and happy to be watchin' our boys all the time, when you go to work." Liz was relieved with her answer and got up and hugged Etta, thanking her. It was settled. Liz was ready to leave the nest behind and go back to work.

The first day she went to school, Liz cried; leaving her twins behind. When she got to the school, she called home right away; and everything, of course, was fine. As she went in to the staff room, she remembered everyone's names. They were all so happy to have her back at their school. They remembered how sweet and kind she was, so likeable.

There had been no other changes with the staff. The only difference now was the grade one teacher was retired; and Liz was the new, permanent grade one teacher. The other upcoming change in staff would be for the grade three's. Mrs. Emms was pregnant, again. If the grade one teacher hadn't retired yet, they were going to ask Liz to come and take over for Mrs. Emms' maternity leave, again. This reminded the staff, that when Liz was there the last time, she was pregnant, too. They all wanted to see pictures of her boys. When she had the boys, she did ask Nancy; from the library, to inform them at the school, that she had twin boys. Someone asked her if they were identical twins.

Liz said, "Well, I'll let you be the judge." When Liz took the pictures out to show them around, everyone fell silent. There were a couple of quiet gasps, but no one said anything. No one there knew her husband was black. Not even Vince Kirkland had met him; and Nancy felt no need to gossip about Liz's family.

Liz showed everyone a family picture and said, "As you can see, they're identical, except James takes after me; and John takes after his daddy." Just then, the bell rang and everyone was relieved. They all went off to their classrooms and Liz did, too. Everyone quietly congratulated her and welcomed her back to working there, with them.

At the first recess, the other staff was quiet, but still spoke to her, asking how her morning was going, and such. She excitedly told them it was a great morning, so far and it was so wonderful to be teaching again.

Vincent sent a note to her classroom, for her to come to his office before she goes for her lunch. She giggled at the thought, she was being called to the principal's office; she must have been a bad girl. It made her smile. When she went in to his office, Vincent pulled a chair out for her to sit down. He said, "Mrs. Allen..."

She interrupted right away, "Vincent, do we have to be this formal? You have always have called me Liz."

He said, "Of course not, Liz. I don't mean to sound so much like a principal, but as a friend. Now, your colleagues and I are respectful and we're so happy to have you here, but we could have a potentially serious problem." She started to get that sickening feeling that she was losing her job, already. She was only there for a few hours, so far.

Vincent continued, "Liz, we did not realize you had a mixed-race marriage. As I said, we here are your friends and we accept that your husband and one baby are black. But, the problem lies in the parents of your students. If they were to find out they could cause a big problem. It, unfortunately could lead to your dismissal, because the parents don't want you to teach their children. I really hope you understand that I and my staff do NOT have a problem with it. We're still your friends and colleagues and we respect you, greatly."

Liz said, "I guess it's the same old racist BULLSHIT! Isn't it Vincent?"

Vincent said, "Liz, we want you to stay. What I am trying to say is please, for your own good, don't let any students know and I'm sure you can be here for many years. We want you here, teaching. We have nothing against you at all: Nor your husband, or son. It just took us off guard, that's all...and we want to protect you and your position, here. The other thing I have to make you aware of is, your black son will never be allowed to attend this school, ever. It's the law, here. I'm sorry Liz, I don't make 'em; I just have to enforce 'em."

Liz stood up and said, "Thank you for the advice, Mr. Kirkland, sir. I'll always keep it in mind, as long as I am allowed to be employed here." She left the office, went to her classroom and closed the door. She ate what she could of her lunch and then she threw up and cried. She didn't go back to the staff room at all the rest of the day and at three-thirty, she drove home without going into the staff room, or seeing anyone else.

That night at home, she was preoccupied and she wasn't herself. Etta was upset to see her so unhappy. This was supposed to be a glorious, happy, fun, first day at school. It was anything but that.

When Joe came home, he found his wife, unhappy and she wasn't herself. She tried to be bubbly, but she couldn't. It was much too hard to put a smile on, this time. She didn't want to tell Joe what was upsetting her, she wasn't ready. Joe knew it had to be something racial. That was the only subject that upset her, this much. He knew inadvertently, it was his fault. He was a Negro. She blamed it on ignorance and hatred.

After a quiet supper, she took the boys upstairs to bathe them. After she was done, she called to Joe, "Daddy, can you read the story, tonight?"

He called back to her, "Yeah honey, I'll be up in a minute. She had them both in their new cowboy pajamas that their grandma had sent and she took them into her and Joe's bed. They loved being in mommy and daddy's big bed. They loved to jump on it. They would often fall down, laughing. Joe met them there and he took the family bible off the shelf and turned to the story of Noah and the Ark. They were too young to understand it, but daddy always made the animal sounds. The boys loved it when he did this.

They would all usually, as a family, end up laughing hysterically about Joe's sounds. He wanted to read this story, not just for the boys, but to hopefully make Liz smile and laugh and maybe confide what was wrong.

After the story, the boys were put in their cribs and they quickly fell asleep. Liz didn't want to talk at all. She couldn't help it, she was still very hurt.

After Etta went to bed, Joe went to Liz and took her face in his hands and kissed her tenderly on the lips. She started to cry, uncontrollably. All she could say was, "I want to go home!" Joe sat in old faithful and sat her on his lap. He just held her and let her cry.

He asked, "When do you want to leave?" He was quite serious.

All she could say, through her sobbing and tears was, "Yesterday!" She didn't want to tell Joe what was upsetting her. She didn't want him to hurt, like she was.

He said, "Baby, I'll take you anywhere you want, any time, but will that take away, or solve the problem? I don't think it will." He wiped away a few of her tears, tenderly took her face in his hands again, looked her in the eyes, smiled and said, "Honey, I've never asked you this before...... but.....did you ever notice that I'm black?"

Her tears turned into hysterical laughter. It was a huge, knee slapping, belly laugh, which she was having a hard time recovering from. As a matter of fact, she was laughing so much, Joe couldn't help it and he was at a full laugh, too. It lasted so long, her muscles hurt.

When they finally stopped laughing and went to bed, she said, "I can't be honest and tell my grade one class, my husband is black and that I have a black son. The children may tell their parents, and I'd be fired. I'd never be allowed to teach in a white school, in Mississippi. Mr. Kirkland and the other teachers at my school can handle it, but I can't let any children know.

Honey, why does God make black and white people, anyway? Why can't people accept others who are different? Mr. Kirkland also told me that John could never attend our school, with his brother, he has to go to a 'black' school, when he's ready, IF there is one running at that time."

She lay beside him and he held her for some time. She became aroused and she started to kiss him, forgetting her troubles. His chest was sore, from the Sickle Cell Disease tonight, but didn't let on. He even hid the shortness of breath, he was experiencing.

As Liz began to fondle Joe, his penis became very erect and he wanted inside of her. She was becoming very excited and took charge. She got on top of him and started kissing him. She slowly made a trail of kisses down his chest, right down to his penis. He was so hard and he wanted her so badly.

After teasing him with her mouth and tongue for a while, she slowly climbed on top of him, straddling him, until he was fully inside her. He was so large this evening and filled her more than he had in some time. It was feeling so incredible to Joe, but he knew he was going to suffer, afterward. His chest was becoming very sore, his breathing was labored and he knew he was going to have an erection afterward that may last hours, but it was worth it tonight. Even if the priapism did bother him for hours later, she was giving such pleasure to him, as well as herself. He didn't want to stop. Sex with Liz was always great, but tonight was better than he'd remembered, in a long time! He wanted to enjoy every second of it and her!

After she was done and got off of him, she lay in his arms and fell asleep, quickly. He suffered for several hours, but it was worth it. He held her for a while, as his chest pain slowly subsided and he eventually got out of bed and went to the living room, until his painful erection went down. He was so annoyed on nights like this, when the sickle cells restricted the blood flow and cause the priapism of the penis. It took three hours tonight, before he was comfortable enough to sleep. It had certainly hurt him, but he smiled, thinking how wonderful it was making love to his beautiful wife, tonight!

When Liz went back to school, she certainly couldn't deny that she was living in a racist society and there was nothing she could do about it. She hoped nothing bad would befall her family because of it, but they were staying in Mississippi, anyway. She was still very accepted at school, by the other staff. Vince was right. None of them had any problem with her, or her black husband and child. She was happy, once again.

By 1950 the twins were healthy, happy three year old boys who could always be seen spending their time together. Whether it was eating, playing, bathing, or whatever, they were always together. It was very rare to see one, without the other; outdoors, or indoors.

When the Allen's moved in, the neighbors did not like having a black man on the block. They learned to tolerate it, because Joe never bothered anyone. He would often offer help to neighbors, when they were doing things, like cutting grass, gardening, or fixing a car, but no one ever took him up on his offers. They eventually learned to live with him being there.

When neighbors first found out about the multi-racial family, they were in an uproar. The neighbors tried to get them moved off the block. Neighbors went to Alvin Diamont and insisted that he kick them out of the house. They were not wanted. The Diamont's said they could not, because the Allen's had a civil right to live there. Alvin would not make them move, because they never caused a fuss, they paid their rent and they were good tenants.

But, by this time, Joe had bought the house from Alvin and Agnes, when Alvin had a small heart attack. He told Liz and Joe, that no one was to know this. It was for their safety. If people thought that the Diamont's still owned the house, there was less of a chance that they would be bothered. He knew, someone could be convicted for destruction of property, to a white man's house, but not to a black man's house. It made sense and that's the way they left things.

Agnes came over to the house once in a while to visit and make it look like she was collecting rent, but Alvin couldn't get there, until he was better. When he eventually visited the Allen's, he thought they had the cutest twins he had ever seen. But the decision they made to let people think it was still the Diamont's house, was the best way for Joe to keep his family safe. The neighbors never knew, for the longest time.

Agnes and Alvin still came over about once a month to have supper and play bridge. Joe and Liz really enjoyed it, when they came to visit. They got to know Etta and liked her very much. Alvin particularly liked her for her cooking and since she always shared her recipes with Mrs. Diamont, Alvin was grateful.

About two weeks after Eleanor and Robert started their relationship, after the twins had come home from the hospital, she had to go back to Chatham. Liz and Joe were so happy for them, for finding each other and falling in love. Liz didn't think her mom would ever love again, after her dad. Robert and Eleanor decided they didn't need to marry. They were frequent visitors to each other's home. About two weekends a month Robert flew to Detroit, where El or one of the boys picked him up and took him back to the farm.

Right from the first visit, Abe and Simon liked Robert. It was nice to have a doctor there, again. No one objected to his having a relationship with their mother. They were quite happy for her. She was smiling and happy all the time now. Eleanor also flew to Mississippi about once a month. She could see the twins and how they were growing so big and happy.

Sometimes when El went to Mississippi, one of the Liz's brothers, or their wives flew with her to visit and it was the same as Robert going to Chatham. Liz would pack up the boys for a weekend and go with him. She usually planned for these trips when Joe had to work over a weekend on a project, for the most part, but, Joe went with them occasionally.

Liz's Aunt Mary and Uncle Patrick had passed on by then and their boys had taken control over the manual operations on the farm and the golf course. Both businesses were thriving still. El got Robert to take up golfing right from the first warm spring weekend he visited her. He could see how much she loved to play and it was an important pastime for the McDonald's and for the Allen's, when time permitted. Liz would take her boys on the course with her. Although there was a no children clause, under the age of thirteen; people knew they were her boys and were tolerant. After all, they owned the course; and the boys were taught early to never get in the way.

Robert had a project in mind. Although there was still the old 'children's clubs' in the attic; which had been cut down, decades ago, they had become very old and worn out. He thought, maybe when the twins were big enough, he could cut down a golf club, or two, for each of the boys and maybe use hockey stick tape at the end to make a small hand grip for them. He was still quite taken with Liz's twins. He looked after them well, over the last few years. They were growing normally and healthy. He would often think back to how tiny James was after he was born. He laughed sometimes when he would see them because James now was bigger than John, by over an inch in height and he was five pounds heavier.

Liz asked her mom one day while she was home in Chatham, for a visit, "Mom, are you and Robert ever going to marry?"

El looked at her and asked, "What made you ask that, dear."

Liz said, "I don't know. You're such a cute couple and, well, why don't you get married?"

El sat down with her daughter and placed coffee on the table, which Caroline always had on. They still always had tea ready, too. It was always ready for family and farmhands, which they had many of, by this time to help with the daily running of the potato farm...like the old days. El said, "Honey, he's not ready to pick up and move here and I'm not ready to pick up and move there. There has to be McDonald's running the farm and I'm responsible for that. The golf course could be sold off, if the family wanted, but it's a money maker and I think we love it too much, to sell it."

El started to laugh. Liz gave her a quizzical look and her mother said, "Remember Christmas of '44: The look on your face about the encyclopaedias; and then the golf clubs. I never saw you so pissed off before, when Joe didn't come back after lunch. We all knew the plan was to drive you crazy and I'll hand it to Joe, his plan worked like a charm."

Liz laughed and said, "Well, I apologized for what I thought of him and his gift, when I needed to study to pass the exams and receive my teaching license to teach in Mississippi. Yep, he made me wear egg on my face for a while, that day." She and her mom laughed.

Then the door opened and Joe and Robert came in from golfing. They had done eighteen holes and were coming in for a late lunch. Joe asked, "What's the joke?"

Liz said, "Mom and I were just talking about Christmas of '44."

Joe started to laugh and he said, "C'mon Doc, let's eat and I'll tell you all about it."

Liz and El took the boys outside to the swings. Liz said "Mom, are these still the original swings that Joe's great-grandpa Jed, put up for Jacob and George Sr.?" She lifted the seats and on the bottom was the names George and Jacob. She smiled. They were the originals, about ninety-two years old.

Her mom looked at her, as they placed the boys on the swings and said, "Well we have tried to preserve them as much as possible. We still bring them in, in the winter and paint and varnish them once in a while. We put new rope on them each spring, but we always put them on the same tree, same branch. A couple of generations of your nieces and nephews have had a lot of fun on them, too."

Liz said, "I'm just glad to see them, again. Joe and I used to love being on these swings. He would push me, then stand on it over me and keep it going back and forth for what seemed to be ages. Mom, I do miss the farm. It was a wonderful life, here...still is! Mississippi is so....different. I can't really explain it. The life, the laws, business, it is so much simpler in Chatham and it will always be our home."

Whenever Liz and her family went to Chatham, they stayed in the Allen house, which they owned. Her brother's family vacated it when Liz and the family visited and they did so, permanently, when Little Mary and Patrick died in a head on car crash. Their sons, Richard and Emmett, both had houses on the farm for themselves and their families, so they didn't need it. Liz's brother moved in there with his family.

Liz felt strange sometimes in the Allen house, when Joe wasn't with her. There was a feeling about the house. She started to see the 'shadows' in the master bedroom. She didn't want to tell her mother, or Joe, in case they wanted to commit her.

When Joe was with Liz and the kids on visits to Chatham he could have comfortably, abandoned their life in Mississippi. He made his mark with Benson and Associates, but he still loved being a structural engineer, for George Benson. He never mentioned this to Liz; he thought she would be upset, leaving her school. She loved teaching, so much.

Pakos Industries, Roy Pakos, in particular, was extremely happy with George Benson and with Joe Allen. The foot bridges and tunnels he designed were great and Joe's first solo job was completed on schedule. Joe received his bonus from George for this project.

Business was busy and Joe was, too. To the others in the office, there was a feeling that there was a friendship between George and Joe. Most didn't mind, or didn't care, except for Ray. Bubba, deep down didn't find it a problem, but he couldn't let Ray know how he felt about it. Bubba was climbing the ranks of the Klan, but was still under Ray's thumb. Ray was sure Joe was getting the primo jobs and Ray's jobs were menial and he was never his own boss, on a project. As time went by, Joe appeared to be George's 'golden boy'. Ray wouldn't stand for this, forever!

Ray Halden still played his pranks on Joe and called him names when George wasn't there, but Joe didn't let it bother him. He let Ray have his fun, just as long as it wasn't his family that suffered. Ray was not a stupid man. He found out where Joe lived and kept his house under surveillance. He knew about the Nigger housekeeper, white wife, Nigger baby and white baby. He also knew about his white mother-in-law sleeping with the Nigger doctor. Joe didn't know this.

Unlike the sheriff, Ray's file on Joe was real. Ray never slipped up and let Joe know, he knew anything. The only thing Ray had wrong was that Joe Allen owned the property and house, at 2 Gilbert Street. Not Alvin and Agnes Diamont.

While George was constantly in charge of all projects, he let Joe reign free for the most part; on his own job sites...he was that good. When Joe was assigned to a job with any other associates, only George was boss.

When people knew Benson had a black man working for him, some people balked. George always went to bat for Joe and he never lost a job. Every one of Joe's designs and jobs, were done to perfection, whether he worked alone, or in a group. It pissed Ray off so much. Ray was getting hotter under the collar, every day. Ray told Klan to leave Joe's wife, housekeeper, and kids alone. His WAR was with Joe Allen.

Joe felt he was in danger, at times. Then at other times he thought, maybe he was imagining it. He never let Liz know about anything serious. She just knew about the name calling and a few pranks and jealousies. Joe was not about to let 'pieces of shit, with bed sheets on' control his life, or try to run him out of town. Every day, when Joe went home he'd leave the office behind and his family was always there, waiting for him. That's what he concentrated on and believed in. That and God!

Ray's projects were getting sloppy and on one of the smaller ones; the client refused to pay, until Ray fixed some mistakes he made, by taking shortcuts. George was so angry, he knew he should fire Ray; but was really uneasy about possible retaliation. He couldn't risk it. He knew it would mean his business. George started spending most of his time on Ray's job sites, more than on anyone else's. He had to hold a tighter rein on him. Sometimes, all it took for Ray to behave was, for George to say, "Maybe we should let Joe help out on this one." Ray would straighten up, right away.

The first time Ray heard this, he blew up. He went in George's office and he knocked over a filing cabinet and started to yell, "DON'T YOU DARE BRING IN THAT FUCKIN' NIGGER. I CAN DO THE JOB, YOU KNOW I CAN: HOW DARE YOU THREATEN TO BRING THE NIGGER ANYWHERE NEAR ME!"

George was pissed about the filing cabinet. He just sat in his chair and let Ray spew. After Ray stopped yelling, George said, "Are you quite done acting like a spoiled child who doesn't know how to play with his playmates?" Ray just stared at him without saying a word. George continued, "Now, you son-of-a-bitch, you pick up that filing cabinet and don't you EVER come in to my office with that behavior, again. You'll find yourself in the unemployment line."

Ray tucked in his shirt, which came out of his pants, during his temper tantrum. He also straightened his tie. Next, he very calmly walked to the filing cabinet and picked it up and put it back in place. He looked at George, and said, "George, I'm sorry, I had a bad night, last night. I don't need extra help with this one. It will be done to specs, you just wait an' see. Your business ain't gonna suffer because of me. But I don't need another man on the project: Especially, Mr. Allen!"

After straightening George's office, he walked back to his desk and got his files and papers out and signed out. The other engineers he was working with were waiting to go to the job site, with him. He remained silent most of the day and no one talked to him, unless they needed to ask a question. No one dared mention his outburst to George.

Sometime after they left, Joe knocked on George's door. George said, "Come."

Joe opened the door and said, "You okay, boss?"

George said, "Yeah, I'm fine. Are you working on your site, today?" Joe nodded and told him he had some office work to do first and then he'd be at his site, the rest of the day. George continued, "I probably won't be there. If you need me for anything, let me know. I'll be here." Joe went back to his desk and worked. He didn't bother George all morning and George never came out of his office, until lunch. He asked everyone who remained in the office that morning, if they needed help on anything. Lorne asked for his help and they both went into George's office.

Joe ate his lunch and signed out. He was on site the rest of the day, and worried about George. While he was dealing with foremen on his overpass he was assigned to, leading in to the north end of town, he couldn't erase the morning and what George went through. Joe didn't know everything that happened in the office, but he could guess. He knew it was bad and he knew that he was the cause of it. Joe thought about Chatham. Since he'd been visiting once in a while, he thought one weekend; maybe he'll just stay there and never return. He was that upset that George was bearing the brunt of grief, just because of him. After his family, George was the only reason Joe was staying in Mississippi. After the morning George had Joe wasn't sure whether to back down, leave him alone, or talk to him later.

About four-thirty, Joe called the office. Maria told him, "Hi Mr. Allen, Mr. Benson is still in his office. He's only come out twice this afternoon. Do you want me to knock on his door and see if he'll take the phone?"

Joe said, "Yes, please Maria." She walked to George's office and asked him and he said he'd talk to Joe. Joe asked, "George, you okay?"

George told him, "Yeah, tomorrow's another day, right?"

Joe said, "Are you up for supper with the family?"

George had a slight smile when he answered, "Buddy, that's the best suggestion I could ever hear, on a day like today. Thanks. I'll be there by five-thirty if that's okay with you."

Joe told him, "That's fine. I'll be there by then, too. See ya later." As he hung up the phone, he picked it up, again and called home. He told Etta that his boss would be joining them for supper. She said it was not a problem she was just starting to prepare it. When Joe asked Etta about the boys, she told him that they were both fine and she told him that Mrs. Liz was home and asked if he wanted to talk to her. He did.

Liz took the phone and said, "Hi honey, everything okay?"

Joe told her, "George has had a pretty shitty day and he's coming for supper. I hope you don't mind, love."

She told him, "That's fine hun, I have some papers to mark, so I won't be much company for a bit but you guys can take care of yourselves. I'll see you later sweetie." As she hung up the phone she wondered about George. She had noticed that he seemed sad of late and maybe a bit lonely. She thought he needed a wife. But, Joe told her, not to match-make. She disappointedly agreed not to.

Joe and George came from opposite directions and pulled in the driveway, nearly at the same time. They laughed about it. As they both got out of their vehicles, Joe went to him and shook his hand, saying, "Well, my friend, did your day get any better, after I left the office?"

George said, "Not until I got your call for supper, tonight."

Joe smiled and said, "Glad we could help. George, before we go in, I want to ask you something. Are you sure you don't want me to leave your company? I mean, you never had trouble like this until I came along, did you?"

George said, "Now Joe, you know I don't want you to leave. Ray is just a complete asshole and I'm not going to let him ruin my business. You are the best damn engineer in Mississippi and I'm not letting you go anywhere, you got that? And, another thing, since you came to me a few years ago, I don't mind tellin' you; you've made me a wealthier man."

Joe smiled and said, "Wow. Now that's a compliment. Let's go inside."

As they went in the house, the boys came running over to the men. James got there first and raised his arms, saying "Up, dada, up."

Both men laughed, as Joe put his briefcase down and picked up his son. He said, "James, have you got a kiss for daddy?" James puckered up and kissed Joe on the lips. He and George laughed. Then James quickly leaned over and wanted George to hold him. As he leaned, Joe let George take him. Joe said, "Do you have kisses for Uncle George?" Just then, James leaned right into George's chest and he gave him a great big wet kiss. Both men laughed.

George sat on the couch with James, on his knee. John was tugging on Joe's pant leg saying, "Up, up." Joe picked him up and said, "Does John have kisses for dada and Uncle George, tonight, too?" John nodded his head and kissed his dad. Joe took him to George and sat him on his other knee. John gave Uncle George a kiss, too, and a big hug.

George said, "You know Joe... I think you are the luckiest man in Mississippi, if not the country. Coming home to these precious boys is the best medicine anyone could have." He hugged both boys, as they tried to wrestle with him.

Liz came in the room and said, "I see Uncle George is having fun. Hi George, hi honey. Everything okay here, do you want me to take them?"

Joe said, "No, it looks like Uncle George is having too much fun." They all laughed.

Liz asked, "Do you guys want a beer? Or, there is that bottle of Scotch, mom gave you for Christmas, if you prefer?"

George said, "I'll have Scotch, Liz, if you don't mind."

She looked to Joe and he said, "I'll have a beer, baby, but I can get it." Liz told him she'd get it, she didn't mind. When she came in the living room with the drinks, James and John were both standing on George's knees and attacking him with kisses. Joe, Liz and George all laughed. The boys were having fun, too.

George said, "Joe, if this don't beat havin' a shit day, like the one I had today. Well, you just can't help it. These little ones love you unconditionally, no matter what shit's been thrown at you."

Just then, James poked George on the nose and said, "Shit," and smiled.

The three adults tried not to laugh, but snickers came out of Liz and Joe. George felt bad, but Liz told him not to worry about it. She didn't want George to feel bad. She said, "It has to happen with every toddler. It's just James' turn to reach out and express himself."

Just then, he started bouncing on George, saying, "Shit, shit, shit!"

Liz said, "If you guys laugh, it's only going to encourage him to say it again. I mean it, don't you guys dare laugh. I'm going outside to pee my pants, now, while you guys sit there and stifle your laughter!"

George apologized to Joe again and said, "Joe, I am so sorry. I had no idea he was going say it, too. Is Liz going to be really pissed at me?"

Joe said, "No, like she said, she's outside laughing her ass off, probably peeing her pants!" The guys laughed a bit, but didn't let Liz hear them.

James wanted down; and George set him on the floor. John was quite content to sit on Uncle George's knee. James toddled into the kitchen; and Etta picked him up. She said, "What'chew up to li'l mister. Is you…are you causin' a fuss?" She hugged him and set him back down.

George found himself cuddling John; and noticed he was falling asleep. Joe said, "Do you want me to take him for you?"

George said, "Don't you dare, this is the best thing that's happened to me today. You'll have to pry him from me, now."

Liz came back in the living room, after composing herself, outside. She said, "Oh George, you look like you could just take him home and raise him yourself. He is so comfortable with you. He loves you. They both do."

George had a tear, as he said, "I wish Margaret was here to see this. She'd be crying and so happy. I wish she was here. I need her too, on days like these."

Etta called them into the dining room. Supper was ready. They had to wake John up for supper. He had dozed off sitting on George's knee. He was tired, but he managed to stay awake during supper..

After supper, Liz said, "Well guys, its bath time."

Joe said, "Honey, maybe George and I can handle bath duty, tonight." George smiled after Joe said that.

Liz was always happy, when daddy took over bath time for her. She said, "James, John do you want daddy and Uncle George to bath you, tonight?"

In unison, both boys yelled, "Yeah," and clapped their hands, excitedly.

Joe stood up and lifted James out of his high chair and George stood up and lifted John out of his high chair and the four went up stairs to the bathroom. They set the boys down and Joe started filling the tub. George started to take the clothes off and they were down to their diapers, when George said, "Daddy, this is your department."

Joe said, "BRUCK, BRUCK, you chicken!" They both laughed and the boys did, too.

Joe took the diapers off and the boys got in the tub. The four of them laughed, played and the men got very wet. Joe and George were soaked to the skin, but laughed constantly. Liz knew this was what George needed, even if she didn't know the reason why. She wanted him to smile and have a bit of happiness in his day, no matter, what his troubles were.

Monday, August 13, 1950 was a hot muggy day, in Mississippi. Joe was still putting up with daily pranks from Ray, up until three days ago, when the pranks stopped. Joe became a little uneasy. He'd rather have the pranks. That, he could handle with no problem. When Ray was behaved and quiet, Joe wondered what he was up to. Was he thinking about doing something more serious, like the manure in the truck? He wouldn't have to wait long to find out.

The Monday morning meeting was under way and as everyone updated where they were on each project, there were very few problems: Except for Ray. He asked if Joe could help out at his site. Everyone was shocked to hear this. No one, more than Joe. Ray, Jesse and Daniel were assigned to a new project. It was a dam, on the Pearl River: Again, out of town. It was a fairly big project and Ray thought, since Joe just wrapped up his own project on the Friday before, he asked George, "Is there another project, or can we borrow Joe for about a week, or so?"

George said, "I'm negotiating right now, but haven't committed to anything, yet. Joe, are you able to sit in on their project, for a bit?"

Joe said, "Yeah, if they'd like me to help, I'd be happy to." That was set. Joe left to go to the job site, when the others did. He drove his own truck out to the site. Joe was feeling great. Maybe after three years, the torment was over. He was relieved, but still cautious. The day turned out to be eventless. Not a bad word, a joke or prank...nothing! This was a good day. Ray even mustered a smile or two, throughout the day. Joe thought to himself, he should mark this on the calendar. He wanted to call and tell Liz, but it would wait until he got home.

About 4:45 p.m. Ray suggested they knock off for the day. Jesse and Daniel were the first to leave. Joe looked around with a very satisfactory smile on his face. He worked with Ray, all day and there were no problems. As he looked around, he saw several cars. This was unusual, because they were not ready to hire the Construction Company and workers, yet. Just then, Joe collapsed on the ground. He'd been hit over the head with a lead pipe.

When he woke up, he was in an old shack somewhere, lying on the floor. His legs were tied together and his hands were tied behind his back. He had a gag in his mouth and his head was pounding. As he looked about, he saw several people, he assumed men, standing around. They all had Klan robes on, their faces covered by their hoods. Joe knew this was bad. Hopefully they would only hurt him and release him. He prayed...hard!

All of a sudden, he heard a voice. It was a familiar voice, he'd heard for about three years. He mostly heard it yelling, not talking, but either way, he recognized the voice. It belonged to Ray Halden. It was unmistakable. Ray said, "Now Nigger, you're gonna 'git yours. 'Da boss-man, Massa Benson, ain't here ta' protect ya'. What'chew gonna do now, boy? Looks like you're on your own, this time...boy. You ain't got no one ta' help you now, you black fucker. I think your family, ain't never gonna forget this day...now what was it that Franklin Roosevelt said, that time the war started, 'A date that will live in infamy', I think he called it. Yeah, I'm sure that's what the man said; a date that will live in infamy."

He kicked Joe in the stomach, really hard. Joe gave a loud grunt, but couldn't speak. He felt another kick, but this was from behind. Someone else kicked him, saying, "This one is from me, Nigger." He knew the voice, too. It belonged to Bubba Shep. Joe's head was really hurting, but he remained calm, for the moment.

A group of four men picked him up off the floor, took off his gag and sat him on a chair. This was so they could hit him in the face and head, more easily. Now, he became terrified. Joe worried about his family. He worried they wouldn't see each other again.

As the Klansmen took turns punching Joe in the face, Ray continued, "What's the matter, Mr. Allen. You look nervous. Hey boys, look, the Nigger's turnin' white, from fear! I think we have him a little scared." They all laughed.

He went on, "I seen yer' wife on the weekend, Nigger. Looked like she was doin' her shoppin' for the week. Yep, she sure is some looker. She's looks like a really sweet piece of meat, we'd all like to taste, right boys?" They all laughed, again. Most agreed with Ray. Joe was in a lot of pain, but now he was angrier, than scared.

Joe didn't raise his head. It hurt too much. Ray took the gag out. Joe said, "Ray, if you, or any one of your asshole cronies, go near my wife,

I'll kill you all. And, believe me, I killed, before!" Just then, Joe thought, he said the wrong thing. Thinking back to the farm the day Liz was almost raped by the farm hand, during the depression. This information was going to get him into more trouble than he could imagine. Because, if he lives through this torture, they will tell the police and Joe can be extradited to Canada, or they would take care of him themselves, with their own brand of justice.

Someone else said, "Is that right, boy? Well, we should oughta check that out." Joe remembered that voice, too. He was sure, it was Sheriff Appleton. He became more terrified. The law was helping this mob. They were part of this. Right then, he knew! He knew this would be the end of his life, one way or the other!

Suddenly, from behind, someone quickly put a rope around his neck. They tightened it, but not to the point of suffocation. They gathered around and several of them lifted him off the chair and they carried him outside. He was horrified. All he could do was struggle as hard as he could. But there were too many men holding him. They carried him to a tree with a large sturdy branch, about nine feet up the trunk. They threw one end over the branch and several men got on the other end of the rope, ready to pull. He saw it coming, now. In a few minutes, he would be dead.

Joe started to pray again. Not to save his life, he knew it was too late. He prayed for God to watch over his family. For Him to give Liz the strength to handle everything she was going to go through, raising the boys without him. He prayed that God would always look after his family.

He thought about the night before, when he took Liz in his arms and made love to her. He remembered how soft she was to touch. How excited she was...they both were. He thought about how much they loved each other. Ever since they were toddlers, on the farm, playing together. They had always been in love. He was never so sure of anything, in all his short, thirty-one years of life.

He thought about bathing his boys and the mushy wet kissed he'd always get from them. They would be growing up, without a father. He silently asked God to help his family deal with all this ugliness and spare his wife from hearing all the gory details of what he was going to endure.

Suddenly, the rope tightened and he began to be lifted in the air. His breathing was cut off. He started to dangle and his feet and legs instinctively, uncontrollably began to kick, back and forth, while he hung. Just when he was nearing the last seconds, they released the rope and he fell to the ground. The men loosened their grip a bit. He could breathe again. What were they doing now? He still had his wits about him. The oxygen to his brain had not been cut off long enough...yet.

He prayed harder. He began now to beg God to spare him any more torture. Joe just wanted them to hang him now, and get it over with. He wanted it to be over, but that prayer would go unanswered for a little while longer. Just as he was praying, the rope tightened up and he was dangling again, much higher this time; he was sure. His breath getting cut off, his legs kicking again, he wanted it to be over. Just as he was blacking out, he dropped to the ground again. This time, it felt like he broke his leg, from landing wrong.

All the time the men were torturing Joe, they were talking amongst themselves, stopping to light an occasional cigar, or cigarette. He couldn't believe that these men could carry on normal conversations and be so casual, while putting someone to death.

While he lay on the ground, the rope tightened one more time. It dragged him to the standing position. His leg really hurt, but he hoped this time would end it, for him. He prayed his life would be over in a moment. He couldn't take the torture. The men started to pull the rope again. Again his breath was cut off, and his legs kicked.

This time, he had some flashes. Some pictures went through his mind. He saw his beautiful Liz. He saw her in her wedding gown. She was the most beautiful bride in the world. Next, he saw his boys: Their sweet little faces, looking up at him. He hoped their fates would be better, in this horrible place...specially John's. He now worried, that John was black! He hoped his boys would be strong, like their mommy.

He next saw the farm. He knew where his resting place should be, with his mom and dad and all the McDonald and Allen ancestors. But, he wanted to stay with Liz, wherever she decided to live. He hoped everyone would understand and accept whatever Liz chose to do with his body.

Everything was getting blacker, he could no longer breathe. His legs stopped kicking, as the final picture went through his mind. His mom and his dad were right beside him. His dad said, "We been waitin' 'fer ya', boy. Yo' mama an' me. We's gonna be t'gedder, now fo'ever. Yo' Lizzy, she be a strong gal, son. She gonna be juss' fine. Little James an'

John's gonna be alright: It juss' be yo' time, son. It be yo' time. All yo' kin be waitin', son. Ya'll c'mon, now, boy....yo' mama an' me's waitin', we's here 'fer ya son. You come on now, boy, it be okay."

As Joe Allen hung dead in the tree, the Klan members took off their hoods and robes, laughing. Ray seemed to be having a great time, patting his buddies on the back, thanking them for doing such a great job, for him.

Sheriff Appleton spoke up and said, "I guess, I gotta make me a condolence call at 2 Gilbert Street. I believe the widow's name is Elizabeth Allen." Everyone laughed!

Chapter 14

Aftermath

SUPPER WAS READY AND LIZ hadn't heard from Joe; whether he was working late, or not, it was very unusual that he hadn't called to let her know. She never really worried about it though, because she was used to his occasional overtime. She knew he had wrapped up his project on the previous Friday and this was Monday. If he was assigned a new one, he would have called to let her know when he'd be home.

She thought about calling George, but she was being silly. It was only six forty-five. She'd known Joe to be getting home at eight sometimes, without letting her know. When he did this, he usually came home with flowers, romance, kisses and making incredible love to her, later! Liz was smiling as she was anticipating the whole nine yards, tonight; just like they had, the night before. It was such a passionate night. Even though he wasn't late, they were just in a very romantic mood! She had thought about it, all day!

She and Etta had fed the boys and bathed them. Etta asked Liz if she could read them a bedtime story, this night. Her reading had become so much better in the last months and she wanted to show off a little, for her teacher. Liz was thrilled and proud that Etta wanted to read to the boys. Etta went down to her bedroom and she came back upstairs with her own bible. This bible is the one the ladies who raised her, gave her the day she left the Rice Plantation, in Arkansas.

When she lived with the ladies in the main house, they could barely read or write. They had a bible which belonged to Etta's mother. They kept it for her and gave it to her when she left home.

Etta had been reading from her bible since Liz began teaching her to read. She liked the story of Moses being drawn from the Nile River and being the deliverer of the Hebrews, out of bondage and out of Egypt. Etta had been taught growing up, that Negroes owe their own freedom from bondage and torture to their deliverer, Abraham Lincoln. At three years old, the boys didn't understand the story of Moses, but it meant a lot to Etta.

After both boys fell asleep, Liz checked the time and it was just after eight o'clock. She decided to call George. As she and Etta were coming down the stairs, to the living room, the doorbell rang. Liz opened the door: In front of her stood the local sheriff. He said, "Good evening, Ma'am. Would ya'll be Mrs. Allen? Mrs. Elizabeth Allen?"

She said, "Yes sheriff, what is this about?"

He spoke again and asked, "Would that be Mrs. Joseph Allen?"

She said, "Yes, what's wrong sheriff? What's this about?"

He took his hat off and said, "Ma'am, I'm sorry ta' tell ya'll this, but, I have some very disturbin' news. It's about your husband, ma'am. He was found tonight, just on the outskirts of town, in a heavily wooded area. He was found hangin' from a tree. I'm so sorry ma'am, but your husban', he's dead. Seems, uh, he committed suicide. I can't tell ya' how sorry I am 'bout this."

Liz put her hand over her mouth and screamed out, "NO, NO, NO, it can't be. He would never kill himself. You're wrong. It can't be my Joe. He's just working late. It's not him. It can't be!"

Sheriff Appleton took Joe's wallet out of his pocket. He handed it to Liz. Her knees buckled and she fell on the floor. As she took the wallet out of his hand, she saw the pictures of the twins inside and said, "Who would do this to him? Oh my God, who could be this cruel?"

The Sheriff said, "Ma'am, as I said, he committed suicide. Ma'am we need to know where to take the body."

Liz looked at him in horror and raised her voice, "What do you mean suicide? He had too much to live for. My husband would never kill himself. We have two small children. He wouldn't. Who found him?" Her head was swimming. She was going to throw up and knew she couldn't make it to the bathroom. She vomited on the sheriff's boots. As she did, she noticed there was a lot of mud and some leaves on them.

Etta was crying, "It can't be, it can't be. Lawdy, no, it can't be him. What does we do Mrs. Liz? What does we do?"

Liz asked her to get a cloth, so the sheriff could wipe off his boots. He was really pissed off. He said, "Well don't 'dat beat all! I just polished 'dem boots, 'dis mornin'. Well Ma'am, where do we take it?"

Liz looked at him and said, "Where do you take what?"

He was pissed off about his boots and became very annoyed with her. He said, "Lady, just tell me where the body goes."

Liz looked at him with contempt and cried, "You may transport my husband to Lincoln Memorial Hospital. I will have our doctor meet us there." She was in shock, now. She couldn't believe his attitude. He was more upset over his boots having vomit on them, than the fact that a good man was dead.

Liz could hear the radio in the sheriff's car. She heard laughter. Then she heard someone say, "Well, looks like we got the coon problem taken care of tonight, for the chief." There was more laughter on the radio and the sheriff tried not to smile, but he smirked. She heard, "He's one happy man tonight. He can't wait to get to work tomorrow." There was more laughter and then the radio cut out. The sheriff tried not to smile, but he couldn't help it. He was sure she couldn't hear the conversation...but she did! Liz saw red and she slapped him in the face.

She said, "You know who did this, you sick son-of-a-bitch! You're in on this, you bastard! You know who killed my husband! I heard the laughter on your radio! Your coon problem was taken care of tonight, was it? WHO IS THE CHIEF?" She grasped the sheriff by the scruff of the neck and continued, "YOU MARK MY WORDS SHERIFF, YOU BASTARD; I WILL FIND OUT WHO KILLED MY HUSBAND IF IT TAKES THE REST OF MY LIFE. I KNOW IT WAS YOU AND YOUR KLAN, YOU MURDERING FUCKER!" The sheriff was a little startled by her language. By now, he was getting more pissed off with her.

She was crying harder and yelling louder, now. "YOU GET YOUR FAT ASS OFF OF MY PROPERTY AND TAKE MY HUSBAND TO LINCOLN MEMORIAL HOSPITAL....AND DON'T THINK I'M DONE WITH YOU YET...YOU SORRY EXCUSE OF A MAN! YOU PIECE OF SHIT!" She slammed the door on his face and he left.

Liz went to Etta and tried to console her. She held her, as she reached for the phone. Liz called Robert's number. He answered, "Hello...Dr. Hathaway."

Liz broke down and cried, as soon as she heard his voice. "Robert, Joe's been murdered."

Robert said, "Lizzy, slow down. Tell me that again."

She cried, "Doc, they're taking his body to Lincoln right now, can you meet me there? I'm leaving in a few minutes. Robert, Joe is dead... please help me. How can I make it without him?"

Robert was shocked. He said, "Honey you stay there. Don't drive; I'm on my way to get you now." As she hung up the phone, Liz was still holding Etta and both were sobbing. Liz called her mother next, while she waited for Robert to come and pick her up.

As Eleanor picked up the phone, Liz cried out, "Mama, help me... they murdered Joe. Mama, please come?" She couldn't stop crying. She spoke again, so fast she was rambling. "Mom, Joe's dead...oh mom... help me...oh God, he's dead, mom. My precious Joseph is dead. Mama, they said he committed suicide, but there's no way! They lynched him, I know it, they lynched him." She just kept weeping and couldn't control it. She said, "Robert will be here to get me in a few minutes and they're taking him to the hospital. Mama, they murdered him. The sheriff is in on it, too...."

Eleanor shouted to her daughter, "Lizzy, slow down baby. I'm coming to you as quick as I can. You just tell me slow, do you know who did it? Does George know anything about it?" Liz slowed her breathing down and Etta was still clinging to her. She couldn't let go and Liz wouldn't let her.

Liz said to her mom, "Mom he's gone. My babies have no father... he's gone. Oh mom, I can't raise them without their daddy..." Her voice trailed off and her weeping became quieter.

El said, "Honey, do you know who did it? Was it the asshole at work?"

Liz said, "Oh mom I've got to call George...wait; it sounds like Robert just pulled in." Robert opened the door and walked in. He found Liz and Etta clinging to each other, crying. He gave a listen upstairs and he didn't hear the boys. That was good, they were still asleep.

He came to Etta and Liz and held them both. He asked if it was El on the phone. Liz nodded her head. He took the receiver from Liz and said, "Hey darlin', I'm here with our girls. How are you?"

El said, "Hi sweetie, I'm confused, I don't understand. I'm glad you're there. Did she really say Joe is dead?" She was sniffling and crying, now. Robert told her he was sure Joe was dead and he was going to stay with Liz every step of the way. He had to take her to the hospital to identify his body. He told her that Liz, the boys and Etta, were his priority. El was really glad he was there for her daughter.

Eleanor said, "Honey, I told Lizzy I'm going to get there as quick as I can. I should be there tomorrow afternoon, sometime. Oh Robert, who would kill Joseph. He was the sweetest man…" her voice trailed off to sobs, as she thought of him as her own son. She'd lost one of her babies.

Robert said into the phone and to the two women he was holding; "Now ladies, I have to take Liz to the hospital. Etta, we need you to be strong. When I take Liz to the hospital, you have to be here with the boys. I'm sorry Etta, but are you strong enough to be here, alone?" She nodded her head. Robert said, "Okay dear, that's a great help."

Eleanor said into the phone, "I'll stay on the phone with her, if she wants."

Robert said, "Good, but I think we should quickly call George Benson, first….see if he might know anything about it." They all agreed.

Liz took the phone and said, "Okay mom, I'm okay. I'll hang up now and call George and you and Etta can talk and keep each other company while we're gone. Is that okay, mom?"

El said, "That's fine baby girl, I'm going to try to call the airline to come as soon as I can get a flight, but tell Etta, I'll call her back as quickly as I can." They hung up the phone and Liz called George Benson.

George answered the phone and Liz said, through her tears, "George it's Liz."

George was happy to hear from her, "Hi Lizzy how's my favorite family tonight?"

Liz was still crying and said, "George, it's Joe. He's dead…he's been murdered. Was he at the office or, on site today? When did he leave to come home? He was lynched." She was crying harder again and George couldn't believe what he was hearing.

He said, "Liz honey, do you know what you're saying?"

Liz was sobbing so much now. "George, he's gone. Someone lynched him. Robert's here and we're leaving for the hospital. I have to identify him. Oh George, what do we do now? I can't go on without him!" She had to set the phone down, she couldn't say any more, so Robert picked it up.

Robert said, "George, it's Robert. I'm taking Liz to the hospital now. We just wanted to tell you, before you heard from someone else."

George said, "I'll meet you at the hospital. Robert, are you sure?"

Robert said, "The sheriff came to tell Liz. We're leaving now we'll see you in a few minutes."

George was speechless. He started to cry, when he hung up the phone. He sat down and put his head in his hands, for a moment, then dried his eyes, grabbed his car keys and left for the hospital. As George pulled into Lincoln Memorial's parking lot, Liz and Robert had just gotten out of his car. Liz saw him drive in and they waited for George to catch up with them. He came up beside Liz and stopped. He put his arms around her and held her. She cried, "George, my Joe is gone. They said it was suicide..."

George angrily interrupted, "THAT'S BULLSHIT!"

She said, "He was lynched. We'll never have him back. Who would do this?"

George looked in Liz's eyes, then to Robert and said, "Ray Halden and Bubba Shep, for starters!" Liz became frightened. She was thinking about Ray, but couldn't believe it was his co-worker.

The three went in to the hospital and Robert took them to the basement. He wasn't sure Joe would be at the morgue, just yet. He checked and they told Dr. Hathaway, "They just called us and said a body, arrived in emergency and they were bringing it down as soon as a doctor declares him."

Robert said, "Thanks...I'm here to do it, if no one has, yet." He took the two with him up to emergency. A nurse saw him come in.

She said, "Dr. Hathaway, are you here to see a body?"

Robert said, "Yes is he here yet?" Just then, two attendants came in front of Dr. Hathaway, with a stretcher. There was a body on it, completely covered. He told the attendants to take the stretcher behind a curtain and he went to look. He needed to see him, before Liz did.

He went behind the curtain and lifted the sheet. It really was his dear friend, Joseph Allen lying there, dead. It hit him hard. It was such a shock to see him that way. The rope was still around his neck and he was brutally beaten about the face and head. The swelling was bad and he was almost unrecognizable. It was a horrible sight, he'd never forget. Robert tried to hold it together for Liz, but he choked a little and he teared up. He took his handkerchief out and as quietly as he could, he blew his nose and wiped his tears, before seeing Liz. He knew he couldn't dissuade Liz from looking at him but she had to, so he asked a nurse to clean him up a bit, first.

Liz overheard him and said, "NO! DON'T YOU DARE. SOMEONE TOOK THE TIME TO MURDER HIM, I WANT TO SEE WHAT HE LOOKED LIKE JUST AT THE MOMENT THE MURDERERS SAW HIM DIE!!!"

George was still holding Liz, while they both cried. He was trying to be brave, so she could lean on him, but he was leaning on her. Robert took her hand and brought them both behind the curtain, so she could identify him.

As Robert pulled the sheet back, Liz made a slight whimper. She looked at his face. There was blood, welts, and bruises. You could tell his cheek bones were crushed, and the rope was still around his neck, tightly tied. They didn't even loosen it, as they brought his body in. Her tears flowed more quickly now, as she said, "Dr. Hathaway this is my husband, Joseph...Jacob...Allen....Jr. She wanted to scream and run away, but she held it together. George was still holding her and Robert was still holding her hand. Both men had tears in their eyes.

A nurse was standing with them. She had a pen and a clipboard, with a standard form on it. She was in the process of filling in the pertinent information. There was a space for the deceased's name, the date, a doctor's name, a witness' name and the family member, who identifies the body.

Within a few minutes, the paper was properly filled out and signed. That was that! Within a moment, Joseph's life of 31 years was officially over. The nurse closed the file folder. This time, a so called, official file folder on Joseph Allen had a piece of paper in it. A copy would be sent to Sheriff Appleton, to place in HIS file on Joseph Allen: The one from three years earlier, when he needed to get his pick-up truck back. The file folder that was empty, would have one lone piece of paper in it; now...a death certificate!

As Liz turned to leave, she couldn't. Her feet wouldn't move. Robert and George tried to take her out of the room. She broke free from both of the men and she laid her head on her husband's strong chest, like she had after every time they made love. This time, she couldn't hear the comforting beat of his heart and her tears fell on him. After a moment, she kissed his swollen, bloody lips and whispered in his ear, "I love you, darlin'. I'll always love you. I promise you, I'll find out who did this. I promise our babies will know everything about their daddy...from Berko Yaba, to this day." She kissed him again and let her tears fall on his face. She thought for a moment that she saw a sparkle of love for her, in his eye. She smiled and said, "I know you do, honey. I love you, too."

A couple of attendants came to take Joe to the morgue. As they wheeled him past the trio, Liz noticed Joe had mud, leaves and a twig, stuck to his shoes. She made a mental note of it and tucked it away. Later, a pathologist would do a post mortem, even though it was obvious he died of asphyxiation...he wanted to record suicide, but Robert convinced him, after explaining the situation to record "suspicious death".

El called Etta back about twenty minutes after the three left for the hospital. Liz's mom said through her own tears, "Miss Etta, are you okay dear?"

Etta said, "Yes ma'am. I'se juss' can't believes it! 'Da Mister, bein' gone an' all. Mrs. Eleanor, yo' daughter, she be a strong gal. She be real strong. God'll see her through, he will."

El said, "I know dear. She always was a strong girl. I just finished making my plans. There is a really early flight out of Detroit, which lands in Jackson, at eleven o'clock tomorrow morning. I'll get my rental car and I should be at the house around lunch time. Miss Etta, how are the boys."

As Etta calmed down some, her speech became better, again, "They're still sleeping like angels, grandma."

El was relieved, "That's good. It's going to be a difficult few days for everyone. They will want to know where their daddy is and they'll need lots of attention."

After some time on the phone, Etta heard a vehicle in the driveway. She said to Eleanor, "I think they're back, now...just a minute ma'am." She left the phone and peeked out the window. She came back the phone and told Eleanor that they were back.

When they walked in, Liz asked Etta, "Is that still mom?" Etta nodded her head and handed Liz the phone.

Tears were starting to fall again, as she said, "Mama, he looks bad. Broken, bloody and bruised. It was horrible." Just then she set the phone down and cried harder. George held her.

Robert picked up the receiver and said, "Hey baby you doing okay? How's the family handling it?"

El said, "Hi doc. I'm okay. How's my baby?"

Robert said, "She's strong, love. She's going to be fine. You raised an intelligent, strong, brave girl. She'll make it through this. She has two very precious reasons, why!"

At that moment, Liz raised her head, wiped her tears and said, "That's right." She wasn't talking to anyone in particular. She realized she hadn't checked on them. She walked up stairs and opened James' door. He was sound asleep. She just looked at him for a moment and said, "Oh my baby boy, how do I tell you your daddy's gone?" She let a tear fall as she closed his bedroom door.

Next, she opened John's door and he was sleeping like an angel, too. She smiled. She said, "Daddy will always be with you boys. No matter what you do, or where you go in life, daddy is always going to be with you."

She closed his door and went into her own room and shut the door. She lay on her bed and cried. She took the box of Kleenex off of Joe's night stand and pulled one out. She blew her nose and just lay crying. She heard talking downstairs, but she couldn't go back down, yet. She needed to be alone.

Robert was still on the phone with Eleanor. He asked her, "Do you want me to pick you up in Jackson?"

She said, "Honey, that isn't necessary, I can get a rental and drive."

He said, "I really don't want you driving, dear."

Eleanor thought about it and relented, "Maybe you're right. I'm sure I won't sleep much tonight. I won't be thinking clearly enough to drive, by then. Yes, if you think you can leave Liz long enough to come and get me, that would be great."

That was settled, Robert would pick up Eleanor from Jackson Mississippi and any one she brings with her. As they finished their conversation, Robert said, "I'm going to stay here tonight, love. Please call if you need anything, or just want to talk. I'm sure we won't get much sleep here, either. Good night, darlin'. I'll see you in the morning. I love you, sweetie." El smiled and said goodbye to him and told him she loved him, too. They both hung up their phones.

As they did, Eleanor thought for a moment. This sweet, wonderful man just told her, he loved her. She never thought she'd hear those words from another man. She never expected to say the same thing, to any man, other than George McDonald. She thought he was the only man, she would ever love. She smiled.

Robert asked Etta to go upstairs and quietly peek in at Liz; to see if she was okay. He did this so he could talk to George, who was now sitting on the couch, with his head in his hands. He sat down beside him and asked if he was okay.

George said, "To be honest Robert, no. I know who did this."

Robert looked at George and said, "You really believe Elizabeth?"

George looked at Robert, very seriously and said, "Yes. There is no way in this world, that Joe committed suicide. We both know he had so much to live for. Yes, I know who it was. It was Ray Halden, and if I'm not mistaken, he was probably with a group of men, who were dressed in white robes and hoods, because they were too cowardly to show their faces. In this group, there would also be a man named Bubba Shep and I have no doubt that Sheriff Appleton, would also be with these men.

Robert, there is no way they will ever be convicted. It will be swept under the rug. It won't even make it to headline news, in the major papers, tomorrow. Joe Allen is dead and no one will do anything about it. Robert, these two people are the best friends a man could ever want. You know that, too. They've opened up and shared their lives with both you and me. We're all family. I think of Joe and Liz as my children and John and James, my grandsons. You're like a brother, to me. What kind of friend, boss or father am I? I couldn't protect Joe. He needed me and I couldn't protect him. I should have had Ray charged three years ago and fired him then...maybe Joe would be alive today, if I had!"

Robert listened carefully to George. He was taken by surprise, to know how highly George thought of him, too. He extended his arms to George, hugged him and said, "George, I thank you for being so open and honest with me and for caring about me so much, too. None of this is your fault. If you did all that three years ago, I think you know as well as I do, Joe likely would have been murdered, three years ago." George had to agree!

Liz and the boys need us, now more than ever. She's a beautiful and strong woman, inside and out. If anyone can make it through this, she can. She's gone through a lot in her life, with Joe. Their love was strong. I never saw two people more in love, than Liz and Joe. They were inspiring."

Etta came down the stairs and told Robert, "Doc, she's sleeping. I also spent a bit of time in the boys' rooms and they're sleeping, too. They looks like they don't have a care in the world. They're so beautiful, they're so..." She started weeping again. Robert got up and went to her and held her. He didn't speak he just let her cry on his shoulder.

The telephone rang. Robert went to get it. He heard Liz answer the extension in her bedroom. It was the sheriff. He asked, "Mrs. Allen is that you, Ma'am?"

She recognized his voice and said, "Yes sheriff, what can I do for you, now...offer up my son! Or, are you satisfied with killing just my husband?"

The sheriff was pissed off. He said, "Ma'am you seem to think there was foul play, here. I told you, your husband committed suicide. Now the reason, I'm calling is to ask if you know where Mr. George Benson might be. I wonder if he might shed some light on your husband's movements today." She went to the living room and handed the phone to George and told him the sheriff wanted to talk to him.

George took the phone and said, "What the hell do you want, Appleton? Haven't you done enough to this lady, today: Why are you bothering her you asshole?"

The sheriff said, "I'll thank you to keep a civil tongue. I'm not the enemy. I wanted to ask you if you know where your employee was today."

George told him, "Well Sheriff Appleton, I can tell you that three employees were together after work. That would be Mr. Allen, Mr. Shep and Mr. Halden: The first being murdered by the other two. Where they were actually located; well sheriff, maybe you can tell me, since you were with them during the murder. Now, don't you ever bother Mrs. Allen again. You keep your fat Klan ass away from her and her family. That goes for the rest of the faggoty, sick, disgusting bed sheet jockeys, you associate with." As he slammed down the telephone receiver, Liz started to laugh.

She sat on the couch and she laughed hard. She couldn't help herself. Once she heard what George said, she started laughing then, everyone just looked at her...and started to laugh. Liz could not stop. The more she laughed, the more her ribs hurt. She was holding them, because they hurt so much...all four of them laughed for at least five minutes without stopping.

When Liz finally got hold of herself, she got up and went into the kitchen. The other three just watched her, as they stopped laughing. When Liz came out of the kitchen, she had the bottle of scotch and several beers. She brought a few glasses with her. She told everyone to help themselves, and poured herself a full tumbler of Scotch. She sat in old reliable and downed her drink, in couple of swallows. After that, she opened a bottle of beer and started to drink it.

Everyone just looked at her. She turned in the chair, so that her legs hung over the arm. She stared at her bottle of beer and said, "Please, everyone join me and raise a glass to my Joe. George opened two beers, giving one to Robert. Etta said she'd take a little scotch. When they had their drinks in their hands, all four of them raised their drinks. Liz said, "Here's to my beloved husband, Joe: A man of pride, intelligence, integrity, strength and wisdom: A man who loved his family and friends. A man I loved more than anyone in the world. A great husband and daddy," she then stood up and walked over to their wedding picture on the wall, held up her drink and said, "I love you, baby!" She started tearing up again and continued, "You rest now, love. It'll be some time, but I'll be with you someday, darlin'." She went and kissed his picture. The three raised their glasses and said, "To Joe, our dear friend." Liz broke down crying again.

Robert held her again, as she cried some more. George was at a loss. He felt like he should do something, but what? It brought his wife's death back to him. He knew what Liz was going to go through, yet at the same time, it was worse, for her. His wife died of cancer. They knew when it would happen, but not with Joe. No one expects murder.

Etta said, "Is anyone hungry?"

Robert said, "Etta, you're a mind reader. I would love a sandwich, if you have the makings. Even peanut butter will do."

Etta said, "Not from my kitchen, you won't get no peanut butter sandwich for supper. Mr. George, are you hungry?"

George said, "As a matter-of-fact Etta, I'd love something to eat."

Liz said, "Etta, the spaghetti sauce is still fresh, from tonight guys, how about spaghetti?"

George and Robert told her it didn't have to be that much. Etta said, "Hush now, it will be ready in twenty minutes, just sit and keep my Mrs., company." She went in the kitchen and the other three, sat with their drinks. Tears rolled down Liz's cheeks, again.

Just then, they heard a cry from upstairs. It was loud and sudden. Liz ran up to see about it. James was screeching at the top of his lungs. She turned on the light and he was reaching up to her. She picked him up and cuddled him. She could find nothing physically wrong. She expected he had a bad dream. She took him and carried him down the stairs. He was still crying and she sat and cuddled him on daddy's chair. She asked, "James, did you have a bad dream?"

He rubbed his eyes, and still had a few tears. He said, "Daddy went away. Why did daddy go?" Just then John came down the stairs hugging his teddy bear, wiping his eyes, too. He said he had a bad dream, too.

John said, "Mommy, daddy went away, didn't he?"

Etta came into the living room to see what was happening. John was sitting on Liz's other knee; as she held both of her sons on her lap, James still wanted to know, "Why did daddy go away, mommy?" No one could believe they were hearing this.

"Out of the mouths of babes," Liz said. But how did they know? How could they? She hugged them both very close to her heart. She said, "We're going to talk about daddy after you two sleep tonight. We'll talk in the morning. How would you guys like all four of us take you back to bed?" They both smiled and thought that they were getting very special treatment from everyone.

All six of them went upstairs and they all put James in his bed and then they put John in his bed. After they all said good night to the boys, giving them each kisses and hugs, the boys each replied good night to everyone, including daddy, who wasn't there.

Etta went back to the kitchen and the three, went back to the living room and picked up their drinks. No one said anything, until Etta came in and said, "Supper's ready folks."

They went in to the dining room in silence each wondering how both boys knew something was wrong and daddy wasn't coming home, again. Etta put the spaghetti, salad and bread on the table. They ate in silence. It was too bizarre to speak about. How could both boys think daddy was gone, at the same time? How could they know something was wrong, with their daddy? As they all ate and thought about it, they didn't realize they were all hungrier than they thought.

When they were done, Etta and George cleared the table. Etta wasn't sure what they wanted to drink, so she made coffee and tea, to go with their dessert. She got George to take the tray with the coffee and tea in the dining room, while she took in the pie she baked that afternoon, in. Liz served the tea and coffee and Etta said, "Here we go folks, I made this lemon meringue pie, just for...Mr. Joe."

Liz started to cry hysterically. She remembered it was Joe's favorite. She also remembered chasing him around the living room with the meringue, the first time the Diamont's came over for supper and to play bridge. That's the day they thought she deceived them, her husband was black. As this went through her mind, she cried so hard, she was feeling sick. She ran to the bathroom and started to throw up. Robert went and asked her if she was alright. She said through the bathroom door, "Yeah, I guess it's been a rough day." She opened the door and Robert hugged her. They went back to the dining room and Liz apologized for getting sick. They all understood.

After dessert, Liz excused herself, "I'm sorry everyone, I guess the scotch and the beer was a bit much for me. I think I'll go to bed. I hope I can sleep. Please, whoever wants to stay, the couch is a hide-a-bed; Etta can get blankets and pillows: Good-night everybody."

Liz went to bed and left everyone to decide what they wanted to do. Robert said, "I'm not on call, the hospital won't need me. My office knows I'm taking a few days off. Someone is covering the patients I have in the hospital. I promised El I'd stay here tonight. I said I'd watch over Liz and the kids, until she gets here tomorrow...uh, I guess later today. It's after midnight, already. Etta, are you okay? Do you think you can get some sleep?"

Etta said, "I don't know Doc. The best I can do is lay down and close my eyes. I gotta keep my wits, she's gonna need hep' wit' 'dem boys." As she said this, tears started welling up in her eyes, again.

Robert put his arm around her shoulder and said, "If you need me, I'll be here." He pointed at the hide-a-bed. He turned to George, "Are you okay, George?"

George looked at him, very tired and said, "I'll be okay. I'll head home, but if you need me Robert, call me. I have some decisions to make about work. G'night."

George left; Etta went to her room, after Robert gave her a hug and kissed her on her forehead. She climbed down the basement stairs to her room and cried herself to sleep.

Liz had brought down a pair of Joe's pajamas, when he was talking to Etta. She laid them on the couch, when he wasn't looking. When he saw them, he felt strange. He didn't know whether to put them on, or not. He decided, since Liz brought them down for him, he would put them on, as a sign of respect. He followed suit, in the house. He cried himself to sleep, too.

When George got home, he went to his kitchen and pulled out a large bottle of whiskey and poured a tumbler, full. For Mississippi being a dry state, people still seemed to know where to get alcohol. It was only beer that was allowed there, legally. But, you couldn't buy it. You had to go to a tavern...or a club to get it. It didn't seem to matter; there was liquor in every other household. There was also lots of moonshine to be had, as well. There were stills all over the state. Most sheriffs looked the other way and some even ran them, themselves. Ninety percent of the Mississippi sheriffs were on the take, anyway.

As George thought what he was going to do, he wept again. The best friend he had in all his life was gone: Brutally murdered. He knew Joe would ever commit suicide. It wasn't in him. He had too much to live for. He went to his linen closet and got out some black material out of a box of material, his wife kept for sewing clothing and patching. He set it by the door, to take with him in the morning.

As he finished his whiskey, he poured another. This one was larger than the last. What would he do at work, in the morning. Should he talk to Ray and Bubba, should he fire them, should he KILL them? He smiled at the thought, just for a second. He shook his head, and got that thought out of his mind.

But before he did, he went to his bedroom. He brought a Colt .45 gun, back to the kitchen with him. He also brought a box of bullets in with him. "What to do," he thought out loud...."What to do?"

James and John popped into his mind. He thought about the time he had a really bad day and Joe took him home for supper. That was the day Ray turned over the filing cabinet. He was afraid, that day. He had a few drinks in his office that morning. He was scared of him, but he couldn't show it to the guys, so he stayed in his office all day.

When he went to Joe's that night, John and James gave George kisses and hugs. He got to help Joe bathe them. He was smiling. Then... he remembered, that was also the day he inadvertently taught James to say "shit". He couldn't help but laugh, now. He remembered Liz telling them not to laugh, it would be encouragement. And then, she went outside and laughed her ass off. While he was starting to become inebriated, he laughed out loud. After a few seconds, his laughter turned into tears: Then to rage.

He picked up the Colt .45 and studied it. He thought about blowing Ray's head off. He would automatically get a death sentence: If not from the judge, or jury, then, the Klan. He worried about his business. If he were to take matters into his hands, to any length, his business would suffer. Was he willing to lose it all?

He was getting very tired. He stood up, staggered to the bathroom to relieve himself and tumbled onto the bed. He was asleep within seconds. Six o'clock would be there, before he knew it and it would be time to get up.

In Chatham, all family had gathered at the McDonald house that night, since it was the largest and would hold everyone, just like at every Christmas. Eleanor was crying most of the night. She wanted to be strong for everyone. It became too much for her. She broke down several times. She wanted Robert to hold her and protect her. She was in mourning for her son-in-law and for her daughter and grandsons. They not only murdered a man, they hurt a family and a community, too.

As word was spread in Chatham, everyone heard about the murder in Mississippi. No one at home would ever believe that Joseph Allen would, or could ever commit suicide. It wasn't in him. Everyone was ready to put on a grand funeral for him. Eleanor had her doubts it would happen at the farm. She had a feeling, the break with two family's tradition, would start now.....in Mississippi.

While everyone expected Liz to bring his body to the farm and bury him in the family cemetery, with his parents and the rest of the Allen's.....she wondered. Would Liz keep him with her? Would she sell the house in Mississippi and move back home? Whatever Liz decided, the family had to support her decision. But, it was up to her.

As Eleanor thought about this, she knew it would be one of the toughest decisions, of her daughter's life. According to their wills, Liz was now the legal owner of the Allen house and property, on the farm. She was also going to be co-owner of the McDonald properties and businesses, when Eleanor passed on. With them owning the house in Mississippi, she now owned it, too. Liz was a very wealthy woman and would be for life. All of these things passed through Eleanor's mind. There was so much for her daughter to deal with, now. She just hoped she would be able to help her daughter handle all of this.

El thought maybe, if nothing else, she could look after her grandsons and help Liz that way. As Eleanor lay in her bed that night, she thought about Joe. She had lost a son. He was a wonderful man. She was so thrilled when he asked her and George if he could have their daughter's hand in marriage. They couldn't have picked a better husband, for Liz. She thought about their wedding and how beautiful it was, about Joe wearing the Kente Cloth Robe. He looked so handsome. His great-grandmother, Afua Kakira, would have been proud.

So many things went through her mind that night. As she stared at the alarm clock, she wasn't tired at all. It was three o'clock and she was still thinking. It was like her mind just wouldn't turn off. As she prayed to the Lord for guidance and strength, the phone rang. She picked it up and she said, "Hello."

It was Robert. Quietly, he said, "Hi Love, how are you doing?"

El was glad to hear him. She said, "Robert is Liz okay? Is there something wrong?"

He said, "No darlin' I just wanted to see how you were holding up. I'm sleeping on Liz's couch. I slept for about an hour, but can't sleep any more. It was a really hard evening to get through. Somehow, I thought you'd still be awake. Are you okay, dear?"

Eleanor smiled at his thoughtfulness and intuition and said, "I'm okay too; as okay as I can be, under the circumstances. I'm anxious to get there. My daughter needs me."

Robert smiled, "Your sweetheart needs you too, darling!"

El smiled and said, "I do miss you too, dear."

He said, "I'm anxious to hold you in my arms, again. Will you be able to get a bit of sleep on the plane?"

She said, "That's my plan. I'm hoping I'll be able to fall asleep. Every time I close my eyes, I see Joe. Hun, how did he look?"

Robert said, "I really don't think I should tell you. You don't need that thought going through your mind. It's bad enough that Elizabeth will remember that picture, for the rest of her life, whenever she thinks of him."

El said, "Was it that bad?"

Robert said, "When you come here later this morning, is anyone coming with you?"

El was a little disappointed that he didn't answer her question, but understood. She said, "Simon and Abe's wives are coming, with their babies. They will be on the plane with me. The boys will come in a few days, when funeral plans are made. Someone has to stay home for the businesses, so my nephews and their families will be home, to look after things."

Robert asked, "Will you be staying with me, love, or with Liz?"

El said, "I'm not sure how things will play out for sleeping arrangements. I'm not sure who is going to be staying, where. I guess we'll decide when we all get there. It's too bad the cradles won't be there for the babies to use, but Liz still has the cribs, for them to use."

When Liz's boys outgrew the cradles, they were shipped back to the farm, for future use, by other family. She hung on to the rocking horses, the boys still loved to play on them and probably would for another year or so, until they would learn to ride bikes.

Robert smiled and said, "Well love, I'm getting sleepy, if you don't mind, just pretend I've just made love to you and I'm just rolling over to nod off. You okay, sweetie?"

She replied, "What a lovely thought, dear. Yeah, I might be able to get an hour, before I have to get up. You're just what I needed, darlin'. I'll see you in Jackson around eleven, hun. I love you. Bye."

Robert replied, "I love you, too dear. Bye."

After speaking to each other privately, they both found a bit of sleep. It wasn't a sound sleep, but at least it was a rest, which they both needed. They would have to be rested and about their wits, later. Liz and the boys would need them both, in a few hours.

Chapter 15

Family Arrives For a Funeral

ETTA WAS UP EARLY AS usual, trying to be quiet in the kitchen, as she was starting to prepare breakfast. She put the coffee on. As soon as the aroma hit Robert's nose, his eyes popped open. For just a moment, he thought he was in Chatham and Caroline had the coffee on. He swore he could always smell it from El's house! He rolled over, expecting to hold Eleanor and when he did not find her beside him, he remembered where he was and what this day would likely hold: Grief, pain, and answering little boys' questions and many more tears.

Just then, he heard two little boys toddling down the stairs. When they saw Robert on the couch, they got up and jumped on the bed. They were so happy and excited to see him there. They were screeching excitedly that he was 'sleeping over' at their house. John yelled, "Dr. Robert!"

James yelled, "Yaaay" as they both got busy playing with him and started jumping on him.

Liz came downstairs saying, "Now boys, leave Dr. Robert alone."

Robert said, "It's okay mama, I really like being attacked by these little munchkins!" He had one in each arm, as he sat up and was hugging them, both. They were laughing and they both kissed him and he laughed, too.

Liz laughed as James said, "Mommy, why is the doctor wearing daddy's 'jamas?"

Liz and Robert stopped laughing. She was about to give an answer, when Etta popped her head through the door.

She said, "Good mornin' everyone. How did we all sleep?"

James and John both said, "Miss Etta." They both jumped off of Robert and got off the couch. They ran to her and both hugged her legs. She bent over and gave them both a kiss on the forehead.

Liz said, "I got a bit. What's for breakfast, Miss Etta?"

Etta said, "Well I have oatmeal on, to start. What does everyone want? Bacon, eggs, flapjacks..."

The boys yelled, in unison, "FWAPJACKS, FWAPJACKS, FWAPJACKS!" Everyone laughed. Etta went in the kitchen and started the flapjacks and the boys ran to their mom and reached their arms up, saying, "Up mama." She bent down and picked them both up and kissed each one, smiling. James asked again, why Robert was wearing their daddy's pajamas.

Liz said, "Well it got very late and he was very tired, so we thought he should stay here and sleep. I just let him wear daddy's pajamas, because he didn't have his own." They were satisfied with the answer and wanted to get down and play. Liz said, "I'll call George to see if he's had breakfast, yet."

She called him and he answered on the first ring. He said he hadn't eaten and he'd be right over. Robert got up and folded the hide-a -bed, grabbed a cup of coffee and excused himself to take a shower and get dressed. The boys were on their rocking horses and they were racing with each other.

After about fifteen minutes, George was knocking on the door and Robert came downstairs, showered and dressed.

Liz said, as she went and hugged George, "Hi George, how are you, today?"

He said, "Don't you worry about me, gal. How are you folks doing?"

They talked about their night and Etta called from the dining room, "Ya'll come now. First batch of flapjacks are ready and so is the oatmeal. Robert picked James off his horse and George picked John off the other one, and everyone went in for breakfast. The boys were put in their highchairs and everyone sat down. Just as Liz was about to ask Joe to say the blessing, she caught herself and she said it.

Everyone dug into breakfast and Etta sat and ate, too. They were careful not to say anything about Joe, in front the twins. They kept the conversation light and laughed about the boys getting sticky with the syrup and Liz said, "It looks like you guys will need a bath, before we get dressed." They laughed again and everyone ate a good breakfast.

George asked if he could help. They both yelled, "Yeah!" Liz laughed and said, "If you really want to, sure. You may have to go home and get changed before you go to work. You are going to work, today?"

He said, "You bet I am. I have to talk to a couple of my men this morning."

Liz looked at him and asked, "Are you sure that's a good idea?"

He said, "I have to. I'm not sure what to say, but I have to go in. I owe Joe that. Besides, I have a black cloth in my truck. It will be placed on his chair out of respect."

Liz smiled and said, "Thank you George, that's really sweet of you. I appreciate it."

John spoke up, "Where's dada?"

Everyone was waiting for this. Liz said, "As soon as we get you guys' unstickied, we'll talk about daddy, okay?" They both were fine with this answer, because Uncle George was going to help bathe them. The boys loved Uncle George helping. They loved to splash him.

Robert said, "Mommy, you go start the water and I'll help get these little monkeys up there...WITHOUT GETTING UNCLE GEORGE AND I STICKY! Right guys?" They both laughed and the men picked them up out of their chairs and held them out at arm's length, so their hands, all full of syrup, could not mess anything up. Liz and Etta giggled at the sight.

The phone rang and Etta answered it. As she did, she heard Minnie's voice. Minnie asked Etta about Joe. The black community had heard about it and Minnie wanted to know if it was true. She quietly told Liz the message and Liz told Etta, "You go ahead and tell her everything, Etta. But for her to try and keep it as quiet as she can."

While the boys were squealing and playing in the tub, Liz and George laughed. It was a fun bath this morning. The boys loved it. While they were in the bathroom, Etta was explaining to Minnie, what she knew. She started to cry, so Robert took the receiver from her, with a hug. He said, "Hi Minnie, it's Robert. Everything Etta told you is true, but please, don't spread it any further than it's gone, already. We're going to have an investigation ourselves and we also don't want the community to become vigilantes: Do you understand, love?"

Minnie was weeping on the other end of the phone and said, "Okay Doc. We's try ta' keep it quiet, but how's our Lizzy and our babes?"

He laughed and said, "Well, the boys are in the bath tub. Liz and George are washing all the syrup off them from breakfast." They both laughed. Robert told Minnie, Liz was okay and that her family was coming this morning. Minnie asked him if it would be okay to come later with her baked goods and some food for the family and friends that would be coming, in the next few days. Robert told her that it would be fine and that was very kind of her. He told her Liz would really appreciate the thought. They hung up the phone and Etta had overheard the conversation. She smiled at Robert for taking the call for her. It was still difficult for her to accept what's happened.

As the boys were cleaned and dressed, they came downstairs; George was wet from head to toe. Robert and Etta laughed and George said, "Liz was right. I'll have to go home to change." There was more laughter.

John piped up and said, "Can Uncle George wear daddy's clothes? Doctor Robert wore daddy's 'jamas." The laughter stopped right away.

Liz said, "C'mon you guys, you come and sit with mommy, in daddy's chair and we'll talk about daddy." George didn't care how wet he was, he wanted to stay to hear Liz's explanation and be there, just in case he was needed afterwards. It was time to get to the office, but this was more important to him. He knew the men would get to the office, gossip and eventually get to work. He wasn't sure who would be in the office when he went in.

On the airplane, Eleanor told her daughters-in-law, Maria and Joan, that she preferred to nap, if they didn't mind. They told her to go ahead; the babies were both napping, too. The girls were both teary-eyed, still: Disbelieving the horrible happenings from the day before.

As Eleanor napped, she had a dream. It started off pleasant enough, with seeing Robert and rushing into his arms. They kissed, hugged and caressed. It was beautiful and as she slept, she had a little smile to her face. She dreamed they were taking a walk, hand in hand in the woods. All of a sudden, she looked up and she saw Joe, hanging in a tree. She was moving around in her seat and all of a sudden, she bolted up in her seat and screamed.

Maria was beside her and she grabbed on to her and held her. She told the stewardess, "It's okay ma'am, she had a nightmare. She'll be alright."

The stewardess asked if there was anything she could do for Eleanor and she apologized and told her, "No dear. I thank you. Please let the passengers know I'm okay and I'm sorry for disturbing them."

The passengers were concerned, but the stewardess told them she just had a nightmare and she was okay. Everyone went about their business again and Eleanor was shaking a bit. She didn't want to tell the girls what it was about. She didn't want to upset them. The babies woke up, but they were both fed and they were fine. Eleanor turned her head towards the window and very quietly wept for her son-in-law. She thought about Liz and the boys. How could her daughter explain and make them understand where their daddy was.

As John and James each sat on a leg of their mom, she started, "Do you guys remember where God lives?"

They both nodded their heads and John said, "In heaven."

She smiled and said, "That's right, John. God lives in heaven. Well, when people stop living, it means they die. To die is to go away and live with God, in heaven. When they go there, that means that all of their family and friends will never see them, anymore. So, daddy is never going to come home, again. Yesterday, God took your daddy to live with him, in heaven. He loved your daddy so much, that he took him to be there with him, forever."

James interrupted, "But why? I wanna see him again."

Liz kissed his forehead and said, "I know sweetie. I want to see him, too. I love daddy, so much and he loved us all so much too. But it was time for him to go live with God." James started to cry.

She hugged him close and John said, "Can't we go see him in heaven?"

Liz said, "No we can't right now. Someday, it will be our time to go to heaven. When we go we will be with daddy again and that will be forever. But, that won't be for a very long time. But God will take very, very good care of daddy, for us! Do you guys understand?"

They both looked up at her, John with his big brown eyes and James with his baby blues; and they nodded their heads that they understood.

She held them both very tight and everyone in the room had tears flowing, now. They all sat in silence for a few minutes.

John was the first to speak. He wiped his eyes, took his brother's hand and said, "Okay mama, as long as God looks after him, he'll be okay! C'mon James, let's ride!" They both got off Liz's' lap and got on their horses, to race, again.

The adults looked at each other and smiled. Robert said, "Lizzy my girl, as a doctor, studying life and death most of my life and the psychology of it all, I don't ever think I've ever heard death put so simply, eloquently and beautiful as you just did, for your boys. You truly are a beautiful, amazing mommy, with so much love and understanding for them." He went to her and kissed her on the cheek. She got up and fell into his chest, buried her face and cried without letting her sons see her. He held her and took her into the kitchen.

After a few moments, she straightened up and said, "I guess I have to plan a funeral now, don't I"?

He said, "There is the whites' only undertaker and the black one, outside of town."

She said, "Obviously, it will be outside of town. I'd like to wait till mom comes, but what about the body, at the hospital. They'll want me to get him out of there."

Robert said, "Don't you worry darlin', he can stay in the morgue today, until you want the undertaker to come and get him. You can wait until your mom gets here. Do you want me to give the undertaker the head's up, about Joe?"

She said, with a bit of a chuckle, "Oh no don't worry, I'm sure he's heard the whole story by now and is expecting him."

He smiled and said "What can I do for you before I leave for Jackson?" She told him to go ahead and call the undertaker and she'd need to talk to the sheriff. She first felt she should talk to a lawyer. She thought there would be trouble. Everyone started their day and tried to make it as pain free for the boys' sake, as they could.

Robert called the black undertaker and he told Robert she could take her time and see her tomorrow, if she liked. That would give her mother time to get there and Liz time to gather her thoughts on what she'd like to have, for a funeral. Robert told Liz and, she was relieved and appreciative.

At about nine-thirty George walked into the office. All his staff was there. None of them went out to their job sites. They all decided they would stick in the office, until they heard from their boss. As George walked into the office, Maria was dabbing some tears from her eyes, without Ray seeing. George walked over to Joe's desk and pushed his chair in and draped the black cloth over the top of it. It would remain there for as long as George felt was a respectable amount of time, mourning his friend.

Ray watched him place the cloth on Joe's chair and said, "Oh come on, now. Really! Are you fuckin' kidding me? What the hell is that for? Do you really expect us to sit here and look at that thing on his chair and expect us to cry for him?"

George said, "I don't expect anything from you. This is a token of my grief. That's something you wouldn't know anything about you miserable son-of-a-bitch. Why the hell are you all sitting here? GET THE HELL TO WORK, THE LOT OF YOU!"

Bubba and Ray smiled. They grabbed their paperwork and left for their job site, with Jesse and Daniel. They headed out to their Pearl River, dam site. As they left, George looked at their shoes. Ray and Bubba's were muddy, with a bit of leaf, stuck to them.

After they left, Lorne spoke up, "Then it's true, boss? Joe was lynched?"

George swung around, grabbed Lorne by the scruff of the neck and yelled, "WHERE THE FUCK DID YOU HEAR THAT?"

Lorne was quite shocked and said, "Uh...Ray said there was a rumor around town, about it: Said it happened last night, after he and Bubba left the site."

George had a bit of a smile inside, but didn't show it. He thought to himself, HA! He caught him: The rumor should be, he committed suicide, if it was to go the way the sheriff said it. He kept this to himself: and as soon as he could, he'd tell Liz and Robert. It was becoming more obvious, the sheriff was definitely in on it: and it was murder.

He explained to the rest of them: in the office, "Joe Allen is dead. Yes, he died by hanging. I'll be helping the family out for a couple of days. When his wife decides when the funeral is, this office will be shut down for the day. I don't want anyone in here. As a matter of fact, I want everyone's key to this office, right now."

Everyone got their office keys out: and gave them to George. The only other ones he needed were Ray, Jesse's and Daniel's. Bubba didn't have one, he was always with Ray. He said, "Don't any of you dare tell Ray or the others, I'm doing this. I don't need extra keys floating around. You can either take the day off, the day of his funeral, or you can go to the funeral with me. If any of you want, you can also go to your job sites, if you want. There will be no one allowed in here, that day. Now get some work done, please."

As Etta and Liz sat down and had coffee, the doorbell rang. Minnie was there. Liz let her in. She had a cake in one hand and a pie, in the other. Etta took the cake and Minnie grabbed Liz and she held on to her. She just hugged her tight, for a moment and Etta came back to take the pie from her. Minnie put both arms around her: and said, "You be strong now, gal. Don't you let them 'gits away wit' it!"

Liz looked at her and kissed her on the cheek. She said, "Thanks for coming, Minnie. You didn't have to bring the goodies."

Minnie said, "You juss' waits here. I be back." She went back out to her car and came back in the house with a large pan of homemade corn biscuits, still warm from the oven.

Liz looked at her and said, "Minnie..."

Just then Minnie said, "You juss' hush, now gal. Your Minnie wants ta' do this, you'se ain't got time to fuss wit' makin' food 'fer company. 'Dat's what I'se gonna hep' Etta wit'." The three ladies went in the kitchen and the boys heard Minnie at the door. They ran into the kitchen and they saw a large chocolate cake, on the counter.

They looked at each other with big eyes and both said, "CHOCWATE CAKE!"

The three ladies laughed and Minnie went to kiss both boys. She said, "Now you two, your Aunt Minnie brung 'dis 'fer ever'body so you gotta ask mama if you can have some."

They both went to Liz and stood before her with a look on their faces, which no mother could ever resist. She picked up James first and said, "Well Miss Etta, you'd best cut two small pieces of that chocolate cake. We seem to have two hungry little boys here." She placed James in his chair and John followed her and she put him in his. Etta brought two small pieces of cake to the boys. Their eyes were big and their faces brightly shone with big smiles. Minnie laughed to see them so excited over her cake.

Liz said, "I don't know about you gals, but I think my waistline can stand a little chocolate cake with my coffee. Ladies, will you join me?" Just then, the doorbell rang, and it was Nancy. She had the assistant librarian take over for a bit, while she ducked out to come and see Liz.

Etta answered the door and escorted Nancy in, saying, "That's timin' Miss Nancy, we're havin' Minnie's chocolate cake and coffee. Join us." Minnie had called her to give her the news.

Nancy gave Liz a box. She stopped by the bakery and picked up some fresh squares and cookies. She had with her, a small bag for each of the boys. They both dropped their spoons and opened their bags. Inside each bag, was a gingerbread man; James took his and bit the head off right away, as he smiled and John started his with a foot, on his. The ladies laughed. Nancy hugged Liz and they all sat down with their cake and coffee, occasionally laughing at the boys' antics.

Liz said, "I dare say, Miss Etta, I don't think our boys here, are going to want lunch, at this rate. They won't have room for it." They all laughed and agreed.

Liz didn't want to talk about Joe's death and they didn't push. Liz just looked at Nancy and Minnie and took their hand and said, "Thank you. You two have been so special to me, ever since we arrived here. Thank you for your kindness. I know I can always count on the two of you to be here, to give me strength."

Just then the doorbell rang, again. Liz went out of the dining room and when she went to the door, Vincent Kirkland and his wife, Lynn was there. Liz was shocked to see her principal and his wife. Since school was still on summer break, she figured maybe they were away. Liz opened the door and welcomed them both in. Vincent gave Liz a hug and a kiss on the cheek, while his wife had tears flowing down her cheeks, Liz hugged her. She didn't know her too well, but was so touched they came.

Lynn had a box in her hand and handed it to Liz. Inside was a fresh, warm peach pie. Liz said, "Oh, how sweet, thank you. You really didn't..."

Vince interrupted and said, "It was no trouble, Liz. It's the least we could do, and I expect you'll have lots of family, coming from Canada, to be with you. We thought this might help out."

She said to them, "Thank you so much. Wow, news does travel fast in this town." They smiled and went in to the dining room. Liz said, "You all know each other, I believe. Sit, please. This is one of Minnie's famous chocolate cakes. Etta brought two more cups and plates, a fresh pot of coffee, and the cake.

The boys were finished their cakes, and Liz said, "Holy moly! Looks like you two will need a second bath. You're wearing just as much cake as you ate." They both had very satisfied smiles on their faces and laughed.

Minnie said, "Don't you worry, now. Miss Etta and I'll wash 'dem up fer ya'." The two took the boys up to the bathroom. They cleaned their faces and hands, and Minnie sang them a song. They smiled as they listened. Etta smiled, too. She loved Minnie's singing. It was a happy song, so there were no tears.

Liz smiled, in the dining room, listening to them, in the bathroom. Nancy said, "Is there anything any of us can do for you, Liz?"

Liz said, "You've already done it: Just by coming over to see me. You've shown me you care. That's the best thing friends can do." Everyone gave her a smile. Nancy apologized and excused herself, saying she had to get back to the library. Liz saw her to the door, and Nancy asked her to let her know when the funeral will be. Liz told her she would. They said goodbye, with another hug.

Liz went back to the dining room, and Vincent said, "I guess this is selfish of me to ask, Liz, but I'd like to get a head's up, if you're moving back to Canada. I'll need to hire another teacher, in your place; Or a temp, if you want time off."

It hadn't occurred to her, until that very moment. She said, "Vince, I'm not offended you asked. I understand. I don't need time off, thank you, and you won't need to hire another teacher. I am the grade one teacher at Philadelphia Elementary School, and that's where I belong. My husband is dead, but that doesn't mean I have to run home with my tail between my legs and hide from reality. I have unfinished business here. This is where Joe and I made our home, and he wouldn't want me to run away. I will be in my classroom at 9:00 a.m., the day after Labor Day." She was proud of herself for making up her mind, and saying so.

Minnie, Etta and the boys quietly had come down the stairs, while she was talking, and heard her. They were happy she was staying. Robert, Eleanor, Maria, Joan and the babies were standing in the kitchen listening, too. Eleanor said, "That's my strong baby girl. Honey, you stick to your scruples!"

Liz jumped up and yelled, "MOM!!! MOM!!! You're here." She ran into her mother's arms and held her. El grasped her daughter, and held her so tight. They both started crying, not saying anything; just crying. After a moment, Liz saw her sisters-in-law, and hugged both of them, thanked them for coming and she kissed the babies.

Robert put his arm around her and said, "How are you doing?"

Liz said, "C'mon in, my school principal, Vince and his wife are here. You just missed Nancy, and Etta and Minnie who washed my chocolate cake, covered twins..."

The boys broke loose and ran to El. "GRANDMA!!" She got down on her knees and hugged both of her grandsons. She was so happy to see them.

After everyone said their hellos, Vince and Lynn told Liz, they had to go, but offered any help she needed. She thanked them, and Vince hugged Liz and said, "I'm glad you're staying. See you soon."

Liz asked if anyone was hungry: That there were a lot of sweets and cornbread biscuits. Robert brought the luggage in, and they sat down to some treats everyone brought over, while Etta put more coffee and tea on.

Just then, there was a knock at the door. It was Alvin and Agnes Diamont. They just talked to Liz at the door. They wanted to pay their respects, but couldn't stay. After talking for a moment, she told them thanks for coming, and she'd let them know when the funeral would be. They both hugged her, and left, with tears in their eyes.

The boys were tiring out and looked like they needed a nap.

Etta asked, "Do you want me to put them down for their nap?"

Grandma interrupted, "Oh, Miss Etta, please let me do it?" Liz told her mother to go ahead, and told the boys she wanted a kiss. They both gave their mommy big wet kisses, and toddled up the stairs, to their rooms, with grandma. When she left James' room, she took John in to his room.

As she put John in his bed, he looked up at his grandma with his big brown eyes and said, "Grandma, daddy went to heaven to live with God forever. But we will see him someday, but not for a long time. Mommy cried."

El had big tears in her eyes, and she couldn't help it. She looked at her grandson and said, "I know, honey. She's crying because she misses him. It's okay to cry. That shows how much we love your daddy. So if you want to cry, it's okay. Mommy won't mind. She loves you and your brother very much. You're going to miss your daddy, too. But, he will always be in your heart. God is looking after him, now. So when we say our bedtime prayers, we can also say hi to daddy, at the same time."

John sat up, and put his little arms around El's neck and said, "Night, night, grandma," and he lay down. She kissed him, tucked him in and quietly left the room, and wept outside his door. She didn't want to go downstairs, until she stopped crying.

The doorbell went, again. This time, it was unwanted company. The sheriff! Liz looked at him and asked, "What the hell do you want?"

He said, "Ma'am, I don't want any trouble, I'm just here to tell you, we completed our investigation, and to the best of our knowledge, your husband died by his own hand. Now, I don't know exactly what your relationship with your husband was, whether you was havin'...trouble, but he took his own life...the simple truth, ma'am." He tipped his hat, handed her a one page report, and said, "I'm sorry about your husband, but I also was asked to relay to you, that the town undertaker, will not handle your husband's funeral. You'll have to go, out of town...if you get my meanin'. G'day, ma'am."

Liz saw red! Blood and she wanted the sheriff's. Robert could see it in her eyes and he was ready. As the sheriff got back in his car, Liz was ready to go after him. Robert bolted across the room and caught hold of her and he held her. She was trying with all her strength to break free from his hold, but couldn't.

She was screaming, "YOU ROTTEN SON-OF-A-BITCH. I'M GOING TO TEAR YOU APART, LIMB FROM LIMB, YOU BETTER RUN, YOU FUCKING PRICK."

Robert was having a hard time holding her, and he whispered in her ear, "Lizzy, don't you make things worse. We'll have an investigation of our own and find out the truth, you hush now, and let him go. That is only the police report. The coroner said, "suspicious death."

The sheriff drove out of the driveway and Liz did not see, but Robert did...the sheriff had a big smile on his face. Robert knew the truth at that moment. Everyone in the house that day- knew the truth, too. Joe was lynched by Ray Halden, Sheriff Appleton, and the KKK.

Robert saw it, all over his face, just in his wicked smile! There was no one on earth that would ever make Liz believe that Joe killed himself.

El went to Liz to hold her and she finally broke free of Robert's protective grasp and she ran out into the back yard. She was walking around in circles, screaming obscenities. The two babies were crying and everyone was shocked to hear Liz go on, so. Eleanor wasn't. It was quiet in the house, at first, but El started to laugh. She tried not to make a spectacle of herself, but she couldn't stop laughing. Everyone thought she was losing her mind. She laughed until she had tears in her eyes. Robert couldn't help it, but he started to laugh, too.

As they watched Liz, out the window, El smacked him on the chest and said, "Now hush, so she can't hear us laughing. We have to just let her go, but stop laughing." She slowed her laugh, and finally stopped. Everyone didn't quite understand, but never said anything. El and Robert just stood watching her in the back yard, letting her rant and rave, and get it out of her system. Neighbors were looking out their windows and wondering if she'd lost her mind. They just kept to themselves.

George stayed at work until each man was gone and he knew no one needed to stay late, telling his men, he'd be there before eight-thirty in the morning, to unlock the office. He went out to Ray's site and asked for his key to the office.

Ray said, "Are you firing us, boss?"

George said, "No, I'm not. I want your key to the office, for a few days." Ray was puzzled, and so were the others, but, Ray, Jesse and Daniel took their keys out and gave them to George.

George said, "I'll be at the office before eight-thirty in the morning to let everyone in. If there are no problems here, I'll say good night, and see you in the morning." Ray told him there were no problems and said goodnight to George.

George drove away, and wanted to throw up. He couldn't stand the sight of Ray, or Bubba. His priority was to get to Liz's and make sure his family was alright. He drove to his home, first, to have a shower and change, and he wanted to take something with him, but he wasn't sure, what. He thought people would already be there with food, and their condolences. He didn't want to go empty handed. He thought for a minute, and he went to his workshop, in his basement. He was working on a carving for the boys. It was meant to be for Christmas, and he wasn't finished, yet. But he made a decision. He would take part of the gift to the boys now, and add to it for Christmas.

He was carving a wooden train for each of them. He had both engines made, and another car. His plan was to carve each one a train that included an engine, a flatbed car, a box car, and a tanker car. To finish them both, would be a beautiful red caboose. They were going to be the same, except for the painting. Each one would have a different colored engine, so they could tell them apart. The other way, was easy...on one, he had painted the words, "The James Express" and on the other, "The John Express". This way, there would be no fighting. He would also paint their names on each car. He was so pleased with himself. He loved his boys.

George couldn't believe how these two little boys, found their way into his heart. Although, they called him "Uncle George", he sort of felt they were like grandsons, rather than nephews. Either way, it didn't matter. They were his family, and he loved them more than anything; just like he did, Liz and Joe.

Joe....he thought about Joe. Hanging from a tree...terrified. His last hours and minutes must have been horrible. He let a tear fall, as he thought of him probably being dragged to a tree, somewhere, and being hung, while surrounded by a bunch of assholes, who were so cruel, to sentence a man to death, for being a different color from themselves. As his tears fell, he became angry with God.

The last time he felt this way, was when his wife died, several years before His wife was a beautiful, happy, woman who was very much in love with George, ever since they were at university, together. He was getting his Engineering Degrees, and she was studying Geology. She was very interested in the ground she lived on. She started collecting rocks, as a child and studied everything she could about geology, all her life; That's where she and George met.

After they married, they started the business, together and were a successful team. The one part of their lives that lacked was children. They were always hopeful, but were never blessed with any They never understood, why God had passed them by as parents, until she was found to have cancer She always seemed to have had, 'women problems'. She was never to become pregnant, in her life.

As the years went by, they prayed, and they hoped, but it was never to be. After an early menopause, she was discovered to have cancerous tumors on her ovaries and in her uterus. There was nothing that could be done for her. Within months of being diagnosed, she was dead. George was angry that God could take a woman with so much love to give him and the world around her. He turned to work. That was all he thought about: Until he started to help out a family of one of his employees.

This family took him to their hearts and he took them, to his. He loved Joe's family and was so honored to be with them, right from the day after the twins were born. Color never mattered to him. He was not a bigot. He just stayed to himself and his business and finally understood their struggles, after coming to know Joe. This was also when he began to understand the ways of the Ku Klux Klan, too. He always disapproved in the Klan, but his life wasn't really touched by them, until Joe came to work for him.

He knew Ray Halden, one of his hydraulic engineers was Klan, but he felt, as long as Ray didn't interfere in George's business and left him alone, he'd leave Ray alone, too. He tried to protect Joe without anyone knowing, but it finally came to a head and George couldn't save Joe. George hoped that the law would get to the bottom of things and the Klan would be found guilty of murder. He knew Joe couldn't commit suicide. It wasn't in him and he would never leave his family like that.

His thoughts turned back to the trains. He had the engines complete and the flat bed cars done and painted, for each train. He would take them over tonight and work on the other cars- and cabooses for Christmas. He was happy he thought of this. He put them both in a box.

After seeing Liz drink the scotch the night before and he'd seen her have a beer with them, and with all the company she was sure to have, he decided he would take her a bottle of whiskey, for her company and he knew she wouldn't be offended. Next, he went into the back yard and cut some roses from his wife's favorite rose bush.

Liz had been to George's house a few times and admired them so much. Before his wife died, he promised her that he would always look after her rose bushes. This was the first time, he cut some off for someone else, but he knew his wife would approve. He cut a dozen, long stems and they were the most beautiful shade of red, Liz had ever seen. She loved them so. He was also going to offer Liz some for the funeral if she'd like, too. He gathered everything together and set off for Gilbert Street.

George rang the doorbell and poked his head through like he always did and said, "It's Uncle George." The boys were still awake and heard him. They both ran to the door, squealed with delight. Liz came to the door and kissed him. He gave her the roses and she was so thrilled. She knew they came from his wife's garden. She hugged him and kissed him again and thanked him. They made her think of Joe and all the times he brought flowers home for her over the years; and she smiled.

George also gave her the whiskey and she said, "Wow...thank you!!! Uh oh, do I see something in the box for two little boys?"

The twins heard her and started to tug on George's pant legs. He moved into the living room, where everyone was and he said hi to Eleanor and Robert and Liz introduced him to her sisters-in-law, Joan and Maria. The boys kept saying, "Uncle George, Uncle George, what's in the box?"

He got down on the floor with his box and gave the boys their trains. Their eyes went so big, George thought they might pop right out of their heads and they had the biggest, sweetest grins. They fell in love with them. He showed each one, their names on the engine and car and showed him how to connect them and that they even rolled, on the floor.

John stood up and went to George and put his arms around his neck and gave him a big kiss on the lips, and a hug. He said, "Tank you Uncle George." Everyone was surprised. Liz didn't prompt him to say thank you and she didn't have to, very often. They were both brought up to be very polite. James got up and did the same thing and George was so happy. She was very proud of her sons.

He turned to Liz and said, "Lizzy darlin', this makes life worthwhile, doesn't it?" At that moment, he thought maybe he said the wrong thing, but as he looked at her, she was giving him a look that made him feel good. She wasn't hurt, or offended by his remark.

Liz said, "George, you're right. They're the strong ones around here." Liz got on the floor and grabbed both of her boys and hugged them. She said, "George, we have two little girls here you haven't met, yet. My nieces are visiting, too." She turned to Joan and Maria and said, "George is the biggest softy when it comes to kids...as if you couldn't tell! The boys just love him." He blushed a little. She turned to the boys and said, "Well guys, guess what time it is?"

Both boys tried to pull away from her saying, "No bed mommy!" Everyone laughed. Liz kept hold of them and hugged them both, again.

She said, "Yes, but you can take your trains to bed with you tonight, how would that be?" They smiled, nodded their heads and liked that idea.

Liz got up and told them to go around and give good night hugs to everyone. As they did, everyone was commenting on how cute they are and sweet. Liz took them upstairs. She washed them, but they didn't need another bath. As they got into their pajamas she said, "Ok guys, say your prayers."

As she sat on John's bed, they both knelt down and John started, "Dear God, thank you for the day, and thank you for mommy."

James continued, "Say hi to daddy for us, cause he's there and tell him good night." They both said Amen, at the same time. Liz couldn't help it. She started to cry, again. Both boys got off their knees and reached up to hug her.

She smiled and kissed both of them, telling them she loved them and she thought it was a beautiful prayer and she was sure God would give daddy their message. She tucked them both in to John's bed, since Maria, Joan and the girls were in James's room. She kissed both of them good night and said, "Now I know you want to play with your trains, but you just be careful not to hurt each other with them. I'll see you in the morning. Nighty night." She blew them each kisses, as she turned the light off and started to close the door.

Just before she did, James said, "Mommy, daddy is okay with God, he'll look after him, don't cry."

She blew them another kiss and closed the door. She slipped into her bedroom and lay down on her bed. She couldn't help it. She cried. She thought about every night that she and Joe put the boys to bed and listened to their prayers and she had no idea how much her boys had grown up, over the last twenty-four hours. They were turning into sensitive, sweet, loving little boys. She knew Joe would be as proud of their behavior, today…just as she was.

She dried her eyes and washed her face. She went downstairs and asked, "Who would like a drink: I know, I want one. I have scotch, whiskey and beer…"

Just then Eleanor said, "Honey, I forgot, I brought you a few bottles of that wine that you like. They're in my suitcase." She went upstairs to get the wine and Liz got the guys a beer and Maria, Joan, Eleanor and Etta decided on the wine.

Liz got out her beautiful crystal wine glasses that she and Joe got for a wedding present. They all had a drink and raised their glasses to Joe' in his memory. Afterward, Liz thought to herself, 'I know you're here Joe, I can feel you'!

Eleanor said, "Honey, will you be okay if I stay at Robert's place?"

Liz said, "Oh, I have room 'for you on the hide-a-bed. Uh, oh...well, I guess it's up to you, mom. Wherever you like is fine."

George piped up and said, "Remember darlin', when you end up with more company from home, you have a couple of bedrooms at my place you can use, too." She was touched by the offer and might need it, depending on how many people were coming from the farm. She told him thank you and she'd keep it in mind.

Eleanor said, "Okay, I'll sleep here." Robert was disappointed, but understood. El continued, "Would you mind if Robert stayed here, too?"

Liz said, "Yeah, no problem. I was just thinking, if I need you through the night...well, never mind, I'm being silly. You go ahead to Robert's if you like."

Robert said, "Honey I'll stay here so your mom will be nearby for you: If that's okay with you, that is?"

Liz smiled at him and said, "Robert, you're always welcome, you know that and George, you too. We're just one big happy family under this roof, right?" Everyone gave a giggle and raised their glasses to Liz.

George said, "Well sweetie, thanks for the drink, but I have to go. I have to get in before eight-thirty tomorrow. You call me at home or work, if you need anything. Just let me know when the funeral will be, or if I can help with anything. Oh if you like, you can have some roses for the funeral, too. Good night, all."

Liz hugged him and told him she'd talk to him as soon as plans were made and thanked him for the offer of his roses. She told him she'd love some. George gave her a kiss and said, "You try and get some sleep, now."

Robert got up and said, "I'll walk you out, George." When the men were outside, at George's car, Robert said, "Appleton was here today. He gave her the "official" police -report. It says, in no uncertain terms, Joe committed suicide, case closed."

George started to get angry again and said, "You're God Damned kiddin' me?"

Robert said, "Liz blew. It was all I could do to keep her from tearing him apart, limb from limb, as she put it. If I'd let her go, I believe, she would have done it."

George was pissed off. He said, "I wish I knew where it happened, because I know we could prove it, somehow, it wasn't suicide. There's no way, he did it."

Robert said, "I told Liz we were going to quietly hire a private investigator to check it out. We're not going to say anything, but just get an independent report, on what they find. I completely agree, he didn't do it; the coroner agreed it was suspicious." George agreed with hiring an investigator and the two men shook hands as they said good night and George went home.

When Robert went back in the house Liz said, "Well, since you're staying here tonight, have another beer! Is George okay?"

Robert said, "Yeah, he's still mad as hell. I just wanted to tell him about the sheriff's report. I hope you don't mind?"

Liz said, "No, I don't mind." She gave Robert another beer and took the bottle of wine in the living room, to top up the ladies' glasses.

Eleanor said, "It sounds like the boys went right to sleep. I'm getting tired, too." No one wanted more wine, so Liz put the bottle back in the fridge. Joan, Maria, and Etta all turned in for the night. There was just Eleanor, Robert and Liz left up.

Liz looked at her mom and said, "Mom, will the hurt stop, some day?"

El said, "Honey they always say it will, but it doesn't ever go away, completely. I still hurt for your dad. Not just the way he died and how he hurt me, but he was my husband. I loved him, so much. I still hurt, some. You and Joe knew each other from birth. You hardly spent time apart, except in university and when he worked in Toronto. It gets a little easier to cope with day-by-day life, as time goes by, but you'll never forget your love for each other. It took me some time to realize, but there wasn't a day that went by, that we didn't love each other. I know he loved me...even when he was hurting me. Honey, you'll always love him, but don't shut your heart off. Someone may come along someday and it might surprise you. Joe wouldn't want you to stay lonely."

Liz said, "Mom, I don't want to think about that. I just want to think about Joe. I miss him, mom."

El came over to her daughter and sat beside her. She said, "You have a lot of wonderful years in you, girl. And, you have two very sweet boys, who love you very much."

Liz smiled and hugged her mother. She said, "I know. I don't know what I'd do without them. I love them so much: You too mom."

Liz gave El a kiss and said, "Good night mom, good night, Robert. See you both in the morning. The sheets and blankets are on the bed, already, pillows in the linen closet. Mom, I moved your suitcase to my room, so you can change there, if you like. Robert, I'll toss down those pajamas you wore last night, if you like."

Robert said, "Yeah that's fine Lizzy, thanks. Good night, love."

After the lights were out Robert held Eleanor as she wept, some more: She said, "I'm sorry. It was such a senseless death. Why Joe? He was a wonderful father and husband."

Robert said, "Honey please don't make yourself sick, over it. You'll need to be strong for her and the boys."

She turned to him and held her hand against his cheek and said, "I know, dear. I love you: Good night darlin'."

He passionately kissed Eleanor and said, "Good night sweetheart." They fell asleep, in minutes. The Allen house was quiet. Tomorrow would be a day of organization and planning.

Chapter 16

Sad Days Ahead

WEDNESDAY MORNING ARRIVED. LIZ HOPED the last two days had been a nightmare, but as she looked around her bedroom. Joe wasn't there. His side of the bed was cold. He hadn't been there. As the tears started to well up in her eyes, there were two little boys trying to sneak into her room. They could barely reach the doorknob and turn it, but grandma was there to help.

Both boys and grandma, just barely peeked around the edge of the door and Liz burst out laughing. It looked so funny, to her. It was like a Three Stooges film. Here, she was looking at Larry, Moe and Curly, peeking to see if she was awake. She sat up in her bed and both boys came bounding and grandma helped them jump on her bed. She threw her arms around them and they tackled her.

Liz said, "SHHH guys, everyone is still sleeping."

They both shook their heads and Eleanor said, "Sorry love, you're the only one left in bed."

Liz looked at her clock and it said nine o'clock. She said, "Holy Shit!"

James said, "Mommy, dat's a bad word, Uncle George said it."

Liz smiled, and said, "That's right, James, mommy shouldn't have said it. I'm sorry." She hugged them both and got out of bed. She put on her slippers and housecoat and went downstairs.

Everyone said their good mornings to her and she took a cup of coffee, saying, "Why didn't anyone get me up for breakfast?"

Robert said, "Well, you can blame your mother and your doctor for that. We decided you needed sleep; more than anything else. As a matter of fact, you were so tired, you slept through everyone eating breakfast; even George was here, on his way to work. He stopped in to say hi and have a coffee. Well, do you feel rested enough for your day, love?"

Liz said, "As a matter of fact, I do. I think I can face the outside world today and go see the undertaker, as soon as I wash and dress."

Etta said, "No you don't Missy, you have to eat some breakfast first, girl." She placed scrambled eggs and toast, in front of Liz. She wasn't too hungry, but she still ate it all. She knew Etta was right, she needed to eat.

The boys were busy playing and not caring what was going on around them. They were happy. James and John both liked having the baby girls around the house. They were like little dolls. Joan and Abe's daughter Maxine was three months old and Maria and Simon's daughter, Christine was six months old. She was more fun. She could roll and smile and giggle. The boys loved to tickle her tummy and listen to her laugh. There were many cute opportunities to take pictures of the little cousins together. They all made the adults laugh.

Liz showered and dressed and asked if everyone would mind watching the boys, while she went to make funeral arrangements. No one minded. After all, they were there to help and support her in any way they could.

Robert drove Liz and Eleanor, just a mile out of the north end of Philadelphia. Out there was an undertaker who dealt with the Negro population's funerals. Liz fell in love with the name of the parlor, "Peace of Heaven". That was the place that would take care of her Joe. She actually smiled as she entered the building.

A kindly looking elderly man, she figured to be in his mid-sixties, came to her and extended his hand to her. He said, "Good morning Ma'am. I'm Sam Waters. Would ya'll be Mrs. Allen? I been s'pectin' ya."

Liz looked startled and said, "Why yes, how do you do." She shook his hand and continued, "But how did you...?"

He said, "Well Ma'am, I'd say you'd be 'da only white woman comin' 'fer my services, an' I'se here to hep' you."

She smiled and thanked him, as he guided them into a private room. She expected the building to be a little more dilapidated, than it was, for a black business. It was a decent place and such a kind gentleman to help her, to boot! She had a good feeling about today. She thanked God, already.

Liz introduced her mother and then he said, "Pleased to know ya'll, Mrs. McDonald, but now, ya'll don't needs to introduce Dr. Hathaway. Robert, how ya'll been doin'?"

Robert said, "Fine Sam, thanks for being here for Liz, Mrs. Allen. Joe's body is still at the morgue at Lincoln Hospital. I've put a release on him, to only you. You will be the one to pick him up, Sam?"

Sam said, "Yes'sir, Doc, I'll git' him, as soon as I hep' Mrs. Allen wit' ever'ting she be wantin'. But, I got a problem. T'day, my hep' is sick an' I gots no one to hep' me git 'da body. Do you 'tinks you could see your way clear to go wit' me an' hep' me wit' it, doc?"

Robert said, "Sure Sam, no problem. I'll go with you and El and Liz can drive my car back to the house and I'll go with you to the hospital and I'll come back here and help at this end, too. El, I'll give a call and you could come back and pick me up, if you don't mind." Eleanor nodded her head in agreement.

Sam said, "Well, 'dat be very kind o' you, doc, 'tanks. Now, Mrs. Allen..."

Liz said, "Please, everyone calls me Liz. Mrs. Allen kind of hurts right now...just a bit." He nodded his head, he understood. Liz said, "Well Sam, first, do you have a problem with their being several white people here for the service?"

He said, "No, Mrs...Uh...Liz. It don't matter what color yo' skin be, if 'dey wants ta' come an' say g'bye to yo' husban', 'den 'deys welcome to come. We's all God's chil'run." She smiled and thanked him. She liked him.

He showed them the caskets and Liz picked solid white pine. Joe loved the smell of pine. She did, too. The lining would be silk. Most couldn't afford it, but Sam kept some in stock, for those who could. It was white silk.

Liz wasn't asking for opinions from Robert and Eleanor, but they both agreed with her. They wanted to be near her, if she needed them, but it was up to her to make the decisions. Eleanor thought everything should be decided by Liz. It was up to her, since she was Joe's widow and if anyone didn't like it, she'd deal with them, herself!

Mr. Waters asked, "Liz, is he bein' interred here?"

She didn't even look at her mom. She didn't want to see a disapproving look. She said, "Well, Mr. Waters, Sam, I hope you can help me with this." She took a deep breath and continued, "I want him cremated and want to keep the ashes, in an urn."

Sam said, "No problem, Ma'am. I can 'rrange 'dat 'fer ya'. It'll cost ya' a bit more."

She said, "Price is no object, Sam."

He said, "Yes Ma'am, it won't be a problem. Do ya'll want him cremated befo' or afta' 'da service?"

She hadn't thought about it and paused for a moment. While everyone waited in silence she finally spoke, "I want him to be laid out, in an open casket, so everyone can see what was done to him. I don't want any make up or facial re-construction done."

Eleanor interjected, "Honey, what about James and John. They have to see him and say good-bye."

She said, "Thanks, mom. I hadn't thought of that. They have to see him, before he goes." The tears started to come. Sam got up and handed her a full box of Kleenex and she laughed, "You think I'll need a whole box, huh?" Sam just smiled warmly at her. She continued, "Robert, do you think he needs much fixing on the face?"

Robert thought for a moment and said, "Honey, maybe the crushed cheek bones could be filled a little, to make them look a little more natural. The cuts and abrasions can be touched with make-up. The swelling from the beating he took, will still be visible, but some of it will have gone down by now. Right, Sam?"

Sam said, "Yes, all 'dat be c'rrect. Does ya' have a picture of your husban'?" He looked at Liz. She went into her purse and took out a photo of Joe. She put it in her purse before they left the house. She thought she might need it. She also brought his half of the marriage kerchief. Eleanor forgot all about that part.

Sam said, "Fine lookin' man, Liz, jus' fine. I can fix him, as best I can, so yo' sons can see him, an' we don't want 'dem gittin' scared...he be lookin' juss' like 'dey remembers him." She smiled, and thanked him again, for all his kindness.

He said, "Now, I has several urns, let me show 'dem to ya'll."

Liz looked them over. She chose a beautiful, manly black one. It was polished granite and she really liked it. She decided the cremation would take place after the people left the service, and Sam offered to deliver the urn to the house to her over that weekend, or, whenever she preferred. She gave him her phone number and address and asked him to call, to make sure she was home, when he wanted to bring it to her. He agreed.

Liz said, "Mom, do you think I could cut a small piece of the Kente Cloth Robe that Afua Kakira made and place it in the coffin, with him? And, a small piece of the McGee Tartan?"

Eleanor said, "Honey, they belong to you. You do what you wish, with them."

Liz said, "Technically, they belong to John and James. I'll explain about them and ask them, both. It's about time they hear the stories about their great-great-grandparents again, don't you think, mom?" She smiled and shook her head.

Just then, Sam said, "Does I detect Ashanti Tribe, maybe from Ghana?"

El and Liz looked wide eyed at him. Liz said, "Yes, that's Joe's heritage. Both of his great-grandparents were Ashanti, from Ghana."

Sam said, "My kin, too. Men stole 'dem way back in mid-1800's. Bad business, 'den. But, we come of it: We's still here."

Liz lowered her head and said, "Some are here and some get murdered, Sam." After a second she continued, "Now, I have a strange request. Do you know anyone who can conduct part of the service in Twi, or Akan language?"

Sam smiled. He said, "Me, Ma'am."

Liz grinned. She was happy to hear this. She asked him if he'd mind translating a part of the service and he said he'd be delighted to. She was ecstatic.

Liz said, "Mom, if you and Robert have anything you want to do, or go for a walk, Sam and I can go over some details and you can come back in a bit; if that's okay?" Everyone agreed.

Robert and Eleanor went out for a walk. Robert knew the area well and there were a couple of elderly residents around there, he hadn't seen in about a week. He had his black bag in the car and he and El made some house calls.

Sam told Liz that he arranged with the black minister, Pastor Brown, in the community to do the service and he would do whatever she requested. Sam told her the reverend was unavailable to meet with her that morning, but sent apologies and Sam would make sure Liz got the service she wanted, down to the letter. She was fine with that. She also requested a choir and Sam said that wasn't a problem, either.

As Sam showed Liz around, he didn't show her the utility room at the rear of the building. This was where he prepared the bodies for burial or cremation. She noticed he had a fairly large hall attached to his parlor, too. This hall was used as the local black church. He told Liz that because the Black Church was bombed a few years earlier by the Klan and the black community could not afford to replace it, Sam decided to build this hall onto his building and that's where the community worshiped every Sunday. He also had another large room, where he used for custom furniture repair and refinishing. This helped supplement their meager income from the funeral business and was appreciated by the surrounding community.

Sam then showed her some traditional funeral services and she picked a very classic, simple one. He said he'd translate whatever she wanted. He also told her it was lovely that she wanted to put a piece of the Kente Robe, in with him. He asked her if he might see it. She told him, that was not a problem, she'd be proud to show it to him and she mentioned that Joe wore it to their wedding.

Sam's wife came in the room with a tray of coffee and homemade cookies. Liz was delighted to meet Honoree. She and Sam had been married since they were thirteen years old. He told Liz they hadn't always been in Mississippi. Their family came from Chatham, Ontario.

Liz's ears certainly perked up at this point. She said, "I don't believe this. I was born in the Chatham Hospital. My family owns a really large potato farm, there. I was raised there, with my husband. As a matter of fact, my mother, Mrs. McDonald owns it. Maybe you've heard of it. Olde McDonald's Potato Farm?"

Sam almost dropped his teeth. He said, "Mrs. Allen. Be you'se 'da relatives of Jed Allen?"

Liz said, "Yes, yes! My Joe is...was...the great-grandson of Jed and Mary Allen."

Sam said, "Hoooweee! Don't 'dat beat all? I'se be 'da grandson of Rolly Waters: Jed and Mary's good frien'. He lived wit' 'dem, 'fer a piece, but he worked on 'dat very potato farm! I believe 'dat 'dey was the very good friends of John and Diana McDonald, 'da owners."

Liz said, "My dad was George McDonald, Jr. His grandparents were Johnny and Diana." Liz was wishing now, she hadn't let her mom and

Robert leave. She was so thrilled. She said, "Oh my Lord, mom isn't going to believe this."

As Robert and El walked around hand in hand, in the slum neighborhood, they stopped at an elderly couple's tar papered shack. The lady was dying of cancer and wouldn't go to the hospital. Robert had been treating her, at home. There was nothing much that could be done, since she refused to go to the hospital. That was where she wanted to die: At home, with her family around her. Robert stopped in to give her husband more morphine, to keep his wife comfortable.

She was happy to see him, but did not have strength to get out of bed. Her husband was with her, constantly. He did not work during the worst of his wife's illness. He temporarily quit his job, to look after her. Their family was supporting them and when she passes on, he'll go back to work.

Robert told El, as they left the house, "That happens a lot, here. These people have been married so long the spouse often stays home to nurse the other, when they're dying. The rest of the family helps to support them, during this time. It's really quite sweet, when you think about it."

El said, "And sad...Robert, you don't get paid out here, do you?"

He laughed. "I do. In satisfaction, that I helped another human being."

Eleanor stopped in her tracks, turned to face him and put her arms around his neck and said, "Darling, that's why I love you so much. You love what you're doing and you're happy doing it." She reached up and they kissed, right in the middle of the road.

There were many people sitting, working outside their shacks, doing different things. Cleaning fish, tending small gardens, beating blankets and rugs...they all stopped what they were doing and looked at the couple. Most people were quite surprised to see their black doctor kissing a white woman.

One elderly woman called out, "Dr. Robert, you 'tinks ya'll should be doin' 'dat, here?"

He stopped kissing El and said back to the lady, "I think it's the perfect thing to do. We're in love!"

The lady called back to them, "Well 'den, ya'll juss' goes right ahead." A few people chuckled, who were watching.

Robert and Eleanor both laughed and walked over to the woman so he could introduce El. The lady just made some tea and asked Robert and El to have a cup. They agreed and sat with her and drank tea. They chatted a bit and when they were done, they got up and both thanked the lady for her hospitality and shook her hand and left. They were both in a little state of shock. Some of that black community, secretly witnessed Joe's hanging.

Never in their wildest dreams, did they expect to find this startling piece of news, today. As they walked on to the next patient's house, El asked, "Hun, do we tell Liz?"

Robert said, "Yes. I'm just not sure when love: Before, or after the funeral. For all we know, maybe Sam is telling Liz the same thing, at this very moment."

They went in to the next house and the patient was a little girl with Spina Bifida. El heard of it, but never knew anyone with it. The little girl was born with a hole in her back. Her spinal column and cord protruded through this hole. Robert was able to find a surgeon to close the hole, but she would never walk. She was now five years old and her mother was at home with her, all the time.

The little girl smiled when she saw Robert come in the house. Although she was five, her mind was that of a three year old and always would be. She recognized Robert and her smile was big and her eyes shone, whenever he came to check on her. She knew the doctor always had a candy in his black bag for her. El thought she was the sweetest little girl and watched her, as she smiled and was immediately thanking the Lord, for her healthy grandchildren.

Her mother told Robert that things were still the same. She couldn't walk and still had to wear diapers. She had no control over her bowel, or bladder; and Robert told her mother that she may likely be that way, permanently. Her mother hoped and prayed this wouldn't be so. As they left, El had a tear in her eye, but was amazed to see how happy the little girl was. Robert and Eleanor held hands and walked back to the funeral parlor, to meet Liz.

When they walked in, Liz heard them come in and ran to them. She was excited. She grabbed her mom's hand and dragged her back to the small room they were in. She said, "Oh my God mom. You won't believe this. Sam's grandfather was Rolly Waters."

El knew that was a familiar name from the family past. Liz said, "Remember the story, Rolly Waters was Jed Allen's best friend from Africa. They grew up in the same village. Mom, Rolly took over as Johnny McDonald's head farm hand, when Jed Allen was dying of Sickle Cell Disease.

Rolly died, just after he found out that his girlfriend, who lived in Chatham, became pregnant. He knew he was going to be a father, but Sally's father took her away. Rolly died of pneumonia. Sally had a boy, she named Rolly Jr., and he had a son, named Sam." As Liz said this, she pointed to Mr. Sam Waters, the undertaker. El was shocked; Robert, too. They couldn't believe they were hearing this, it was too fantastic! They were so happy to hear, they had such close family history and another 'common thread'.

At home, Etta was busy keeping the house clean and preparing food, for many people, for the next few days. James and John were well cared for. They had their cousins to watch over. They were so excited by these baby girls. They watched everything their mothers did with amazement, and amusement. Joan and Maria tried to keep them happy and laughing. It worked. They were very happy with their cousins and they did not get under foot, at all. Etta was pleased, since she was so busy.

Joan and Maria asked Etta if it would be alright if they took the boys for a walk. She said it would be okay, if they wanted to go. Of course, the boys jumped at the chance. Etta usually took them for a walk during the day and wasn't sure she would have time.

Liz still had a carriage in the garage, from when the boys were smaller. The ladies got the carriage out of the garage and both babies fit into it comfortably. The boys were 'big boys', now. They could walk alongside, with their aunts, holding their hand, making the walk much longer. But, no one minded.

The ladies decided to walk for a few blocks and then circle back. They had a lovely time, looking at all the beautiful gardens. James and John wanted to dawdle and play on the way, as they usually did with their mom and Miss Etta.

As they were walking, the littlest baby, Maxine woke up crying. They boys wanted to know what was wrong. They wanted to see what was wrong with their cousin, so they tried to climb up on the carriage. John said, "What's wrong with baby?"

Joan said, "I think she's hungry. Do you think we should go home and feed her?"

James said, "Yeah...she sounds real hungry to me. Can we eat, too?"

Maria said, "I think Miss Etta will have lunch ready when we get home." The boys got excited and picked up speed a bit.

When they returned home, Etta was making sandwiches for everyone. She had all kinds of desserts for everyone and lots of tea, coffee and milk. After she placed everything on the dining room table, she took the boys to the bathroom to wash their hands. She asked if they had fun on their walk and they both told her they liked walking with their baby cousins. She thought it was so cute the way John and James seemed to dote on the babies.

Etta was not sure when to expect Liz, Robert and Eleanor, so she decided she would make something fresh for them, when they came in. Everyone sat to eat their lunch and Joan was feeding Maxine, at the same time. The boys watched very attentively, as they ate their bologna sandwiches.

Just then, Liz and El came into the house. James and John were still keeping their eyes on Maxine, but when Liz came into the dining room, they both turned to her, with mustard faces and said, "Hi mama!" They showed her what they were eating as she came to their high chairs to give each one a kiss. They saw El and both said hi to her, too. They thought they should also show grandma what they were eating, so they showed her their bologna sandwiches, too.

Etta said, "Well Mrs. Liz, Mrs. Eleanor, I was just about to give them their milk. All three smiled at each other. Liz went to the kitchen and brought out two glasses of milk. James and John looked at it and both stopped eating. James said, "Dat's not milk, mommy."

Liz said, "Sure it is. It just happens to be different. Do you remember our colors?" John nodded his head. Liz asked him, "What color is milk?"

He said, in a coy, matter-of-fact way, "White, silly mommy!" Everyone laughed.

Liz held up the glass and asked, "What color is this?"

James piped up and said, "It's brown!"

Liz said, "That's right. Now, I just want you to taste it. It's special milk, that grandma thought you both might like to try. Eleanor had picked up some 'Nestle Quik', chocolate powder, which turns ordinary milk into chocolate milk. They both tasted it and liked it. They thought it was a great treat, and thanked grandma.

After lunch, the boys and the girls all went down for naps. The phone rang and Liz answered. It was Robert wanting El to come to the parlor and pick him up. He was finished helping Sam take Joe's body from the hospital to the funeral home. Liz said she'd tell her mom that he was ready to be picked up.

Liz wanted to ask some questions, but they could wait until he came back to the house. As El was getting ready to pick Robert up she said, "Honey do you mind if Robert and I go out for a bit?"

Liz said, "No, not at all. You'll both be here for supper?"

El said, "Oh yes dear. Is there anything that I can do for you, or pick anything up for you?"

Liz said that she couldn't think of anything. She kissed her mom and asked if she remembered how to get back to the funeral parlor. She did.

When Eleanor got back to the funeral parlor, Sam and Robert were talking. She wondered if maybe Sam told him anything he knew about Joe's hanging. He did. He told Robert the same story, the woman told them.

She got out of the driver's seat of Robert's car, so he could get in. She went around and got in to the passenger side and she asked, "How bad does he look, Robert?"

He said, "Hun, I'd prefer not to tell you."

She said, "Okay. I have a surprise for you."

He smiled and said, "Really...?"

She said, "We have a few hours to ourselves this afternoon. I asked Liz if she minded me being out of the house for a bit and she said that she'd be fine. She didn't mind, at all. She had lots of company to keep her busy. So, my darling, what do you think we should do for the next couple of hours?" She grinned, coyly. He grinned too and drove towards his house. They both had the same thing in mind. Each other!

Robert unlocked his door and they went through. When they got in, he pulled El to him and kissed her. As he did, he forgot that this was one of the days that his housekeeper, Mrs. Martin came in to clean. She was startled by them coming in. She had everything done, with the exception of washing the floors. Robert told her she didn't have to wash them, since he hadn't been there for a few days and was not going to be in that much for the next few days coming, due to helping Liz and her boys get through this very difficult time. Robert told her that there could be some of Liz's family staying in his house, over the next few days and he would let her know what her schedule would be, when decisions were made.

As Mrs. Martin collected her pay from Robert, she said goodbye to Eleanor, also giving her condolences, on the loss of her son-in-law and asked her to pass it on to Elizabeth, too. El was touched and thanked her. Mrs. Martin didn't know Eleanor very well, but she did know Liz. She liked Eleanor and she felt that she and Robert were a good match. She told Robert she'd be back in a few days, or whenever he needed her to come over.

Eleanor wanted Robert, so much. She'd been missing being in his strong arms. As Robert was saying goodbye to his housekeeper, El went in the bedroom. She wanted to make love to him. She decided, she was going to take control of the afternoon, if Robert didn't mind. She knew this would surprise him, since she still was a little shy about making love, sometimes. She preferred it at night, when it was dark. She was shy about having sex in the daylight, or with the light on. She was insecure about her body.

She had no reason to be. She was a beautiful, shapely, fit, sexy woman. She had no reason to be insecure, but she was. Robert loved Eleanor's body, just like her George had. Both George and Robert, would take their time to caress her, all over. They loved the way she felt...so soft and sexy. They both were very sexy men themselves and they were the only two lovers she had in her life.

Each man was so different. She knew both loved her very much and she loved each of them, too. There were times that she would think about the differences between the two men in her life. Although George had hurt her so badly, she still loved him. But, there was a large part of her heart that belonged to Robert, since they had started seeing each other. She knew, he would be the only other man, she would ever love.

As Robert went into his bedroom, it was darkened, by the blinds being closed, but there was still a bit of daylight shining in. El was already out of her clothes and under the covers. She gave him her sexiest smile. Robert smiled at her and said, "I think my lady has a wonderful idea. As he knelt on the bed, he leaned towards her; she put her arms around his neck and pulled him on top of her, kissing him so passionately. He became excited right away.

As she let go of him, he got up and took his clothes off. He was hard with excitement, just looking at her. His penis was so large and she wanted him: All of him. She couldn't wait. As he started to enter her, she reached an intense orgasm and was disappointed in herself, for climaxing so quickly.

Robert told her not to worry he had faith in her, that she would be able to reach that point again, before the afternoon was over. She flushed a little, but she was still very turned on. He wanted to please her so much, that afternoon. He wanted her to know how much he loved her and wanted her.

As they stayed in bed making love, they didn't let the horrors of the last couple of days creep in to the bed with them. They tuned out the world, for this brief afternoon.

When they were both spent from their afternoon of lovemaking, they didn't want to fall asleep, because Eleanor didn't want to be away from Liz, too long. She also wanted to get back, to help Etta prepare supper. She got up and wrapped a sheet around her and excused herself to the bathroom. She called out to Robert, "Hun, I'm going to have a quick shower, if you don't mind."

Robert said, "Okay, I'll get a towel for you. As he came in the bathroom, he saw her form through the frosted shower curtain. He loved her body, so much. He loved to hold her and caress her. He asked, "Babe, do you mind if I join you?"

She hesitated a second or two and then she said, "Sure, come on in." With the light on, she wanted to try to get past her shyness.

As Robert stepped in the shower, he couldn't help himself. He became hard again, as he held her, caressing her and kissing her. This was a first for both of them, as they made love in the shower and they both thoroughly enjoyed the experience. She was doing things with Robert she never would have, with George. She started thinking, she was letting go of some of her prudishness and fears about her body and her sexuality. It felt great!

When they finished and got dressed, they embraced for a bit. After a minute, or two, she started to cry. Robert asked, "What's wrong, love?" El started to shake and she cried so hard, she couldn't speak for a moment. Robert just held her close to him. He lay on the bed with her again. She lay in his arms, without speaking. He knew she would be alright shortly, so he just waited patiently, until she calmed down enough to talk.

Eleanor said, "I feel so damn guilty, Robert. I wish I didn't, but I do."

He lifted her head to bring her face closer to his and he looked in her eyes and said, "Why do you feel guilty darling?"

She spoke in between sobs, "I'm so happy with you, Robert. I love you and here my daughter has lost the only man she ever loved. I think they loved each other right from their births. I feel guilty for being in love with you, and happy. I feel guilty for doing what we just did for the afternoon, while she is going through the hardest pain she'll ever experience, in her life.

I know you're going to tell me not to feel this way, but I can't help it. I think she will shut herself off and not let another man into her heart, even over time. I said the same thing about myself, when George died. But, you came along and proved me wrong. I love you." She was still weeping for her daughter.

Robert said, "I know love. But you have to teach her that life goes on. You went on, after her dad died. I know how much she loved Joe and he loved her just as much. That was unmistakable. She has to go on, for her sons. She is mommy and daddy, now."

El smiled at him, as she got up off the bed and pulled a couple of tissues out of the box, to blow her nose. After she did, she kissed Robert and said, "Thank you. You always know what to do, what to say. How did you ever stay a bachelor, all your life? You know women and any woman would be so lucky and honored to have you as a mate."

Now it was his turn to blush. He said, "I'm afraid you give me too much credit, dear. I'm just a man who never found the right woman, until a few years ago. All my life, I've been looking for the one woman who would claim my heart and soul...while me carefully observing others' relationships. I've seen good ones and I've seen bad ones; and have learned from my observations."

She smiled at him, as she wiped her eyes. She kissed him and she said, "Thank you."

He said, "I'll always be here for you...and Liz and the boys. You don't have to go through anything alone. I'll always be here, for all of you." He kissed her and said, "We better get going back to the house." She agreed and they left.

Liz and her sisters-in-law had a good afternoon. They talked about her brothers, and the farm. She filled them in on details of the funeral. It was going to be held on Friday. That was in two days. Both Abe and Simon had talked with Liz on the phone. They wanted to let her know how much they loved their big sister and when they hung up the phone, the boys started making their plans to go to Mississippi.

Liz's cousins, Emmett and Richard had a couple of good foremen, who looked after the workers at the golf course and at the farm. They trusted these foremen to fill in for them, while they were gone for a few days. It was the same around the house. Eleanor and Caroline trusted the girls that were hired to assist Caroline, years earlier.

Edwina and Jane still lived off the farm. The girls lived happily together in a one bedroom apartment in Chatham, above one of the stores across the road from the livery.

Although it was not really used as a livery anymore, it was primarily a blacksmith shop, as well as a gathering place of men. It was their place to catch up on news and gossip. The livery was still owned by decedents of Adam and Jeffrey White, as was the general store. It was still called Lavalle's General Store, in memory of the Lavalles' who perished in the mid 1800's in the tornado.

The blacksmith shop was still in use, as there were many horses and ponies that needed shoes and the shop was always busy, because of all the farms in the region. The farmers also needed to hear the local gossip.

Both foremen and the two housekeepers, stayed at the farm, just during the family's absence. The family had no worries with leaving their employees, in charge. The ladies would keep all the farm hands fed and the house in order. The golf course and farm would run smoothly, while the family was away. Eleanor didn't worry. Her priority was her daughter and her grandsons.

Everyone at the farm, made their arrangements to go to Mississippi. Caroline had been invited to come as well, since she'd known Liz and Joe for a long time. She was like family. Eleanor told Caroline to leave the cooking and cleaning to the two ladies and fly with her.

Emmett, Richard, their families, Caroline, Abe and Simon, were not all able to travel on the same flight. There weren't enough open seats, so they split up and went down on two flights. The wives, their children and Caroline, joined El and went on an early morning flight and the four men, left on a flight in the afternoon. It all worked out, that everyone would be at Liz's house by Thursday night.

The family rented three cars. Emmett's family and Caroline went in one, Richard's family went in one and when the men landed later that day, they drove the other one. Caroline had never taken a trip, since she was hired by Eleanor. She could have. Eleanor was always offering her time off, but she chose to stay on the farm. It was her home, even though she was an employee.

Liz was so thrilled, seeing the first and second cars full with her family. She embraced everyone and broke down, each time they hugged her. She couldn't help it. The twins were awake and everyone enjoyed seeing them, in their own home setting. Before the men arrived, everyone decided where they were going to sleep. Robert gave his house for Emmett and Richard and their families; while Liz's immediate family was staying at her place. Everyone would have a bed to sleep in, for the few nights they were in Mississippi. There was no need to get motel rooms.

By the time the men arrived, supper for everyone was over, but Etta and El made sure there was a hot meal when they arrived. Liz had tears in her eyes again, when her brothers and cousins stepped out of the car. She went to the car and Abe got out. Simon was getting out the other door at the same time. They both came to her and held her. She cried, they both were in tears, too. Their mother could not stand the pain her children were feeling. She came and embraced them and the four cried, while everyone went back in the house, to give them some privacy. It was a moment, they would never forget.

After about five minutes, the family inside the house let the twins run out to their mom. It brought four instant smiles. Abe and Simon picked up James and John, who were happy to see their uncles. There were hugs all around for Liz's family circle.

Everyone went in the house and the children were all put to bed. Now that all the company was there, Liz said, "Mom, I have to run out to Sam's. Can you take care of things here?"

El said, "What are you doing dear?"

Liz told her, "I'm taking the marriage kerchief, the McGee tartan and the Kente robe, for him to see and cut a small piece off, so he can put it in the coffin, with Joe.

El said, "Honey, do you want me to go with you?" She told her mom that she wanted to go by herself and that she wouldn't be long.

When she arrived, Sam and his wife were having tea and asked her to join them. She said she would be delighted. As they drank their tea, she showed Afua Kakira's robe to Sam and his wife, their eyes opened wide with amazement. They both loved it. It was in remarkable shape, seeing as it was close to one hundred years old. Sam said, "It's a shame to cut a piece off."

Liz showed him where there had been a couple of other pieces were cut off and it didn't show. Sam got Liz the scissors and she cut a piece, the size of the marriage kerchief. She began to sniffle and she asked Sam to take her to Joe.

Sam apologized, but he hadn't had time to do his make-up, or fill in the cheekbones, but he was embalmed and still on the table. She said it was alright, she wanted to see him, anyway. Sam took the pieces of cloth and placed them in the coffin and he gave Liz privacy, to be with her husband.

As she looked at Joe, she tried to smile. She said, "Honey, I love you. I know you loved me, too…and, the boys. We're going to miss you, baby." Then she started to get angry. She kept her voice low and said, "Joseph, how can you leave us now? We had so much living to do. Now you're gone and I have to do it on my own. I ought to slap you in the head for this, you know."

Liz touched his face and it was so cold. The tears started falling down her cheeks. As she bent over to kiss his lips, her tears fell on his face. She quickly apologized to him for getting angry. She knew he would understand.

She pulled a tissue out of her purse and wiped her tears off of Joe's face. As she did this, she could swear she saw a smile on his face. Was it her imagination? She wasn't sure, but somehow, she felt comforted.

Chapter 17

The Funeral

As Liz drove home, after seeing Joe privately, she still had a few tears. She felt guilty for getting mad at him. Although she knew better...she saw him smile.

After Liz got home, El asked if everything was alright. She said, "Yeah...we're okay." All the adults spent the next few hours talking and telling family stories. There was laughter and tears and Joe's life was remembered warmly. Liz was happy...until the house was quiet and she went to bed.

As she climbed into her cold, lonely bed, Liz remembered making love to Joe. She remembered him holding her while she cried, while she laughed, when she got silly and she held him, while he told her what he put up with at work. Now she knew. He didn't tell her everything he endured. She was angry again, but that subsided into tears. She softly wept for what seemed like hours before she fell asleep.

She didn't want to dream, but it came anyway. She dreamed about the times they played on the swings. The ones she recently had asked her mother about that summer, while visiting Chatham. She thought about high school and university. Her dream carried through the happy moments she shared with Joe.

Then, there was something dark. It was something she'd never experienced. It was nothing they shared together. She was walking hand in hand with Joe. She didn't know where they were, but it looked beautiful. It was a secluded wooded area. He had the sexiest grin she'd ever seen. She knew what was on his mind. He stopped and kissed Liz.

As they kissed passionately, he guided her to the ground. It was a soft leafy area, but a little muddy. He made sure it was the cleanest area and they lay down and made love. She was so happy. After they were finished, things were a little strange. Joe got off of her and then disappeared. She was alone, all of a sudden and she became scared. She'd never experienced the scene, she was dreaming. It was out of place. She rolled around in the bed, but never woke up.

In her dream, she stood up and all of a sudden, she had all her clothes on, again. But, she hadn't put them on. She was alone. She called for Joe and he didn't answer. She said, "Joe, this isn't funny, please, come and get me." He never came. She heard rustling in the woods behind her. She became more afraid. She wanted to hide. She found a large tree, with a large mound of dirt beside it. She got down on the ground, so she was out of sight.

She waited, while the noise got louder. Then she saw it. There were several things marching towards her. They were white. They looked like triangles. She thought that was odd, but she was spellbound. She couldn't stop watching. As they came closer, she became confused because in the middle of these triangles, there was a man. He was being dragged along with them. This was a black man.

As the group turned, she could see well: The black man was Joe! She gasped, in horror. She couldn't move. It felt like there was a thousand pound weight lying on top of her. She was paralyzed. She couldn't talk, or scream. She wanted to scream her head off. She couldn't. It wouldn't come.

She watched as they had a rope around Joe's neck. She knew instantly, these were Klansmen, and they were lynching her husband. She tried and she struggled, but still couldn't move, or make a sound. She watched as men pulled the rope and lifted him off the ground. She watched as his legs kicked and they dropped him to the ground. This happened again and the third time....her Joe died!

Liz sat up in bed and screamed loud. John and James were sleeping in Liz's room and woke up crying, too. El and Robert heard them from the living room hide-a-bed, where they were sleeping and they ran to her room. Eleanor flung the door open and ran to the bed. She held Liz in her arms. Robert came running, too. He immediately went to the boys, who were sleeping together on a mattress on their mom's floor. He held them both for a moment, but they wanted mommy. Abe and Simon came running, too. Their mother said "It's okay boys, you go back to sleep. I'll take care of your sister." Liz apologized for the scare and they went back to their rooms.

By then, Etta and Caroline were upstairs, too. Caroline was bunking in with Etta, for her stay over the few days. Etta didn't mind, she enjoyed the company. They really got along well with each other. They too, were told that they could go back to bed, that Robert and El were seeing to Liz and the boys.

Robert picked up the boys, one in each arm and carried them to Liz, who was still in her mother's arms. She saw that Robert was bringing the boys to her and she let go of her mother. Robert set them on the bed with her and she let them both under the covers with her. She wiped her tears and John said, "Is mommy scared?"

Liz looked at him, with a tender motherly look and said, "Honey, mommy just had a bad dream. It's okay. I'm sorry I woke you guys up." She kissed each one and they both laid down, one on each side of her.

James asked, "Can grandma come to bed, too?"

El said, "I'll lie down beside you, until you go to sleep, how's that?" He smiled and nodded his head. Robert stayed in Liz's room, waiting for them to go to sleep, which only took a couple of minutes.

Robert walked over to the bed and whispered, "Honey, do you want me to put the boys back on the mattress for you?"

Liz said, still wiping some tears away, "That would be fine, thanks Robert."

After he put both boys on the mattress and covered them up, he said, "Does anyone feel like talking?"

Liz said, "Now that I've woken the whole house up, I think I'd like some tea." Quietly as possible, the three left the room and crept to the kitchen. Liz put the kettle on for tea and sat down. She placed her face in her hands and wept some more. El came behind her and bent down to hold her daughter. Robert sat beside Liz and held her hand, as well.

Liz looked up, wiped her eyes again and told them about her dream. As they listened to her, they looked at each other, in shock. Not just because of her dream itself, but because the dream she was describing, was so exactly the same story the eye witnesses had seen and told Robert and Eleanor, the day before, while Liz was with the undertaker. They felt they had to tell her what they knew now and get it over with, and accept the consequences.

Liz looked at her mother and Robert in horror, when they confirmed that it wasn't just a dream, it was the truth. They had heard it all the day before. Liz tried to keep her voice down, as she said, "How could you not tell me about it, yesterday? Why were you keeping it from me?" She was filling up with anger, now. She felt she should have been told about it. She said, as she broke away from her mother's grasp, "Mom, how could you keep that from me? I can't believe you guys never told me you heard about his lynching!"

Robert spoke up and said, "Liz, your mother and I were trying to find the best time to tell you, but I guess we were wrong. There really wasn't a 'best' time to give you the information we had. I'm so sorry dear. It's really my fault." El was crying, too. Robert put his arms around both of them and kissed them both on the cheek, as the kettle was boiling away.

Liz calmed down and said, "Mom, you guys should have told me. I'm going to have that dream in my head forever. It was so vivid. I was right there and I couldn't save him. Mom, I tried to scream and save him, but I couldn't! I couldn't save my Joe!" Liz was at the stove, trying to make the tea and she set the kettle back down, sat on the floor and cried harder, as quietly as she could. Through her sobs, she said, "Mom, they tortured him. They tortured my husband: How do I ever live with that, now?" Eleanor got on the floor with her daughter and held her. Robert got down, and held the two of them. All three wept and forgot about the tea.

After about ten or fifteen minutes of crying together, Liz wanted to get up off the floor. They all decided they didn't want the tea. Liz was tired, and didn't think she could stomach anything, right then, but she didn't want to close her eyes, either. She also knew she needed sleep, so she could handle the twins, the family and the funeral. She looked to Eleanor and asked, "I feel like such a baby. Mom, would you mind lying down with me, until I fall asleep?"

Her mother stroked her hair and said, "Of course I don't mind, dear. I seem to remember you lying down with me a few times, after your dad died." She was choking back tears, again.

Liz smiled and said, "You're right. I forgot about that."

Robert asked, "Will you both be okay? Just remember, I'm a yell away!" They assured him they would, and they'd call if they needed him. All three headed back to bed and Liz prayed for sleep. With her mother beside her, she drifted off and the rest of the night was dreamless.

Friday August 17, 1950 Liz woke up, in her mom's arms. It would be a day to remember, forever. As she woke up early, the boys were just waking up, too. John asked her, "Mommy, are you better from your dream? Did grandma help you sleep, too?" He was looking at his mother, with his big innocent brown eyes. As she looked at her son, she hadn't realized he looked so much like his father, these days.

Eleanor said she'd go help with breakfast. Liz smiled at John and said, "Come here sweetie, both of you." John jumped off the mattress and James joined him as they went to their mother's bed. They both kissed their grandma, and they climbed up on the bed. One sat on each side of Liz. She never heard any other commotion and that was fine with her. She just wanted to cuddle with her boys for a bit, before facing this dreadful day.

As James was climbing on the bed too, she also noticed that he looked like his dad, too. Except his skin was white and he had the most beautiful blue eyes, she'd ever seen. She smiled, as best she could. She didn't want to cry, but the tears fell down her cheeks, anyway. John looked up and put his little finger on a tear. He asked again, "Mommy, are you still scared of your dream?"

Liz thought for a moment then said, "Well, mommy did have a bad dream and I did cry, but I feel better, now that you and James are with me. Now, mommy needs a hug." They both stood on the bed and tackled her with hugs. She was happy. She loved her sons so much.

As they giggled and tackled Liz, Eleanor came back to the bedroom and knocked on the door. She said, "Honey, is everything alright in there?"

Liz laughed, "Yeah grandma, come on in, we're all having hugs."

Eleanor opened the door and both boys turned and said, "Hi grandma."

They both kissed their mother on her cheeks then scampered off her bed to see grandma, again. El bent over and picked them both up. Robert was behind her and the boys were excited to see him there, too.

Just then, everyone heard both baby girls cry. James and John wanted to be put down, so they could check on their cousins. They wanted to see why they were crying. Liz told them to knock on the doors, first. They did what they were told and the boys were welcomed in each room to see the babies.

Liz and El went downstairs and found Etta and Caroline making breakfast. As everyone was coming down the stairs Robert said, "I'll get dressed and go over to my place and see that everyone is up and get them over here for breakfast and I'll also get into my suit."

Eleanor said, "Okay, dear. We'll see you shortly; oh, but here, stay and have a quick coffee, first." He kissed Eleanor tenderly and he playfully patted her behind, with a devilish smile. She smiled back and hand him a coffee.

Liz looked at the boys. They were in the living room, watching their cousins being fed, by their mothers. Abe and Simon were still in bed, to catch a few more minutes of sleep. Liz thought she might let them sleep a bit longer, but then she had an idea. It may be cruel she thought, but she loved it.

She gave James and John each a pot. Then she gave them each a spoon. She told them to go upstairs and wake up their uncles. As the boys marched up the stairs with their kitchen drums, they were happy to be helping mommy get her brothers up.

Both Abe and Simon jumped out of bed thinking the country was going to war. They forgot where they were, from the surroundings. They both were a bit confused then looked at the boys. They smiled. This was Liz's doing, they both thought.

A minute or two later, Simon came downstairs holding James and Abe was carrying John. They brought the boys to Liz and thanked them for their 'wake-up' call. She laughed, hysterically. Eleanor and Robert laughed, too. She was glad to see Liz smiling and playing pranks on her brothers, like she always did whenever she was with them. Robert finished his coffee, kissed El and drove home.

At Robert's house, everyone was up and was getting washed and dressed. Robert said good morning to everyone and Emmett asked how Liz was, today.

Robert said, "She seems good, right now. She just sent the twins with pots and spoons to wake up her brothers." Everyone laughed. After they were all dressed, Robert changed into his suit and they all went back over to the Allen's house.

Etta and Caroline made lots of breakfast. Caroline didn't feel out of her element. She was teaching Etta how to cook for an army....just like she made every day, for the farm workers.

When Robert and the others arrived, they were happy to be there. They knew Liz needed her family. Everyone started to sit down to eat breakfast and the doorbell rang. A second later, the door opened and George poked his head in and said, "Hey, it's Uncle George!"

James and John were not in their high chairs yet and they ran to the door to greet him. He picked them both up and they hugged him and kissed him on the cheeks. Liz went to the door and gave George a hug and said, "Just in time for breakfast, George: C'mon in."

George went in to the dining room and the table was full, so was the kitchen table, but Robert found a chair for him and they all squeezed together and George sat to eat breakfast, too. The conversation was light and they talked about everything, except Joe and the impending funeral. Liz didn't want to think about it, yet. The time would come, soon enough.

Everyone got in their vehicles to go to the Funeral Parlor. Liz's car was the first to drive up. She was surprised to see many of the black community standing outside the building.

As she got out of the car with Eleanor, Robert and the twins, Liz wondered why there were so many of them standing there? They didn't know Joe. She was sure they didn't. As she walked toward the building, she saw the sheriff's car. She was mad. He was the last man she wanted to see. She saw many other vehicles and wasn't sure who they all belonged to.

George parked his car and caught up with Liz. He said, "I can't believe this, Liz. I can't believe that the sheriff had the balls to show up, here." He looked around the parking lot and he continued, "I don't believe it. Ray Halden and Bubba Shep are here, too. That rotten bastard has nerve. Do you want me to throw them out, for you?"

Liz said, "No George, I want to meet the men who murdered my husband."

Sam Waters met her at the door and said, "Good mornin' Mrs. Allen, well looky here. You got a couple o' fine, handsome young fellas, here. 'Dey looks like 'dere papa, 'fer sure. Let me take ya'll ta' 'yer seats." Sam's wife was playing the organ. Liz had asked her to, and she agreed to play all the music for the funeral.

Just before Sam accompanied Liz inside, one of the Negroes came to her and said, "Mrs. Allen, now I knows, none of us really knows yo' husban', but we knows what happened. We juss' wants to show ya'll we's sorry 'fer it happenin' and well...'dat's it, ma'am."

Liz said, "I thank you, all." She looked at the crowd and said, "I know there is not enough room for you all, but you are all welcome to come into the chapel, for the service, if you like." She didn't realize the chapel had already been filled.

When Liz walked to the front of the room, she heard several people gasp. Although many people knew either her, or Joe, not everyone knew they were a multi-racial couple and had multi-racial children. She held the hands of both of her boys and she held her head high. Her mother walked behind her, with Robert and George. Next were her brothers, their families and their cousins, with their families.

When Sam got the family to the front of the room, he closed a large curtain. This was so that they could view Joe, privately. Robert lifted James and Liz lifted John. They were brought over to see their daddy, briefly. Clearly visible, was bruising and cuts, but Sam had done the best he could to cover them up. Undertakers had to use shoe polish to mask facial scars and bruises, since there was no make-up available to cover the skin of a black person, whose skin turns a dark ashen gray color, when they die.

Liz saw his wedding ring, on his finger and Sam had placed the piece of the Kente Cloth, McGee Tartan and the Marriage Kerchief in his hands. The whole family was quite happy to see he had done this for her.

John said, "Mama is daddy sleepin'? Can't he wake up?"

Liz said, "Honey, remember we said that daddy is going to sleep forever, but is going to heaven to live with God."

James said, "I want daddy,"...and started to cry. The crowd which gathered for the funeral were able to hear the boys and they felt sadder, for it. After everyone was finished saying their goodbye's to Joe, Liz let El and Robert take the boys away from the coffin and they tried to reassure them, with hugs and kisses. They both calmed a bit, as Liz turned back to Joe and kissed him and said, "I love you."

The pastor had not arrived yet, so when the family was viewing the body privately, George Benson, asked Sam, "Mr. Waters, there's something troubling me. You may not be able, or free to help me. Joe's death was attributed to "suicide", but we know that was NOT the case, he could never take his own life...Were there any marks on Joe's body to indicate a 'lynching', which several persons claim to have witnessed."

There was a lengthy pause, while they awaited Sam's reply. With hesitation and carefully chosen words, he said, "Professional ethics prevents me from givin' a d'rect answer, 'dat might be repeated in 'da paper, but I has ta' count heavily on you'se keepin' 'dat secret 'fer me. I've provided services, in 'da pass' 'fer several folks, who been killed by lynchin'. Well 'dem marks on Joe's body 'dey looks juss' like 'dey was 'da same ones, I seen befo' and ya'll can't beat yer'sef in 'da face' like 'dat."

"Thank you Sam," George replied, "You can be assured, that what you have just said, will be kept in the strictest confidence."

News of Joseph Allen's death spread rapidly throughout the community, both white and black. The Philadelphia weekly newspaper, a "white" publication, provided very few details, but registered mild suggestion that Joe died by his own hand. The sheriff's office insisted on them saying this...and no suggestion of an inquiry was made. Reaction of the local population ranged from seeming indifference, on the part of a couple of his co-workers and police officials, to deepest grief by family and the black community, even though most had never met him, or knew of him, until his death.

Many, who knew Joe, respected him for his honest openness and friendship to everyone, regardless of race, creed, color, or religion. But, inherent prejudice prevented his service, or burial taking place in town. The sheriff wanted the tone to reflect Joe's 'suicide', but Liz had other thoughts.

Liz signaled Sam that he could open the curtains and go on with the service. The funeral home had been filled to capacity an hour before service time. She took a look and saw who was there. George pointed out all of the other engineers from Benson's. Liz and Joe's friends and some of Liz's colleagues were there. Additional chairs were put out to accommodate the crowd, including some who were sitting outside. Fortunately, they were able to hear the service, as the windows were open, in an attempt to lessen the mounting temperature, inside. It was too late to move everything into the hall. Sam never expected such a large crowd. It was the biggest, he'd ever served. Everyone seemed comfortable, despite the hot day.

Sam had seated everyone where they should be and before she sat, Liz looked around; and saw the room was packed full of black people, even taking up standing-room only. There was a chord of the organ. The first hymn that was played and sang by the choir was, "Take My Hand, Precious Lord".

Liz and Joe loved this hymn. To them, it was to symbolize Jesus taking them home to heaven, after they pass on. Liz just didn't think she would be requesting and hearing it, this soon. Liz was happy with this choir's rendition. It was soulful and beautifully done. If one looked around the chapel, you could see tears flowing from every black face. These were mostly the people who didn't even know Joe, or Liz. There were few tears from white people. It was only from those who knew and were friends with Joe or Liz. Liz noticed the other engineers Joe worked with, were sniffling, too. They all showed their respect for him, with their tears.

Ray and Bubba, stood with the sheriff, deputy and several other men, all with their arms crossed throughout the whole service, showing no emotion whatsoever.

When the choir finished the first hymn and sat down, Pastor Brown came to the podium, welcomed everyone and drew their attention to the printed service leaflet which they had received. All of the black people were handed a leaflet, although most of them could not read it. He stated that Joe's tragic death had struck an extremely harsh blow to all of Joe's family and his friends. This could, if left in itself create a sense of futility, resentment and even feelings of hatred. But, he emphasized, "We must rise above this seemingly natural and totally justified reaction. With God's help, we can rise above our grief and claim his promises now and for the days ahead. Joe was a very special person to his family and to his friends, where he served in so many ways for the common good."

The pastor concluded his introductory remarks by requesting that all present join in offering thanksgiving to God, for Joe's life. Then he invited everyone to join him in prayer.

"Dear Heavenly Father, come to us and heal our broken hearts, strengthen us to overcome all that would defeat us and allow us to sink to the level of those that rise up against us. As Jesus forgave His enemies, help us to forgive ours. May we defeat them as He did with the power of love. We ask this in His name, Amen."

The service continued with Patrick, who was the family patriarch, being the oldest male family member on the farm, now. Liz had asked if he would read the 23rd Psalm and he told her he would be honored to read it. The whole family loved Joe so much they would do anything that was asked. Everyone stood, with the choir leading the Black Hymn, "I'm Gonna Live So God Can Use Me", then, Pastor Brown followed with the reading of St. Paul's Letter to the Romans 8. Then he asked Eleanor to step forward.

She talked of what a wonderful son-in-law Joe was, and what he meant to her, and the rest of the family. Next, Robert stepped up and gave a heartfelt testimony as to Joe's faith and what he had meant as a friend, and what a good father he was to James and John. George Benson spoke of Joe's character, and what a great employee he was, as well as a true friend.

Liz spoke of her and Joe's daily reading of the bible, and how he lived by its precepts. She talked lovingly of him and ended with, "Let us honor his memory by following his example."

As each person had spoken about Joe, it was clear there were "common threads" throughout his life, which touched each and every one of them, in such similar ways.

The choir and congregation joined in singing "I Am So Glad Jesus Lifted Me". Pastor Brown then came forward again, and standing in the center aisle, he thanked all of those who had assisted with arrangements and participation in the service. "I stand before you as one whose heart is filled with sorrow as we share this terrible loss. But, let us look at our reasons for being here. We come to express our love and support to Joe's family. We come mindful of the shortness and uncertainty of human life. We come to thank God for Joe and for the consolation of our Creator's presence here and now. Let us love and support one another that we may rise above all that would defeat us and claim the victory that God alone can give. Let us all say together, "Thank you Lord for the life of Joseph Jacob Allen." Let us pray, "O Lord support us all the daylong of this earthly life, until the shadows lengthen and evening comes, the busy world is hushed. The fever of life is over and our work is done. Then Lord, grant us safe lodging, a holy rest and peace at the last." The Pastor then repeated the same prayer in Twi language, which surprised the black community, since some of them knew exactly what he was saying.

The choir then proceeded out, slowly singing in beautiful harmony, "Amazing Grace". It was Joe and Liz's favorite hymn' ever since the first time they had heard it in their own church, when they were growing up in Chatham!

Chapter 18

Celebration of Life

L IZ WAS SO IMPRESSED WITH the service. She was truly happy and believed that Joe would have liked what she and Sam had arranged. The endings hymn "Amazing Grace" was a commonly used one for funerals. Although it was about two-hundred years old, she had studied it and found it was written by a man who, at one time made a living shipping slaves from Africa, to the new world. When the Lord spared his life one night on the ship, he had a revelation and penned "Amazing Grace". She was sure Joe would like what she picked. It was started by the choir, but everyone joined in for the last two verses.

Afterward, Liz asked Sam to leave the coffin open, so the black folks could file past and they could all see what Joe had gone through, on the last day of his life. It was getting very stuffy inside and Liz wanted to go outside, if anyone wanted to talk to her, she would stay for a while.

The sheriff was first. He said, "Now ma'am, you know he done it, hisself. Nothin' can change 'dat. I'm just sorry 'fer ya' and 'yer family. Good day, ma'am". He tipped his hat and walked to his car. Several men stood with the sheriff by his car and Liz could tell. These were the men who murdered her husband. She was sure of it.

She walked over to the sheriff's car, while Robert and George quickly caught up to her, they warned her not to do anything to cause more trouble, for her and her family. George went with her to introduce her to the men. Robert stayed with her, like a protective father. Eleanor was glad to see this.

When they got to the group of white men, George started, "Fellas, this is Mrs. Allen." He went through the whole group. Robert and George quickly made introductions of these men who were standing around with the sheriff. They all worked in town and didn't really have anything to do with Joe, or herself, except she recognized them from many stores and other businesses they had frequented, for the last three years. She did not shake their hands, either. She just gave an indifferent nod. She looked them all, up and down. She knew who they were. KLAN! She was disgusted and she told George she had to get back to her family. She just swallowed her pride and said, "Thanks for coming, gentlemen." They all had the nerve to show up! Liz was courteous but angry at the same time. Then George moved to another group of white men, standing apart from the crowd. He took her to meet "Benson's Associates". She'd never met any of them before.

As George introduced each one of his men, they shook her hand, telling her how sorry they were and that Joe was good to work with and that they respected him. They assured her that he and his talents would be missed...Ray just grunted! She couldn't tell if they were lying. She shook hands with each one and thanked them for coming, even Bubba. George left Ray until the end. He said, "Liz, this is Ray Halden, another of my hydraulic engineers."

Ray tipped his hat and coldly said, "Ma'am." Liz did not put her hand out to him. He never put his out to her. She just gave a cold hard stare of contempt for a moment, not saying anything. Ray suddenly felt uncomfortable...everyone knew she meant business.

As she walked back towards her family, she could hear Ray snicker. She wanted to slap his face. She never turned back to look at them, she just kept walking. She didn't look at George, or Robert. She just said, "All those men with the sheriff were in on it...Ray and Bubba, too. They all had mud covered boots, with bits of leaves, just like Joe and the sheriff. They didn't have the decency to clean up their boots after they did it. I know who the men are, that murdered my husband." A tear rolled down her face and she said, "And there is not one God Damn thing I can do about it. The fucking sheriff is part of it, I know it!" She did not let the men see her cry.

All the white men got in their cars and left. All that remained at the funeral parlor now was Liz's family, her close friends and the people from the black community. They wanted to show respect. She was touched. They also had a surprise for her. Sam had arranged it.

Liz did not want to hold a luncheon, or anything, where she would have to stay in a room with any of these men, who were responsible for Joe's death. She wouldn't have been able to stomach it. Besides, she didn't want any of them near her children. Deep down, she knew they would be at Joe's funeral. She had read that sometimes, it was customary for Klan to show up at the funeral of the ones they murder, just in a boasting and defiant way. Whatever the reasons they had, she was sickened by it. She figured that she was just going to thank everyone who came and go home with her family.

After all of the unwelcome element left, the community started to walk away from the funeral home. Sam came to her and said, "Liz, the community has a surprise for you. Please have your family follow us. It's not too far. It's walking distance, but we can drive, if you prefer."

She asked, "Is it too far for the twins to walk?" Sam told her it was just two farms down the road. She thought it would be okay and the boys could be carried, if they needed. Abe and Simon preferred to drive their families. Liz had forgotten about the baby girls. She said, "Oh, you're right, it would be a bit of a stretch for you guys. Let's all drive."

Sam wanted to wait a bit to let the people get ready for them to arrive. He said to Liz, "Does anyone need one mo' look, or can I close 'da coffin?"

Liz asked the family and everyone said no. She looked to her mother, then to Robert and said, "I think I'll take the boys for one more look, so they can say a proper goodbye. It was hard to do, while everyone was waiting for the service to start."

El said, "Honey, as long as you think it is the right thing to do, I'll come with you."

Liz said quickly, "No, mom. I just want the boys with me." Eleanor smiled an understanding smile and let her go in by herself, with her boys. Even Sam and his wife stayed outside.

When she took the boys to the coffin, instead of picking them up and holding them, since they were too small to see; she brought two chairs and placed each of them right near the head of the coffin. She picked up each boy and placed them on a chair, while she stood between them and held her arm around each one. She said, "If you don't want to be here, I can take you back to grandma."

James said, "I want to see daddy."

John said, "Me, too."

She smiled and waited for the questions to start. As she did, there was silence for a moment. After a moment, John asked, "Mommy, can I touch him?"

Liz looked at him and said, "Yes, where would you like to touch him?" He pointed to his chest and she guided his hand to the spot he pointed out.

As he set his hand on the spot he wanted, he broke loose from Liz's hand and started to push on him and said, "Daddy, wake up daddy. It's wake up time. You have to stop sleeping, now!" Liz cried. She wasn't sure she would make it through this.

She didn't realize it, but James was also touching his father. He was rubbing his shoulder, and trying to wake him up, with his brother. Liz took both of their hands and said, "Guys, daddy will never wake up. God is going to take him to heaven shortly. When the nice man, Sam, comes back in here, he will close this lid and God will come to get daddy."

John said, "Mommy, can we wait and see God take him?"

She said, "No sweetie; God won't come if anyone is watching. Honey, he's kind of like Santa Claus. He won't come either, if anyone is watching." This, they understood. She continued and asked, "Do either of you want to give a kiss, before he has to go?" Her tears were flowing fast. She couldn't stop them.

They both nodded their heads. First she lifted John and she held him over his father. He gave him a sweet kiss on the cheek and said, "Night, night, daddy. Have fun in heaven." As she set him on the floor... her tears were uncontrollable. This was taking its toll on her.

She lifted James over his father. He too, gave him the sweetest little kiss. But, at the last second, he threw his arms around Joe's neck, as far as he could and cried out, "Don't go, daddy. Don't go...I need you here!" Liz gently pulled him back and he was crying hard now. She sat on the chair and held him.

After a few moments, James changed his demeanor and asked, "Mommy, can I go see grandma and tell her I said goodbye to daddy, now?"

Liz said, "Yes sweetie, I'll be out in a minute".

When both boys looked up at her, she burst out laughing. When they each kissed their father on the cheek, some of the black shoe polish, used in place of make-up, came off on their lips. They looked hilarious. They wanted to know what was so funny and she reached in her purse to get her compact. She showed them what they looked like, in her mirror and they laughed. She explained the shoe polish to them and it broke the tension for a few moments and gave them a laugh, while she took out a tissue and wiped it off each of them. James and John ran out the door, where Robert and El picked them up, for a cuddle and they were laughing, trying to tell them about the shoe polish kisses. Liz remained inside.

Liz looked at Joe and said, "Honey, I'll miss you so much." She paused and turned angry, "How can I go on without you, you bastard?" After a few seconds, she said, "Baby, I'm sorry, I shouldn't have called you that; I'm so sorry honey, please forgive me." She touched his lips and said, "Oh honey, I'm going to miss these...for several reasons." She chuckled at that. She was thinking about all the times they made love. She loved his lips. She touched his chest and said, "This chest is the sexiest one I've ever seen. I'll miss it, too." Then she started to cry even harder and said, "I can't do this without you, darling. I need your help to bring up the boys. I can't do it alone."

She felt a breeze come across her face. It blew her hair for a few seconds. It was Joe. She knew it. She knew he was in the room with her. She looked around and saw nothing. She looked back in the coffin and there was nothing amiss. Was she imagining it? She wondered. She wasn't afraid she knew he was telling her something. But what was it?

She asked, "Honey, I can't let you go. I can't bury you in Chatham. I need you here! I hope you can understand. I'm not ready. I thought the only logical thing to do is to cremate you and have your ashes at home. I'm sorry, if this is not what you intended, but I can't let you go, yet. I promise you'll be there with your mama, daddy and the others, someday. I just can't do it right now. Baby, I hope you understand. Please understand?"

She waited for a few moments and when she thought she was done saying what she needed to, she started walking away. She had only gotten five steps away, when she felt the breeze, again. The curtains were not moving. The breeze was just on her face. She turned back and went to his coffin, again. As she looked at Joe's face one more time, she thought it looked different. She thought there was a smile. She knew it wasn't possible.

Sam had explained some of his procedures to her a couple of days before, which she had insisted on knowing. She knew the eyes and lips were secured shut, but she still saw a change. She saw a smile! She was confident that he heard her, he understood and it was okay. She knew she made the right decision, even though all of the family before him had been interred in the family cemetery, on the farm. He would be the first one in the history of the McDonald and Allen families to be cremated.

When Liz came out of the parlor, she nodded to Sam. He quickly went inside and closed and secured the coffin. Liz managed to keep a smile on her face. The boys ran to her and wanted her to pick them up. She didn't have the strength. Robert picked up John and El picked up James, again. They both reached over and hugged their mom.

Sam came out and said, "Okay folks, if you'll just follow me, there's a place to park your vehicles, where we'se goin'." Everyone got in their cars and Sam started down the road. He turned in the driveway of the second farm and he got out of his car. Everyone got out of theirs. Sam led, with Liz and the boys, first.

He opened the door of the barn and inside was a big surprise. The black community had painted, and decorated the inside of this barn, and it almost looked like McDonald Hall, in Chatham. There was the picture of Joe, which Sam had placed in a frame and there was food, galore. All of the blacks were there, waiting for Liz and her family. Each and every one of them had a smile for Liz and the boys.

The family stood in awe, looking around the barn. Sam said, "How did I do, arrangin' 'da barn, Mrs. Allen?" Liz stood in amazement. Her childhood came back to her. Even though it was a funeral, Liz and the family were so happy. The community wanted to help her and her family, to celebrate Joe's life. The family couldn't believe what they were witnessing.

Just then, Liz walked over to Sam and put her arms around him and hugged him, whispering, "Thank you," in his ear. She backed up and asked, "Sam, how did you know about the barn?"

Sam said, "Well ma'am, it seems 'dat my grandpa Rolly tole' his son, my daddy, 'bout 'da great 'celebration barn', an' paintin' it a couple o' times, an' since you wasn't takin' yo' husban' home, I'd bring a bit o' home, ta' ya'll. I hopes ya'll doesn't mind."

Liz said, "Thank you, Sam." She looked around at all the people and said with a tear in her eye and a smile, "Thank you all, for this wonderful surprise!" She took a deep breath and continued, "Well, let's get on with celebrating my husband's life." Everyone clapped and then there was music. People brought their instruments with them and played, for the rest of the day. Some even brought African instruments, which were either heirlooms brought over from Africa, or some that were recently carved, within the last few decades. They would use them through the night to sing African songs, and American songs, too. She was thrilled to see and hear them, so was the rest of the family. Joe would have loved this party. There were lots of children there and the boys had a great time playing with them.

Everyone came to Liz and introduced themselves. She was so happy to meet them all. Their kindness would never be forgotten. Sam cautioned everyone, before the funeral, not to talk about witnessing the hanging, unless Liz insisted on hearing details.

The feast was appreciated and as the family got to know the people, they talked for hours. They talked of Joe's life and family history, of both families. From Jed and Mary: Diana and Johnny, right through to that day. There were so many similarities, having all their new friends' ancestors come from Africa, as slaves, too. There was camaraderie, amongst them. They all thought Liz to be a wonderful person and everyone loved her twins and her family. After the supper hour, no one wanted to leave. The people who lived at the farm, offered a bed for the twins and the two baby girls, but Joan and Maria decided that they would rather take the babies home, to Liz's and put them to bed.

Maria asked Liz, "Would you like us to take John and James and put them in bed, too?"

Liz said, "Well, they look tired and I'd really appreciate it. You don't mind?" They told her they would be happy to take the boys home, for her. That way, she could stay on and continue celebrating, with her new friends. Eleanor offered to go too and come back later, but Maria and Joan said they could manage. That way, El could stay around, in case Liz needed her.

There was lots of moonshine and the music went on far into the night. Liz was so happy her white friends were staying, too. There was

Vincent and his wife, Lynn who came with a couple of teachers from her school and their husbands. Minnie and Nancy and the Diamont's were there and even Mr. Pakos and a few other men, whom Joe worked on projects with, were there. Liz was very impressed. She knew, regardless of color, Joe was highly regarded and respected, in Philadelphia, Mississippi. The family all relayed their stories and fondest memories of Joe and Liz.

A few of Joe's co-workers heard about the celebration and decided to go later in the afternoon, not sure at all that they would be welcomed, but went anyway. Jesse Snow and all of the Canadian-born engineers came to Liz and asked if they could join in the celebration, of Joe's life. George was by her side and she looked to him, then she smiled and said, "Of course you're welcome to join us...next to his family you guys were closest to him, here in Mississippi. Welcome, gentlemen!" They were relieved and she gave each one a warm hug. She knew they did respect Joe and had nothing to do with his death, she was sure of this!

Liz went out of the barn for a moment to get some fresh air. As she did, Marteen popped into her head. She thought about Joe joining both her and his father, whom he'd never known. Joe was born after Joseph Sr. died of the Spanish Flu.

Liz let some tears come. After all, it was such a sad state, that Marteen was gone, too. She was sure they would have forgiven her for having the affair with Liz's dad, by now. She didn't know if Eleanor would have been able to. She didn't concern herself with this thought too much, right now. Her mom was so happy with Robert, now. Liz smiled...she knew her mom and Robert was a good match and that her dad would be happy for them.

Liz went back into the barn and smiled again. She was so touched that Sam and his friends arranged all of this. It was too bad that Joe couldn't have seen the barn decorated, in his honor. These people didn't even know him and the outpouring of love and care and respect for a man they didn't know, was overwhelming.

About 2:00 a.m., she was getting tired and it was time to go. Liz stood on a bale of hay and asked for everyone's attention. She said, "Ladies and gentlemen, I'd like to thank you for having this celebration, to honor my husband. It looks like you went to such extremes to throw this party and I...my family and I, want to thank you, from the bottom of our hearts. We'll never forget any of you, for doing this. I know Joe would be happy...slightly humbled...but happy. If there is ever anything that I can do for you, anytime, please don't hesitate to ask...and I mean it! I thank you again, and good-night." She hoped she could repay the black community, in kind someday, for what they did for her .

The audience clapped and they all said goodnight to Liz and her family, before they left. The crowd stayed on and celebrated some more. Liz and the family drove back to her place. Her close friends were also invited to join them at her house. They were all getting tired, but they'd had fun this evening and still wanted to talk about Joe, some more. When Liz's family and friends got back to her house, she put out her wine and beer, scotch and whiskey, and Liz insisted that her family and friends join her, in her toast to her husband.

After everyone had a drink in their hand, she raised her glass to her wedding photo and cleared her voice to speak. "To the sweetest man, I've ever known: A man who has faced life with its struggles and overcame them.

Joe was the love of my life and always will be. I think from the moment I first set my newborn eyes on him, I'm sure I saw his face and fell in love. I feel it in my heart. I know he loved me, too. I never doubted that for one moment, in our lives together. We've had thirty years to love each other and an eternity, to continue loving each other.

He will be missed. His family loved him so and his children will grow up knowing the stories about him. We will all help to keep fresh in their minds, how much their daddy loved them. It's going to be a tough road ahead, for their mommy, but I know with God's help, I can do it. I believe in the Lord's strength, which I can only hope to draw on. The bible tells us in Psalms 119:53, Horror hath taken hold upon me because of the wicked that forsakes the law. Psalms 22:14 My strength drains away like water, all my bones are dislocated, my heart is like wax, it melts away inside me, and finally in 118:14, The Lord is my strength and song, and is my salvation. Dear Lord, I need you now, like I've never had before.

My dear, sweet Joseph: Rest now with God. With God's help and our family, I'll be strong enough to go on without you and make you proud. I promise darling, I will move heaven and earth to have the men who killed you, punished: Even if it takes my whole lifetime." She had to pause for a few tears. Everyone in the house was now crying, including the men; she continued with her glass raised and her head held high, her voice crackling. "Honey this toast is to celebrate your life, not mourn your death. I know you would have wanted it this way. So sweetie here's to you. I love you!"

Everyone else said, "To Joe," and they all took a sip, while the tears were flowing. Everyone said that it was a beautiful toast. Liz was sure that was all she wanted to say and smiled at everyone. Then she sobbed uncontrollably.

Eleanor held her and her brothers came to her, too. They held each other, while they all cried. The rest of the family watched, with heavy hearts, but didn't want to intrude. Liz needed her mom and brothers most, now. After a minute, she said, "I don't know about all of you, but I'm going to bed." She wiped her tears, finished her drink and said good night to everyone. She climbed the stairs to her lonely bed, while her twins slept on the mattress on her floor. She fell asleep as soon as she lay down. She hadn't even put her nightgown on, yet.

Vincent and his wife, along with the few teachers who were there, bid them all a good night and left together. Nancy and Minnie had come together and they left at the same time the others did. George stayed a little longer.

Robert gave Richard the keys to his house and the family said their good nights and left to go sleep. They said they'd be back in the morning for breakfast. Simon and Abe and their wives went upstairs, leaving Robert, George and Eleanor alone. Etta and Caroline cleaned the kitchen, and excused themselves for the night.

George and Robert opened another beer and El poured herself another glass of wine. She was tired, but didn't want to sleep, yet. She wanted to talk about Joe some more. The men listened to her stories and enjoyed them. Before they knew it, it was going on 4:00 a.m., and they were tiring out. George had a little bit too much to drink and was not able to drive home. Eleanor got a blanket out and said, "Well, you can sleep here, if you'd like." She was pointing to old reliable.

George said, "I hope Joe wouldn't mind, if I slept on his chair." El smiled and nodded approval. She knew Joe wouldn't have minded, one bit. Robert and Eleanor were still sleeping on the hide-a-bed. All three fell asleep quickly. They were all very tired.

Saturday morning everyone got up refreshed; and Etta and Caroline were making another monster sized breakfast for everyone. There was nothing that Liz had to do. She just visited with the family and they all had a nice time together. They shared laughter and tears again, talking about Joe, some more.

The twins kept everyone smiling, all day. They were fun to be around. They fussed over their baby cousins, constantly. They couldn't understand why the girls could not sit on the rocking horses. They wanted to play with the girls, but they were too little.

Everyone went outside for the afternoon. It was a beautiful, sunny day and they all enjoyed having a Saturday to themselves and not be working. Simon said, "You know ma, I could get used to time off from the farm." He had a devilish grin for his mother. Both boys loved to tease their mother at every opportunity.

One of the things about the McDonald's was their sense of humor: From Johnny and Diana, through to Liz, her brothers and Eleanor. Both boys pulled pranks on their mom, every chance they got, too. There were many practical jokes throughout the years. She smiled and said, "You just watch it boys, the farm won't run itself, you know. Behave yourselves, or I'll fire your asses and you'll be out of the will." Simon smiled and hugged his mother, letting her know he was just kidding and he loved their farm.

Everyone started talking about the potato farm and the golf course. They were truly blessed, that they had their ancestors, with the foresight, determination and the know-how, to run these very successful businesses.

Sunday arrived and Sam knocked at the door around lunch time. Liz answered and she saw him standing there with the urn she'd chosen for Joe's ashes. She'd forgotten that he would be along with them, as soon as the cremation was completed.

She welcomed him in to her house. She said, "Hi Sam. I guess that's for me?"

Sam said, "Yess'um. Is ya'll ready for 'dem? I can hole' 'dem if you'se not ready."

Liz held out her hands to take the urn from Sam and said, "Oh Sam, of course. I'll take them. I was just surprised to see them so quickly. Please, come in and have a coffee, or some lunch with us." Sam handed her the urn and she placed on the mantle of her new fireplace. As she did she remembered back about six months. George and Joe had just built a new fireplace in the living room. She remembered thinking to herself, 'I need something special to place on the mantle'. Well, now she had something…very special.

After a really good, old farm Sunday lunch, Sam left and everyone headed back to Jackson to catch their plane. There was enough room on this flight, to fit the entire family. They would all be traveling together, this time. The whole family took the better part of all the seating on the plane, going home. It was sad for Liz, to see them all leave. She was already starting to feel very empty and lonely, inside. El decided she would stay on, a few more days to help her with the boys. Liz would appreciate the help with them, for a few more days.

George also went with everyone to say goodbye. All three rental cars were turned in, in Jackson. Liz would drive her mom to the airport, when she was ready to go home. Liz cried, as she watched the airplane take off. Robert and El put their arms around her and held her. She was glad she left the boys at home with Etta for the afternoon. They both needed a nap. They were put back in their own rooms and would rest, until their mommy came home.

When Liz, George, El and Robert came back to her house, they sat in the living room. Liz sat in old reliable and stared at the urn. She said, "I guess life goes on now. Folks, would it be too much, if I asked you to go out for a while? I need to be here alone for a bit. Would you all mind?" George, Robert and Eleanor understood and they went to George's house for an hour or so. After a couple of drinks, they went back to Liz's place for supper. She was a new person. She was happy and content. The boys were awake and sitting on her lap, talking about their daddy…and they all knew she could face the world, now!

Chapter 19

Back to a Normal Life?

I N JUNE OF 1950, THE Korean War, or "conflict", as they liked to refer to it had started. Joe Allen was exempt from the draft, due to his Sickle Cell Disease. This was one time his wife Liz was happy for the disease. When Canada entered, there were boys who worked for their family's farm and the golf course who had to go. Cousins Emmett and Richard were exempt because they were too old. Abe and Simon, Liz's twin brothers were needed to run the farm, since they had government contracts again; with their potato supply, for provisions, overseas. Eleanor said many prayers of thanks for this. After the funeral, Liz remembered these thoughts, as she heard daily news reports from Korea. She never knew that Joe had been fighting his own personal war, every day since they had moved to Mississippi.

Two weeks after Joe's funeral, in August of 1950, Eleanor had to leave Mississippi and get back to the farm. Even having Abe, Emmett, Richard and Simon away during the funeral, meant four less men to do the work, needed.

Liz knew it was time for her mom to go. School would start again in a couple of days and Liz had to pull herself together and get back to work. She wasn't sure how she would handle being alone with the boys. The two weeks before school were spent on long walks and talks and playing with the boys, answering tough questions. Liz was glad her mom was still there for back up, for those two weeks. They would ask each night, during their prayers, "Mommy, can we talk to daddy, like we talk to God?"

Liz told them, "Yes you can talk to daddy, but remember, just like God, he can't talk back." They would always get upset. They wanted him there, or they wanted him to talk to them. They missed him a lot. Some evenings one or both would cry and Liz tried to be strong, but after tucking them in and going to bed alone, she would cry herself to sleep.

One night John asked, "Mama, did daddy go away 'cause me and James were bad?"

Liz broke out crying instantly and grabbed them both and held them tightly to her bosom, not knowing what she would say next. She had to wait a moment before she could compose herself, before she could answer. El heard her cry and came up the stairs, but didn't butt in. She waited at the door, to see if she was needed. Liz calmed down and said, "Honey, daddy loved you two, and me, more than anything in the world. He would never be upset with you, no matter how good, or bad you think you were. Daddy knew you didn't mean it if you were bad; just like I do.

I know you miss him. I really miss him, too. Daddy went away... well...because sometimes, bad men do bad things. They sometimes hurt other people and daddy was a person who got hurt. They hurt him so bad, that he died. His heart stopped working and that's how people die." Just after she said it, she regretted it. How could she explain it and fix it, so they could understand.

John said, "But mama, if daddy's heart stopped, how can he still love us?"

Eleanor came in the room and she sat on the bed. She put her arms around her daughter and grandsons and said, "Boys, it's true that daddy's heart stopped working. But remember, when we talk about God, sometimes you hear about the Holy Spirit?" They both nodded their heads. They remembered.

El continued, "Well, the Holy Spirit isn't anything you can see, or touch, or hold, or hear. But it is always around you. Just the way God is. Well, daddy is like that, now. He is a spirit, which will always be around you. That means his love is always around you. You can't see him, feel him, or touch him, or hear him, but his love is always there for you. It's around you every day, whatever you do, or wherever you are...and he's around mommy, too. Do you understand?"

They nodded their heads again and smiled at their grandmother. They stopped crying and Liz couldn't say anything. Her mother had come through for her, again: Like she always had, all her life. She could always count on her mom to have the answers for her, when she didn't. Both boys smiled and James patted his mom on her shoulder and said, "It's okay, mommy. Daddy still loves you, too; even though you can't see him." She smiled more and the tears kept coming. Right then, she knew she had two of the very sweetest, loving, sensitive sons, in the world. They were there for her, this time.

Every evening, during those two weeks, Robert came for supper, or he would cook for them at his place. Or, Mrs. Martin might be there and would cook for them, if Robert was going to be late at the office. Etta was invited during these nights too, but she felt she should let the family have private time alone together, before El had to leave.

Etta would usually visit Minnie on these evenings and they would talk for hours. There were so many new people coming to town, Etta met several new friends, who took room and board at Minnie's. Minnie and Etta were the best of friends. They went shopping together, they went to church and choir practice and they often baked at her boarding house together. Etta liked being with her and helping her with her baking, which by now, Minnie was selling out of her home. Etta didn't miss her life on the plantation at all except, she periodically thought about the women who raised her. She did love them and missed them.

George Benson stopped by every few days after work, but made sure he called Liz every evening to ask how she was doing. He would let her know what was being said at work about Joe if anything. He was listening for Ray to screw up, somehow. He needed evidence that he killed Joe. But, where would he take this evidence? There was nothing he could do, unless the sheriff and deputy were out of their publicly elected jobs. He needed to take it to a new sheriff. That could take years. He would bide his time. He was sure, their day would come.

When El was ready to go home, both women cried a lot. Robert drove to Jackson with Eleanor, Liz and the twins. The ladies hugged and held each other. They didn't want to let go, but they had to. It was time for Liz to stand on her own two feet. She'd never been alone before, other than at university. She had to be strong for her sons, now.

Robert and Eleanor bid farewell. They were glad they had this much time together, even if it was wrought with tragic circumstances. Robert would visit Eleanor soon, but he had to catch up on some work. It would be at least three weeks, before he could go to Chatham, but the first time he went, Liz and the twins would go with him.

Liz went back to Philadelphia Elementary School and on that first day, her colleagues were glad to see her. She asked Vincent to let them know she'd prefer not to dwell on Joe's death, at work. She would prefer that everyone act like they did, before. She knew it might be hard for them, not to ask questions, but she didn't want to risk crying in front of her class.

The only thing her friends did for her was, they placed a lovely vase of flowers on her desk, with a small card pinned to them that said, 'Mrs. Allen, just a note to let you know, we're thinking of you!' It was signed front and back, by all the staff at her school. She was happy. They were beautiful and she'd never forget how touched she was, that they did this little gesture for her. No one mentioned Joe.

Vincent had a few calls from parents of Liz's students. As word got around that she had been married to the "Nigger" that 'committed suicide', they questioned if she was fit to teach their white children. Vince Kirkland had only five parents call about it. He thought 5 out of 22 students was not bad. He was ready with his answer. He told each parent, "We have been fortunate enough to have Mrs. Allen teaching at this school for almost three years, now. Your children have the benefit of having a teacher, who graded the highest mark in Mississippi's history, on the board exams. She came from Canada you know and she was a much respected teacher there, too. When her board exams were graded, the Governor of Mississippi personally came to give her, her teaching certificate. Not only that, he also presented her with a personal letter from the Oval Office. She had a congratulatory letter from President Truman personally, about her high scholastic marks. She is also the mother of two very beautiful twin boys. Yes, your child is in wonderful hands and we don't dwell on the tragedy she has recently been through and it is our hope that the parents of our students let her do her job and get on with the business of teaching grade one, to our town's children."

On that first day with his answer to the parents who called him, he was proud of himself for handling the delicate situation and they all agreed to keep their children enrolled in her class; and did not insist on her removal from her post. He never told Liz about the phone calls until years later. Liz was glad, because she probably would have cried and maybe made the terrible mistake of quitting her job.

She loved her class. She was thrilled to be back to work. It took her mind off her husband, but she was even happier to go home to her boys every afternoon. They loved to wait and watch out the window for her to drive in the driveway. That first day she came home from school it occurred to her that Joe's pick-up was still sitting in the driveway. She thought she should do something with it. Did she really want to keep it? Did she need two vehicles? As she got out of the car Joe had bought for her when the boys were born, she considered the fate of his truck. Liz still loved her car, but did she need the truck, too. She thought she would talk it over with her mom and Etta and if she was going to get rid of it, she would likely give it to the farm in Chatham, to use.

Also that first day of school, Etta was happy to be looking after the boys on her own, again. They were very well behaved most of the time when they were alone with her, but she had a little trouble as soon as Liz left for work, that first morning. They both cried. When she asked what was the matter, John said, "Miss Etta, Mommy is going away like daddy. We will never see her again, will we?"

James cried even harder and said, "Miss Etta, why did mommy go. Did she go see daddy? Why can't we go see him, too?"

Etta thought carefully about her answer and she began, "Now, you two boys juss' hush, an' come sit wit' yo' Miss Etta." They both climbed up and one sat on each side of her while she tried to explain. "I guess you boys are a little young to remember, but yo' mama left every day at this time, to go to her job. She's done it for the lass' few years, since a while after you boys were born. Do you remember what yo' mama does?"

James said, "Mommy is a teacher."

Etta said, "That be right. Well, she went to work last year and the year before and now she's gone back to work, again this year. Every day, she went to work and every day, she comes home to you boys. Now believe me when I tells you, she went to work today and she be comin' home later, when her work day is over. I promises, you bot', she be back 'dis afternoon." Etta temporarily had her hands full, but they both accepted her answer. Fortunately she had the television...and, although she hated to use it...bribery.

The boys loved the television. Their favorite shows, though, were not aired until the early evening hours. So, Miss Etta promised, if they were good and stop crying, they would watch their shows as usual. If they kept crying, or they were bad through the day, they could end up going to bed without seeing them. It would be up to mommy, when she got home.

The usual routine had the family eating their supper at 5:00 p.m., every night. After supper was over, the boys loved to watch "The Howdy Doody Show", which aired Monday to Friday, from 5:30 p.m. to 6:00 p.m., and that was followed by "The Kukla, Fran and Ollie Show", which aired, Monday to Friday - 6:00 p.m. to 6:30 p.m. After that, it was bath time and off to bed. The boys loved Buffalo Bob Smith and his marionette and the puppets kept them both laughing, Liz, too. Etta would usually peek around the corner of the kitchen door, into the living room and would watch them giggle, with their mom. It brought a smile to her face.

Although they were too young to remember it all, their dad let them listen to the "Lone Ranger" shows on the radio, whenever he could catch it. The same was for the television show. He thought they might like him, and Silver, and Tonto; as much as he did, growing up.

One of Etta's favorite times of the day, was when her program was playing on the radio. Monday to Friday she faithfully listened to "The Guiding Light". It was what was known as a soap opera; named that due to the sponsor of the show. It was a company whose main products were soap related. The show was the continuing story; of people's lives, their woes and triumphs, in a fictitious town. She loved it; it had been running, on the radio since 1937. She was hoping that someday it would be adapted to television. That way she would be able to watch it, instead of just listening to it and imagining what the characters might look like. Her program was on while the boys napped, every afternoon.

After the boys watched their programs in the evening, Etta would put on the "CBS Evening News", with Douglas Edwards, as anchorman. She would turn the sound up a bit, so Liz could hear from the bathroom, where she was bathing the twins. Liz made sure to never miss the daily news. She needed to know what was going on in the world. She also liked Etta to keep up with it, too. It gave them so much to talk about, when the boys were in bed. Liz would also talk to her class about these current events. Even though they were only six years old, she would try to put things into perspective.

During 1950, the news program they liked to watch changed its name to "Douglas Edwards with the News". Etta didn't understand the change, but she figured most folks liked the man, so CBS changed the name. She found him too stuffy, too uppity; Liz liked him.

Liz and Etta would always watch "Toast of the Town", on Sunday nights. It was a variety program, hosted by Ed Sullivan. There was also "Meet the Press"; another news program and Liz would never miss "I Love Lucy", on Monday nights. The two women bonded during these times and as they shared their evenings, watching television, if Liz wasn't working on the next day's class lesson. They would talk and laugh and sometimes cry, when they talked of Joe. They became the best of friends in these first few years of Liz's widowhood. Liz would come to think of Etta as the sister she never had.

So, that first day of school in 1950, Liz went back to work, the boys decided they would stop their crying and not jeopardize their favorite time of day. It wasn't just the television shows themselves. It was their favorite time of day because mommy always sat between them with an arm around each one. She would watch the shows with them.

Etta also promised them that first day and every day after, when their mom went to work, they could watch for her through the living room window, in the afternoon. They could both sit in front of the window, on their rocking horses and watch for mommy coming home and when she finally made it through the door, they jumped up to her and wanted to be picked up and give hugs and kisses. She laughed at her boys and it was a good start to the new school year and she thought of it as the first real day, of their new lives.

Nineteen-fifty, was also the year of the beginning of "Brown vs. The Board of Education". Liz was happy to hear about it, as was Vincent and a couple of teachers she worked with. Most Mississippians saw it as a downfall and a tragedy, if it were to come to fruition.

Black people were tired of their children not having an education, or walking long distances, to get to a black school, when there was a white one, within blocks of their homes. There were no buses to transport black children to their schools. The black people wanted integration! The whites didn't! The NAACP, or National Association for the Advancement of Colored People, wanted to take a stand. It would likely be the biggest, in their history.

The NAACP, was founded on February 12, 1909, on what would have been Abraham Lincoln's one-hundredth birthday. Its founders consisted of two colored people, one Jewish person, and three white people. Included were one white woman and one black woman.

Their Charter Mission reads:

> "To promote equality of rights and to eradicate caste or race prejudice among the citizens of the United States, to advance the interest of colored citizens, to secure for them, impartial suffrage; and to increase their opportunities for securing justice in the courts, education for the children, employment according to their ability and complete equality before law".

Jews were also very prominent in the NAACP. Not only did they provide funding, but were represented in the organization's beginning.

In 1914 the NAACP, with its following of six-thousand members, fought for and won the right for blacks to enlist and fight in World War I. Then in 1915, the organization protested, nationally against the release of D.W. Griffith's new motion picture, "Birth of a Nation". The movie glorified the Ku Klux Klan. The movie was released anyway and it was accepted by the country. Especially in Mississippi

They also spent so much time trying to fight lynching of blacks, by white men. They fought for ten years to try to get federal legislation, to ban lynchings. In the NAACP's office in New York, every time a black man was lynched, they would display a black flag, in their window. Liz found out years later, in New York, they'd heard about Joe's lynching and hung their black flag for him, too! She was touched. They'd also been fighting for desegregation, for decades.

When Liz heard that her husband was having racial troubles at work, she remembered reading about "civil rights". Although it was in the constitution, it was barely in place by the late 1940's and 1950.

The NAACP had been fighting for this for so many years and getting, virtually nowhere, until a man in Topeka, Kansas, named

Oliver Brown, let them use his personal experience as their cornerstone case.

Rev. Oliver Brown had to walk his eight year old daughter, Linda, to her black school every day. Each day they would walk about a mile to school in the morning and the same trail home in the afternoon. They walked through rough terrain and a dangerous railroad switch yard. There was a white school only about seven blocks from their home.

When he went to register his daughter at the white school, the principal refused. The school board backed the principal, saying that segregation provided other aspects of life and segregated schools prepared black children, for the segregation of adult life. So many black parents were in the same situation, all over the country.

Rev. Brown went to the local NAACP and requested their help. This was perfect! It was the right time and climate, to make a crucial move. Rev. Brown was not the sole plaintiff. The NAACP used Brown's name, with his permission, to spearhead the case. There were other cases of the same problem, in other states. There were nearly two-hundred plaintiffs around the country. Many cases would join the 'Brown' case, in the years to come and the ones, who previously failed as individual cases, joined in support.

Liz would follow the news on the progress of the NAACP and "Brown vs. Board of Education". She prayed for the outcome, that segregation would be abolished. She would, however, keep her thoughts and comments to herself, or she would only talk with her principal, once in a while about it, since he was in agreement with her. There were teachers in her school, who would fight to keep segregation and she wanted to keep things peaceful at work, by listening to their philosophy, but not commenting on hers.

Desegregation was the topic every day, at the school. Liz would listen and wait. She was sure that the Brown case would lead to desegregation in the schools. After all, there were some desegregated units fighting in Korea, together. Albeit: As white soldiers were dying, they were replaced by black soldiers, hence, the desegregated unit. At least it was a start. This was, of course, with the exception of the all black troops who fought in the Civil War.

As time moved on, the town forgot about the 'Nigger, that committed suicide'. Liz didn't! She still wanted to see justice done to the men who murdered her husband. After Vincent came to her defense, with parents of her students, she was fairly well respected and accepted as the teacher of the grade one students at Philadelphia Elementary School. But, as people found out about her black child, they just tolerated it. She and Etta tried to keep the boys protected, at all times. She didn't trust the white community, with the exception of her white friends. The black community admired her. She and her twins were welcome there and treated with respect.

Liz took the boys to visit Chatham about every five or six weeks. She would still join Robert, when he went to visit her mom. Liz would always ask Robert on these trips, "Why don't you and mom get married?"

He looked at Liz with smiles, each time she asked this question. He would always say, "Liz, your mother and I don't need a piece of paper to prove we love each other. We're happy with the way things are. And, while we're on the subject, do you think you'll ever marry again?"

Sometimes she would look away and say, "Joe was the love of my life. I could never accept someone else." He would give her an understanding smile and pat her hand, sometimes. He never pushed the issue. Neither he, nor Eleanor would press her on it. If it was meant to be, it would. God would see to it.

On the visits back home, the boys would get to play on the family swings, which they loved and they got to ride on the tractors, out to the potato fields. The family and all the farm hands loved having the boys around. They were always making everyone laugh and smile. They were so sweet and friendly. No one minded looking out for them.

It was the same on the family golf course. The boys were often around while their mom golfed. Although the rule was no children under twelve on the course, the twins were always accepted by the patrons. Liz usually dropped the boys off in the club house. The staff looked after them and they had fun, while their mom was on the course.

Everyone was welcome at McDonald's Golf Course. It didn't matter if you were white, black, Jewish, or whatever. You were welcome to golf there. The McDonald's mostly ran the golf course, just for the love of the game. It was still a money maker and they had the cheapest green fees, in all of Ontario. Golfers found that this course had some of the most challenging holes, too.

Every once in a while one, or the other, or both of the twins would go out on the course with her. They would stay with her and walk the course. Periodically, they would run ahead and pick up her ball and bring it back to her, because they thought it got away on her. Everyone would laugh.

While golfing by herself one unseasonably warm day in the fall that first year Joe was gone Liz was up to the double hole. The one they duplicated from the farm, decades earlier. It was par 5 and she had done it, in 4. She was so thrilled, she jumped, excitedly. She turned around, twisting her bad ankle and said, "Joe did you see that, I did it in four. I finally tied you." All of a sudden, she realized Joe wasn't there. She had been so sure he was behind her to hear her. She started to cry and couldn't continue with her game. She was in physical and emotional pain.

She slowly, painfully dragged herself back to the club house. When she jumped, she forgot herself and landed wrong on her permanently damaged ankle. She hurt it bad, but didn't want to tell anyone. She felt bad enough about Joe. She didn't want to worry anyone about damaging her ankle, again.

Her boys were at the club house, entertaining other golfers with their high-jinx. By the time she arrived, she had been able to stop the tears. But she was limping so much worse than usual and needed to sit down, desperately. When she hobbled in, the boys saw her and ran for a hug.

She picked up John, because he got to her first. Then James wanted up, too. She dropped in the first chair she came to and then had both of them sitting on her knees and her ankle was causing so much pain, but still never said anything. After the boys got down, she saw her mom and Robert arrive in the clubhouse. They were going to play a round and El asked Liz, "Honey, did you want to go out with us?" But Robert could see she was in much pain.

Liz said, "Mom I can't, I really hurt my ankle out there on our hole."

Robert looked at her ankle, which was swelling quite badly. He said, "What did you do, girl?" He came to her and touched her ankle and she screeched in pain. Robert said, "El, we have to get her to the hospital in Chatham. I think she's broken it again, even with the plate and screws in. It could be very bad hon, they could have to open and repair it again, but she needs to go now."

Liz started to cry, it was so painful. She didn't want anyone to know that she was imagining Joe was there. She thought they might commit her. She tried to smile at the thought of him, but the pain was too bad.

She told them she jumped and landed wrong. Then she had to walk all the way back to the club house, dragging her clubs. She was on the family's favorite hole. The thirteenth; which is the furthest hole away to walk back from.

Robert carried Liz to Eleanor's car and El said, "I'll drive Liz's car and take the boys back to the farm with me. Caroline will take care of them. Then, I'll come to the hospital." James and John weren't sure of everything that was going on, but they heard the word hospital and started to cry; thinking their mommy wouldn't come back, just like daddy. When she went to the hospital to see him, he never came home again. Liz hugged and reassured them as best she could. When they were a little calmer, everyone left and Liz was on her way to the hospital, possibly to have more surgery on her bad ankle.

On the way to the hospital, with Robert, she started sobbing, uncontrollably. Robert knew she was in pain, but he thought it was more than that. He asked, "Sweetie did something else happen out there, today?"

She turned to him and through her tears, she cried, "I miss him, Robert. I'm angry; he left me and I want him back. I miss him so much. I am in so much fucking pain, over his senseless death and now I probably broke my fucking ankle, again...I'm so fucking pissed off. I need my Joe back." Robert did not respond, but he understood. He pulled into the parking lot and went in to get a wheelchair. After Liz got in it, she said, "I'm sorry for my tantrum, Robert. Please don't tell mom about it, she'll just worry". He smiled.

When they went in to the emergency room, an older doctor, Dr. Smith recognized Liz. He knew she was Dr. George McDonald's daughter and Dr. Marteen Allen's daughter-in-law: Both respected by everyone who knew them around the hospital. After he found out what happened and examined her, he told her how sorry he was to hear about Joe. Dr. Smith knew the whole family. She smiled a weak smile at him. He sent her for an x-ray.

Eleanor arrived at the hospital and was chatting with Dr. Smith while Liz was in X-Ray. He told her to expect surgery, in Toronto. As soon as she knew, El called the farm, to prepare Caroline. She thought she and Robert would be taking Liz to Toronto. When Liz came back from the X-ray Department, Dr. Smith gave her the news. She was going to Toronto for surgery.

When the doctor looked at the x-ray it was determined that her ankle was badly broken, once again. The bone that the plate was attached to was broken above the plate. It was a very bad break indeed. They had no idea how she ever dragged herself and her clubs, back to the clubhouse. The doctor said she would have to go to Toronto, to the special Orthopedic Surgeon, Dr. Terrence Henderson. Liz looked to her mom and started to cry.

Eleanor put her arms around her daughter and held her. Dr. Smith left the room and called Toronto General. They were getting hold of Dr. Henderson and would relay the message, about a patient coming in from Chatham with serious fractures, which would require immediate surgery. He happened to be on call that weekend. Liz was very lucky.

Dr. Smith ordered an ambulance. Liz didn't want to go without seeing the boys, but she had to. El wanted to take her to Toronto herself, but the doctor said she was better in the ambulance. She could be closely monitored and Dr. Smith was going to give her some morphine for the pain, anyway. She would likely sleep all the way to Toronto, but she'd be closely observed by the ambulance attendants. He recommended El drive to Toronto and meet her there. The ambulance was ordered and picked up Liz. Dr. Smith gave her a good dose of morphine and he was right - she slept all the way.

El and Robert drove the cars back to the farm and El packed a bag for Liz. Word got around the farm about what happened and they all pitched in with the twins. When grandma told the boys about what was happening they cried. James said, "Mommy IS going away like daddy!" El said, "Honey, mommy only hurt her ankle. Remember when she was in the clubhouse and you saw her crying?" They both nodded their heads, yes. She continued trying to make the bad news as minimal as she could for them, "Well, she broke her ankle again and it needs an operation on it, to fix it up again."

John said, "Why can't we see her?"

Robert stepped in and said, "She has to go to another hospital to see a very special doctor, to fix it. He doesn't live around here, so she has to go there." He wiped some tears away from John's eyes and blew his nose.

As John hugged Dr. Robert, he asked, "Does she still love us?"

Robert said, "Of course she does, darlin'. She didn't want to go without seeing you boys, but she had to. Do you know what a doctor's order is?" They both shook their heads. Robert continued, "Well, that's when a doctor tells someone something and they have to do it. He tells them something for their own good…to make them better. Mommy had to follow her doctor's order so she would get better and get home to you guys quickly. She didn't have a choice. She had to go…even if that meant she didn't get to see you both, before she left. They have to fix her ankle as soon as possible, so she can come home and get better.

You know boys, when she comes back from that hospital she is really going to need both of you to help her. She'll be walking with two sticks, called crutches and she will need you two, to help her get around the house. You'll have to look after her, for a change. Do you two think you can do that for her?"

They both smiled and nodded their heads. James said, "We will look after her really good, Miss Etta will, too!" They were going to be fine.

They said goodbye to grandma and Dr. Robert. Caroline and their aunts and uncles would look after James and John, until Liz got back to the farm. Robert brought all his things with him and decided on Monday, when he went back to Mississippi he'd fly from the Toronto Airport, since he was so close to it. Eleanor packed a few things for herself and they planned to stay in Toronto at a hotel near the hospital. El was scared for her daughter, but as always, Robert was there for her with his support and his love…and love for this wonderful family who had accepted him into their lives, over three years earlier.

On the drive to Toronto, Robert said, "Honey, I think I should explain about Dr. Henderson…he is really the top orthopedic surgeon, well, I'd say in the province, if not the country."

Eleanor felt good to hear this. She said, "I'm so glad Dr. Smith is sending her there."

Robert said, "I know him, love. He, George and I were at McGill, together."

El looked at him for a moment and said, "Are you sure it's the same guy?"

He said, "Yes dear, it's him. Are you going to be okay with this?"

All she could do was nod her head and then she smiled, reached over to take Robert's hand and she kissed the back of it. She said, "I can take it…I have you with me, don't I?" They smiled; she kissed his hand again, and they drove north, to Toronto; only about forty minutes behind Liz's ambulance.

When Liz arrived in Toronto, she felt that she had dozed off for only a few minutes, but they told her that she'd been out about three hours. When she arrived at the emergency department of Toronto General, there was an operating room ready and Dr. Henderson was almost ready for her arrival. There had been a bad car accident, before she got there. He was in another operating room, doing surgery on one of the accident victims. Liz's ankle would have to wait until he was done.

He left orders to give her more morphine if she needed it. He had personally talked with Dr. Smith, in Chatham and he was aware of her accident and her previous break and repair. Dr. Henderson requested that the x-rays come with her to Toronto, as well. The ambulance attendants gave the x-rays to a nurse when they arrived and she placed them where Dr. Henderson would be scrubbing and he'd study them there, before sending them into the operating room where he could refer to them before and during the surgery.

Within the hour, Eleanor and Robert arrived at Toronto General. They were guided into an examining room, where Liz was drowsy, but awake. She was so happy to see them she wept and reached for her mom's hand. She said, "Mom, how did the boys take it?" She told Liz it was rough at first, but Robert took over and explained things to them and now they want her home because they are going to be her personal helpers and will be looking after her, with Miss Etta's help. Liz grinned and said, "That's my boys!"

Just then, a man walked into the examining room and said, "Okay Mrs. Allen, I'm Dr. Henderson. I'm head of Orthopedic Surgery, here at Toronto General. I just looked at your x-rays, and we have some major repairs to do. I guarantee you will walk again, but I don't know if you'll need help with a cane, or crutches, but you will walk again." He looked up at Liz's company and he blinked his eyes. As he held out his hand, he said, "Dr. Robert Hathaway, how are you old buddy? I take it you all know each other quite well?"

Robert said, "Yes, Terrence. Let me introduce this lovely lady, on my arm. This is the widow, Mrs. Eleanor McDonald. She was married to Dr. George McDonald, from McGill. And your patient is their daughter.

Dr. Henderson grinned and couldn't believe it. He said, "It's a pleasure to meet you both, but I'm sorry about the circumstances. Wow, what a surprise, Robert. McGill was a lifetime ago. Mrs. McDonald,

Mrs. Allen, I was sorry to hear that George passed away a few years back. You have my sincerest sympathies. He was a good friend to me at McGill and one of the finest surgeons, of our times. I'm sure Robert feels the same way.

So anyway, I'll get you into the O.R. sweet lady and we'll fix that ankle and tibia, as best we can. I better let you all know; it is going to be a long surgery. It will be several hours...about three, or four I expect. I need to do some major repairs in there, by the look of these x-rays!"

Robert said to Eleanor, "Well honey, I guess we could go check into a hotel nearby and get some rest. Terry, would you recommend a hotel for us, close to this hospital?"

Dr. Henderson told him, "Yes, the best is the Royal York, on Front Street. It is Toronto's pride and joy. It is built over by Toronto's Union Station. I guess you could say it is equivalent to New York's, Grand Central Station, just on a smaller scale. As a matter of fact, it is only a few blocks away, a couple of minutes by car. You could leave your car there and take the street car. That's probably the best. Then you don't have to worry about parking here and paying the day rate!" He looked back to the gurney and said to Liz, "Okay dear, let's get you in there. I'll have to remove the plate and pins and put new plate in and probably one on the ankle. But don't worry love, you'll be fine. I'll take care of George McDonald's little girl! Let's go." Dr. Henderson and a nurse took Liz into the operating room and Eleanor and Robert got directions to the hotel from another nurse and went to get a room.

When they walked into the hotel lobby there were a few stares; for the black and white couple but they ignored it. They were used to it and dealt with it. They opted to carry their own luggage and went to their room. They didn't want to be a bother to anyone. As they walked into the decadently decorated room, they knew this was a real treat for them, both. This was the 'big city' and they were amazed at the beauty of the hotel and fascinated by the city's sights and sounds.

There was a good restaurant in the hotel, but they ordered dinner from room service. They treated themselves to a lovely steak dinner and champagne. The hotel was a special occasion, but unfortunately under poor circumstances. As they ate their dinner, they thought of Liz and the boys. Robert hesitated, because he didn't want to betray Liz, but he felt he had to. He said, "Dear, Liz misses Joe a lot. I think she's having a harder time, than she is letting on." He stopped there and would say no more.

El knew that he must be betraying a trust, but she was curious. She also didn't want to get him in trouble with Liz. She said, "I agree with you. Maybe I should go back to Mississippi when she goes home. I'll feel her out about it. I think you'd be quite happy, if I did, too." They both grinned at each other, thinking the same thing...more time together.

After their supper, Robert called the Toronto Airport and reserved a seat on the Monday flight to Jackson, Mississippi. Then he called Detroit Airport and cancelled his, Liz's, and the boys tickets for Sunday. Next, he called George Benson. He asked if George would pick him up in Jackson on Monday. He told him that was not a problem. He'd meet his plane in Jackson.

Robert and El arrived back at the hospital before the surgery was over, but were told it was going well. They only had about thirty minutes to wait, until Terry came out of the operating room, and went into the waiting room, where he found Robert and Eleanor.

He said, "Wow, she sure did a number on it folks! She had a Trimalleolar fracture of the ankle...oh Robert, how about I leave it to you to give the details to Eleanor, you're a doctor." They laughed. He continued, "The best way to fix this fracture was to secure a plate and screws along the back of the tibia, down near the ankle.

She also had a Tibia shaft fracture, above her existing plate. I removed the old plate and screws and placed new, longer ones in and she now has one on each side of her tibia. She's got quite the metal supply in her, now!" Eleanor couldn't help it, she giggled.

He said, "I'm not quite sure how she managed so much damage, but I'm sure the previous break and surgery had something to do with it. Obviously her tibia bone was no longer as strong as it should have been. Regardless of the plate, she broke the bone, above it. The ankle fracture, I think was a really unfortunate twist, when she landed from her jump, but believe me, she will be alright. She will, however have a limp, but shouldn't need a cane or crutches. I don't want her running marathons, but she will be able to golf, which I hear is where the injury happened and I hope her cheerleading and jumping tendencies, calm down. She does sounds like her father's daughter. I'll bet she's a fireball, right?" Eleanor and Robert nodded in unison and all three laughed."

A nurse came in and told them Liz was waking up. All three went in to see her and the doctor told Liz everything he had just told her mother and Robert. She understood, but wanted something for pain. Terry ordered morphine and it was put in through her IV. It started to work, almost right away.

Liz asked how long she had to stay there and her doctor asked what she did, where she lived, etc. They told him she lived in Mississippi and that she was a teacher and had three year old twins at home. Terry said she could go back to Mississippi, when he felt she could, but needed help at home and could not get back to work, yet. He suggested that she stay off work, until the January session started up, again. That would give her more than six weeks to recover. She hated to hear that part because she loved her class.

Liz asked, "Am I going to walk? Am I still going to limp?"

Dr. Henderson said, "Yes, you will walk but, very likely with a limp, but I'm not sure how much until you heal. I didn't know how bad it was before I met you, but you should certainly be well enough to not have to use a cane, or crutches the rest of your life. You'll need physical therapy in Mississippi, which I'm sure Robert can arrange for you to get you walking, but NO weight bearing for six weeks. It WILL take TIME, my dear! Use it wisely. Rest and play with your children, for a few weeks. They'll grow up, before you know it!" He bid everyone goodnight, but turned to Robert and Eleanor and said, "Robert, I'm still on call tomorrow, but would you and Eleanor be my guests for dinner tomorrow evening?" They looked at each other and said they'd love to. Liz was fast asleep.

When Liz woke up on Sunday morning, she felt pretty good. She didn't need any morphine, but the doctor insisted she have a little. She remembered Robert, after having the twins had told her not to wait until the pain is too bad. She agreed it was a good idea to just have enough to keep comfortable. Dr. Henderson was telling Liz what a 'study horse' her dad was. He said, "We always tried to get him to loosen up on weekends and come out with us, but he always stayed in, studying."

Liz was smiling. It was nice to hear something good about her father again, from a new person in her life. She laughed and told Terry her dad was always like that. He read and studied everything he got his hands on. She told him about her twin brothers and the big farm...and their golf course.

Terry knew about the potato farm, but didn't know about their golf course: Terry was a self- proclaimed golf nut! Liz said, "Well, that's all there is to that! You have to come to Chatham. Are you off next weekend?"

He said, "As a matter-of-fact I am I'd love to come down!"

She said, "There's lots of room on the farm, you won't need a hotel room, or anything. You can meet the family and golf to your heart's content. I'm sure Robert will be there, unless he's on call in Mississippi."

"Unless who's on call in Mississippi, young lady? Are you gossiping about me?" Robert smiled as he walked in the room, with her mom.

Liz was sitting up, bright-eyed and smiling. She said, "Oh, hi. Guess what? Terry said he'd love to come to Chatham next weekend and golf. I told him you might be there, if you weren't on call at home."

Robert shook Terry's hand and said, "I'm going home tomorrow and I'll try to book it off so I can come up. I'd love to golf with you Terry. Sounds like a great time. You'll love the farm and the family. How is our girl this morning?"

Terry said, "Great. She's only taken just a bit of morphine. But says she feels good. Now mother, is she the type of girl that says she's fine.... just to get out of here?"

El said, "Well Doctor, I would have told you before yesterday, YES, but I think she knows how important it is to heal and heed her doctor's advice. Right my dear?" Liz blushed and smiled, but didn't answer. She giggled, with the effect of the morphine.

Everyone laughed. She straightened up and said, "I do want to see my boys. After all, their dad just died a couple of months ago. They need me."

Terry was shocked. It hadn't occurred to ask about a husband. He thought, if she had one, he'd be there. Robert said, "Joe was killed by Klan." Terry was shocked and disgusted at this news and commented on how barbaric Mississippi sounded. He gave Liz his condolences and dropped the subject. He asked her if she could stay here, in Ontario, or go home, if she was released.

Liz said, "Well mom, I guess maybe I can stay on the farm for a week and then go back. I think I could go to the farm tomorrow, on crutches, if that's okay. I'm very experienced on them, from the last time I did this and Robert is my family doctor."

Terry said, "Well, I guess under those circumstances, I think that would be alright. I'll release you tomorrow, IF I think you're up to it and you can go to the farm for a bit, then I'll assess you there next weekend, when I come. I'd like you stay in Ontario a bit longer, then we'll see if you can go to Mississippi." Liz agreed reluctantly and then asked her mom to call Vincent and tell him about her accident and tell him that she would call him, when she got out of the hospital. El promised she would.

Liz dozed off occasionally that Sunday, while Robert and El took the day to see the sights of Toronto. They met Terry for a great dinner; they would get Liz and go home the next day, if all was okay.

Monday, Robert went to the airport and flew home, while Liz and Eleanor drove back to Chatham, after Terry watched how Liz handled her crutches...and he knew he was going to see her in five days. He also knew Robert would be able to take her stitches out, in Mississippi, when it was time. As they left, they gave him directions to get to the farm. He told them he'd see them Friday night and he was looking forward to it.

When they got to the farm on Monday afternoon, the twins were having a nap. As soon as they woke up, they came downstairs and saw their mom. They excitedly ran to her, to hug her. After she kissed them both, they were full of questions about her leg, her cast, her crutches and when were they were going to go home. She answered all their questions and held both boys close to her. She didn't want to ever leave them again, if she could help it.

She wanted to sleep in her house, the Allen house, that night. But her mom thought she should stay in her house, in case she needed help through the night. She stood her ground and she slept in the Allen house, with her boys.

After getting them to sleep, she lay in the bed and drifted off. When she woke up in the middle of the night, she felt like she was being watched, so she sat up, and looked around. There was no one there, but she still had the feeling that she was being watched. She wasn't scared; she figured it was Joe's family, like they had both felt, in the past. But she was disappointed. She didn't feel Joe's presence there. This upset her. She looked to the wall and suddenly the family spirits were there, but there was an obvious empty space! Joe's spirit was missing!

Friday evening came along and both Robert and Terry arrived. Robert had a surprise. He brought Miss Etta with him, to help with the boys, on the trip home. It was still unseasonably warm, and the two doctors golfed all weekend and got reacquainted. Etta and Caroline made sure everyone ate well. No one let Liz do anything. She sat down a lot, she hobbled around a bit and tried to play with her sons.

As Liz rested, she remembered that Joe had left a box of his old books in their attic. She got Abe to help her get into the attic and he brought out Joe's books. When Joe was young, he was very interested in 'The Lone Ranger'. He started collecting all the books that were written about him and throughout the years, collected all thirteen. He had also seen some of the movies, in Windsor when they were growing up. The last book he collected, was written the year that he died.

Liz got them out, dusted them off and started reading them to the boys. The twins were so excited about these stories. Liz made a mental note to herself to make sure she kept purchasing any more written and make the set as complete as she could. It would be a gift from a father to his sons. She would take them back to Mississippi, when she went.

The Monday after Terry visited, he decided that Liz could go home. He released her into Robert's care in Mississippi and he was just a phone call away to advise them, if he was needed.

Liz, Etta, the boys and Eleanor all flew back to Mississippi, that Monday morning. Robert had left on Sunday, as usual. Liz was glad to be going home. She hoped she would feel Joe, when she got home. She hoped he would be there, in spirit. He wasn't in their house, in Chatham.

Chapter 20

Life at Home

WHEN LIZ HAD ARRIVED AT the Chatham farm after having ankle surgery in Toronto, she called Vince to let him know she couldn't go back to work until after the Christmas break. He was disappointed, but understood. The substitute teacher he'd called in could stay right through until Liz went back, in January. Liz had never used any of her sick days in the years she had worked at Philadelphia Elementary School, so now was the time to use them. She had some time off, with pay.

When Liz went back to Mississippi, after having the surgery, her mom went with her to help out with the boys for a couple of weeks. Liz was so relieved.

After Liz was finally home, she called Vince again, to see if things were going well for her substitute. She also told Vincent to say hello to her class and that she missed them all. A few days after she was home, she received flowers from Vincent and the other teachers. She also received a letter, and a picture, from each of her students. She was delighted and sad at the same time. She missed them.

George came by the first night she and the boys were home and made sure they were alright. They were happy to be home and George was happy to see them all. He was even happier, when he saw that Eleanor had come with them, to help look after everyone.

Christmas 1950 was spent in Chatham. Liz wanted the boys to be surrounded by lots of family and friends. It was their first Christmas, without their father. Robert and George were invited to join the family at the farm and both came.

Liz's ankle had healed very well and she had just a slight limp, this time. It was not as bad as the first one and she felt great. She was thrilled with her recovery and always would try to remember not to overdue things. She didn't want another surgery. Two were enough.

As she lay in her cold bed, in the Allen house that Christmas Eve, she thought about a story she heard, growing up. Jacob Allen, new father and widower, lying in that same bed. His new son Joseph (would be Sr. someday), beside the bed in one of the family cradles and seeing shadows on the wall. This was on a Christmas Eve too. She wondered if the spirits would come to her this night.

She fell asleep wondering and when she stirred at 2:00 a.m. she looked at the bedroom wall. She saw the outline of several figures...with one missing. It was a brief sighting but, she still couldn't feel Joe. She was *so* sure that he would be there this Christmas Eve.

Liz and Joe both had visits from the spirits over the years, while they were living in that house and whenever they would visit the farm. Neither was afraid of them. After all, they were family. Liz could always talk to her mom about the shadows and their visits. Eleanor had known about the shadows in the Allen house for decades. Almost since the time she arrived in Chatham, from Scotland. She believed in the shadows, too.

Liz wanted to feel Joe, but he wasn't there. Why couldn't she feel her husband? She loved him so much and wanted so desperately to feel him, there. It wasn't meant to be. She slept again, and was awakened at 6:45 a.m. by two little boys jumping on her, asking if Santa had come. She and the family spoiled James and John, with presents. It was a nice Christmas and the twins never cried once. She did...at night. George had brought his gifts to the farm. He had finished carving and painting the other wooden cars, for each boy's train that he gave them, after Joe died. They loved the train cars Uncle George made, to complete their trains. The train cars were their most cherished gift.

When January 1951 rolled around, Liz got back to school. Her friends were happy to see her and so were her students. The twins stayed home with Etta and fell back into their routine.

That year, there were to be new things in the air. The boys would be turning four years old and there were new shows to watch on the television and mommy was still reading the Lone Ranger, series to them. They loved story time, with mommy.

Since they loved cowboy characters, Liz let them watch the new Roy Rogers Show. The boys would come to love cowboys and Indians, on the television, the radio and books. Liz couldn't take the boys to the movies, together. She had to take James in one door and sit with the white people; and Etta would take John, in the colored door and have to sit in the balcony with him. It was awkward and sad to Liz to have to do this. But, until there was desegregation, it must remain this way. She and Etta would have to follow the law.

She didn't want to give in, but there were some great cowboy serials and feature films in the theaters. Since the boys loved them so much, Liz felt it was unfair for them to miss what they loved, most - cowboys and Indians. Etta didn't mind sitting in the balcony with John, but he would ask, "Why can't we sit with mommy and James?"

Etta didn't know what to say. She tried to explain that they had to sit up there, because their skin was a different color. That was just the way things were in Mississippi. He didn't understand, but he never forgot those words, 'because their skin was a different color'. He was puzzled, but accepted the answer, for the time being.

On the sports front, there was the formation of the L.P.G.A., or Ladies Professional Golf Association, the year before. Liz followed the women golfers, in the papers and on the television and radio reports. She would watch and learn. She got some great tips and tried them out, when she was home, in Chatham.

Liz followed the Brown vs. Board case that was really just getting under way. She kept her fingers crossed for desegregation. She wanted it before her sons were ready to be enrolled in school. If they called for desegregation, she could have John and James in her grade one class together, in 1953.

Liz decided that she would teach her class a bit about Canada, because that's where she came from. She taught a little of its history and geography. She always had great teaching methods to keep the children interested. She would always involve her students in some kind of project and they learned so much from her.

In 1952, the Dominion of Canada and all the Commonwealth countries, lost their reigning King, when King George VI died and the throne passed on to his daughter, Elizabeth. She would take the name, Queen Elizabeth II.

The class followed along with this news, because Liz fashioned her lesson after a fairy tale princess to a queen. She kept her class interested. On June 2, 1953, the first coronation of a queen was televised around the world. With time zone difference, it was on much too early, in the States, so Liz asked her class to ask their parents if they could watch the evening news. Liz would discuss it the next morning. Her students became so enthusiastic about the coronation that Liz wrote and let her class perform and play about a princess who becomes a queen. Vince gave permission for Liz's class to perform their play, in front of the school. All the students and teachers loved it.

As September 1953 was upon them, Liz had to now start to deal with the trials and tribulations of a pair of school aged multi-racial twins, who had to spread their wings, test the waters of emotions from love to extreme hatred, molestation and homosexuality; how would she ever handle it all? The trilogy continues......

Printed in the United States
By Bookmasters